THERE IS
HAPPINESS

THERE IS HAPPINESS

New and Selected Stories

BRAD WATSON

W. W. NORTON & COMPANY

Independent Publishers Since 1923

This is a work of fiction. Names, characters, places, and incidents are the products of the author's imagination or are used fictitiously. Any resemblance to actual events, locales, or persons, living or dead, is entirely coincidental.

For information about permission to reproduce selections from this book, write to Permissions, W. W. Norton & Company, Inc., 500 Fifth Avenue, New York, NY 10110

For information about special discounts for bulk purchases, please contact W. W. Norton Special Sales at specialsales@wwnorton.com or 800-233-4830

Manufacturing by Lake Book Manufacturing
Book design by Beth Steidle
Production manager: Gwen Cullen

ISBN 978-1-324-07642-1

W. W. Norton & Company, Inc., 500 Fifth Avenue, New York, N.Y. 10110
www.wwnorton.com

W. W. Norton & Company Ltd., 15 Carlisle Street, London W1D 3BS

1 2 3 4 5 6 7 8 9 0

FROM THE WATSON POEMS IN *Blue Angel* BY MICHAEL PETTIT

O to be a Blue Angel
burning, becoming wholly and finally air!
Watson knows how, step by step, the soul
can die in the living body. He'll make sure
they go together, and when they do, go quick.

—FROM "BLUE ANGEL"

Watson still dreams wreckage, recovery,
an impossible headlong drive toward
what is durable, what is abiding,
what is, unlike our lives, everlasting
somewhere before us, or somewhere behind.

—FROM "MOBILE HOME"

Only now can he look back in wonder
at those outlaw years he spent on the run,
one calamity after another
chasing him all over the planet, whoosh
all that bystanders got of him passing
into his next incarnation, Watson
the perpetual work-in-progress and . . .

—FROM "KOYAANISQATSI WATSON"

Who would have figured, least of all him,
he'd arrive into the sweet, forgiving
light of this evening? And who would complain
of sunset, its breezes and clarity?
Not Watson, not yet divine but willing
to accept divine grace with grace: *Amen.*

—FROM "HEMICENTURIAN WATSON"

Contents

Foreword

BRAD WAS BRAD WATSON'S MIDDLE NAME. THE NAME HE was supposed to go by was Wilton. Wilton Watson. What a mouthful. What could such a name portend for a white Mississippian born in the summer of 1955? Well, anything could happen and some things even did. He didn't dream of becoming a writer, certainly. A presence on stage or screen perhaps. He was good-looking, a bit roguish. He had charm, that Southern charm. He fathered a child and got married when he was but a junior in high school. It seemed he was always getting married and fathering a son and getting divorced, but that happened only twice. Then suddenly he was forty and had written a wonderful book, *Last Days of the Dog-Men*, a collection of stories. Each one excellent, assured, funny, startling, heartbreaking, wild. And within each, its blazing core, its irreducible essence, was a dog—a memorable, tragic, honorable, thoroughly realized dog. "A dog keeps his life simple and unadorned," Watson states quite correctly. "He is who he is and his only task is to assert this." Watson's dogs are close to divine, his people—strange, piteous, futile, and fickle things—hardly. In the title story, a wife euthanizes her faithless husband's dog Spike, just to be mean of course, but compounds the evil by confessing that after the fatal injection she begged the dog not to die, to come back to her, to them, the marriage.

Only occasionally does a human rise to the level of redemption, achieve that state of faithful abide, that is a dog's natural condition. "Bill" may be the saddest, dearest story of the lot when an old woman and her aged "trembling" poodle Bill share a last dream howl, a pure wordless language of grief and goodbye.

Last Days of the Dog-Men, with its iconic sepia-colored cover photograph of two madly confident dogs in flight, won some prizes and was allowed to nudge against the cold cruel gates of establishment success. His next books were permitted to do the same; a boisterously engaging novel *The Heaven of Mercury*, another collection, and a second novel, the quiet and riskier *Miss Jane*. The novels were more deeply lyrical than the stories, wide-focused on a lifetime in a single, long-past place. They were roomy, like a big old Lincoln, generous with meanderings and asides.

> A mockingbird sat somewhere nearby . . . belting a rep-
> ertoire . . . ohmygodhelpme!, ohmygodhelpme!, dearme
> dearme dearme, lookahere!, lookahere!, boogediebooge-
> dieboogedie, therewego therewego therewego, who,
> me? who, me? stick close! stick close! stick close! stick
> close!, I don't know. I don't know. I don't know.

But it was, I believe, the short story in which he delighted and at which he excelled, that American treasure that American readers are so wary of, resisting its surprises, attentiveness, and demands. The good short story tells us something very alarming about ourselves and our puzzling sojourn on this earth, our situation, as it were. It is the perfect vehicle for delivering us to ourselves, an experience we instinctively wish very much to avoid. A good story gives us a glimpse—and the glimpse is so surprising, so varied yet unequivocal, so ruthlessly complete, that it does awaken us in some manner, if not protect or prepare us.

This glimpse is the short story's gravest gift and Watson is a maven at slamming our souls with it. In "Visitation," an unhappy father awkwardly attempting to engage with his estranged and fearful son doesn't recognize his child or himself after his palm is read by a woman in a sleezy motel. In "Terrible Argument," a couple seasoned in marital discord find there are limits to choreographed rage. In "Uncle Willem," a prank involving a much-delayed sunrise drives a simple man literally out of his wits. In "Agnes of Bob," a woman quietly drowning in a public swimming pool has a vision of her long-dead husband cleaning bream and throwing the heads still gasping for air to their old bulldog, "tossing fish heads around the yard like balls." She feels "on the brink of a wonderful vision, as if in a moment she would know what Pops had seen as he passed through his own heart and . . . into the next world."

The next world(s) are always near in these stories, so unlike the visible here-and-now one where people just get "scattered carelessly into this life or that," and Watson enters them with unguarded joy. He dips into the consciousness of boys ("Eykelboom") and dogs ("Seeing Eye"), and ex-cons ("Dying for Dolly") but more arcane ways of being pose no challenge, either. Two of my perversely favorite stories here are pure grotesque. One explores an awareness of the "mighty defecation" of a leopard escaped from a zoo "steaming in the wet, glinting, close-clipped grass" of freedom. The leopard has brought down and consumed a zookeeper (for whom he had long cultivated a hatred). Now digested and transformed into fresh scat, the man, or rather his remaining consciousness, finds a measure of relief "at the sensation of (relative) light and air."

In the other, "There Is Happiness" a gruesomely embellished wig stand provides comfort to none other than a homicidal lunatic before ultimately speaking to her of life's grim verities and death's dominion. Yes, the wig stand speaks. Its skin is shrunken and hardened and its eyes are black as if burned in a fire of deep understanding. Its name is Elizabeth Bob.

Such freakish flair is not uncommon in these stories, but neither is straightforward melancholy realism like the powerful "Crazy Horse" or antic forays into male meltdown like "Are You Mr. Lonelee?" The mix, the shifts in intent and tone, makes for a heady experience, a soulful half-comic songbook of cries and fears and play.

Ohmygodhelpme dearme dearme stick close I dont know I don't know . . .

William Gass has noted that every real book is a mind, an imagination, a consciousness. The reader reading "dreams the dream of the deserving page."

In the accomplished "Aliens in the Prime of Their Lives," the story that lent its name to Watson's second collection, a young couple, totally unprepared for their impoverished and inevitable future, rent a sweltering attic apartment a block away from a mental institution. After a visit from a cheerful twosome in rumpled pajamas who claim to be from another planet, certainly *not* the nearby facility, they cycle through a number of pleasant scenarios—some quite immediate (a lovely breeze enters their awful home, a wide bowl of cold fried chicken and a Tupperware of potato salad appear in the previously empty Frigidaire)—while others unfold in a serene and fulsome future complete with a well-tended farm, a perfect child, and a fine church-singing voice. All that happens is more than a dream, but it's still necessary to awake from it. So does life require. Or, as one figure from a blurry past informs our unnamed hero: "You have to go back to where you came from."

Wilton Brad Watson died in the summer of 2020, suddenly, of cardiac arrest in his home in Wyoming, two weeks shy of his sixty-fifth birthday. Here is a generous portion of the work of a swiftly passing lifetime. Bountiful is the deserving page. And the dream, both imagined and remembered (the difference being not great), is the peculiar one of life and its conversions. The moment

it ends seems hardly stranger than all that has transpired before.
Brad was ever striving to glimpse a vision appropriate to his characters' essence—perplexed, anxious, done with it, or hopeful, as
that glimpse might be.

On his death notice are the last lines of *The Heaven of Mercury*.
It is one of the most striking, unabashedly lovely endings of any
novel I know.

> He wandered toward a spot of color in the distance and
> when he got close he saw that it was a bush filled with
> preening monarch butterflies . . . resting and soaking up
> the sunlight . . . They seemed to shiver under his rapt
> attention. He felt such an outpouring of love for them,
> he thought he would weep. They seemed hardly able
> to contain their delight that he was gazing upon their
> beautiful wings.

—Joy Williams

THERE IS

HAPPINESS

DYING FOR DOLLY

I WAS IN THE PEN FOR A CRIME OF PASSION WHILE THE whole country was making such a big thing out of her boobs: are they real, are they not, look at the size of those things, etc. The gay boys put on shows wearing big blond wigs, tight short skirts. They chose the small, delicate boys to do it, boys with those clear-as-a-bell backwoods voices, and stacked them with brassieres begged off the great fat cafeteria maids, triple-E cups they stuffed with loaves of light bread. and I wouldn't be telling you anything if I said what was done to those boys back in the cellblock. Smokes and dope and money changed hands. Everybody in the joint was a little obsessed with Dolly in those days.

It was right around then that I started singing a little, strumming the guitar at night, and then during the day as people started telling me I had some talent. You can get in a lot of practice in prison. Pretty soon I was playing little gigs during mealtimes and out in the yard during exercise hours. "Dying for Dolly" was one of the first things I wrote. That would be good and bad for me down the road. Even the guards warmed up to me after I came up with "The Big House Blues," which in case you don't know it is a ballad of a guy who was a guard at a prison which was left unnamed, who had a problem with a wife who couldn't stay out of the honky-tonks and kept fooling around until he caught her with a service station operator and killed them both. He ended up in his own prison, the real one and the one in his head, and all his old buddies guarding him and having to draw away.

One of my buds, a jailhouse lawyer named Webb Spenser, wrote to the local television station, and I guess it was a slow news week because they came out and did a piece on me playing in the yard and talked to the warden and some guards and to Webb, and damned if the network didn't pick it up, and that's how I landed a recording contract before I even got out of prison. They came down and we cut the record live, in the yard, with all the inmates whooping it up. I was a hero. They called the album *The Big House Blues*, with seven of my songs and covers of "Folsom Prison Blues" and "Kaw-Liga" and "Your Cheatin' Heart," and put out singles of "Cheatin' Heart" and "Folsom Prison," with the flip sides the title song and "Dying for Dolly," and pretty soon all four were getting airtime. I insisted we get some of my buddies among the prison population to sing a chorus in the Cash song, and made it so they'd get a little piece of the royalty with every album sold. I just want to point out I wasn't ungrateful. All of us paid our dues but nobody got any better dividends from it than yours truly. On the day I was released, the recording studio and the warden threw me a big party in the chow hall, and the warden came up and put his arm around me.

"Marlon, stay out of trouble, son," he said. "You might find success is just as hard to handle as what you came from."

"Don't you worry, Warden," I said. I winked at him. "I think I can handle the sunny side of the street."

Still, you can imagine my surprise when I got a call from my agent that afternoon telling me Dolly Parton had a show on the road, using local artists at all the stops. She'd heard I was getting out and wanted to know if I'd be in the show when she stopped in Birmingham just three days hence. I said, "What do you think?" The agent said the plan was to sing "Dying for

Dolly" and maybe "The Big House Blues," and maybe do a little skit with Dolly, since they were taping all her road shows so they could put together a network special from it, and who knows but what I could end up a part of such a show. I thought, This is it, the big time.

I bought an old Dodge convertible at a lot in Atmore with some of the advance money on my recording contract, and filled it with regular unleaded, folded the top down. I was due up in Birmingham in two days but I had to take care of some business, first.

The back roads to Tuscaloosa are beautiful in the fall, with the weather cool and the grass growing thick and tall right up to the edge of the old highway through the fields, doves busting from it like they're flying out of your fenders, everything sweet and green. I was cruising through a valley of deepening light, the sky so blue you could almost taste it, the colors of the ripened hay and corn softening until what light was left seemed to come from within them. I hit the long slow wooded grade from Moundville into T-Town right at dusk, and the streetlamps were flickering on when I pulled up to the little clapboard house on the bluff where Charlotte grew up. Down below sat the ghost buildings of the old dead paper mill beside the river. From the house's screen door there was TV light flickering. I stepped onto the porch and rapped softly on the doorframe, and a little ghost rose from the recliner in front of the television. Charlotte's mother.

She came close and looked through the screen at me for a minute like I was the saddest thing in the world, like I was the messenger of all her sad life and failures as a mother and as a wife to a man who used to beat the hell out of her about once a week. She was a toughened old woman, though. She'd had her flat brown hair cut either by a barber or her own shaky hand and wore a house robe faded from red to old rose.

"Well, we heard you was getting out," she said. "She ain't going to divorce you now, Marlon, not with you making all that money as a singer."

"I ain't making a lot of money yet," I said. "They get ex-cons pretty cheap."

"You will, though, they all do," the old woman said. "And you know Charlotte, she ain't going to let go of a sugar daddy."

"How come she didn't divorce me while I was in the pen?"

"I don't know," the old woman said, munching her gums. "Just lazy, I guess, always was the laziest gal."

"I'm not going to let her bleed me dry. Who's she shacked up with?"

"Some fellow sells condominium homes," she said.

"On the coast."

"You known that. She loves the beach."

She said the man had his own cabin down on the peninsula near the fort on the bay side, and told me how to find it.

"Don't you hurt him, Marlon," she said.

"I ain't going there for that," I said.

I gave her a hundred-dollar bill, which she stood there and studied like it was some kind of puzzle, then she tucked it into her robe pocket. I got into the car and drove back the same direction I'd come. Old 25 is beautiful at night, too, but in a completely different way, like driving down this crusty trail in the blackness just racing to stay in your headlights' cone, and what creatures come into your vision are huge moths, night hoppers, and smaller insects spattering the windshield like raindrops. I had to scrub it for half an hour when I stopped for gas in Bay Minette.

I took it slower down through the little towns along the way to the beach, Loxley and Robertsdale and Foley, little towns that before I went in had welcome signs that said things like A NICE PLACE TO LIVE, A TOWN YOU WILL LIKE, but now were nearly obscured by billboards about restaurants and condominiums and golf courses. The hurricane had come through the year I got sent up, and wiped away all the old beach shanties, and since then developers had taken cover like beavers. Just on the other side of the canal I pulled over and slept awhile in a big Baptist church parking lot, and when I woke up it was getting on into the morning, a bright sun in my eyes. I picked up a sack of biscuits and a cup of coffee at Hazel's, took my shirt and shoes off, and sat on a bench at the public beach and had my breakfast. It's still plenty warm for beach sunning in Alabama in October, plus the crowd's thinned out. You think there's nothing like the sound of the waves and the salt air when you've been inland awhile, just try it when you've seen nothing but institutional green walls and barbed wire and smelled shit and piss and disinfectant for four years and heard the grunts and moans and weak cries for help through the night. I was sitting there stuffing biscuits into my mouth, washing them down my dry throat with scalding coffee, tears pouring down my cheeks. I guess people strolling by on the beach thought I was a lunatic.

The old winding road out to the fort opened up after a few miles of tall pines and palmetto into mostly flattened dunes. It was easy to find the place Charlotte's mother had described, once I'd breezed past it and saw it out of the corner of my eye, tucked into a little grove of skinny pines on the bay side beyond the last curve, just like the old lady had said. I pulled into the shell drive-way, parked, and knocked on the flapping screen door.

Her man came to the door, a man with the ridiculous name of Lardo Inabinett. I guess it made customers remember your name. He wore his thick black hair short and blow-dried straight back, a mink pelt glued to his head, and his eyes bulged like a fat Arab's. He wasn't fat in the body, but his head was the head of a fat man, set up on a long neck.

"She's on the beach, back at the bay," he said. "Her mama called and said you were coming, so she said for you to go out and meet her there." He offered me a beer, but I declined. "Miz Jenkins said you weren't looking for trouble," he said.

"Indeed I'm not," I said.

"I was half hoping you'd come to take her back," he said with a nervous laugh. "She sure likes to spend money, that gal."

He was one of those skinny-legged boys who wore loose polyester dress pants and kept juking his balls in a way that made the change rattle in his pockets. I wanted to ask him did he have one twisted up in there or was he just nervous.

I walked out back and down a sandy trail through the pines to the bayside beach and looked both ways, and there was Charlotte laid out on an orange towel, wearing sunglasses and a little bikini. I strolled down, looking her over as I did, and feeling more out-of-place than ever in my Kmart shirt and flaw-bin jeans and cheap Dingos cracked with age. I hadn't worn them since going in. And there she was, her beautiful brown slim feet splayed in the sand, knees up and doing a kind of slow Charleston to some tune in her head, and hands spread onto the sand, too, like she was holding on to the earth. Looking at her lying there near-naked made me want her all over again. The way a long-reformed junkie still dreams of a fix, I suppose.

"Nice tan," I said.

"Look at you," she said, not opening her eyes behind the sunglasses. Then she sat up and did open them, and even behind the dark lenses I could see their oddly almond shape that always loosened something in my groin. Her hair was pulled up into a thick bunch on top of her head. "I always thought you had a nice voice. How come you never wrote any songs for me?"

"I have, now, but I wouldn't feel flattered if I were you."

She lay back down on the towel, half smiling.

I said, "How come you never divorced me while I was in prison? I know it's not because you loved me."

"How do you know that? Besides, being divorced from you

would've been worse than being married to you. Nobody feels sorry for a divorcée. A woman's husband in prison makes her an interesting character."

I stood there a minute. Out in the bay there was a shrimp boat with its booms out, dragging, and behind that a new gas rig. Mobile was low and hazy in the distance. I imagined those boys on the shrimp boat watching us through the glasses, and I imagine Charlotte did, too.

"Well, how about it now?" I said.

"What?"

"Give me a divorce."

"You got some nerve," she said in a lazy way, "asking me for a divorce. I should be demanding one from you. But, no, I won't do it."

"Won't ask me or won't give me?"

"Whatever," she said, then she sat up again. "Marlon, you might still owe me something. Let's wait and see."

"Suit yourself," I said. "I'm going to file, anyway."

"On what grounds?"

"It was your cheating that drove me to what I did."

"History, Marlon. Kind of warped thinking, anyway."

"You're living with this condo fellow."

"Oh, Marlon," she said, "who's going to care about that? Here," she said, tossing me a bottle of suntan lotion. "Put some of this on your face, you're red as a beet." I guess I'd gotten sunburned lying asleep in the convertible and then later on the beach with my breakfast.

I left her there and went back to the car. It wasn't there. Neither was Lardo Inabinett. There was a note back in the kitchen that said he'd just borrowed the car to run up to the store, but when he wasn't back in an hour I went back down to the beach.

"Well, he might not be coming back," Charlotte said, rising

up on an elbow. "Some fellow came and repossessed his car last week, one of them Ford Expeditions, like he was some cowboy."

"You mean you think he stole my car?"

"Condos might be big here one day, but right now this is still just a beach town that got blowed away in a hurricane. Lardo used to be in mobile homes, he made real money then."

I waited another hour back at the house and then called the police. I gave them a description of the car and Inabinett. They said they knew who he was, and kind of laughed. Charlotte came back to the house and fixed herself a drink from a half-gallon bottle of Gordon's gin, starting with gin and tonics, and in a little while I let her fix me one, and when the tonic ran out she started just pouring gin over ice, and when the ice ran out we started swigging it from the bottle.

"I haven't missed you one bit, Marlon," she said, swaying like a buoy anchored to the kitchen sink by her ass. Her nose and high cheekbones turned apple-red. When she came at me I gave in and we went at it right there on the kitchen floor. I mean, it had been a long time, your judgment's not right. I can hardly remember it—hard-rimmed humping with a sandy edge, a vision of peach-colored skin and that pinkness about the seams, raw and humming. Some time during the night old Lardo comes back, he's drunk, too, and Charlotte hits him with that empty gin bottle from across the room, and next thing I know we're on the road, together, and Charlotte's got a little glossy black handbag full of cash.

"Don't worry about Lardo," she said, "poor old son of a bitch, he hasn't got the brains God gave a mullet. He's good-hearted, though."

I said, "Charlotte, about that money."

"Joint bank account," she said. "When Mama called and said you'd showed up, I told Lardo to go close me out." She leaned over and ran her lips along my stubbled jawline and licked my ear and breathed into it, "I never stopped thinking about you, baby."

I didn't believe a word of that, but I'd let myself get into this with her, and I was hungover and she was still my wife. So I figured I'd take her on up to Birmingham and after the show we'd sit down and do some hard talking and I could take her back down to Tuscaloosa, drop her at her mama's, and think about what to do next.

And I was turning all that hard stuff over again in my mind, how Charlotte ran around with that boy and made me lose my mind for a while. I knew the boy, he worked for me in my own shop. And when I came home early from the hunting camp that morning, and she's still asleep in the bed, the covers a tangled heap on the floor, the smell of booze so strong in the room, and her white Victoria's Secret brassiere she'd ordered with my credit card blackened with the perfect black print of a man's hand, engine grime, I knew that hand, it was still in the room and resting on Charlotte's soft, white, beautiful rump. I was pretty much out of my mind after that, I don't even remember doing what I did, though no one else would have roped that boy to the hood of my truck beside the eight-point I'd brought down at dawn, and only a man in his rational mind would have reasoned that, buck-naked, the boy would succumb to exposure, and when they picked me up I was eating eggs in the City Café, I don't know how long I'd been riding around. It could all happen again, I feared, there was still something that happened in me whenever I looked at her. I guess she was just too much my type.

The show in Birmingham was to be in the old Alabama Theater just because Dolly liked the place, I'd heard, and she was going to do three performances so most of the people who wanted to see her would have a chance to. We'd have just one afternoon to rehearse, which was all right since I already knew my songs, of course, and I figured the skit wouldn't be a big deal, if she decided to do it. I'd been to court, I knew all about memorizing lines and expressions, I'd been good enough at it to sway a jury from murder two down to manslaughter.

A stage manager showed us around, gave me a little dressing room backstage. We'd seen Dolly's bus out back of the theater when we'd driven in and figured she'd stay in there most of the time, but before the first rehearsal she came by and introduced herself. It's quite a shock, after the billboards and magazine covers and tabloid stories and photograph spreads, to see she's such a dainty thing. And there's that something about Dolly, you know, that makes her seem like your sister or a good-hearted neighbor down the street, or maybe somebody from your church coming by to bring you fried chicken. Except she's wearing a skintight jumpsuit made of thin little slices of what looks like emerald that cling to the delicate bones in her shoulders and drape across a low-cut front that advances her intimate scents to within an inch of your nose. It makes for a strange chemistry of desire. I stepped back and introduced Charlotte.

"Well," Dolly said, "I'm so pleased to meet you, Charlotte. Well," she said, "what a nice surprise." So I could tell she knew something of my story and didn't know quite what to think.

Her two huge bodyguards in their Calvin Klein cowboy outfits and Ray-Bans began to take a cool sort of interest in looking over me and Charlotte.

Charlotte said, "I always knew we'd forgive each other," and we all stood there a second or two, all tongue-tied for different reasons, I guess. Then Charlotte stepped forward and gave Dolly a little hug and a peck on the cheek, and it wasn't until then I thought about how we both must stink of b.o., gin, and wild fucking. And I could feel my heart really sinking, like I knew I'd made a big mistake but had to ride it out and hope for the best. Even then, though, already I knew I'd taken the wrong fork in the road, should have left Kilby grounds with a flat fare-thee-well and never looked back at the life that sent me there. I broke into a little sweat just thinking about it.

"Marlon," Dolly said then, with renewed aplomb, "I just want you to know you got a real genuine talent, I could tell that the first time I heard you sing that song about me, and I think God has smiled on you, finding you a way out of a life of crime and unhappiness. And even though you must be strange to do what you done to that boy back in Alabama," and she kind of looked at both us for a second, and Charlotte smiled back as if someone had complimented her hair, "there must be something in every one of us that can understand the kind of pain that made you do it, and, well, I think that's why people like your music. I think you're an example of what's great about our country and I'm proud to have you on my show."

Looking at her, hearing her voice, smelling her mixture of light perfume and perspiration, her little dainty presence there bigger than life, it sort of bouyed me up again and I felt a little better.

I cleared my throat and said, "Well, thank you, Dolly. I'm real proud to be here."

"Well," she said, and patted Charlotte on the hand, "y'all just make yourselves comfortable, now, and Charlotte, honey, if you need anything at all while we're rehearsing for the show you just holler and somebody'll take care of you," and before she could let go of Charlotte's hand Charlotte grabbed her little hand in both of hers and said, "I have just always loved your singing," and Dolly tried to move on by saying, "Well, thanks," but Charlotte didn't let go of her hand and my heart jumped as the bodyguards stepped toward her, but Dolly stopped them with a gesture from her free hand.

"I love that new group of Dolly chorus girls you got in your show now," Charlotte said, just gushing.

"Well," Dolly said.

"I was a dancer in high school, wasn't I, Marlon. That's when Marlon was first attracted to me, watching me dance in modern dance." And with that she let go of Dolly's hand and kicked one leg up so high in the air, I tell you, it was astonishing, and Dolly and the bodyguards were somewhat arrested by it, too, for in those soft and faded short jean cutoffs you could plainly see Charlotte still had a beautiful leg, and tanned, too, and though I was alarmed, my blood thickened in a moment of remembering her kicking those legs up in the air to show off while I climbed onto the bed from the footboard headed for ecstasy, those days.

"Aw, well, honey, that's amazing," Dolly said, and there was another moment of us all just standing there feeling stupid and everybody, except the bodyguards, smiling. Then I saw one of them, the bleached blond one, slip his own little smile no bigger than a comma, and I wanted to laugh out loud. Dolly said, "You know, I tell you, old Marlon's got a good career ahead of him and you ought to just get up there and get involved with him, be a part of his act in some way, you know, sing backup maybe."

"Let me try out for your girls," Charlotte blurted then.

And then Dolly'd had enough, too, though, and even as she and the bodyguards moved away was saying, Well honey that'd be great but we've been on the road awhile already and everything's set up you know and I would but it's just not something you can change a horse in the middle of the stream and Marlon I'll see you in rehearsal in a little bit, right, now 'bye, and they were gone out the side stage door to Dolly's bus. I pulled Charlotte into the little dressing room.

"Goddamn, woman, are you out of your mind?" She tore into me then, and tore into Dolly, said that snotty bitch, she can't sing anyway, a no-talent boob job and on and on and on until I just slapped her, it was done before I knew it, and she took in a breath, then started beating hell out of me with both hands, trying to scratch me, until I grabbed her and held her down on the bed. I know it's ridiculous but it's true that in no more than a minute we were at it again, not fighting. I guess a chemical attraction is nothing but a senseless animal wildness, and when we were finished we were both on the floor dragging in air and clutching our guts like we'd run a mile full-speed and done a hundred sit-ups. When she fell asleep I slipped into my clothes and went out onto the stage, where I heard people talking and shoes shuffling around on the stage boards. When I get out there the stage is full and in the middle is Dolly, dressed now in a pink sweatsuit and a baseball cap with the Dollywood logo on it, and you can see that underneath it her hair is cropped short.

"Just about to send out a reveille for you, Marlon," she sings out, then she turns to a band tuning up in the pit and says, "All right, y'all ready?"

The first thing we practiced was one of those big musical numbers with a western twist, and the deal called for about two dozen Dolly look-alikes as the dancing chorus, all of them clopping and clogging around in boots and buxom buckskins. This was a silent rehearsal so there wasn't any singing, just the music, which was taped for practice. Dolly was going through the number, too, with a kind of bland expression on her face, and seeming to whisper the words of a song to herself as she went through the steps. The pink sweat suit she wore was nylon or something, and when she danced near me I could hear it make a sound like the foil being peeled from a Hershey's kiss.

Meanwhile all the other Dollys were spinning and bobbing into my vision and smiling at me or leering at me like they were having real fun, and one of them swear to God goosed my ass as we spun out of a big complicated twirl like a wagon wheel, and I couldn't for the life of me tell which one it'd been, but I didn't suppose it mattered. Next thing I know the number's over, everybody takes a bow, and from way back in the seats comes a solitary clapping, slow and hollow in the empty theater, and everybody looks up for a second and I see it's Charlotte sitting back there alone, and when I see her she gets up and walks out the back and when I follow her I just see her headed out of the lobby and onto the street, and I let her go. I hoped she'd just get on a bus and go home, or back to Lardo on the Gulf Coast. But I can't say I believed in my heart that that was her plan.

I went back to rehearsal after we had a short break. We blocked out this skit the writers had dreamed up about a struggling country music singer, name of Marlon, who meets a struggling young lady country singer, name of Dolly, who's working as a waitress in a café, and they talk about where they come from and how lonesome they are and sing a song about the old values and good cooking back home and what success really means and all that crap. Then we started doing it with lines.

I guess I was a little stiff, since I thought the whole thing was embarrassing. So Dolly stops to lecture me on how to loosen up and be natural. She's still wearing her jumpsuit and baseball cap and her tennis shoes, and she stood there with her hands on her hips. She didn't look so much like a star just then, but I liked her.

"Marlon, it's just like when you was a young'un and you'd get up in front of your family and horse around. It ain't a bit of difference, when you get right down to it. Just be yourself."

Well, I could have told her that while other young'uns was horsing around in the parlor in front of all the relatives come together for a Sunday reunion, I was helping my old man throw up the Aqua Velva he'd drunk that morning while my mama finished off a six-pack of Jax, but I didn't say anything except, "Well, I'll try, Dolly."

Still, I was having a pretty rough time of it until I took a good look around the set, and saw all the garish decorations, the curtains all made of frilly lace like on fancy underwear, big golden stars hanging everywhere, and all those Dolly impersonators sitting in those folding director's chairs, watching, and the peculiar thing was that I loosened right up. I figured that the whole business was much stranger than I'd ever thought, so who was I to be nursing my ego in a situation like this? Looking back, I think that was Dolly's attitude, too: that what the public wants is much stranger than you ever figured it was when you were growing up in a little three-room shack and thought all anybody ever wanted was a pure voice singing an honest song. I let go and had a hell of a time, and we got it down in just two more tries.

"Well, I think I like you, Marlon," Dolly said when we wrapped it up, and she gave me a little pat on the ass and a wink and made that little *skitch*ing sound you make in your cheek to make a horse gitup. "You got gumption."

"Well, I like you, too, Miss Parton."

"You just make sure you call me Dolly, and let me tell you something else." She took me by the arm and we sort of strolled backstage toward my dressing room. We stopped in the hallway, there was no one close by.

"I know you must still love your wife, and you want to get your life going again—and excuse me for butting into your business but I'm going to be out of here in a couple of days so I might as well tell you what I think, and I got a good eye for trouble, so here goes: That girl's got problems, Marlon, and no matter what you might think you owe her you don't owe her your life." She put her little hand on my chest and looked me in the eye, then patted me on the cheek. I wanted to cry. "Maybe you ought to send her home for a while, till you get your bearings. You got a great opportunity here, Marlon, and I think it'd be just great if you could make the most of it. I believe in you."

"Thank you, Dolly."

Then she kissed me on the cheek and went away. I couldn't even see her going and I hopped into the dressing room and sat on the sofa in there till I got myself together again, and then I took a nap.

And after that, when I woke up later on, there's not a whole lot more to describe except the bitter end. After her appearance at the rehearsal that day, Charlotte disappeared. The show was great. They had my choreography down to a simple part right in the middle of all those swinging and clopping Dollys, and when it was time to sweep me off the stage it was done by a couple of those girls hooking their arms into mine. And when it was time for the skit they just set me down out there and said to say my lines, and I did, and when I flubbed one and got embarrassed Dolly just slapped me on the arm and said, "Come on, now, Marlon, this ain't Shakespeare!" and laughed, and it just brought the house down, and my lines came right back to me. And all this time, I'd sneak a look over the audience, and no sign of Charlotte, but pretty soon I stopped even thinking about that. When it was time to sing they stood me out there and raised the curtains, and halfway through "Dying for Dolly" I heard the audience start laughing and clapping and there was Dolly come up behind me. She started in and we finished the song together, and I'd had not a clue. We went right from there to what we'd rehearsed, a duet of "The Big House Blues," and the whole audience jumped out of their seats into a standing ovation. It happened the same way in all three shows, and it was at that moment, the ovation, in the very last show, that I saw Charlotte stumble into the aisle and start toward the stage. I knew it was her, in spite of the huge cheap blond wig on her head and the short, shiny minidress and the steep, tiny high heels—I thought they were why she was stumbling till I got a look at her face, all fleshy and strange with gin, the dregs of which she hurled in a pint bottle toward us up on the stage. All she got out before the guards grabbed her was something about That big-titty whore something, and the guards dragged her toward the nearest exit, the one off to one side at the base of the orchestra pit.

I was back in my dressing room dealing with the embarrassment over that and the crushing regret from so much else that the incident had brought up in my heart, when there was a knock and two plainclothes cops came in, and I stood up to greet them and apologize for Charlotte's behavior. I said it was my fault she was there and I shouldn't have brought her, and if they'd go easy on her I'd take her on home to her mother's and pay for any damage she might have done in the theater or if she hurt one of the guards. The two cops stood there a second, both short men with short, styled haircuts and poker faces. One stood looking at me and the other's eyes sort of cut around the room, looking.

"We didn't come over for that, Mr. Peak," the detective who'd been casting his eyes around the room said, "though I guess now I'm glad we came when we did."

I just looked at him a minute, and he and the other cop looked back at me. The other cop reached behind him and shut the door on the people—some of the stagehands and maybe others from the entourage. I looked back at the detective. He could've been somebody I knew, maybe somebody I'd gone to school with, his face just now starting to beef out under the jaw with his wife's cooking, and his eyes more tired than hard or cold but looking as if they didn't have a whole lot of humor left in them. I wanted to ask him did we know each other in school, was he from Tuscaloosa originally, but I didn't. I said, "What did you come here for, then?"

"A warrant for the arrest of you and Mrs. Peak," he said, pulling it out, "for assault and robbery of one Lardo Inabinett down in Gulf Shores." He looked up from the warrant. "Mr. Peak, I believe this is a violation of your parole."

The finale number, minus me, was still playing out on the stage when they led me out the side stage door to the car. Charlotte was already in the back seat. We rode back there with our hands cuffed behind us. We didn't talk on the way down, and about halfway there she vomited onto the floor at her feet, then sat back up and leaned her head on my shoulder.

"I guess I'll give you that divorce now, if you still want it," she said, and then she pretty much went to sleep.

I never did see Dolly again in the flesh. Lardo dropped charges on Charlotte, said it'd all been me, and I guess they're back together, living down at his place on the coast. She pretty much got all my record money. The old cons in here weren't surprised to see me back, and when I heard that my head tingled like someone had tossed it, guillotined, into a kettle of boiling water. It's the way things happen in the world, they said. But I won't sing for them, and it's hurt their feelings, so they want to give me a rough time. I keep to myself. Webb Spenser's gone, paroled just a couple of weeks after I was. He sends a note every now and then but doesn't visit. The wispy boy, my cellmate, killed his mother. When I showed up he traded himself to a homo lifer for one of the costumes from the old Dolly shows. There's a sweet rankness about him, a decomposition. His bone-white skin's gone soft with fear and his eyes have sunk darkly into their sockets like prunes. He's wasting away, wants me to save him. In the evenings, after lights-out, he stands in silhouette and straps on the big Sunbeam bra stuffed with toilet paper, pulls on the wig, and sings "Coat of Many Colors" in his quivery, atonal moan. It's all I can do not to kill him. I've got two mad-men's strength running in my veins and my muscles have turned to jelly. I could fling myself to pieces. He says, "Show me how it's s'posed to go, Marlon," he's on the floor, doubled up in some pain. But my voice has faded to an aged whisper, and I can't hear a note in my head.

EYKELBOOM

WHERE HAD THEY COME FROM, THE EYKELBOOMS? THE other boys suspected Indiana, Illinois. Some crude and faceless Yankee state. The Eykelbooms had emerged and emigrated from it. It was a tiny, deeply threatening invasion. The boys watched them unpack their moving truck, which was actually a dump truck, their belongings piled into the bed and covered with a large heavy tarp. The truck belonged to Eykelboom's father. No one else on the street owned a real dump truck, and this might have been cool had the owner of the truck not been Eykelboom's father.

They weren't neighborly, of course, aside from Eykelboom himself, an only child, who tried to befriend the other boys, to no avail. His parents made no effort to help their son or to make any friends, themselves. His mother almost never appeared outside the house, except for trips to the grocery store, and his father did only when he drove the dump truck to and from work, blowing his customized musical horn to announce his arrival, which everyone came to truly despise, or when he was mowing the grass on weekends. He did this shirtless, as if to show off his physique. He was tall, with a big rectangular head, a flattop haircut that wedged to a point over his small, square forehead, and droopy, arrogant eyes. Long loose limbs that looked apelike and strong, huge hands and feet, but thin and wiry legs as if he'd descended from a jackrabbit or some fleet herbivore. As he pushed the lawn mower back and forth across the grass, he sucked in his gut like a movie actor. You could always tell that it was sucked in because it wasn't muscled, just smoothly concaved by the sucking. Eykelboom walked around doing the same thing, sucking in his belly, sticking out his chest, atop which stood the same long neck, slack face, flattop haircut. He was slighter and softer than his old man, gangly. He ran with his head thrown back, legs flailing, chest thrust forward as if to break the wire.

Eykelboom's old man didn't like Eykelboom much, either, which was a pretty awful thing, even to the boys.

The boys wore cut-off jeans and faded torn T-shirts, went barefoot or in begrimed old sneakers without socks. They had blackened fingernails and knuckles, tired boy eyes, scarred knees and elbows and ears, snotty noses, unwashed hair spiked with sleep and itchy with sand, scabby stubbed toes, unbrushed teeth flecked with tomato peel and pieces of grass. They got around on foot or on one of a squad of bent and banged-up bicycles that seemed interchangeable and were left crashed into shrubbery or tangled at the center of a forlorn front yard or askew in the street like the rusted remains of extinct, mechanized animals.

Eykelboom, neatly dressed, clean, quiet, was not a trouble-maker, as far as the other boys could see. Yet every so often his father would come out of their house, call to him, and stand there waiting. Eykelboom's face would blanch, he would freeze for a moment, then mutter something fatalistic and trudge over to his old man. Together they would turn and go into the house, and the boys wouldn't see Eykelboom for a couple of days, maybe even a few. They might see him being driven to school by his mother instead of taking the bus, but he never looked out the car window. At school, he kept his head down, staring at the book on his desk, sat alone in the cafeteria, and somehow disappeared at recess. Then one day he'd be back, attempting once again to be their friend. What he had done to bring down his father's wrath no one knew. Some private transgression. But once the boys realized that they could use it against him, they did.

Of course, it was common in those days for parents to hit their children, with everything from hairbrushes to toilet brushes, flyswatters, switches, bare palms, rolled newspapers, and folded belts. But, usually, there was a good and obvious reason.

The boys couldn't be sure, but it seemed like Eykelboom's old man did it just to do it, to keep the boy in check. Secretly, they envied him this. Their fathers were generally ineffective, weak. They were low-ranking white-collar, nervous, inattentive, soft, unhappy. In a way, they were not even there.

I'd like to see it, the older Harbour twin said. I'd like to watch.

That's pretty sick, said the boy named Wayne, a brooding olive-skinned boy whose father was a temperamental judge whom everyone except Wayne seemed to fear. You're a fucking freak, he said.

Wayne and the older twin wrestled, making high whining sounds, and then stopped when Wayne pinned the twin, who got up and walked off up the hill toward his house, sulking. Wayne stood there panting, looking after him. Then he stared for a while at Eykelboom's house before heading off toward his own, without speaking to the other boys.

EYKELBOOM WAS NOT SUPPOSED TO PLAY in the big drainage ditch at the end of the street, down near the turnaround. It was not a cul-de-sac, as no one had ever heard of the term. Plus a cul-de-sac should have houses rimming its perimeter, houses with neat yards and diagonally symmetrical lots, whereas one part of this turnaround was bordered by a bamboo-filled ravine, another led to a rough dirt path to a small bass-and-bream lake that was infested with water moccasins, and a third section opened up to a big new house with a low-lying front yard that filled with brown water every heavy rain. Just before you reached the turn-around, on the north side of the street, a buried storm drainpipe that ran from the top of the hill down to the bottom emptied out into the drainage ditch. The sandy earth there had eroded into a small gully that threatened to undermine the street itself. The boys built dams in the storm runoff that came from the pipe, dug treacherous caves into the sandy bank, hid in the ditch to lob dirt clods at cars that had come down their street by mistake, thinking it a throughway. Their parents didn't worry about the ditch, thinking the boys had sense enough (they did not) to be careful and look out for themselves. But Eykelboom's family was from some place very different, and Eykelboom's old man did not allow him to run loose. He was expressly forbidden to go into the big drainage ditch.

Nor was he allowed to run loose in the dense tract of vir-gin forest that began just behind the houses on the north side of the street. These woods were owned by a cantankerous old man named Chandler, who lived in a large old plantation-style house perched on the edge of the woods as if he were the resident troll whose mission it was to guard them. Chandler had once owned the land under the boys' houses, too, before the developer bought it from him and paved what had been a dirt road to the lake and built a dozen small ranch-style houses on a dozen small lots, six on either side of the street. At the end of the turnaround was the big house that the developer had built for himself.

When Eykelboom declined to go into the woods, the boys called him a coward and headed in without him. He stood in the street and watched them cross a vacant lot to the section of barbed-wire fence where they normally entered the woods. Then he called out, *Wait, I'm coming*, and ran to join them.

There was a creek that ran the length of the woods. At its low-est point it widened into a series of waist-deep, muddied pools, creating a swamp. In the clear, shallow areas of the creek higher up, there were minnows and tadpoles, and crawfish to catch. But the pools were murky and more likely to harbor snakes and snapping turtles, so the boys avoided them.

They took Eykelboom on a tour of their main trails through the woods. They pointed out areas that even they hadn't explored, then doubled back and showed him the layout of the creek from near its source down to the pools. When the boys saw that he was standing on a spot that had been weakened by the creek's current they exchanged glances but said nothing. The bank gave way and Eykelboom plunged into a pool up to his belly. The boys pulled him up, but he was inconsolable.

My dad's going to kill me, he said.

Why don't you just get wet all over, and you can say someone sprayed you with a hose? the older Harbour twin said.

It won't work, Eykelboom mumbled. It won't matter.

Why don't you just go change before he gets home from work? She'd tell him.

Well, someone else said, we'd better hide out in the ditch and hope you can dry in the sun before your old man comes home.

It was the younger (by five minutes) twin who said this. The twins were not identical. The younger one looked like a boring businessman shrunk to the size of a child. The older one was taller but scrawny as a starved stray cur.

Eykelboom reminded them that the ditch would only make it worse. He looked like he was about to cry. A couple of the boys felt sorry for him, along with a vague annoyance.

Actually, Wayne said, the woods would be worse.

He seemed very calm. Eykelboom was bringing something out in Wayne.

It's not just someplace you're not supposed to be, Wayne said. It's trespassing. We could all go to jail just for being here.

The boys looked at Wayne. They knew that the woods'

owner, Mr. Chandler, hated them because they built forts and camped out in there and of course made campfires, which meant that they could potentially start a forest fire and burn it all down. This was a small and pristine forest where some boys just a few years older than these swore they'd seen an ivorybill woodpecker, supposedly extinct for longer than the boys' parents had been alive. But the boys' parents seemed to think nothing of their trespassing in Mr. Chandler's woods. If they knew that Chandler hated the boys being in there, they showed no sign. Chandler sometimes used his shotgun when he detected the boys' presence in his woods, striding into his great backyard and firing off loads of birdshot that pecked down through the broad low canopy of leaves like a shower of rain. Once the middle McGowen brother took a pellet on the pad of his pinkie finger. The finger stayed swollen for a week. His older brother advised him to say it was a bee sting.

Now, after Wayne's words, the boys were having visions of prosecution for trespassing, a previously unthinkable prospect. A squad of deputies would be dispatched to the woods to round them up and take them to juvie lockup, inking and logging their filthy little fingerprints, taking their urchin-esque mug shots, interrogating them, hauling them to court, tossing them into some kind of Boys Town chaos of a prison.

Then Wayne said, There's nothing else you can do. You have to go hide in the ditch. It's too shady in here. You'll dry out in the sun and your old man will never know.

The boys all knew he wouldn't dry out there. It was a humid day. One of those days when their mothers had to leave the wash on the line for a second or third day to dry it fully. The boys knew that Eykelboom was fucked, either way, that it was just a brief matter of time before his old man would come home in his ridiculous vehicle, rolling down the hill blowing his ridiculous melodious horn as if everyone, as if anyone, would be delighted to know that he was home again, home again, and that as soon as he went into the house and said, Where's Ikey? and Eykelboom's mom said, I don't know, he's been out all afternoon with the other boys, Eykelboom's old man would be out in the street himself, hands on his hips, so you could tell even with a T-shirt on that he was sucking in his gut to look like he did calisthenics and never ate anything other than raw lean meat, calling out Eykelboom's name in a voice that said as clear as God's that he was planning on putting some kind of hurt on Eykelboom.

They waited, squatting low, watching the dirty water trickle from the big pipe and down the drainage stream. Every few minutes one of them climbed up to peek over the rim of the ditch to see if a car was coming down the hill. On the far wall of the ditch were the ruins of the caves they'd built earlier in the summer. They'd built four of them. Wayne's had been the most elaborate, with two chambers, the smaller just large enough for Wayne to crawl into and curl up like a baby. They'd come out one morning to find them all destroyed. Someone had taken a shovel and caved in the caves. Someone afraid that his child would be in there when the sandy soil above collapsed and smothered him. It could have been anyone, really, someone's parent or even a city worker cruising by on inspection. But the boys knew it had been Eykelboom's father. They imagined him sneaking down there in the middle of the night with a shovel and a flashlight. No one else had really seemed to notice the caves. No one else hated the ditch. No one else was so aggressive. Their fathers did not take action. The boys' fathers tended to ward off worldly trouble with idle, halfhearted swats as if at lazy bees. Eykelboom's old man, although odd, even laughably weird, was potentially frightening, very humanly alive. They couldn't even greet him, *Hello, Mr. Eykelboom*, without getting a smirk in return, as if they had tried to speak but had failed because they were retarded. Sometimes he even laughed at them. They were terrified of him. They wanted not to kill him but for something stronger than themselves to crush him.

As for Eykelboom's mother, they knew nothing, although they assumed that she was at least somewhat like their own mothers, sometimes angry and sometimes sad, obsessed with the outrageous burden of housework and cooking, even if they had paying jobs as well. Women who rushed out of their back doors to smoke, pacing, on the patio or in a lawn chair as far from the house as possible, who could not be spoken to until it was bearable for them to be in their lives again, which could take minutes, hours, or days.

A car came down the hill and the boys hunkered low. It whooshed past fast and unseen and turned into the long drive of the developer's house at the end of the turnaround. The developer and his wife zoomed up and down the street, and occasionally waved but never stopped. The boys had waved back when they were younger and the street was newer but they did not anymore. They realized that they were negligible. Occasionally someone's dog or cat that lacked sense or agility was crushed beneath one of their big, sleek cars. The developer's wife would come and apologize. She seemed gigantic, loud. Her teeth were enormous. They feared her. Like their parents, they toiled in the developer's fields like serfs, outwardly quiet and obedient. They took out their need for violence upon one another.

After they heard the developer's car door open and shut, they heard Eykelboom's father's dump truck turn onto their street. They heard it come over the top of the hill and slow with a throaty downshifting of gears, and heard the horn blow out its melody, the opening bar of "Dixie," which was idiotic, not to mention deliberately provocative, given that he was from Indiana-land. They heard the truck lunge into the Eykelbooms' driveway and stop. They heard Eykelboom's father get out and go into the house.

Eykelboom's eyes in his long, heavy head were wide open, limpid, staring at nothing. He squatted there very still, wet and steaming in the sultry heat. Then they all heard the Eykelbooms' front door open and shut again. Eykelboom seemed to be holding his breath, his lips trembling. His father called out in a hard low tenor, a voice all the stranger for being rarely heard in regular speech.

Emile! he called. Emile!

He called Eykelboom Ikey only when he wasn't mad.

Eykelboom closed his eyes, took a deep breath through his nose, and let it out.

I better go on up, he said.

Wayne said, Let's sneak out the back way into the woods.

The boys looked at Wayne. He was looking at Eykelboom in a way that was meant to seem very casual but was actually very intense, as if no one else were there but Eykelboom and Wayne.

Eykelboom said, It'll just be worse if he has to come get me.

He squatted there a moment more, then stood and said, I'll see you guys, and climbed the side of the ditch and onto the street. They could see his father standing beside the dump truck, waiting on Eykelboom, who trudged along like a boy condemned, arms at his sides, big flattop head hanging down. His father didn't even glance at the boys peeking up over the edge of the ditch as he slowly pulled his belt from its loops, folded it in half, and stood waiting, yea, like an executioner, the leather belt hanging from his big, bony right hand, his wire-rimmed spectacles gleaming in the light. When Eykelboom reached him, neither said anything. The father turned and followed Eykelboom through the carport and into the house.

The younger twin said, derisively, You guys, in an exaggerated Yankee accent. Then his brother said, in the same tone, Emile. He said, He's beating the shit out of Emile right now. The three McGowen boys said nothing, their small similar mouths squinched up.

The middle brother looked at Wayne, who was staring at the Eykelbooms' house with his eyes half closed and his mouth slightly open, as if he were daydreaming or lobotomized or asleep on his feet. Then just his eyes moved and he was looking back at the middle brother, who felt electrified by his stare and struggled to look away.

IT WAS A WHILE BEFORE they saw Eykelboom again.

They almost forgot about him. They forgot to hate him.

Then one day he stepped out from behind a large shrub that grew wild in the middle of the vacant lot and followed them into the woods without their knowing it. One of their forts was a four-story treehouse built with lumber stolen from an outbuilding below Mr. Chandler's house. It was an old servants' quarters house that had been overtaken by kudzu and brush and it was far enough away from the main house and dilapidated enough that they had been able, like insects or spirits, to dismantle it from beneath the kudzu's cover. The boys worked at it, slipping pieces of the little house into the throat of the woods without once alerting Chandler.

They'd built the treehouse on a hill, the first floor six feet above the ground, using three large straight pines as its foundation beams. The trees formed a rough triangle and the boys had nailed the floor joists into the trees, laid the floorboards across these, built the walls without openings except for a narrow strip between the wall and the next floor, and then nailed on more boards to form a flat roof, which served as the floor of the next story, until they had four levels. They'd stolen the remains of a roll of tar paper from a construction site and laid sheets of this over the roof of the top room. The only entrance was a small hole in the floor next to one of the trees, which they climbed using pieces of two-by-four nailed into the trunk as a stepladder. There was also a hole in the ceiling of the top room, so that they could stick their heads out and watch for the approach of Chandler or one of their parents. Once the twins' mother had drunk too much gin and wandered into the woods and been lost until the boys found her, standing in a small clearing in her nightgown, barefoot and weeping.

On this day, one of the twins was on the roof for only a minute or so before coming back down.

He said, Eykelboom's down there.

The boys were incensed that Eykelboom had followed them to this fort. It was their newest and grandest fort and they had not shown it to him when they had given their tour. Wayne climbed up through the lookout hole and then climbed back down. He looked at the oldest McGowen brother, who turned to the middle brother and said, Go down there and tell him to go away.

What if he asks to come up? the middle brother said.

He can't come up, Wayne said. He's not allowed.

Make him leave, the oldest brother said. Go on.

The youngest McGowen brother watched them from a dark corner, his eyes bright with excitement.

The middle brother slowly made his way down the ladder steps, floor by floor, and stuck his head out of the entrance hole when he reached the lowest level. There stood Eykelboom, gazing into the woods with a stoic, if forlorn, expression. The middle brother figured he had heard their discussion. Eykelboom fixed a strangely calm expression on him, and said nothing.

Ikey, the middle brother said. You have to go away.

That's right, Emile, one of the twins said from inside the fort.

Eykelboom looked suddenly angry.

I'm not going away, he said.

I can't let you in, the middle brother said.

You don't have the right, Eykelboom said. I can stand here all day if I want to and you can't do anything about it.

The middle brother pulled his head back through the entrance hole and looked at the other boys, who had climbed down to the first level to listen and watch.

It's a free country, Eykelboom said then, louder. Which was such a Yankee thing to say.

Fred-e-rick, Wayne said in a mock-tired way, drawing out the middle brother's given name, a name that everyone knew he did not like. Climb down there and make him go away.

The middle brother whispered back, How?

Wayne's eyelids fluttered. He was smoothing the paper on a cigarette he'd lifted from his old man's pack. The boys had been planning to smoke it. Wayne put the cigarette into the corner of his mouth and spoke.

Beat. His. Ass.

The middle brother did not want to go down there and beat Eykelboom's ass. Eykelboom was big, and like his brothers the middle McGowen was small. But he couldn't not do it. He would become lower than Eykelboom. With a swelling of sadness and doom in his heart, he descended the two-by-four ladder to the ground.

Eykelboom had crossed his arms like a stubborn, determined person on a television show, like in a musical movie or something. He was even taller and broader than the middle McGowen brother had realized. He reached out and gave Eykelboom a push, to no real effect, and Eykelboom looked away, reddening. The middle brother pushed him again, harder, and Eykelboom let out a high-pitched wail of rage. He flailed at the middle brother with his long heavy arms, landed one big blow against the middle brother's head, and turned to leave.

The middle brother reeled and his head rang with the blow but then he heard something and saw Wayne peering at him through the entrance hole. Wayne said, Are you going to let him just do that to you?

The middle brother caught up with Eykelboom and leapt

onto his back as if he were riding piggyback. Eykelboom twirled like an off-kilter top but the middle brother hung on, afraid to let go. They spun toward one of the fort's foundation trees and slammed up against it. The middle brother fell off without a word and Eykelboom ran away toward his house, keening in his outrage and grief. Possibly it was outraged grief. The middle McGowen brother lay on the ground, stunned. Wayne stuck his head through the entrance hole and looked down at him for a moment.

Way to go, he said. Come on up.

The middle brother roused himself slowly and climbed back into the fort. The boys lit and smoked Wayne's cigarette, passing it around. The middle brother took a puff and passed it on.

You did good, his older brother said to him.

But he didn't feel good about any of it. He was using every bit of will he had not to cry, which would have made it all even worse.

EYKELBOOM DISAPPEARED. HE WINTERED in his brooding or became spectral as a ghost, there but not there in any evidence. Then summer came again and he drifted or sifted back into visibility, though he kept himself peripheral and quiet. He didn't try to merge. He didn't speak much or look at anyone directly. He'd changed, still angry but also disaffected, detached. The boys saw him do things on his own. Leave his house and go into the ditch without apparent concern then disappear out of it into some other place, down to the lake, or into the woods, emerging hours later seeming unchanged. Sometimes his old man would be waiting on him, sometimes not. It didn't seem to matter. He affected or displayed a studied nonchalance, leaving his father to look weak somehow as he stood waiting in the driveway holding his belt, or sometimes just balling up his rawboned workingman's hands as if they contained all his rage, his face showing nothing.

Once Eykelboom stayed out in the woods all night by himself at one of the boys' forts, the oldest one, now abandoned deep in the woods. The boys found the evidence days later. Ashes and burnt logs in the pit from a fire they hadn't made. A ball of blacked foil in the ashes that had helped cook something they hadn't eaten. What looked like Eykelboom's big sneakers' prints in the soft dirt around the pit. How he had got away with that, they had no idea. Then they realized that he probably hadn't but didn't care.

Things began to happen. The long-abandoned shack on the lake's far bank burned down. It had once been a caretaker's cabin. The boys had planned to steal its lumber for a new fort. The police, in the paper, called it arson. A girl's stolen bike was found broken and bent down in the bamboo. A row of new saplings in the Porters' immaculate yard was destroyed, every trunk snapped. The twins' dog Bummer, a giant golden retriever so ancient that he never left the carport anymore, disappeared one night, his body never found. The boys knew it was Eykelboom. Wayne went up to him and said so.

He said, We know it's you doing all this crazy shit.

So what if it is? Eykelboom said.

So you'll pay for it, Wayne said.

Says who?

If you killed Bummer, the older twin said, you deserve to die.

Eykelboom stood there with his chest poked out, like his old man, staring back at Wayne.

Says me, Wayne said. Says we.

You can't hurt me, Eykelboom said. You can't prove I did anything. And you don't hate me any more than I hate you. So fuck you.

None of the boys had ever actually had those particular words said directly to them before, nor had they quite used them yet. Wayne stood chest to chest with Eykelboom. Then Wayne gave him that half smile and walked away. Eykelboom didn't move. He looked around at the other boys. They looked back for a moment and then went home. Before going into the house with his brothers, the middle McGowen brother glanced back. Eykelboom was still there in the fading light in the vacant lot across the street from his house, looking at nothing.

He didn't exactly disappear again. He slipped in among them now and then, silent or all but so, like a strange intelligent dog, a stray. He slipped in when they were out in the twilight, one minute not there and the next minute beside them. It was spooky. One night, in just such a moment of quiet apparition, they heard Mr. Chandler's horse down in the woods. It sounded as if it were being attacked. The shrieking sound it made prickled their skins. Chandler often let the horse run loose in the woods, but never so far as they knew at night. More than one of them had been almost run down while walking along a narrow trail, hearing the hooves very suddenly near, diving aside as the horse came galloping by in a heavy-heaving, wheezy blur. He was a big bay stallion. When he got out of the barn he needed a run, and there wasn't a lot of open ground in the woods. The meadows tended to be small, no more than thirty or forty yards across. So this horse was a woods horse and he ran the trails. And maybe, they figured, that desire to run the trails was also a product of fear, because the older boys always said they'd seen bobcats in there. A couple of them even said they'd seen a panther, or had heard it scream. The boys themselves had neither heard nor seen sign of a bigger cat, but a panther was not out of the question. In this place, in this time, in this small town bordered all around by woods and rural land, any animal wanting to broaden its territory needed only to cross a few two-lane, tree-loomed roads into this or another swath of undisturbed forest. There were deer in Chandler's woods, so why not panthers, too? When Mr. Chandler's stallion ran in the woods, he ran like a horse with his tail on fire, or a horse with a big cat swiping at his flank, a horse who never knew from which tree something might leap onto his back and sink fangs into the ridge of his long, exposed neck. In short, whenever he got his exercise, this horse was effectively mad with terror. You didn't want to get in his way.

They heard the horse call out again. At first they stood very still and listened, and then Wayne said they had to go see. He came back from his house with a pair of flashlights, and Eykelboom followed them in. They made their way across the vacant lot, through the fence, down the trail toward the swamp, the horse's trembly bellowing growing louder. Soon they saw lantern light glowing down in the swamp, and heard the voices of men in between the sounds of the horse. They left the trail and entered the swamp, picked their way across muddy grass islands toward the yellow glow. The air was chilled and stank like rotten roots and sewage.

Kerosene lanterns hung from swamp tree branches, illuminating the horse, which was up to its withers in one of the black mud sinkholes. Two men who lived in old cottages behind Mr. Chandler's house were trying to get the horse out by levering him with thick pine boards stuck deep in the muck on either side of him. Mr. Chandler, his boots and pants heavy with mud, a battered town Stetson jammed down on his head, held a rope that was clipped to the stallion's halter. The men helping were mud-caked head to toe, as if they'd emerged from the swamp itself to free the beast from their own sightless world. The boys stood in a bunch just outside the dissolving rim of the lanterns' light, perched on soft hummocks of unstable swamp grass and moss, constantly shifting their feet to knobs of firmer ground.

The boards and the men and the lanterns and Mr. Chandler's harsh commands made the horse more afraid, and he bucked helplessly in the sinkhole. He strained and trembled, struggling to pull his forelegs free, pushing with his powerful hind legs.

Every now and then he raised his head and his neck went rigid and his large eyes rolled around in fear and that awful sound they'd heard from the street came from his throat, through his long clenched teeth.

The middle McGowen brother heard Eykelboom just behind him. Eykelboom said quietly, If it was my horse I'd go ahead and cut its throat.

The middle brother looked over his shoulder and saw Eykelboom staring at the horse, as they all had been, but he didn't seem disturbed. Eykelboom pulled a Boy Scout knife from his pocket, opened the blade and felt the edge with his thumb, then folded it and put it away. The middle brother almost said, Are you in the *Scouts*? but didn't.

The men and the horse worked so hard their bodies shuddered with fatigue. Finally the horse was able to free his forelegs and in a series of scrambling lunges he was out. He shook his big head and yanked the halter rope from Mr. Chandler's hands, knocking the old man into a sinkhole. He splashed straight for the boys, leaping from little island to island, busted past them with a blast from his nostrils, jumped the creek, and galloped away in the dark toward higher ground.

Help me out of this goddamn hole, they heard Mr. Chandler say to the other men. One of them leaned down to give him a hand, then took a lantern down from a tree branch. Mr. Chandler reached up for the other lantern and when he swung it around he saw the boys standing there like silent swamp elves.

You boys get the hell out of here, he said. You stay the *hell* out of my woods.

As they were leaving they heard him ask one of the men to repair the fence around the swamp the next day. He said something about those little heathens having cut it. The middle McGowen brother wondered if this was true. If it had been Eykelboom. Or Wayne. He thought it was the kind of thing that either one of them might do, Wayne just to do it. Eykelboom with some inscrutable sense of purpose. Even a boy could tell that it was Eykelboom against the whole world.

Using Wayne's flashlights, they made their way back down the dark trails and crossed the fence out of Chandler's property. When Wayne said to Eykelboom, You know he's going to be waiting when we come out, they all stopped. Eykelboom stood there for a minute. Fuck him, he said, I'll just stay here. He turned and walked back into the woods.

When the boys made it to the vacant lot they could see Eykelboom's old man standing alone in his front yard, lit by the streetlamp two houses down, waiting. He held something in his hand that wasn't a belt—a stick of some kind, thin like a thrashing cane. The boys stopped and looked back toward the dark woods. They glimpsed the faint contrast of Eykelboom's white T-shirt farther down the trail.

Eykelboom's father spotted them and called out, Where's Emile?

When he began to move toward them, they took off running.

They leapt over the fence back into the woods. When the younger twin caught his foot on the barbed wire and fell, hollering, they stopped to see if he was okay. But Eykelboom's father was still coming toward them through the vacant lot, the stick in his hand, and they took off running again down the dark trail. They listened for Eykelboom ahead of them as they ran. Instead they heard his father, following. They ran in the dark on the trail that followed the creek to the crossing upstream. They tripped over vines and roots and stumbled in ruts but kept going. They scrambled down the upper creek bank, jumped the creek, and ran up the other side. They heard Eykelboom's father far back on the trail—he had no flashlight and didn't know these woods—calling out to his boy. The boys called out then, too— Eykelboom! Emile! Ikey! they called in turn.

They searched for an hour or so, then made their way back

to the street. They left the woods at a different spot, crossed the fence behind the Porters' yard, and peered out from the side of their house. A police cruiser was parked half on the street, half in the Eykelbooms' yard. Eykelboom's father was talking to a cop near the open door of the cruiser. His mother was there, just outside the carport, in a house robe. A couple of people stepped out of their homes, curious.

Cautiously, the boys went over. Eykelboom's father stiffened when he saw them. He still had the stick in his hand. He looked at the cop, then at the boys.

He said, What have you little bastards done with my boy? What have you done? I'll fucking kill you if you've hurt him.

It was hard not to run.

Then Wayne said, We didn't do anything to him. What're *you* doing with that stick in your hand? What were *you* going to do to him before he ran away?

What do you mean ran away? Eykelboom's father said. The cop peered at the boys from beneath his visor.

That's right, Wayne said then. He beats Ikey all the time. He made him run off.

The cop's narrowed eyes moved from Wayne to the other boys to Eykelboom's father. He looked at the stick.

I'll handle this, Mr. Eykelboom, the cop said. Please put the stick down and go inside your house for now.

Eykelboom's father didn't move, just stood there with the stick gripped in one hand, staring at Wayne. The boys tensed, thinking he might rush them.

Mr. Eykelboom, the cop said again.

Eykelboom's father slowly turned his head to look at the cop, then at the stick in his own hand. He gripped the stick even harder and went inside, walking past his wife without seeming to see that she was standing there in her robe and slippers, pale and speechless, her face drawn tight as if there were no teeth in her head.

The cop asked the boys questions. Had they seen Eykelboom in the woods? Did they know where he might be? He got on the radio, talking.

There's a swamp in there, Wayne said, and told him about the horse and Mr. Chandler and his men. The cop studied him for a long moment. Then he got on the radio again. He said something into the mic about Mr. Chandler. In a little while an old pickup truck grumbled down the street and parked next to the cop's cruiser and Mr. Chandler got out, wearing clean clothes. He talked to the cop, glanced at the boys, shook his head. The cop said something else and Chandler shrugged. The cop got on the radio again. Chandler lit a half-smoked cigar he'd pulled from his shirt pocket, leaning against his truck, gazing into the shadows of his woods.

Eventually, two sheriff's deputies dressed in hunters' overalls went into the woods with high-beam flashlights. Soon another cop pulled up with a dog in his car and they went in, too. Neighbors came out and gathered near the cruisers, whose lights were whirling and lighting up the homes and windows and trees in the yards. People shared coffee and beer, smoking, speaking in quiet voices. Occasionally someone said something that made others laugh and then stop themselves. Mrs. Eykelboom had followed her husband inside. After a while the neighbors went home. Chandler got into his truck and left. The boys were called home by their parents. The two youngest McGowen brothers watched from the dark window of the bedroom they shared, in their house next door to the Eykelbooms'. They saw the deputies make their way out of the woods, looking beat. The cop with the dog came out. The police talked among themselves. Their radios squawked. They turned off their cruisers' flashing roof lights. Then an unmarked black car arrived. Two men in suits got out and went up to the carport. They talked to Eykelboom's father at the door. It looked like Eykelboom's old man wouldn't let them in. Then he closed the door and the cops all left.

For days the police and deputies searched the woods with a pack of hunting dogs. A helicopter from the National Guard base flew over low and slow, a couple of military men in the bay looking down, searching. Drown teams pushed heavy rakes through the muck pools in the swamp. They dragged the pools near the end of the creek, then the lake below the turnaround. Police checked the bus and train stations, though the boys had never known Eykelboom to have money that he could have used for travel. Outlying farmers were queried, their barns searched. The local TV anchorman seemed to hint that something had been wrong among the Eykelbooms, but in a very cagey way. No one ever reported, *It is said that Eykelboom's old man regularly beat the holy shit out of him.*

Among themselves, the boys knew that was why, idiots. Weeks passed like time underwater. Winter came and went, then spring. The Eykelbooms, Mr. and Mrs., moved away. Their house sold within a month. This time it was bought by an old man who had worked at the creosote plant. Newly retired, the boys' parents said. Occasionally, the retired man's grandson came to see him and spend the day. He was a shy boy, but nice enough, with a small face and downy blond hair. But his grandfather wouldn't let him play with the boys. When they approached, the grandfather came out and gave them a dark glare and called his grandson back in the house.

Wayne went off. He didn't move away, or disappear like Eykelboom, but he stopped hanging out with the other boys. They rarely saw him. The oldest McGowen brother had become interested in other things, as well, and pretended the younger two did not exist.

The boys effectively disbanded, a tacit dissolution. They abandoned their forts. It was said that Chandler now kept wild dogs in the woods and fed them deer he shot from his back porch and dragged into the woods to a clearing just below his house.

Then, one late summer night, the woods burned, flames leaping up to the low evening clouds and turning them red and orange. Forest crews managed to contain the fire, but the woods were destroyed, their ruins like a blasted, ghosted battlefield, stumps and blackened fallen trunks releasing swirls of smoke into winter. Spring seedlings worked their way from the dirt, but before they could begin to grow, a man in a backhoe churned through the mud and dug a long trench from the lake to the swamp, draining it. Another crew laid in large concrete pipe and installed storm drains on what looked like concrete chimneys emerging from the pipe. Then they covered the pipe with dirt. A grader smoothed and leveled the land. The Developer had been waiting, knowing that Chandler would sell. During all of this, a policeman kept watch, in case there were human remains. There were no remains. No one would ever know what became of Eykelboom. If he was alive somewhere, the boys felt sure that no one knew who he really was. They believed he had made some kind of miraculous escape. Into some other life that he had made up and now occupied, somewhere else. He had passed himself off as older, used his outsized body to get a job in construction, a factory, an oil field. He rarely spoke to anyone, no more than was absolutely necessary. He was a mystery to everyone who knew him now, wherever he might be.

They all grew older, in the visible world, scattered carelessly into this life or that. The boys' parents sifted into their private, forgotten histories, crumbs of memory in a landscape of stained tablecloths and kitchen floors.

The two younger McGowen brothers, having survived their older brother as well as their parents, had become drinkers, and sometimes when they were together, drinking and talking, the middle brother would mention Eykelboom. Together, over time, they dismissed the old theory of escape and began to envision Eykelboom deep down in what used to be the swamp. They imagined that the sinkholes there were deeper than anyone had ever known. In spite of the elaborate drainage system the developer installed, the area where the swamp had been was never developed. It had never stabilized.

The brothers imagined Eykelboom there, preserved and whole, curled up in a cold, fluid clay, drifting very slowly with the earth itself. His fists lay knotted against his cheeks, his knees to his chest, his face closed tight in an infinite, chilled gestation.

THE ZOOKEEPER AND
THE LEOPARD*

THE ZOO AT LATE EVENING NEVER FAILED TO CREATE IN
Walston, after two or three tokes on his one-hitter down by the
meerkat pen, looking down across the rhinos' pit, the illusion of
great isolation among wise and indifferent, almost godlike beasts
in a wilderness kingdom suspended somewhere slightly above
the surface of the earth. He leaned on the rhino railing and gazed
at the meerkats, who stood very erect and big-eyed on the hump
in their pen, looking back at him in alert and intense curiosity.
Every now and then their leader gave off a low chirrup. A large
bird, an African gray, flew over low just then, the sound from
his broad wings like the airy pistons in an old riverboat, like the
one in *The African Queen*, Walston's favorite movie. The parrot
was a regular flyover, did not belong to the zoo, and everyone,
Walston included, figured it to be an escaped pet now living in
the thick swampy woods between the zoo and the river, which
separated this southern part of the city from the old downtown.
Briefly, Walston considered what the results would be were he

---

* The author excerpted this story from a novel in progress he was tentatively
calling *The Man-Eater of Marigold Park*.

able to let everything go, open all the cages, primates and predators and birds and herbivores and snakes—everything. By God,
if he thought it would work and some rogue wouldn't kill him,
he'd do it. He'd let all the birds out first, the aviary birds, from
parrot and parakeet to spoonbill and truly frightening secretary
bird (talk about harkening dinosaurs), then he'd fling open the
gates to the game animals, the gazelles and impalas and dik-diks,
then the larger herbivores—the elephants, wildebeests, rhinos,
and water buffaloes—then the monkeys and apes, and finally the
bears and big cats, and he'd scramble up and watch it all from
the safety of his observation tower in the center of the zoo complex, having raised the ladder behind him, turn on the radio
and television up there, and wait for the chaos to begin. The
zoo was going down, anyway, just like this old moldering city,
so why not? That's what he would do, were he clever enough,
and sober enough. But since he was not, and knew it, he would
stick to his more modest plan, then leave town with the hundred
grand in his duffel along with his clothes and make Mexico, most
likely, before anything happened to make anyone the wiser. The
absence of the monkeys would no doubt be reported right away.
But it would be a day or so, given the way things worked around
there, before anyone noticed the absence of the leopard.

He stumbled over toward the gate to the rhinos' corral, startling the meerkats back into their tunnels, then drifted with his
half-empty bottle of Old Forester through the zoo's winding
sidewalks, to the monkeys' island. He could see some of them
in the moonlight, perched on the pitiful limbs of the artificial
trees sunk unto the phony island's concrete base. He set the
Forester down carefully next to a line of dense shrubbery and
then pushed his way into the shrubbery and disappeared for a
moment. A few more monkeys emerged from hiding to watch,
and now they were lined up on the branches of their phony trees
like an audience. They tensed and stirred with anxiety when

the shrubbery shook violently for a moment and then Walston reemerged struggling with a long two-by-ten pine plank, which he dragged in their direction, causing all but a few to hop toward the other side of the island. When he dropped one end of the plank onto the top of the fence around their island, the monkeys began to yip and shriek and run to and fro, stopping momentarily to look at Walston and the plank, then scamper in panic again. Walston ignored them. He got hold of the other end of the plank and shoved it hard as he could, running with it until the far end bounced down on the ground on the other side of the moat around the island. He held his end so that it remained atop the fence, so that now there was a plank bridge for the monkeys to cross to freedom whenever it might come to them to do so. He stood there catching his breath for a minute, watching the monkeys run amok and then gradually settle down and sit on the ground and on the branches, looking at him, looking at the plank. Look at Walston, look at the plank. Scratch their heads and armpits. Then he retrieved his bottle of Forester, took a good plug from it, replaced the cap, and made his way toward Carnivore Alley.

He passed the large aviary. A solitary shriek from somewhere high in its alcoves, from some recalcitrant species, seemed tunneled from the prehistoric past and sent the tiny hairs on his neck and along his spine quivering and electrified, receptors. He rounded a bend into the cats' area and approached the pits with their stagnating pools of water disdained by the cats except in moonlight. He passed the phony mountain outcropping lair of the cougar, the quarter-acre savanna of the lions. He could see them, their massive heads alert and watching him. He stumbled past the micro-jungle behind glass that was the home of the jaguar, which he feared even more than the lions because of its unfairly smallish area and its constant mad, muscular pacing during the day and the way it eyed intently, moving its massive blunt head on its neck like a curious bird, any small child that wandered up or by on foot, in a stroller, or in its parents' arms. Then Walston moved swiftly across the zoo path and a few yards down to the leopard's den.

The leopard was hidden, somewhere back in the bamboo and bramble in its corner. During the days, it often perched on the swinging platform built for it close to the bars that separated it from the sidewalk, in between which of course was a rail and a pit. The leopard, too, had a way of noticing small children and babies, but unlike the jaguar it did not seem excited by their presence. It only gazed at them, panting lightly in the heat, as if yes it, too, would love to kill and eat them but it was smart enough to know that it could not. On some level the leopard understood captivity perfectly well. The jaguar either could not entirely process this or was just a bit insane in its life of pointless and inextricable captivity in which the hunt, and violence, and fresh blood were as removed as the memory of an animal's dream. Either way, for Walston this actually made the leopard more frightening. A more intelligent big cat did not exist. And this was why he had chosen to let out the leopard instead of another cat. A tiger, had he one to release, would certainly create a more immediate terror. A lion would be a more spectacular event, even less disposed to make itself invisible. But the leopard would be, in the end, much more effective. And the leopard's famous appetite for monkeys, and skill at catching them, was why he was releasing the monkeys. Give the old boy a little native game to munch on for a while. The few deer left in these woods would soon clear out. Stray cats and dogs hapless enough to have taken up residence in the woods would be taken. The possums and raccoons would be decimated, or leave, or become savvy in the case of the raccoons. But soon, soon enough, the little city of Marigold would begin to miss its urban stray cats and dogs that had managed to elude the animal control units, which would seem a strange but favorable mystery. Then a little later the farmers closer to town would have their dogs taken, if unchained or unfenced, and eaten on the spot if chained or fenced. People within the city limits would begin to miss their beloved kitties and lapdogs and yard dogs. And then the real hue and cry would go up. This is what Walston wished he could stay around to see, but it would not be wise. He would enjoy quite enough imagining it all from his hacienda somewhere in the mountains of central Mexico, sipping the local mescal and pondering whether to simply whore around or convert to Catholicism and take a lovely little Mexican bride. Mexican whore, Mexican bride. Angel, or devil. A fine way to ponder out one's days. Walston went around back of the leopard's den and used his key to enter the feeding berths, leaving the door open behind him, propping it with a rubber stop. Even in the berth, with the door to the viewing area closed off, the scent of the cat was strong, something like he imagined smelling salts would put off, with the additional tangy tinge of feline urine. Walston took it in as if huffing a deep breath of fresh air in the country, then coughed. He heard a rustling on the other side of the berth door, then the unmistakable cough of the leopard himself, in response. He would have laughed if he hadn't been afraid he would piss himself.

THE FEEDING BERTHS WERE SIMPLE concrete floor areas behind the viewing environments, which the animals could enter by way of a small steel door that could be opened or closed by the feeders with a long-handled tool. Normally one would see that the cat was not in the berth, lock the door between there and the environment, open the door to the berth, leave the meat on the floor, exit, and use the tool to open the access door again.

Near the leopard's feeding berth Walston paused, listening. No sound of heavy breathing. Nothing of its acrid, fetid scent. He sat on the concrete for a moment, his back against the cold concrete wall opposite the berth cage. The Forester and weed were working a great fatigue upon him, and he wanted to make sure his wits were about him before he made his next move. He took a last pull on the bottle, finishing it off, and went over his plan again in his mind. It was difficult to keep it quite straight, and this was why he'd kept it simple. He felt for the butt of the Army .45 he'd shoved into his belt, was relieved to feel the solid steel and wood of it, before cursing himself for having forgotten the simplest and most obvious part of his plan, which had been to shoot one of the monkeys and bring it along as distraction and bait. But he didn't have the strength or will to go back and do all that now. He'd made sure that the leopard hadn't been fed in several days and so it wouldn't really matter if he gave it something as scrumptious as a monkey or not. Regular feed meat would do.

He set the empty bottle aside, heaved himself upright, and went over to the cooler. He reached in and hauled out a large chunk of thawed meat of some kind—either horse or old beef—set it down about five feet from the feeding door. Then he went next door to the jaguar's feeding berth, checked to be sure the jaguar was not in there, reached in the tool and tested to make sure the access door between the feeding berth and jaguar environment was securely fastened. He fumbled out his keys and opened the door to the berth. Here he would retreat and lock himself in until the leopard had exited the building. Then he opened the door to the leopard's feeding berth just a crack, hastened back toward the jaguar berth, closed the cage door behind him, and sat again on the floor, feeling exhausted. He would need a bit of rest here after the leopard's departure before he would have the strength to get up and out to his truck, which he'd parked just off the access path nearby earlier in the day.

He wished again he'd had the moxie and the wherewithal just to let everything out, everything. He imagined the great chaos that would arise. He would watch the leopard eat a bit, eyeball him, and then most likely take the rest of its meal and wander out onto the grounds. He would wait a bit longer for the presence of the leopard and the other big cats to panic the other creatures, who with any luck would mostly exit the rear of the zoo, having had time to either see the gate Walston would have swung wide open or to see or hear other animals leaving from that vicinity. The cats were sure to follow, their curiosity taking them out toward the tract of woods in any case, a much greater likelihood really than any of the other animals, although he figured the birds, primates, and smaller mammals would gravitate that direction. It was possible, which gave him its own measure of satisfaction, that the larger herbivores would lumber their dumb way onto the four-lane loop around the city, this northern section of it between the zoo and the river and the low soybean fields there, and cause great havoc among the early commuters. Surely the primates and some of the birds and possibly all of the cats would make their way through the tract of woods and to the outskirts of the city itself, possibly crossing the river west of town and making their way into the outlying residential neighborhoods, with any luck creating great havoc for the city's authorities and, in particular, the city's Chief Animal Control Officer, to whom Walston referred ignominiously as the dogcatcher. He took particular delight in this because the dogcatcher was in fact a member of the social elite in this town from his membership in one of its oldest and most respected families. In addition, he was a much-decorated military veteran, retired as a high-ranking colonel, and had plenty of money. Everyone knew the dogcatcher had wrangled the job because he was bored, and he liked power no matter what form it took, and the position of Chief Animal Control Officer, appointed by his friend the mayor, was a relatively easy way for the dogcatcher to wield power and still feel as if he were at least semi-retired, which was retired enough for a man of his disposition and energy.

Thus, to call him the dogcatcher was a high insult, albeit one the zookeeper (formally known as Zoo Manager, but he knew the dogcatcher referred to him as the zookeeper, and he even referred to himself as the zookeeper out of a studied demonstration of humility to his staff, even though he had attained his status because he was in fact a veterinarian and planned to support himself in Mexico by running an illicit clinic, to stay off the law enforcement radar) had not yet mustered the courage to use in the dogcatcher's formidable presence.

He could hear in his mind a herd of tiny deer clattering by on the asphalt path just outside and he laughed to himself.

The dogcatcher had become the zookeeper's enemy after having seduced the zookeeper's wife at a drunken fundraiser for the zoo in March. Since then, the zookeeper figured, the affair had progressed. His wife was never reachable at home when he was at work, anymore. She often ran two-hour errands in the evening, returning with a can of tomato paste or a jar of olives from the store, pleading boredom and distraction in the aisles. Though the zookeeper and his wife had no pets, his wife's clothing was now often clung to by short coarse hairs that came off on the car seat and the sofa. The dogcatcher, though nearly seventy years old, had the reputation around town as quite the cocksman. Known for ravaging the bored wives of his fat, alcoholic club buddies and playing their jealousies off one another at cocktail parties throughout the season, the dogcatcher was apparently highly amused by the catfights that inevitably ensued after martinis and the dogcatcher's prolific flirtation on dimly lit patios and in the recesses of broad, manicured lawns. As well as by his cuckolded club buddies' astounded refusal to believe that anyone would want to ravage the sagged, wasting bodies of their wives.

But the zookeeper's wife was not sagged or wasting. She was the hot and hot-tempered daughter of a supposed-gypsy fortune teller who operated out on the old south highway, a woman the zookeeper had managed to marry in spite of her family's nearly murderous opposition. He'd seduced her with his Honda motorcycle and flights in the Cessna 150 he shared with two friends from the air base. Through their influence he'd once secured tower permission to buzz the zoo with his wife while he was still wooing her, sending animals on scampers that were abbreviated versions of wildlife scattering on the savanna from the swoop of an aerial hunter's plane. He'd lied and told her of upcoming expeditions to Brazil and Tanganyika to collect specimens for the zoo. He'd told her of exotic foods and drink from these and other source countries. He'd even made up one country, which he'd named Loolandia and claimed was a tiny, isolated island just northeast of Madagascar, where it was rumored there lived a unique primate beast who spoke an ancient quasi-humanistic language and lived entirely on the flesh of its enemies: monkeys, chimps, lemurs, great cats, rivals within its own clan, and the occasional human who washed up on its shores. He suggested to her that it was the fabled missing link. What did the supposed gypsies' daughter know, a smart girl but unworldly, her education choked off by the cord of possessive paranoia wound about her neck since birth by her jealous, latently incestuous family? He'd never have met her had he not encountered her running away one afternoon down the blistering-hot two-lane highway, wearing only a long nightshirt, and barefoot, her black eyes smeared with tears, her brown fingers soiled from some kind of violent encounter with her own starved and ravenous heart. She'd leapt onto the back of the Honda as soon as he'd stopped, before he could even beckon her aboard, and sank her long ragged nails into the flesh below his ribs as he gunned it on down the highway and into the furrows of a clear-cut acre just below a distant curve in the road.

Since those days, however, the zookeeper's wife had become quite worldly, in a small-town way, and the delightful source of society column gossip in the daily newspaper, *The Argonaut*. She was a social autodidact to a keen degree. Her combination of curiosity, burgeoning lust, vengefulness, and suspicion—all the result of her virtual domestic enslavement for twenty-five years—gave her a foul mouth and a forward nature, so that her sexual modus operandi generally was to embarrass or even insult a man with presumptuous remarks about his genitalia or prowess. He either withered or rose to the challenge and grappled with her in couplings not unlike wild beasts' whose mating rituals were typically violent and quick, though persistently repeated for sometimes hours at a time. To keep the zookeeper complacent she had for many years followed such illicit encounters with sexual attacks on the zookeeper himself when she returned home, dashing his suspicions by blowing his mind out with extraordinary orgasms she'd learned to elicit by secretly reading an ancient tome of gypsy sexual practices she'd found between the mattress and box springs of her parents' bed. It was perhaps because they knew she'd read this book that they were so wild to keep her in the house until she married a proper gypsy man, although the family claimed in public to be descended from Abyssinian Arabs of the shimaglle class and lived in a wooded compound of Creek Indian ruins made from the historic local orange-red brick and sandstone. But those plans had been dashed by the zookeeper's effective abduction of her, and since then her family had been dithering over whether to kill the zookeeper or not, whether it would be more disgraceful for her to stay with a *gadjo* zookeeper or be the widow of one. This they discussed and argued over, often coming to blows, every evening at the family's long, communal supper table in the ruins of what they called the compound's villa.

The zookeeper had considered various modes of revenge on the dogcatcher, from an anonymous letter to the editor about his adulterous nature, sugar in his municipal fleet's tanks, to darting him with a rhino tranquilizer as he stepped into his backyard some evening to take a territorial piss. But on a recent evening he'd had a stroke of brilliance and realized the best way to harass the dogcatcher was by humiliating him professionally, and his elation at the idea had prevented his drawing a sober breath ever since. Surely a leopard, the most dangerous cat among all the big cats, the most stealthy and intelligent, the most vicious killer, a notorious lover of dog meat, would wreak havoc among the dogcatcher's most influential constituents, the well-fed owners of various sleek and exotic canine breeds sleeping stupidly and complacently on the screened back porches of Marigold mansions, snoozing lap dreams on their hundred-dollar doggie beds from L.L.Bean, or trotting between the hedgerows and impotent topiaries down the lawn.

HE'D BECOME A LITTLE LOST in his daydreaming mulling over this, resting behind the cage door inside the jaguar's feeding berth, when he blinked and saw that the leopard stood just on the other side of the cage door, watching him. A sickening fear crept through him like a sluggish bolt of deadly current, and he thought for a moment he might throw up. Saliva flooded his mouth and he spat it out to one side. And when he looked up again, the leopard was gazing at the cage door itself, and pawing it tentatively, the way a housecat might paw half-heartedly at a toy. The leopard hooked its paw gently around the lock to the door, which swung open toward it so that it leapt back, surprised, crouching, tail switching back and forth. And then it raised its eyes to see Walston sitting there, the passage open between them, in a freeze, his eyes very wide. Walston pissed himself, could not move for a moment, and then against what would have been better judgment began to edge himself away toward the far corner of the jaguar's berth, trying to tug the pistol from his belt but it was stuck by its hammer, which had become wedged beneath the belt. The leopard watched him until he reached the corner of the berth, and then it crept swiftly through the open berth door and crouched there, facing him, ears laid back. Walston tugged desperately to free his pistol. The leopard snarled. Walston managed to pull the pistol free and fling his hand in the leopard's direction, but he had neglected to chamber a round and now he was trembling so violently that he could not do that. Nor could he be silent. He screamed. He saw the leopard move toward him, the cat a spotted blur of speed, then he experienced a concussive blur into blackness, into nothing. He was alive, but not breathing, his neck snapped. Just before he expired from the blood flooding the left side of his head and oxygen deprivation, he regained consciousness. Just for a moment. Just before he felt the long teeth squeezing into his windpipe, the huge head of the leopard buried into his neck like a lover's. Just for that moment, before he was gone, the zookeeper regained his vision as if in a blossom of consciousness before blacking out, and was eye-to-eye with the cat's dilated, green-and-yellow-rimmed pupil not two inches away, the short hot wet snorts from its nostrils in his ear.

NORMALLY, THE LEOPARD WOULD STASH the kill in a nearby tree for safekeeping and return to it later, when he was hungry again. But he knew he would not return to this place. He'd dragged the zookeeper outside the jaguar's feeding den, not wanting to eat where the other animal ate, and fed on one of the zookeeper's legs for a while, then rested. He sniffed the air, reaffirmed the absence of any other threats. He bit down into a firm grip on the back of the zookeeper's neck and swung him around, knocking the head on the open cage door and inadvertently slamming it to. Dragging the zookeeper's body between his legs, he padded from the feeding area into the open air of the zoo, now grown silent after the general commotion stirred by the noise he made making the kill and by the scent of blood that had permeated the air.

There was a near-full moon up, not ideal. Yet nothing seemed amiss. He paused to lift his tail and mark the entrance to Carnivore Alley, then made his way along the footpath to the zoo's boundaries, taking his time, as apparently calm as only a large cat can be. His passage caused a great pall to fall over the cages and pens and pits, with the monkeys and chimps and gorillas quietly ascending to the tops of their perches, in the far corners, and the small animals zipping into their holes, and the large herbivores shuffling to the far edges of their areas, and the other cats going still, half crouched, eyes dilated, watching the progress of this beast who must be a ghost cat to have entered the world of the human beings, strolling down their paths, breathing their air. And then the other cats began to pace, growling low in frustration and envy and confusion. The large herbivores trotted en masse hither and thither, spooking one another until they fairly stampeded from one end of their pits to another, the monkeys and apes began leaping about and chattering, then screeching, the birds fluttered and flew about madly, knocking against the wire walls and ceilings of their aviaries, the iguanas and snakes flicked their tongues all about their glassed little caves fetching particles that whispered *leopard*, and the hyenas knocked one another in their restless jealous avarice until one attacked another and they became a chaotic bloody high-yelping melee of black and brown fur and blood on pink torn flesh and bloody grimace. By the time the leopard, the zookeeper's carcass firmly in the grip of his jaws, leapt to the top of the hurricane fence on the zoo's south side, dropped the zookeeper's carcass onto the ground on the other side, picked it up again, and forded the creek there—by then, the zoo's ten acres, with its rich array of animal and bird life, its cool green flora of oaks and mimosas and sycamores and great stands of rustling bamboo, the flowering fruit trees, azaleas, and camellias along its manicured paths, the shrubbery thick with heavy-scented gardenias, honeysuckles, and magnolias, had blossomed into an unspeakably beautiful garden of madness, the leopard its envoy to the sleeping city, his heart singing with lust for prowling, stalking, watching, killing, and the godlike invisibility of observation from the dense-leaved limbs of sturdy deciduous trees.

But that would come later in his new freedom, which already felt as natural as if he'd never lost it—after a couple of days leisurely feeding on his kill. The leopard had not tasted fresh meat, or warm blood, for a long time. He had an intense and instinctive craving for the rich blood and tissue of the organs. Though it was more work, the combination of this craving and his long-cultivated hatred of the zookeeper compelled him to crack open the skull and devour the brain with relish. After raking out the viscera he ate the heart, but the liver was fouled.

HE HAD SLEPT IN THE HIGHER BRANCHES of a massive live oak between the fairways of holes one and three at the country club, and late in the afternoon watched with intense curiosity the golfers walking by, stopping to swing at the balls, calling to one another. Once a short, sturdy woman pulling a little cart behind her stopped right beneath the tree, hunted around for a ball, found it, hit, and walked on, pulling her cart. The leopard had been tempted to leap down on her just for the sheer fun of it, as leopards will sometimes do. But there were other golfers nearby, and he didn't want the trouble of dealing with them. His meal was almost digested but not entirely just yet.

Finally night fell and the last golfers were only occasional gabbles of laughter and speech erupting small and distant from the lights at the bar and grill beside the eighteenth hole. The leopard made his way carefully down to the largest, lower limbs of the live oak, leapt down into the grass of the rough, and stood there testing the air and waving his tail lazily back and forth. He was curious about the bar and grill so he began to walk in that direction, in no hurry, a sleek and shadowed solitary figure in the silvery light. He paused on the fairway of the long, silent number five hole and made a mighty defecation, scratched a clump of grass at it, then went on his way. The large scat lay steaming in the wet, glinting, close-clipped grass. It was the zookeeper, of course, some facet of his vestigial consciousness relieved at the sensation of (relative) light and air. At the oddly, fleetingly familiar scents of cut grass and irrigation water. Of the way a waxing moon might indicate itself so softly, so infinitely, to the blissfully closed lids of one's eyes, through a window open at evening, when he was a child. [Watson note to self: Other parts of the zookeeper's consciousness will be in other piles of excrement, fading from the larger ones and barely there in the smaller ones, until they're all decomposed and he's vanished.]

FOR IT HAS BEEN WRITTEN, and is true, that more than any of the other great predators, the leopard lives only in the moment, not in memory, not in any world other than the one he walks through just then, and he takes it all in, but it is as God might take it all in, as if it is all his, as if it all exists only for him, in that moment, and any other mode of existence is, literally, inconceivable.

For the creature with the ability to live as such, every moment is timeless as the ages. It is a kind of immortality, in truth. As close as any living creature in this world may achieve.

Thus they are gods.

SEEING EYE

THE DOG CAME TO THE CURB'S EDGE AND STOPPED. THE MAN holding on to his halter stopped beside him. Across the street, the signal flashed the words DON'T WALK. The dog saw the signal but paid little notice. He was trained to see what mattered: the absence of moving traffic. The signal kept blinking. The cars kept driving through the intersection. He watched the cars, listened to the intensity of their engines, the arid whine of their tires. He listened for something he'd become accustomed to hearing, the buzz and tumbling of switches from the box on the pole next to them. The dog associated it with the imminent stopping of the cars. He looked back over his right shoulder at the man, who stood with his head cocked, listening to the traffic.

A woman behind them spoke up.

"Huh," she said. "The light's stuck."

The dog looked at her, then turned back to watch the traffic, which continued to rush through the intersection without pause.

"I'm going down a block," the woman said. She spoke to the man. "Would you like me to show you a detour? No telling how long this light will be."

"No, thank you," the man said. "We'll just wait a little bit. Right, Buck?" The dog looked back over his shoulder at the man, then watched the woman walk away.

"Good luck," the woman said. The dog's ears stood up and he stiffened for just a second.

"She said 'luck,' not 'Buck,'" the man said, laughing easily and reaching down to scratch the dog's ears. He gripped the loose skin on Buck's neck with his right hand and gave it an affectionate shake. He continued to hold the halter guide loosely with his left.

The dog watched the traffic rush by.

"We'll just wait here, Buck," the man said. "By the time we go a block out of our way, the light will've fixed itself." He cleared his throat and cocked his head, as if listening for something. The dog dipped his head and shifted his shoulders in the halter.

The man laughed softly.

"If we went down a block, I'll bet that light would get stuck, too. We'd be following some kind of traveling glitch across town. We could go for miles, and then end up in some field, and a voice saying, 'I suppose you're wondering why I've summoned you here.'"

It was the longest they'd ever stood waiting for traffic to stop. The dog saw people across the street wait momentarily, glance around, then leave. He watched the traffic. It began to have a hypnotic effect upon him: the traffic, the blinking crossing signal. His focus on the next move, the crossing, on the implied courses of the pedestrians around them and those still waiting at the opposite curb, on the potential obstructions ahead, dissolved into the rare luxury of wandering attention.

The sounds of the traffic grinding through the intersection were diminished to a small aural dot in the back of his mind, and he became aware of the regular bleat of a slow-turning box fan in an open window of the building behind them. Odd scents distinguished themselves in his nostrils and blended into a rich funk that swirled about the pedestrians who stopped next to them, a secret aromatic history that eddied about him even as the pedestrians muttered among themselves and moved on.

The hard clean smell of new shoe leather seeped from the air-conditioned stores, overlaying the drift of worn leather and grime that eased from tiny musty pores in the sidewalk. He snuffled at them and sneezed. In a trembling confusion he was aware of all that was carried in the breeze, the strong odor of tobacco and the sharp rake of its smoke, the gasoline and exhaust fumes and the stench of aging rubber, the fetid waves that rolled through it all from garbage bins in the alleys and on the backstreet curbs.

He lowered his head and shifted his shoulders in the harness like a boxer.

"Easy, Buck," the man said.

Sometimes in their room the man paced the floor and seemed to say his words in time with his steps until he became like a lulling clock to Buck as he lay resting beneath the dining table. He dozed to the man's mumbling and the sifting sound of his fingers as they grazed the pages of his book. At times in their dark room the man sat on the edge of his cot and scratched Buck's ears and spoke to him. "Panorama, Buck," he would say. "That's the most difficult to recall. I can see the details, with my hands, with my nose, my tongue. It brings them back. But the big picture. I feel like I must be replacing it with something phony, like a Disney movie or something." Buck would look up at the man's shadowed face in the dark room, at his small eyes in their sallow depressions.

On the farm where he'd been raised before his training at the school, Buck's name had been Pete. The children and the old man and the woman had tussled with him, thrown sticks, said, "Pete! Good old Pete." They called out to him, mumbled the name into his fur. But now the man always said "Buck" in the same tone of voice, soft and gentle. As if the man were speaking to himself. As if Buck were not really there.

"I miss colors, Buck," the man would say. "It's getting harder to remember them. The blue planet. I remember that. Pictures from space. From out in the blackness."

Looking up from the intersection, Buck saw birds dart through the sky between buildings as quickly as they slipped past the open window at dawn. He heard their high-pitched cries so clearly that he saw their beady eyes, their barbed tongues flicking between parted beaks. He salivated at the dusky taste of a dove once he'd held in his mouth. And in his most delicate bones he felt the murmur of some incessant activity, the low hum beyond the visible world. His hackles rose and his muscles tingled with electricity.

There was a metallic whirring, like a big fat June bug stuck on its back, followed by the dull clunk of the switch in the traffic control box. Cars stopped. The lane opened up before them, and for a moment no one moved, as if the empty-eyed vehicles were not to be trusted, restrained only by some fragile miracle of faith. He felt the man carefully regrip the leather harness. He felt the activity of the world spool down into the tight and rifled tunnel of their path.

"Forward, Buck," said the man.

He leaned into the harness and moved them into the world.

CRAZY HORSE*

ROBBIE STARTED COMING TO CRAZY HORSE AS SOON AS HE could stilt himself around on his casts without crutches. His legs were so badly broken in the crash that he was hospitalized for a month. For a couple of weeks they didn't know if he'd keep the legs or lose them. Then they inserted pins, layered on the full-length casts, watched him another couple of weeks, and sent him home to recuperate with his mother.

Which was a lot worse than being in the hospital, he said.

He said, "If I couldn't wipe my own ass, I'd be in trouble."

Often, in the early afternoons, he was the only person in the bar except for me, and I was running it. I was running it into the ground, but I was hardly even aware of that.

One thing I'd done was make a deal with the man who owned and serviced the pool table, who let me use quarters marked with red fingernail polish. When he emptied the coin bucket he gave me back the polished coins. I said it would increase his business if I started the games, and it did, so I played a lot of eight-ball and got pretty good. Pretty consistent double bank. Simple straight or angled, no-bank shot, forget it.

I must have played eighty to a hundred games every week.

---

* This story was still in progress at the time of the author's death.

And for a while there I played at least five or six games a day in the early afternoon with Robbie, who moved around like some life-size tin soldier, stick on his shoulder like a parade rifle, cantilevered over the table to make his shots. And he was good enough that often as not I had to use my marked quarters for at least half the games. If I ran out, I just polished another roll and kept going.

That's one indication of how I ran Crazy Horse. Another would be letting my friends drink free if they minded the bar while I played a game of pool. And toking up in the cave-like room in the back, behind the bar, which made my father nervous. And another would be keeping no books, not a single notation. All Crazy Horse served was canned beer: Bud, Busch, Miller High Life. When the canned beer got low, I called the distributor, re-stocked, paid the driver with cash from the register, and that was that. I probably had customers who had a better idea of my profit/loss margin than I did.

I didn't care. I was eighteen, married with a one-year old son, when we got the phone call telling us my older brother was dead. He'd been running Crazy Horse, a moldering, underleaf-green, concrete block bunker in the old neighborhood east of downtown near the cemetery where they'd buried the Gypsy Queen back when that was a big deal. Even the cemetery was decrepit by then. The little package store my father ran, a tiny affair on the street corner of the same lot, had no name at all. Just "Package Store," "package" being the Southern euphemism for a bottle of liquor in a paper sack.

Sometimes in the middle of our afternoon games the pay phone on the wall by the bar would ring and it would be Robbie's mother, drunk, raving, cussing me out for being a bad influence on her boy. Then she'd tell me to put him on, and I'd hold the phone out toward him on its metal cord.

He'd just shake his head, a vacant smile on his plow blade face.

"He doesn't want to talk," I'd say, then have to hang up in the middle of her Cuss Soliloquy, because it was so obvious she could have gone on and on.

I let Robbie drink for free, of course. He was underage, so I couldn't *sell* it to him. So technically she was right.

But not only was he the miracle survivor of the wreck that killed my brother, on his left, and Steve Youngblood, on his right, he had a history of surviving wrecks that killed others. It's almost as if he was touched, in that way. These two shattered legs were the worst thing that ever happened to him, in a vehicle I mean.

He'd survived this last wreck because of those legs, is what he finally told me, after a lot of eight-ball and Budweiser on a Monday afternoon. Because he was sitting between the Bronco's two front bucket seats (it was a three-on-the-tree), legs stuck straight out beneath the dash, and because that Knox boy's car came flying around the curve, airborne, and hit them halfway up the grille, his legs got trapped there and kept him from going through the windshield, which is what killed Youngblood. My brother was killed when the steering column came up and smashed him in the face. I'll never forget my father looking into the casket during the private family viewing and turning away in tears. "He's crushed," he said. My mother held it in, and it pretty much killed her, in time.

We closed the casket for everyone else.

One night I and my wife and baby and mother and aunt were in the living room at my parents' house watching television, and we heard my father's car pull up in the drive, heard the car door shut, and he stumbled into the room, drunk, plopped onto the couch, put his head in his hands, and sobbed.

"I can't stand it," he said. "I just can't stand it."

It says a lot about my family that no one went over to comfort him. We were all paralyzed by his grief and our white, Southern,

Protestant inability to deal with emotions. We sat in our places as if frozen there by some science fiction machine, unable to move or even speak. In a while he got up and went down the hall and to bed. No one said much of anything then, either, and soon my wife and I gathered up our baby son and went home.

Years later, for some reason, it was this moment I thought about when I looked down on my father in his own casket. Aneurism. He didn't look bad, for a corpse, but something was off. It was his almost luminescent silver hair. They'd combed it straight back from his high forehead, a style I'd once suggested he adopt, but he insisted on brushing his thin forelock to one side. He was awfully vain about it. So I asked the funeral director to please adjust, and he rushed to do so. Then Dad's friend Woodrow came up and stood beside me, looking at Dad. Stone-bald Woodrow wasn't an emotional man, but he was one of my father's oldest friends. He made a little hitching sound in his throat.

"Henry always had the prettiest hair," he said.

YOUNGBLOOD WAS OUT CELEBRATING the birth of his own first son. Robbie was along just because he was always looking for someone to attach himself to. No one was paying attention to that kid. There was his mother, the drunk, his older brother, who had his own life, and his father, who'd shot himself in the head a few years earlier. No one ever said why. No one blamed Robbie's mother. It was just something that happened, in the master bathroom in their nice big house on Poplar Springs. After that, lacking her husband's income, Robbie's mother lived in a little white house with asbestos shingles and a stoop instead of a porch. She drove an old Ford Country Squire wagon, no panels, with a busted left rear spring like it was dragging a club foot. Drank and smoked like a barfly but always at home. Robbie lived with her simply because he had no interest in working a job, and anyway the police could have forced him back home because

CRAZY HORSE | 65

of his age if his mother had demanded it, and she would have. He had no interest in going to school, either, after dropping out of tenth grade. Since she slept in every day, so could he, and it wasn't hard to get out of there before she came to and around. And it wasn't hard to stay out until she passed out again. Sometimes he misjudged and caught hell from her until she gave out or he walked out, waiting in the shrubbery as the noise inside died down and he could hear her snoring through the open window of her room.

My brother was out because earlier that evening, in Crazy Horse, his wife had been insulted in a nasty way by Jack Flanagan, who had lost his mind. Everyone knew Jack had lost his mind but even so it was appropriate that he deliver an apology to my brother's wife, and my brother was driving around—with Robbie, who'd been in the bar, and Youngblood, who'd also been in there celebrating, and my brother's wife and his wife's friend Leah on the Bronco's back benches—looking for Jack, in order to persuade him to apologize to my brother's wife. I'm not sure exactly what Jack had said. I'm not sure I ever knew, if that ever got clarified. Even so, that's why my brother was driving them all around after midnight on a Friday/Saturday. They'd just stopped by the bowling alley. Jack was here not fifteen minutes ago, someone said, so they headed up winding, narrow Ludlum Road to continue their search.

And what happened next was so absurd as to seem impossible, but it's true.

JACK FLANAGAN HAD LOST HIS MIND for no particular reason after his father died of a heart attack and left him $100,000, which was a lot of money in those days. He quit his job, became a gym rat, got drunk bar hopping every night but Sunday, and on Sundays just rode around in his car, drinking. He picked fights and pummeled his opponents near to death, until most bars wouldn't let him in and the ones that did tended to be the rowdier ones, including Crazy Horse.

On the night he killed my brother and Steve Youngblood, crushed Robbie's legs, partially paralyzed Leah Scarbrough, and nearly killed but only concussed my brother's wife, Jack had left the bowling alley and, it so happens, parked at the other end of Ludlum Road, in the shadow of Roy Fields's service station there, waiting on Dee Knox to pass by on his way home. Jack knew where Knox was drinking, just up the road at Porter Wagoner's bar, and that the only logical route was for him to take a right onto Ludlum, so he was waiting. Knox had offended him in some way and had escaped a beating, somehow, but Jack intended to catch him on his way home or follow him all the way and beat him there. And when Knox did make that turn, and Jack took out after him in his car, my brother and Robbie and the others were leaving the bowling alley headed in the opposite direction, toward Jack and Knox, who were traveling at about eighty miles an hour when Knox hit the dropping curve around which his car would collide with my brother's Bronco. Jack had braked and slowed for the curve, though the terrified Knox boy had not.

I don't remember now if Jack stayed and tried to help at the scene. Everything was confusing, everyone in a state of shock— the living, anyway. I don't think Jack was charged with anything. It was his word against the Knox boy's, I guess. There was a time when, I suppose, I would have been assigned a blood revenge, I would have had to kill Jack Flanagan. But I was not. And Jack Flanagan went away somewhere, and then later his wife and child went away, too. They disappeared from our hometown as if they'd simply vanished. That's the way it finally felt, once we began to wake up from our dumbfounded disbelief, confusion, and grief.

MY BROTHER WAS NOT AFRAID of anything. Most likely Jack Flanagan would have bested him in a brawl, but that wasn't under consideration. The point was my brother believed that Jack should apologize to his wife for insulting her in Crazy Horse that night. He would not have walked up to Jack and taken a swing, would not have gone up and cursed him, goaded him. He would have said, reasonably, that Jack had been rude to his wife and should apologize for it. It's very possible that Jack, after some calming talk, would have done that very thing. But my brother wasn't worried about what would happen if a fight couldn't be avoided. He would be all in, and if not defeated then Jack would not come away unhurt, big and strong as he was. My brother was not a big man. He was on the small side. His friends called him Crow, maybe because of his crow-black hair, maybe because he kind of looked like a crow, just a bit, in the face. Because I was his little brother, they called me Little Crow, although by the time of his death at twenty-two I was taller than he was. But that didn't matter, it was a manner of speaking. Also I would never be the man my older brother was, all around. Small as he was, he was formidable. He had no fear, was a natural athlete, strong for his size, and quick. And smart—some people didn't know that, as he had no interest in college and didn't show off. But to speak to his toughness as a small man who wasn't afraid of confronting the much larger and stronger Jack Flanagan, I'll tell an anecdote told to me by one of my brother's friends long after his death.

"We were all out at the lake," this friend said, "and I didn't know him yet. Back in those days, you know, I kind of liked to fight. I enjoyed it. I said to Finn Samson who was sitting beside me on the beach, said, 'I'd kind of like to fight that guy.' And Finn looked at me and grinned and said, 'You don't want to mess with that little fucker.' And I took another look at your brother, studied him, and I realized old Finn was probably right. So I didn't fight him, and I'm glad of it. We were good friends after that, all the way up till he died."

AT THE TIME OF ROBBIE'S COMING to Crazy Horse in the afternoons in his casts, I was dealing with it all by smoking a lot
of marijuana, drinking beer, and spending most of my waking
hours in the bar. My father didn't have the will to chastise me,
set me straight. It was hard for him to care whether we made it
or not. He was drinking a lot of his own stock, too, in the little
package store. He scolded me for smoking weed in the back, but
a year later he'd be borrowing one of my homemade marijuana
pipes, smoking up with his old childhood pal, Sweetpea. A couple of middle-age white guys wearing gold jewelry around their
necks, navigating a white Buick Wildcat through the country-
side, ripped, listening to Willie, Waylon, Merle, Conway Twitty.
Tall, skinny Sweetpea, with his long, swept-back yellow hair and
mellow baritone, helped amp up the cool factor for my father
enough that Dad didn't seem entirely ridiculous.

The fact was my wife had moved out, taken herself and our
son to live with her parents. And because we'd been renting our
basement apartment from her two old maid aunts who lived
upstairs, I had moved back in with my parents as well.

My mother had taken a sick leave from her job at the medical
clinic. She sat in the recliner and watched television most of the
day. She still made dinner most evenings but they were ghosts of
her famous Southern country fare. More often we ate bacon and
tomato sandwiches, ground beef and bean casserole, hamburgers,
Hamburger Helper (which she'd never stooped to, before) and
the Chik-Steaks and hot tamales we'd order out from the Triangle and Mrs. Benson's tamale kitchen in the projects.

So my mother sat in the recliner in our relatively new brick
ranch house on that dead-end street and watched television and
smoked cigarettes. In summer the foliage sagged like thin shed
skin from its branches. Our backyard regressed to wild weeds
and storm debris. Paint was peeling. Inside the house smelled

of mildew and cigarette smoke. She'd been given a prescription of some kind of tranquilizer that was a predecessor of modern antidepressants. She was hardly there, anymore. I slept in my old room, with my younger brother, while my older brother's room remained empty, the door shut, everything my brother had owned still hanging in the closet, sitting in the dresser drawers, perched on top of the dresser. Fishing rod leaned in one corner. Shotgun and rifles on the rack on the wall. My mother had gone over to his and his wife's apartment—she seemed to blame my brother's wife for the accident, for putting him in the position of looking for Jack Flanagan, more than she blamed Jack, himself—swept up all his belongings and replaced them in his old room, then shut it up tight. As if some part of him were still alive in there, his ghost, and everyone acted as if that were indeed true. Also, in the middle of the night, more often than not, my younger brother—with his fine features and long, silky brown hair—would have his dream, whatever it was, and sit up like someone rising in the coffin from death, pulling his upper body up straight into a seated position, saying words I could not make out, in zombie fashion. I would call his name in a loud whisper, tell him to wake up, to shut up. He would slowly turn his sleepwalking face (though he never actually got out of bed) to me, stare with big, doe-brown, unseeing eyes, then lay himself back down again and sleep like a normal person.

I knew I had to get myself out of there somehow, and soon. I considered sleeping in the bar, but it smelled too strongly of spilt beer, piss, and so much cigarette smoke that little sticky rivulets of tar ran down the walls at the pace of slow time. I would have had to sleep on the pool table. I would have to wake up every morning in a dive bar. It wouldn't matter that it was my own.

Finally, the only thing to do would be to surrender, beg my wife to take me back, try again, start over, and that's what I

would do, but that's another story. That would come only after
I'd hit bottom, and that would take a while. I got out of my parents' house by sleeping in my old VW bus, stumbling across the
gravel lot to it after closing up. I showered in the shower room
at the public pool at Highland Park. And in the meantime, there
was Crazy Horse, and part of Crazy Horse was Robbie Love.
Something about that boy got ahold of me. He'd been the closest
person to my brother the moment my brother died. And he'd
been conscious. I wanted to know exactly what he'd seen, but I
couldn't bear to ask.

NIGHTS AT CRAZY HORSE were hoppin'. Sometimes I thought
my brother's death had increased business out of sympathy, but
the truth was he was widely loved. Starting around five or six on
weekdays, and midafternoon on Saturdays, we started filling up.
Not a big bar, and not a window in it, just a vestibule to the one
door for in and out. It would never pass a fire inspection these
days.

I ran the A/C in the cold or cool weather that late winter and
early spring, to suck out some of the cigarette smoke, but I kept
the old gas space heater going at the end of the bar to balance
it out. One night Dub Coleman passed out on his stool and fell
onto the heater, caught fire, and rolled off onto the floor. No one
went to help him, just stopped drinking and watched, waiting to
see what would happen next, until he moaned and rolled over
and put himself out accidentally.

Our town, the younger people in it, had a need, a craving,
for raucous bars run by younger people who let customers do
whatever they wanted, who did not demand a particular deco-
rum, whose bars did not attract respectable middle-class people
of a certain age, neither the old drunks. Bars that didn't attract
any people who would remind us of what we would certainly
become one day, of our futures, which we declined to explore. It

was the mid-seventies, and the summer of love was gone, dead, the war in Vietnam finally abandoned to shameful history, drugs were mundane and boring, deadly, marijuana was no longer fun, all the funny weed poisoned by the government down in Mexico and all the new stuff heavy Colombian fare that smelled bad and turned you into a lobotomy case if you weren't careful with it. The worst-off among us did quaaludes with their beer, or went dry and turned on to heroin. Monster Man, for instance. When I said to him that he should watch out for that shit, he stared at me, his features slack, and said, "No, man, it's the best." And that was as much as he could say, dropping back into his fog. And why not? Monster Man was always doomed. I've never known anyone who sustained as many serious head injuries. Once something—maybe a radio knob—made a perfectly round dent in his forehead about an inch wide and deep, to little effect. When he cleaned up, a few years later, he fell asleep at the wheel of his eighteen-wheeler and jackknifed it on the off-ramp not a mile from his home. That one killed him. At the graveside service, his sister looked over her shoulder at me as if I were somehow to blame. People like Monster Man, and like Robbie, like Cecil Hart, who made innocent drunken fun of that man leaving the Pizza King and the man came back with a .38 and shot him through the heart. Bo Logan, thrown out of Lewis Webb's truck against a tree a half second before the truck hit the same tree and cut him in half. Max Blackburn thrown in jail for being too high and OD'd on PCP, dying on the bare floor as his cellmates and the jailer paid no mind. Stephen Page, with his Honda and Marlon Brando looks, choking on his own vomit in bed down the hall from his sleeping or passed-out parents. Wright Hawthorn back home alive from Vietnam, drowning in six inches of water out at the lake, his friends just a few yards away. You had my mother numbed down to almost nothing. Father drunk down to a heart attack at forty-eight. Younger brother strung out on

quaaludes and bad pot. All of them and more with their destinies
visible right there on their faces, in their eyes, plain as if a voice
were speaking from there, telling you not to place any of your
foolish hope in this one here.

I had thought my brother immune to all that, invulnerable.
He was a natural sportsman who would quit jobs come deer season and disappear. He was a spendthrift who borrowed money
from me, the miser, though when he worked he made three
times what I made at my part-time job after school in construction. He tried to teach me how to hunt and fish, as these were his
passions, but at the time I couldn't care less, only did it to please
him or try to. He set me on a deer stand at the club he belonged
to, and a sizable buck came trotting over the hill straight toward
me, stopped, turned sideways, and looked in the other direction toward the dogs and men that were driving him through
the woods. Trembling, I blasted away, emptied the twelve-gauge
into the beautiful animal, which nevertheless died slowly. I stood
and watched it, feeling sick. The other hunters came up, smeared
my face with the blood. But when they tried to tie the buck's
scrotum around my neck with a piece of string, I balked. Their
faces fell, and I knew I was disgracing my brother but at the time
I didn't care. Back at camp, I washed the blood from my face,
took a hindquarter, and went home.

Nevertheless, just two months before he died, when I was
home for Christmas, he took me out hunting again—he belonged
to a different club by then. We saw nothing. And during a break
from our stands, we stood together and smoked cigarettes,
talking of nothing. Brother talk. He looked at me, that cocky
grin on his square-jawed face, his old-fashioned horn-rimmed
glasses slightly askew, his one green eye and one brown eye
behind them, and said, "I haven't gotten a decent shot in three
years and you go out just one time, stand behind a fallen-down
tree, and a goddamn buck trots right up to you and says, 'Shoot

me.'" So we finally had a good laugh about that. It was the last time I saw him alive. He'd tried college and said no thanks. Got past his twenty-first birthday, then his twenty-second. Got married, settled down, was learning cabinet making when he wasn't running the bar. He seemed happy. Other young people, mostly crazy ones but not always, died all the time. It was that way in boring small towns. But I didn't think my brother would ever die. He had too much life in him, more than other people did. The thought of that being snuffed out, in any way, was so inconceivable that such a thought never entered my mind, until it happened. And I wasn't alone in thinking that. Not only my family but also his friends felt the same. Any death cracks the world in some way. My brother's seemed to break it apart.

It only took about six months of Crazy Horse, six months to bankrupt it, close it down, leave it to sit there, boarded up, empty, until years later someone bought the lot and bulldozed it all down. I don't know what's there, now. I haven't been back.

Everyone thought the bar had been named for Neil Young's band, but my brother had named it for the great Oglala Sioux warrior, who could summon himself into the spirit world during battle and suffer no harm. Who knew no fear and died resisting the enemy, betrayed. A man whose ways were understated but bold, who had true visions, borne out in the end. Who believed that the spirit world is the real world, and we are but shadows cast dimly from it.

I DID, FINALLY, GO TO MY WIFE and beg her to take me back. I promised, because she demanded it, that I would stop drinking, stop getting high, stop hanging out with my decadent friends, that I would join her family's Baptist church, get a decent job, enroll in the local junior college, start acting like an adult. Like a husband and father. I was nineteen years old, and it was time. A church friend rented us his family's brick bungalow on a nice street in the north part of town. My father-in-law got me a job at the lumberyard, working in the woodshop, where they let me come and go for classes anytime I liked. I got in more than thirty hours a week, made good money, and liked the older guys I worked with.

I made an earnest effort. I cleaned up. Attended Sunday morning and evening services, Wednesday services, supper. I went around with another guy to do what they called "witnessing," entering people's homes like Mormons and talking to them about Jesus and the church. This was deeply embarrassing, but I did it. I taught a youth Sunday School class. I sang in the choir, somewhat tenor. I was baptized wearing a white saintly robe in the big glass tank in the wall behind the choir. I was cold sober for almost two years, except for the occasional bourbon with the elegant fifty-year-old widow who lived across the street. She was one of the most respected people in our town, and so my wife considered my occasional bourbon with Mrs. Wilding to be acceptable, perhaps even honorable, as she was not only a very respectable person managing her family on her own, but also a person of upper middle class wealth. That she liked to have a bourbon with me every now and then was considered to be a good sign.

My God those bourbons were delicious.

My parents divorced. There'd long been the strain of emotional distance, and the loss of their firstborn child was too much. My mother began dating an old friend who'd been in love with her in high school, before she married my father. They drove around in his enormous powder blue two-door Bonneville with white leather seats, sipping bourbon and water from little jelly jars. My mother sat with one leg tucked beneath the other, like a teen. The man who would become my stepfather, Clarence, beamed at having finally gotten a date with his high school dream.

My father moved to Jackson and rented a place in a cheap

complex of prefab apartments. When I could muster the will to visit him, I endured the stench of an older bachelor's abode, with its filthy bathroom tiles and the general odor of unwashed socks. He liked to sit in his La-Z-Boy and watch *The Benny Hill Show* and cackle over Benny's stupid sex jokes. He was recovering from a triple bypass, out of work. He'd let his body have its way and let his mind go idle. It was depressing, but I understood.

My younger brother was gone in his fog.

They were all surviving however they could.

My wife and I moved upstate so I could attend the university in Starkville. I didn't like the idea, didn't want to go. I liked my job, liked our house, liked my bourbons with Mrs. Wilding, and though I did not like all the church business I had a feeling we wouldn't last very long away from our families, even only ninety miles away. And indeed we would not. Just two months in she realized I didn't love her anymore, and I wondered if I ever had, and then I was alone up there and miserable. And sometime in there I got the news that Robbie Love was dead. Like his father, he'd done himself in. I had to wonder if his mother would get herself off the hook for this one, her youngest child. I couldn't believe it wasn't her fault somehow.

Grant Holifield, who'd been out with Robbie that night, told me what happened.

When Robbie turned eighteen he got the money his father had left him in his will. His mother tried to sue him for it because he wasn't yet twenty-one, but lost, and Robbie went on a long drunk of his own. He wasn't violent like Jack Flanagan, being of slight build, though he bought a big revolver and liked to wave it around, laughing at whoever freaked out over that. He started wearing cowboy boots to increase his height and walked like John Wayne drunk, a kind of controlled wobbly sideways staggering gait. With his new money, he finally moved out of his mother's house, though he'd slept elsewhere

as much or more often than home, anyway. He didn't rent a
place of his own but just kept sleeping around on people's sofas,
floors, right in their beds with them, fully clothed. He slept
on bar floors and, when it was warm enough, in little clearings in the woods. He slept in other people's cars, sometimes
cars belonging to people he didn't even know, scaring them
half to death when they found him there the next morning.
Once a half-blind old man didn't notice him passed out in the
back seat of his '61 Rambler American and drove him around
town all morning, to the drugstore, his barbershop, the hard-
ware store, took lunch at the new McDonald's, and when he
was headed back home Robbie almost gave him a heart attack
by sitting up and asking if he could pull over at a bus stop so
he could catch a bus downtown. He smelled bad and wouldn't
bathe until his straw hair stuck to his head as if wet and his body
odor became overwhelming enough to elicit universal, loudly
expressed disapproval.

Since the demise of Crazy Horse, a new popular bar had
popped up on State Boulevard, between the junior high school
and the local state mental hospital, in an old log cabin refur-
bished by a big man nicknamed Mimi who'd been a good friend
of my late brother's. Robbie, a regular, was in there with Holifield, hitting it hard. Holifield was by then the only person who
would put up with Robbie's difficult ways. They'd been friends
since elementary school. He practically made himself into Robbie's valet, took care of him, drove him around, let him sleep
on his own sofa most nights, tried to make sure of it, in fact.
Robbie was drinking whiskey he'd poured into an empty beer
can and just about blind with it. He had the big pistol, a Dirty
Harry Model 29 .44 magnum revolver, jammed into the front
of his jeans, handle and half the cylinder visible to anyone who
looked, and when he was drunk enough to make even easygoing
Mimi nervous about it, Mimi persuaded Holifield to get him

out of there. Which Holifield did, one big hand on skinny Robbie's arm as he John Wayned himself through the crowd of other drunks outside to Holifield's car.

But before they got out the front door Robbie said, "Wait, phone call." He found a quarter in his fob pocket, dropped it in, dialed, and after a moment he said, clear as if he was sober, "You ready now? You ready for it, bitch? 'Cause I'm coming over. Right now. You better be ready." He hung up, they went out, and Robbie told him to drive to his, Robbie's, mother's, house. Holifield tried to take him to his own house but when they pulled up there Robbie put the gun's barrel to Holifield's sweaty neck and said, "We going to the old bitch's house right now, Grant. Let's go." So Holifield backed out of his driveway and drove them to Robbie's mother's bungalow, going slow till Robbie waved the pistol at him and said, "Speed up, motherfucker, I ain't got all night."

His mother was standing in the open doorway, stoop light on, flanked by two policemen. "Don't get out, Robbie," Holifield said but Robbie was half out of the car so Holifield stopped and Robbie, the .44 huge in his small, almost childlike hand, staggered into the yard as the cops pulled their weapons and told him to stop, to not come any closer. His mother just stood there, mouth open in disbelief. Holifield thought Robbie would be gunned down, except that he did stop, called out, "Hey?"

Then he said, to his everlasting credit, "Get a load of this," and fired a .44 magnum round into his own right temple. It obliterated the left side of his head. Sent it in a wet cloud up into the streetlights. It looked, Holifield said, like he'd set off a bomb in the left side of his brain.

I WENT HOME TO ATTEND THE FUNERAL, at the same funeral home that had buried my brother almost three years before.

The crowd was big, not as big as my brother's, but bigger than I'd thought it would be. People loved Robbie after all. No one believed he'd had a chance to do any better than he had.

Out on the funeral home's porch Holifield was holding forth to a handful of guys standing there smoking.

"Fucking amazing," Holifield said.

"Who got the gun?" another said.

"Cops got the gun. I guess they gave it to his mother, after all was said and done."

"I wonder what she did with it?"

"I don't know, but I bet she didn't give it to Eddie." That was Robbie's older brother, the quiet one. "Probably ate it, monster bitch."

"Swallowed it whole, fires .44 mag rounds out her ass."

"Out her old ironclad—"

"God don't even want to think about that."

Inside, Robbie's mother, her big dyed red hair a mess, sat near the coffin, comforted by a group of women her own age and younger. Eddie stood to one side, no expression but a stern stillness on his face. Robbie's mother wept and wailed. But she got in her very last victory over that boy. The coffin was open. The undertaker had done his best, but the left side of Robbie's head looked as if he'd clapped a big clod of Bondo onto it and smoothed it out as well as he could. It was horrifying. What kind of mother would open that coffin, invite everyone to see her baby son, let them see exactly how awfully he had betrayed her one last time?

I didn't go with Holifield to the graveside service. I left the funeral home and walked the three miles to my mother's house on the north side of town. I didn't want to see anyone. But that's where my own car was. I had nowhere else to go.

It was the end of something. The end of our lives as we'd thought we would live them. My brother's death had torn us apart, and Robbie's death brought it home to me finally. We were all adrift, and no one survived it very well. That's why I'm telling this story. I've held it in all the rest of my life, but this is the story I most have to tell.

In my life I can't really believe that there's any other worth telling.

LUDOVICO TAKING HIS BATH

IT HAPPENS EVERY MORNING AT SIX O'CLOCK, LUDOVICO
taking his bath. Moehanid is in a shallow sweating sleep when
Ludovico pads heavy and naked to the tub and pushes the hot
water tap with his big fat toe. Locked in his room, Moehanid
imagines the scene: fat Ludovico shivering beside the tub, waiting for the water to rise. The pipes wail like freight train brakes,
then knock into their beat like bongo players, muted gongs, tiny
jackhammer crews in the walls, *bong boom brrrrang!* He hears the
water slosh, then a soft *hup!*

For three days after Moehanid shut himself in, Ludovico
tried to appeal to him. He knocked on the door, speaking softly.
"What are you doing, Hanid? Are you alive? Are you sleeping?" He walked back and forth outside the door (Moehanid
could see it in his head), shoes stretched to the obscene shapes
of his toes, the backs crushed beneath his thick heels so like
the hard pink rumps of chimpanzees in the zoo or the *National
Geographic*, so that he clopped, back and forth, Moehanid wondering, Horses? Goats in the house? Twisting into the sheets. In
the evening stray cats yowled and screamed in the crawl space
beneath the floors.

" 'Hani?" Ludovico squeaked through the keyhole. "Hey, Moe?"

"Go away," Moehanid said. "Don't speak to me." Sometimes he called out in his delirium, heard his own voice from outside himself and sat up to listen. He spoke to the keyhole. "It had better not be you," he said.

Moehanid had never liked his roommate. From the first time he met him in the student union, in the small group of internationals huddled in the coffee shop corner, Moehanid had been appalled. He was in engineering. They were all in engineering or business. Moehanid was nearly finished in civil.

He dreamed of designing a vast irrigation system fed by ancient rivers running miles underground, of replacing the arid dunes with lush crops and oases where lovers would stroll cobbled pathways lined with fountains and palms. But this Ludovico, when asked about his interests, says, "Human factors," arrogantly waggling his head. "To provide the link between man and machine. Otherwise, you design these beautiful monsters which no one understands and no one can use and which turn on us. Like Frankenstein."

"Frankenstein?" says Ahmed Bsaibes.

"A film," Ludovico says, "a movie. You want to understand Americans, go to the movies."

Moehanid couldn't remember when the big one had arrived on campus. He materialized fatly out of the hot and smoky Southern air. Moe thought his grossness not a benevolent state—it was the manifestation of a greedy soul. This was something Moehanid could just tell. His eyes were like folded flesh in his face, his breathing thick and forced and somehow intimate, like the sound a child hears when the doctor lets him listen to his own quietly rasping chest. Sweat formed a sheeny slick on his skin, beading in the coarse hairs on his fingers, his massive flesh like viscous sacks of oil inside his clothing. But most of all and most justly Moe disliked his smug behavior, his cozy presumptuousness, as if by being foreigners in a provincial state they were all tacit comrades. He had once overheard Ludovico tell an American instructor who was meeting with a friend of theirs, "You should not be so hard on foreign students," and had to restrain himself from telling him off. It was embarrassing to the friend, but Ludovico didn't seem to notice and slurped daintily at his heavily creamed and sugared coffee and smiled. "No matter," he said later, thumbing through a *National Geographic*, "you have only to look here, in their magazine, to see how superior they believe themselves to be. Everyone in here, many of them shown without clothing, is considered to be some sort of specimen, you see. We are no different, in their eyes. Subhuman. Go to the movies, who is the villain? The Arab. The Spaniard. The African. The Russian. The Indian. The villain is a white man, an American, then he is crazy, insane. But the villain is a foreigner, it is just his natural state, to be the villain."

He was everywhere, always in the union, always in the cafeteria, the coffee shop. If Moehanid wandered wearily far up into the library stacks late at night, into the region of raw metal shelving and cool unfinished concrete floors, there would be Ludovico at Moe's favorite nook, sequestered or wedged into the small space perfect for Moe but an ergonomic impossibility for Ludovico, the human factors expert. Moe sadly eyed the desk supporting the overflow of Ludovico's flesh, the small square window that gave suggestively onto the lovely desolate lamplit street below. Ludovico would say, "Hello, my friend. All this hard work will pay us well in the end," or some such infuriating banality. In his fat hand resting on the worn wood of the little plank desk, Ludovico's pencil looked like a strange, immaculately beveled twig, and Ludovico in his distracted study ran its point over his lips like a woman applying makeup.

But when Moe's money was cut off, his parents missing, the

flat blank fact of the occupation the only thing in the news, he had no choice but to accept Ludovico's generous offer of a room in the small house he rented near campus. Moehanid couldn't pay his apartment rent, and his friends were married or lived in the dorm. Of course no one was living with Ludovico at the time—who would? Moehanid tried to earn his keep. He took a humiliating job delivering pizzas, but he earned only enough to pay Ludovico a decent share of the rent and food costs, not nearly enough to move out on his own. When the fighting began he could no longer even get through on the phone. He bought cheap plastic mounts for the pictures of his mother, father, and little brother Wahlid and set them up on the dresser in his room. They seemed to look out from the photos into nothing. He couldn't make contact with their eyes.

There was a peculiar deadness on the campus, it seemed. He passed a small war rally one afternoon on the steps of the union, with seven or eight silly American students waving an American flag, and an even smaller counterdemonstration consisting of three slouchy students who appeared disgusted—whether to be there or because of the war, Moe could not really tell.

He began to sense something he had never noticed before, or let himself notice, believing it to be insignificant or a self-indulgent illusion: a certain undercurrent of hostility, directed vaguely toward him in the hallways, on the sidewalk, or especially away from the campus, from the ordinary people who lived in the town. His nerves sang with a new and numbing self-consciousness, as if he'd been struck like a tuning fork against the solidity of this sudden awareness. It was an emotion he'd completely shut out up until now as false, a waste of time, a weakness, a projection of his own insecurities. And especially a distraction from achieving what he had come here to do, which was to get an education so he could go back home and take care of his family.

And then, after days of watching CNN around the clock with Ludovico in their den, there was a call. His mother's voice on the telephone sounded so small he could imagine her only as a voice, not as his mother, but some small electronic reproduction of her, saying, "Oh, 'Hanid, they cut off his head," and sobbing until his father took the phone away from her and told her to lie down. "It's true, 'Hanid," his father said, "your brother," and then his father began to weep himself.

Moehanid had visions of Wahlid's head in his dreams, its eyes rolling back in shock, its mouth stretched into a wordless O. He could not rid himself of the image.

He dreamily attended his classes. He drank beer late at night at a bar near campus where baseball played on the television to the sound of country music from the jukebox. A tall girl in jeans and a loose halter top came up to his stool, swaying to the music, holding a bottle of beer above her head, leering at him. Moehanid could see her small pale breasts jiggling inside the top. He put his arms around her waist and danced with her, despair and lust at odds in his heart. She pressed herself against his groin and he pressed his lips against a tiny breast that slipped from the side of the halter top.

Then he was yanked away and thrown crashing against chairs and a table to the floor. A blur of thick pale faces above him. They picked him up by his shirt and pushed him out through the door to the street. His head banged against a power line pole.

He focused on a boy with bristly blond hair and an angry flat face. The boy hit him in the jaw. His cheek on the hard grainy concrete, Moehanid heard the guy's voice in his ear.

"Why don't you go home, you greasy Arab son-of-a-bitch, coming over here to go to our schools and then call us American pigs, you goddamn sand nigger."

A blow cracked him hard in the ribs. Stumbling home he found Ludovico in the den, watching TV.

"Your father telephoned," he said, "just now."

Moehanid stood in the stroboscopic TV light, Ludovico's bulk shifting in black-and-white, the whole room a broad fluid sketch in grainy pencil. It made him dizzy.

"What?" he said, his dulled mind grating against his pain and apprehension.

"I should not say, 'Hanid. It's not for me to tell you such things."

He received no answer when he called on the phone, the noise in his ear like the haunted trilling of a species long extinct.

"I am very sorry," Ludovico conceded, sadly eyeing the small bowl of roasted nuts in his palm. "I'm sorry that this falls to me." He plucked one from the bowl and munched it, then breathed deeply. "Your mother has expired. Your father said that her heart was not good."

Moe felt the radiating waves from the television set pass by him like silent wisps of a desiccated breeze, parching the insides of his mouth and nose and the surfaces of his eyes. It was hard to breathe.

"I am very sorry," Ludovico said. "It's a tragedy."

"Her heart was very good, you son of a whore," Moe said.

Ludovico looked up slowly, chewing. Moehanid was enraged by his bovine gaze. He lunged and pressed his fingers into the soft flesh around Ludovico's neck. Ludovico gagged, his peanuts flying across the floor as he sank back into his chair before taking Moe by the armpits and flinging him off.

"You crazy man!" he cried, hacking. He looked at Moehanid. "Have you lost your mind? What happened to your face?"

Moe got up and walked calmly to his room and locked the door.

THE FIRST FOUR DAYS IN BED he went without food or drink. His stomach was empty but the thought of eating made brackish liquid ooze from his glands till he leaned over the bed and spat mouthfuls of it onto the floor. Once in a dream he thought a victory parade went by, but it was a parade like the Macy's parade on TV, with huge floating corpses bloated and black-eyed attached to their wires. On the fifth day he emerged from the bedroom, walking with one hand on the wall to the refrigerator. Ludovico's cat, crouched under the kitchen table, one orange ear torn and bloodied, watched him and cried for milk. Moe wolfed down half a pound of cheese and then grabbed a jug of milk. Trembling and twisting the plastic cap off with his teeth, he gulped almost all of it before his stomach flopped and emptied itself onto the linoleum floor. He dropped to his knees. His eyes would not focus. He moved like a baby crawling, arms wobbling, down the hallway to the front door, down a shiny narrow path through the dust. He reached the door handle, pulled, and when the door gave he inched forward and squinted in the sunlight. For some time he lay there like a dazed lizard, until he saw a large blurry figure approaching on the sidewalk.

He barely reached his room before Ludovico, shoes clopping like animal hooves, entered the house, called out " 'Hanid! Stop!" and rushed down the hallway, banging into the walls. Moe used what strength he had to heave his body against the door, slamming it shut. He reached up and slid the bolt.

"You come out of there! You can't stay here anymore!"

There was a pause. "Do you hear me? Moehanid?" Moe wouldn't answer. "You die in there!" Ludovico said. "Fine! I will pull out your corpse."

Moehanid heard him clop away. In another part of the house two shoes hit the floor. First one, then an audible grunt, then another.

Moe's stomach growled and tightened. He retched, but there was nothing more to throw up. He lay back and pitched into sleep as if knocked in the head and dreamed he was at work delivering thousands of pizzas, his car filled to the ceiling with them. Whole pizzas muscled their way up his gullet, baked in his fiery middle. The teeth of lean blond hunting dogs in doorways snatched the pizzas from his hands, a nightmare of their pale blue eyes, their muttering growls and sudden high-pitched conflicts, the piercing yellow of their pain.

The scrubbing of a toothbrush niggling in, like an insect very close to his ear, gargling, spitting, running water, gurgling down the drain, and a tiny, distant, incessant, rustling, scratching, whispering—how terrible to hear every sound in the world. Twisting in and out of uneasy sleep.

Fingers twisting a milk bottle top. The fitful whine of kettle steam, *hooo hooo*, he whispers hoarsely, and feels the whole room become heavy and wet: Ludovico breathing through the keyhole.

"Get! Get!" he croaks. "Get away!"

Out of the depths of his soul there is a low growl, a nasally guttural howl. Arched creatures of blackened iron, long teeth and holes for eyes, yowling huge and distant in vast tunnels of dead stinking air. They lick the sweating pipes and snort in the cool dank air beneath the flooring, the bed, beneath his eyes. Lean black cats with shrunken human heads, filed teeth, and spiky hair. One with Wahlid's head steals along the wall of his room.

"Wahlid, what did you see with your eyes?"

Wahlid's hoarse voice whispered, "The moment after the blade passed through, I saw the man standing with his arms in the air, a bloody giant against the sky. And the big blue world turning away."

On the mantel, the head sat neatly like a trophy.

"Wahlid," Moe said, "I am so dry, my heart has turned to dust." The room was abuzz with emptiness. He pressed his cold lips to the sheet in his fists. He'd kissed his mother once, through a veil she wore, and cried. Shush, she said, lifting it, it's me. He listened for sounds of life in the house. The whole world was so dark and empty and still, not even a crack of light under the door, no willowing grayness around edges of window shade, no breeze whispering against the sides of the house, no tap of rain-water from the eaves. A vague fear of the very still and silent birds perched in the room, their beaks parting with anticipation, their barbed tongues aquiver. He listened for the faintest rustling of their vanes. It could be ages before morning, another marking of time, the rude and raucous noises of Ludovico taking his bath, the machinery of distant pumps, plumbing, and valves, rattling to life within the walls of the house. Opening of ancient flood-gates flooding the world.

BINARY ECLIPSE

THE CRONUS TWINS ALWAYS GO TO THE GYM TOGETHER, always work out in sync—you might say. Balding, they shave their heads. Black dress socks in black high-top sneakers. Pale legs like young birch trees. Knees like the trees' low limbs sawn off and gummed over. Their torsos, full heavy feed sacks. Their arms, long bolognas bent and crimped where elbows would normally be. Their faces, fiercely noncommittal. Each stares into the gym's mirrored wall, during and between sets, but never looks at the other. Between sets their mirrored flexing is not parallel, does not mirror the other's, but achieves a kind of strange choreography, like the shuffling of elephants in a pod. One has large ears, the other small. One looks very old, the other young. One speaks American, the other Chinese. One thinks quantity, the other thinks form. One, life as continuum; the other, death by swift and violent annihilation. One, love; the other, indifference. One, beauty; the other—swans on a pond who will be named, entirely unknown to the swans themselves, by an intelligent colony of bonobos on the shore.

ARE YOU MR. LONELEE?

I THOUGHT I HEARD A WOMAN SNEAKING UP ON ME IN THE grass. This is the predatory season for women, when men lie pale and naked in their yards like dazed birds. I let my head drop casually over the side of the lawn chair, open one eye, look. No woman. It could have been the birds.

You never know what will come up from behind. I take a shot from my flask and shift in the lawn chair. Even the mailman, crossing the yard to the neighbor's house, can make me jump and stare.

Two days ago this woman snuck up on me and watched me for five minutes before I knew she was there. I jumped up and the beer resting on my stomach spilled.

"Look out, there, cowboy," she said.

She was stunning. Very young, tall, and tanned, wearing jeans and a T-shirt that didn't cover her browned belly, where there was a single gold ring piercing her navel. Her hair, maybe a natural blond, was cut short and stood up on her head as if she'd been shocked, but her expression was calm. She sat down on the edge of the lawn chair and took a sip of what was left of my beer.

"Are you Conroy?"

I nodded and glanced at her navel. "Who are you?"

"I'm working on that," she said with a little laugh from her throat. She drained the rest of my beer.

"All right," I said, for I'd been trying to loosen up a little the last few months.

"I got your name off the mailbox," she said.

I INVITED HER IN FOR A COLDER BEER and she didn't leave for two days. I think she was just hungry, mostly. I took a shower and when I came out she was at the kitchen sink, ripping bites off a cold roast chicken I'd had in the fridge since Friday.

During those two days, she took about eight showers, walking naked from the billowing steam of the bathroom and padding about the place drip-drying or coming up to me and pressing herself into my clothes until I was wet, too, and when I took them off she pulled me into the bedroom, or onto the sofa or the floor. She pinned me down and rode me, come to think of it, like I was one of those mechanical bulls in bars. I think she even slapped my thigh one time.

I looked up at her from the laundry room floor, my head wedged into a pile of wet towels. "Really, you know," I said, "I think I need to know your name."

"Sylvia," she said.

"Sylvia," I said. "All right, then."

But you can never tell what will come up from behind. I take another shot from the flask and close my eyes, let the sun burn the liquid out again. I'm getting brown, burning down to the muscle. All I seem to want is purge.

FOUR MONTHS AGO, MY WIFE DIED. I've tried hard not to think of her since, but it's proved almost impossible.

My house is full of her things: leftover prescription bottles,

a makeup kit, patent leather shoes and sneakers and dainty sandals, a diaphragm that she called her "bonnet," hair curlers, old
grocery lists, wrinkled blouses packed into the backs of drawers, notes asking me to meet her at church that night, hundreds
of useless pots and pans, dumb aphorisms on lacquered plaques,
sheets and towels with the initials of her maiden name sewn
in. The list could go on. I can't seem to throw or give any of
it away. I sleep with one of her favorite old quilts at the foot of
my bed.

A month or so after her death, I decided I was going to get
away from the house for a while, rent it out, let someone else
bother with the mess. I put an ad in the paper and almost immediately this enormous, red-faced, blond-haired woman answered.
I interviewed her in my den.

It took me a minute to realize how fat this woman really was.
She had trouble getting through the front door. She sat down
and took up half the space of the single bed I used for a sofa, and
I heard the old springs groan as it sagged. I couldn't tell if that
embarrassed her or not. I really didn't know what to think.

I rented her my house, though. Partly because I'd have hated
to refuse her just because she was big. But also I had the feeling
that the house would be safe with her. She promised not to sit in
my wife's old rocker and I rented the place to her then and there.
I couldn't believe she'd brought it up herself. It almost made me
feel worse than if I'd said it.

MY WIFE AND I HAD RUN a two-person ad shop downtown in
the Threefoot Building. I often worked there until very late so
I'd fixed it up with a small daybed for catnaps. There was a men's
room down the hall where I could take bird baths. I lived there
for almost a month.

Things went fine until one night Crews, the night watch-
man, dropped in on me with a bottle of Ezra Brooks.

"You look like you could use a drink, Mr. Conroy."

Crews was retired from the city water and sewer department. He carried a fat radio to call the cops if he had to, but no gun. He was tall, shaved his head to hide the gray hair, and generally had the air about him of a man of leisure. He walked like a hip cat, paddling his palms to the rear as he strode the halls like he was walking with some ease through water. Now, having knocked on and opened my office door, he stood in the opening, his old eyebrows raised.

"Well," I said, "I don't think I've had a drink in three weeks."

Crews held the bottle up, hand poised to uncork the top.

I thought about it a moment and motioned him in.

"What's with the 'Mr. Conroy'?" I said. "Just call me Conroy."

"Oh, yes, last names," Crews said. "Like gentlemen." He'd already been into the bottle and was affecting a dapper air.

"Oh, yes," I said, going along. "At the club."

"Indeed," Crews said. He poured me a slug of the bourbon into one of the Dixie Cups he'd brought with him.

We had a pretty good time. Crews had a finger-snapping little shuffle dance he did. He sang "Good Morning Little Schoolgirl." I did Tom Waits grumbling through "Long Way Home." We kept slugging the whiskey. I walked over to the window, unzipped, and lobbed a stream down eleven stories through the neon light of old downtown. Crews ran over and stuck his dirty old SECURITY cap under me, rasping out a laugh, and said, "Man, you gon' get us both arrested." I went ahead and emptied into his cap. He became sober-looking, thoughtful, then shook the cap out and put it back on his head, doubling over into that raspy laugh again.

"Hot damn," I said. "Are you crazy?"

"I'm not crazy, man," he said. "I'm just drunk."

Then he got thoughtful again, uncorked the bottle, and dropped the cork to the floor. He nodded at the wedding band I still wore on my finger.

"You're a married man," he said. "Where's your wife?"

"My wife's dead. If it's any your business."

He cocked his head and looked up at the ceiling. I thought maybe he really was nuts.

"Your wife ain't dead," he finally said. "I know your wife, seen her up here with you many a time. I saw her yesterday, hanging out with some strange-looking dudes down at the Triangle, eating some of them Chik-Steaks."

I felt myself flush, and my mouth flooded with saliva like I was going to throw up. I went over to the window again and spat.

"Just get out," I said.

There was a half inch of bourbon left in the bottle. Crews drank it down and then walked to the door. He stopped, turned around.

"*My* wife," he said, "has been dead for nine years. Heart attack. Only forty-seven years old." I looked at him, and he looked back at me as if he'd never had a drop to drink in his life, and calm. "I don't need to manufacture no grief," he said then, and walked out.

I felt pretty rotten then. How to say it, except straight-up. My wife wasn't actually deceased.

She was an oddly pious woman I'd married because, I suppose, we were both studying public relations at the same school, took almost all the same classes, and just didn't really know anyone else. We were shy and awkward and it was just easier to be around someone as painfully self-conscious as yourself.

She was pious, but I always thought there was another side to her trying to get out somehow. In bed she cussed like a Marine and got crazy, which was fine, but she'd cry about it afterward, and she might even ask God to forgive her, lying there in the bed naked next to me. It was like she'd been possessed and then left behind in her pale, timid shame.

She was on her scooter one day, making a quick trip to the post office, when she hit a slick spot, went down, and banged her head pretty hard on the pavement. She'd left her helmet at the office. When she woke up four days later, she was a different person. She was not the woman I had married. That would have been all right with me, to tell the truth. I'd been having some serious second thoughts. But it wasn't all right with her.

She said I was a nice man but kind of boring. She said she was thinking of moving in with Majestic 12.

I said, "Who's that?"

"Well, they're artists. Painters," she said, leaning her head to one side and sticking a finger in her ear. The finger in the ear was a peculiar habit she'd picked up since the accident. As if she were listening to something inside there, receiving signals about what she should do or say next.

She took the finger out of her ear.

"They live in this big Victorian house up on the ridge south of town, by that old radio tower. It's kind of like a commune. I mean, you don't have your own room or anything, you just sleep where you want to, with whoever you want to, or by yourself, it's up to you. You know what I mean?"

"Not really."

"I mean," she said, holding her arms out and shaking her fingers like they were wet, "none of this bullshit."

She put the one finger back into her ear and wandered off into her studio, which was empty because she'd taken all of her old paintings, of puppies, quaint storefronts, and still lifes of fruits and flowers, to the dump.

And she moved in with Majestic 12. They smoked a lot of dope, painted with oils, were obsessed with alien visitation and abduction, and rode Harley-Davidsons. After weeks of trying to coax her home with letters, phone calls, knocking on the door to the big Victorian and being turned away by one Majestic 12 or another, I gave up. I didn't even have the heart to file for a divorce. I just kind of pretended to myself that she'd died.

And that's the way I've left it.

AFTER CREWS LEFT I DROVE TO MIDWAY, an all-night boot-leg joint, bought a bottle of sour mash, and hit the streets. I was working some things out of my head, and it wasn't pretty. I saw a group of teenage girls walking home from the bowling alley, and whistled and yowled at them from my car. I took a pellet pistol that for some reason I had in the glove compartment and shot out a couple of streetlights in a new subdivision north of town. I'd never smoked but I bought a pack of Lucky Strikes from a convenience store and chain-smoked them as I drove around, coughing and slugging the whiskey. I got out into the country and saw a big vegetable garden, with tall corn and bean vines strung on poles, glowing in the moonlight beside a house, and I steered the car into the driveway and across the yard and mowed down the whole little crop and got back to the road and hauled ass. Then I felt so bad about that little garden that, for the rest of the night, I just drove around and drank the whiskey, trying to forget.

At four a.m. I was so crocked I didn't know where I was and got lost. I'd had nearly a whole bottle of whiskey and all my reckoning finally collapsed. I ended up in front of my house somehow, jamming the spare key into the lock, the pellet pis-tol hanging from my other hand. I completely forgot about the enormous woman I had rented to, forgot she was living there at the time.

I was still on automatic, moving through the living room with my free hand outstretched in the dark, my eyes nearly swol-len shut with booze, sleepwalking toward the bed fully clothed.

But I'd fallen just halfway to where the mattress should have been when I hit something soft but firm, bounced off onto the floor, and rolled over onto my back, dazed—only to see this massive shape blot out the moonlight coming through the bedroom window. She screamed, a high-pitched one for such a large woman. Then I screamed, too, to let her know she was not the only hysterical person in the house, and plinked off a pellet at her before I could think about it.

She paused, then screamed again, and didn't stop until she had pulled a giant Navaronnean handgun from the bed-table drawer and fired off a deafening round. I dove for the hallway just as she fired again, taking off a hunk of doorjamb above my shoulder. She screamed again and I heard something wrench and then a kind of twanging. I lay tense for a moment, then turned around to see her broad behind framing the area where the lower half of the bedroom window had been. She'd tried to dive out through the screen.

I ran around to the back door, but when I stuck my head out she fired at me from her hanging position. The bullet popped into the asbestos siding of my next-door neighbor's house.

"Miss Duke!" I shouted. "It's Conroy, your landlord. Don't shoot."

"Conroy! Oh, God."

I peeked around the doorjamb and saw that her arms were hanging limp, and she was kind of bouncing, her arms jiggling around, the big gun still clutched in one hand.

"Help me," I heard her whisper. Her head hung down, her mussed hair all around it, nearly touching the dew-laced grass. I pushed and heaved at her, she grunted and pulled, until finally she came free and sat back onto the floor. She shook her head and wiped her eyes.

"Oh, my God," she said in a soft voice. She looked up,

saw me, seemed confused for a moment, and then she slowly raised the revolver again and pointed it at my head there in the open window.

I ducked just as it went off, over my head and into the little stand of trees behind the house. I scrambled to the car and peeled out. Twice more I heard the gun's *Caroom!* slam and echo into the night, and soon after the distant wail of sirens.

When I cruised past the house the following afternoon her car was gone and the front door stood wide open. Inside, dressers were torn apart, the closets in disarray. A trail of parachutelike smocks led to the bedroom and I walked on them back and forth. They were printed and embroidered with little-girl things, teddy bears and Raggedy Anns and bluebirds, plantation waifs in sunbonnets, all feminine and soft.

I moved back in.

MISS DUKE FILED CHARGES and I spent a few hours at the police station with a lawyer, working things out. She had no permit for the pistol she'd shot at me, and I certainly didn't want to press charges of attempted murder, so her lawyer persuaded her to drop the charges of breaking-and-entering and assault. The pellet I'd shot at her had sunk a couple of inches into one of her arms. I paid for her outpatient surgery to have it removed.

A few weeks after it was all over, I made the mistake of spilling my heart to a lady down the street, a nosy old widow named Mrs. Nash. She'd been bringing me jars of fresh homemade soup and chili ever since I'd come home, and she seemed very nice and concerned, so one day I broke down and told her everything. The worst was that I'd confessed I was about to die of being lonely, that I wished I just had a good friend, and so on. After that, people on the street just looked away when I drove by, and their awful children got a kick out of calling me on the phone. It would ring in the middle of the night and when I answered some kid would be on the other end.

"Hello, is this Mr. Lonely?"

"Who?"

"Is this Mr. Lone-lee?"

"No, this is not Mr. Lone-lee."

"You must be lonely," said the boy's voice.

"You kids cut it out," I said.

"Oh, please don't be lonely."

Mrs. Nash told them everything. The phone rang one night about twelve-thirty and I answered it without speaking.

"Hey, mister, there's a naked fat woman in your front yard and she has a gun."

I was furious.

"I'll kill you," I shouted into the phone.

Even so, I crept to the window and peeked through the drapes. The shrubs and trees stood silvery black in the evening, very still. Something small and quick darted over the lawn, and I wanted to run out there, run it down, and rip it to pieces. I went to the library and saw a group of Harley choppers outside the door, but didn't think anything of it. Inside, I was thumbing through a book when, glancing up, I saw the face of my wife peering at me from the other side of the shelf. She walked around and stood there staring at me. She wore a full set of tight black motorcycle leathers. Her hair was jet-black and cut in a pageboy. A big gold nose ring, the kind they actually used to put onto bulls, hung down over her upper lip. A pair of heavy, strapped, chrome-buckled boots came up to her knees.

"Hey, Conroy," she said. "You don't look so good." Then she smiled and leaned on the bookshelves. "How's the old homeplace?"

"I don't know you," I said. I put the book back in the same place I'd taken it from and walked out.

On my way home Majestic 12 came out of nowhere and roared past me on their Harleys. I saw a slim black leather-clad arm flip a wave at me from a quivering pattern of red taillights that disappeared into the night like a spaceship.

THINGS HAPPEN.

Last night Sylvia and I were going at it, in the bedroom for once. But she lost her head, forgot where she was. Her eyes were closed, and she was humming to herself, and I could see her eyes darting back and forth behind her pale bruised lids. I was a little mesmerized. But then something emptied my mind and left everything quiet.

I lifted my head and looked at her, but she didn't notice. She was murmuring, "Pedro," in a kind of whispering moan. "Pedro, baby, oh, man. Pedro."

I couldn't go on.

She went still and opened her eyes. "What's the matter?"

"Who's Pedro?" I said.

I could tell she felt awful about it.

"Oh, shit, I'm sorry, Conroy. I didn't mean it. I just spaced out."

I felt like an idiot for caring.

"Oh, fuck, Conroy," Sylvia said. "I mean, that's not even his real name, man."

"What?"

"I mean"—she kind of wiggled her hands—"it's just a pet name."

"What's his real name, then?"

She sat there a moment looking at the opposite wall, then shrugged.

"Wayne. I haven't seen him in, like, weeks, I guess."

"It's all right," I said. "It's not a big deal."

I rolled over and looked at the darkened bedroom ceiling for a while.

"I'm really sorry, Conroy," she said then. "Don't be upset."

"It's okay," I said. "I'm sorry about Wayne."

It took me hours to go to sleep. Bad dreams kept me restless. They were all dreams in which I said the wrong things, did the wrong things, dreams in which I forgot the names of people I'd known for a long time.

Early this morning I got up and came out here with my lawn chair and my flask. An hour or so later I heard her voice behind me.

"Well, goodbye, then," she said. "I'm going."

I raised a free hand, waved it. I heard her retreating footsteps in the grass.

I went back into the house, just to look around, really. I walked around the den for a minute, then into the kitchen, where I washed a dish. Then to the bedroom, where I found my bed neatly made up, the pillows fluffed. It was the first time I'd seen my bed made up since I didn't know when. Since I'd shown the house to Miss Duke, I suppose. I went into the bathroom, pressed my bare feet on the cool tiles, looked around. I noticed that Sylvia had stolen all my shampoo and soap. I looked into the closet. Half my towels and wash rags were gone. I thought for a moment, then went back into the bedroom and looked at the neatly made-up bed. Sure enough, my wife's old quilt was gone. I went through the kitchen and the living room. Something was missing from one of these rooms, I knew. But I still haven't figured out what.

I went back out to my lawn chair and I've been sitting here all day, listening. When I close my eyes the world seems full of sound. Traffic on the highway half a mile away. Children shouting on a playground at the neighborhood school. Dogs barking to other dogs, those dogs barking back. Telephone ringing in a house somewhere. The knockity-knock-knock of a roofing crew. Birds scratching in the shrubbery for grubs.

A breeze drifts through the live oak leaves, cooling the sweat on my burning skin, dropping me into the kind of sleep that's deep as death, or the underworld, a whole other life you never knew you were living. It was nice, for a while. Only the sound of the blood rustling quietly like the ocean in my veins.

AGNES OF BOB

AGNES MENKEN, MISSING HER LEFT EYE, AND BOB THE BULL-
dog, missing his right, often sat together on their porch, Agnes
in her straight-backed rocking chair and Bob in her lap. Together
they could see anything coming, Bob to one side and Agnes to
the other. They always seemed to be staring straight ahead but
really they were looking both ways.

Whereas Bob's bad right eye was sewn up, Agnes had a false
one that roved. It was obvious to her that people often had trouble telling which eye was the good one, so sometimes she would
look at them awhile with the good one, and then when they'd
become comfortable with this she switched and looked at them
with the false one, which was clear and had the direct hard-
bearing frankness of detachment. In her good eye's peripheral
vision she could see the general distress that this caused.

Despite his years and his sewn-up eye, Bob was as stout and
fit as a young dog. He stayed that way naturally, as dogs of his
type will, having the metabolism of all small muscular animals.
He was tight, compact—much like her late husband, Pops, but
just the opposite of Agnes, who was lanky. Officially, he had
been Pops's dog, the son he'd never had, she supposed. In that
way Agnes had felt at best like a stepmother, standing just a little
apart. Pops and Bob had understood one another, shared a lan-

guage of some kind that only they'd understood, whereas Agnes could never tell if Bob was listening to her or not.

Nevertheless, she and Bob had become closer in the year since Pops had died. They had their routine together. Bob ate twice a day, morning and evening. He got to stay outside in the fenced backyard as long as he wanted during the day. At night he slept on Agnes's bed, down near the footboard. And every evening, once early and once late, she let him out to pee in the yard. A neighbor wandered out back to look at the moon would see the light on her back porch snap on, the door creak open, see Bob come flying out onto the grass, snarling and grunting the way Boston bulldogs do, dashing around in the dark near the back of the yard. But Agnes hadn't the patience with him Pops'd had, how Pops would sit at the kitchen table smoking, sipping coffee, waiting till Bob sauntered back up to the door and barked to be let back in. Now, Bob would hardly have time to pee before the door creaked open on its hinges again and Agnes started in on him, saying, "Where are you? What are you doing back there? Go on, now. Go on and do what you're gonna do. What are you doing? Come on. Come on in here and finish up your supper. I want to go to bed. Come on in this door. Where are you? Please, Bob. I'm tired, boy. What are you doing out there? Come on in here. Come on. Come on." Then Bob would stop, sniff around, shoot a quick stream into the monkey grass, lob a fading arc to the bark of the popcorn tree, and then leap back into the light of the porch. And she would pull the door shut, turn all three dead bolts, snap off the kitchen light, and feel her way along the hallway to bed.

EXCEPT FOR THE HOUSE NEXT DOOR on her east side, where the professor lived with his wife and two little girls, this seemed to Agnes like a neighborhood of widows. Next door on the west side was Lura Campbell, eighty-four, who insisted on driving every day. She did all right once she got out of her azalea-lined driveway, but she had the worst time trying to back herself out. On this morning, Agnes lay in bed and listened to Lura's old Impala wheeze to a start, clank into Reverse, back up a little ways, and then *screee*, into the azaleas. Clank clank, into Drive, pull forward. Clank clank, into Reverse, back up. *Screee*, into the azaleas. Clank clank, into Drive, pull forward. Clank clank, into Reverse, back up. *Screee*, into the azaleas. All the way down her driveway. Drove Agnes crazy. She'd said to Lura, I don't see why you feel like you got to get out and go every morning. Well, I like to go, Lura said. I don't see any sense in going just to be going, Agnes said. Well, Lura said, I just have to get out and go somewhere, I can't sit here at the house.

Agnes did not want to end up like Lura, an aimless, doddering wanderer driving down the middle of the street in her ancient automobile threatening dogs and children. She hoped that something would happen to ease her on out of the world before she got that way, that she would die in her sleep or simply somehow disappear, whisked into thin air by the hand of God. She had made her peace with God, though she'd never liked religion. She certainly wasn't afraid of God, like she had been once without realizing it. She would face God like she would anybody else, with dignity and demanding a little respect in return. She'd never willingly offended God, had only ignored Him a little, like everyone else. But recently she had silently said, If it comes a time when it's convenient to You, go ahead.

She thought, Maybe I'll see Pops, and with two good eyes.

She fished her glass one out of the little dish of solution on the bedside table, popped it in, and eased her legs off the side of the bed. As soon as her toes touched the cool bare floor, Bob was there, leaping into the air around her like a circus dog.

"Get," she waved at him, shuffling into the kitchen to make coffee. "Get."

The coffee made, she poured a cup, took it out to the porch, and no sooner had her bottom touched the chair than Bob jumped into her lap, circled, and settled in his sphinxlike pose to observe the traffic.

Carolyn Barr and April Ready walked briskly by, swinging their arms like majorettes. They waved, Agnes nodded. The women, in their sixties, had the legs of thirty-year-olds.

"Amazing, Bob," Agnes muttered. "I bet I know why their old boys kicked off."

She and Pops had had what she'd considered a normal life, in that regard. Toward the end, Pops got to where he wasn't interested, and she didn't mind, much. The truth was, they'd never really gotten over the embarrassment. She'd always figured more sex would've been a good thing, but she'd never brought it up with Pops. It seemed frivolous. They'd never talked about sex, never even used the word. She'd always worked, just like him. Forty years! Forty years at the power company for her. He'd kept books at the steam feed works, never retired. A chain-smoker with Coke-bottle-thick glasses, he came home smoking, seemed like steam from the works leaking out of his thick windows onto the world. When he had his attack, he fell into a pile of foundry sand and suffocated.

The day Pops had died, the widow Louella Marshall (a Baptist) had come by. Her husband, Herbert, had been dead for ten years, and since then she hadn't so much as had coffee with a man. She'd married her church, is what she said. Agnes couldn't stand her because she seemed so smug, and Agnes couldn't believe she wasn't a phony, a religious bully who was scared to death of dying herself, afraid she was going to hell for having secretly wished her bullying husband would die and leave her alone. Agnes wasn't afraid of going to hell, but when Louella sat in her armchair and made like to comfort her by saying God had taken Pops to be with Him in heaven, she had gotten so angry she took her coffee cup and saucer into the kitchen and dashed them in the sink. She didn't pretend to have dropped them.

After that, for a while, she frequently had a dream in which she was swimming out in the middle of the ocean, strong as one of those nuts that used to swim across the English Channel. But then there was a roaring sound, and she'd look up and see it was the edge of the world, and a beast would rise up with the body of a dragon and the face of Pops, which then changed into the dog face of Bob, and she awoke in her bedroom where the blue night-light made the damp air seem like water and the breeze through the window sounded like ocean swells and it took her some minutes to calm down and hear Bob down at the foot of her bed, grunting and thrashing in some dream of his own.

She had realized then that she was afraid of dying, and afraid of what had happened to Pops. But she could not be like Louella and believe that this was God's will, that he had singled out Pops like an assassin. She decided that she would face the possibility of her own death with dignity, by inviting it in, leaving the door unlocked, and that in that way she would be in charge and unafraid. We all know death better than we think, she said to herself.

The only one who'd said anything interesting on that day at her house had been poor Lura Campbell, who had sat tiny and quiet on Agnes's huge old sofa and sipped her coffee and said, when there'd been a long quiet spell in the room, "I think if I had it to do all over again, after Lester passed away, I'da done some traveling."

Louella Marshall said, "Well, Lura, where in the world would you've gone? To Florida?"

"Oh, I don't know," Lura said. "I'da just got into my car and gone."

Lura and her car.

———

AGNES DIDN'T SOCIALIZE with any of the widows. She tended the yard and looked after Bob and kept the house fairly clean and watched for rare birds at her feeders. She didn't see many rare birds, which was natural seeing as how they *were* rare, but the occasional chickadee or purple finch made it interesting enough.

Warm days, she sunned in her lounge chair on the patio out back, her eyes shut tight against the glare and the heat, talking to Bob the whole time. She could hear him grunting and snuffling and rooting around like a hog. Whenever he was quiet she raised up and looked, to see if anyone had walked up, and then lay back down. She hated sunbathing, but it was good for the psoriasis, and it helped fight her natural pallor, which made her feel like those little cave frogs she'd seen once on a trip to the mountains with Pops. Little red eyes and the rest of them clear as a jellyfish, you could see their little hearts pumping and their veins jumping, like their skins were made of glass.

Sometimes she volunteered to take the little girls next door to the pool. Swimming was good for her, the doctor said, and Agnes had always liked the water. She wasn't much on the surface, since she was too slim to float, but she liked to be underwater, moving along in steady breaststrokes like a long slow fish. She liked the look of things underwater, the silent and bright world that seemed strange in the way that a dream is, very intimate and distant at the same time.

After a swim, lying in the sun beside the pool was easier than tanning in her buggy backyard with Bob always snorting around. She'd take a brush and brush her wet hair straight back and forget about it. She couldn't do anything with it anymore, it was getting so thin and frizzy. The gray she didn't care about. She pretty much let Sherilyn just chop it short and do it up in a little permanent. She got it washed once a week. She knew short hair made her neck look longer, but there wasn't any way around that. Her good eye was a little smaller than the false one and a little reddened from strain, her nose was a little long, and her back was bent just a little forward because of less-than-ideal posture. She could see this when she walked past a storefront window and saw her reflection. Now, to boot, her fingers were swollen with a mild arthritis and there were the faded, healed reminders of a few small sores on her arms and legs from the psoriasis. It was a good thing she never cared much about appearances. And after a swim, with her muscles tingling from the exercise, she cared even less.

Nevertheless, a tan seemed to help all of that, and helped create a natural vigor, and in her mind's eye she sought a dignity in the way she looked and mentally compared herself to a tall gray crane beside a bay or a lake, and she tried to carry herself with that dignity in mind. She walked slowly and deliberately, like a crane, and without thinking kept her eye fixed that way, like they did when they were fishing or just stalking along.

IT WAS A NATURAL COMPARISON, given her interest in birds and the three feeders she kept in her backyard.

"Look at that, Bob," she'd say. "I believe that's a towhee pecking around down there." Bob stared at her, jaws clamped. Then he let his tongue out again and started panting.

She sometimes forgot it was Pops who'd first started watching the birds. Feeding them, anyway. He built the feeders in his shop out in the garage. Then he started to read about them a little, and he'd keep track of when they came and went, and he'd sit with her in the kitchen sipping coffee and looking out at the feeders in the spring and announce their arrivals from Argentina, Paraguay, Brazil, and Venezuela, Peru, and Colombia, and Costa Rica. "Flown here nonstop from the Yucatán," he'd say. "Made a little stop down on the coast."

And he took her down there one time in the season. They put on their sun gear, light long-sleeved shirts and khaki pants and tennis shoes and light socks, broad hats, sunglasses, and binoculars. They drove down the beach road to the old fort and camped out for two days on the grounds with a bunch of odd ones who called themselves birders and walked the sandy trails and Pops made notes in a little spiral-bound notebook.

One day they were standing on the beach and birds started to fall out of the sky.

"Oh," one of the birders cried, "it's a tanager fallout." A momentary alarm shook Agnes, naturally associating the word with its nuclear meaning. But then she caught on, birds plopping to the white sand all around them. Bright red birds with black wings and black tails, and dull yellow birds among them.

They'd stood still, as had all the others for some minutes, and then people began to get down on their hands and knees and take close-up pictures of the birds, who were too exhausted to move another feather. People picked them up and stroked them and set them back down. Before they could stop him, Bob— who'd cautiously sniffed at one bird—began taking them into his jaws and dropping them at her and Pops's feet like gifts. Some of the birders got upset and started hollering like fools until Pops got Bob back on the leash and kept him from retrieving any more tanagers.

"He ain't a retriever," Pops said later. "He's built for killing small animals. He knows we like the birds, I guess."

That day, Agnes had stood there, the startling scarlet birds falling around her, and listened to the surf bashing at the sand, and she could see the churning tidal struggle down at the point, at the mouth of the bay. She looked out over the Gulf and thought about the birds having crossed all that water without even a rest, and she thought about the fishes and other creatures that traveled beneath those waters, strong and free as they pleased, roaming without the boundaries of continents or countries or cities and towns or jobs or houses or yards, and the idea of the freedom of such a journey stirred in her something like joy and something like frustration. She didn't know what to do with it, this feeling, and she felt so strange standing amid these people struck wild with wonder over the tanager fallout while all she could feel was the most curious detachment from it all.

SHE DECIDED SHE NEEDED TO GO to the pool and on a whim thought it'd be nice to drive Lura over there with her. If Lura liked so much to go, then she'd give her somewhere to go to. She knew Lura wouldn't swim, but it might be nice for her to sit in the shade and watch the others. Agnes put her swimsuit on and slipped a slightly faded sundress over it, got into her sandals and sunglasses, and went over to fetch Lura.

Lura was sitting in her automatic chair and she fumbled for the button, pushed it, and the chair began to rise slowly until it slid Lura out onto the floor on her feet and then sat there like a sproinged jack-in-the-box while Lura went into the kitchen to get Agnes a bowl of homemade ice cream.

"I don't want any ice cream," Agnes said. "Let's get in my car and go over to the swimming pool."

"I made this cream last week and it's still good, but I can't eat it all," Lura said.

"I thought," Agnes said loudly then, thinking maybe Lura didn't have her hearing aid in, "that I would give you some*place* to go, instead of just wandering. And you wouldn't have to drive."

"Well, I like to drive," Lura said, fiddling in her silverware drawer. "I can drive just fine."

"I didn't say you *couldn't* drive, Lura. I just thought you might like to go someplace with *me*."

"Well, I can drive us to the pool," Lura said, like someone who'd been insulted.

Agnes felt her stomach knot up just thinking about riding with Lura, but she could see what this was turning into and went on out and got into Lura's car and rolled down her window. After what must have been a quarter of an hour, Lura finally came down her back porch steps wearing a light cotton dress with a floral print and carrying a wide, floppy garden hat that looked like a collapsed sombrero. She put the hat onto the seat between them and got in behind the giant steering wheel of the Impala. She looked like a child driving a city bus, Agnes thought.

Then Lura began her driving ritual. She pulled on her white cotton gloves and fished her keys out of her purse, chose the proper key, and inserted it into the ignition. She pumped the accelerator pedal one time with the toe of her sandal, then turned the key. The old engine turned over once, coughed, then died with a hydraulic sigh. Lura pumped again, turned the key, the engine wheezed once, caught, and Lura held her foot down until the car roared like a dump truck. She let it die back, and gently pulled the gear stick down into Reverse. The transmission made its familiar clanking noise, Agnes felt the bump of the car into gear, and Lura placed both gloved hands on the wheel and peered into the rearview mirror as she began her journey out of her driveway. Obliquely, and true to her lights, she leaned the Impala's right fender into her pink azaleas, and the thin and agonized atonal chorus of stems against paint and metal began.

"Oh, Lord," Agnes muttered. "Here we go."

Clank clank, into Drive, Lura pulled forward. Clank clank, into Reverse.

"Lura," Agnes said. "Lura." Lura pressed on the brake pedal and looked at her.

"Why don't you use the side mirror?" Agnes said.

Lura looked at her blankly.

"If you just keep your left fender close to the bushes on that side, you'll be all right," Agnes said.

Lura said, "I couldn't see the rest of the car if I did that."

"You don't have to see the whole car," Agnes said. "Can you see the whole car when you're moving ahead? If you keep it close to the bushes on your side, the other side will take care of itself."

"I do all right," Lura said. "Well, I can't use the side mirror, I never have."

"Lura, it's just easier," Agnes started to say, but Lura's toe had strayed from the brake pedal and the car's high idle propelled them backwards. Agnes, looking into the mirror on her side, thought for a moment that they would make it clear out of the driveway and into the street by accident, but then Lura realized what was happening and yanked the wheel, and the car jumped the curb and plowed into the bank of azaleas with a paint-rending screech. Lura kept one hand on the gearshift, pulled the stick clank clank into Drive, and the car shot forward into the driveway and jerked to a stop.

"Look at that," Lura said, disgusted. "Agnes, will you just let me drive?"

In the end, Agnes got out and waited on the sidewalk until Lura had gotten the car into the street. Then she got in and they drove at Lura's steady fifteen-miles-per-hour pace to the pool.

Lura took a couple of spaces near the gate, put the broad straw garden hat back onto her head, and they walked on in.

"Well, here we are," Lura said. "You go on in. I'll just find somewhere to sit down."

"I'm going to get some sun before I swim," Agnes said. "Why don't you sit over there under that awning and get yourself some iced tea? I'll take one of those loungers over there and stretch out."

"Well, that sounds good," Lura said. "I don't see how you can stand that sun. I'm glad I wore my hat. Whew." She adjusted the hat and began working her fingers out of the white cotton gloves as she made her way over to the refreshment area.

Agnes walked down to the deck behind the diving boards, spread her Panama City Beach beach towel onto one of the cedar chaise lounge chairs, and eased herself down. This was the last time she'd ever go anywhere with Lura. Lord, what an old biddy. She decided not to fool with the suntan lotion. She hoped Lura wouldn't wander off and strand her, or worse yet totter off and fall into the pool and drown. She decided to alert the lifeguard to that possibility. He was a strong-looking boy and very capable, she was sure. She looked at him, sitting up in his high chair, twirling his silver whistle.

She got up and went over to the chair.

"Young man?" she said.

The lifeguard looked down at her. He wore black sunglasses and she couldn't see his eyes.

"Yes, ma'am," he said.

"Would you keep an eye on that elderly lady over at the refreshment stand? I'm afraid she might wander off and fall into the pool."

The lifeguard looked down at her for a moment, then over in Lura's direction.

"The lady with the big hat and the sunglasses, ma'am?"

Agnes looked and saw that Lura had pulled out her pair of giant, squared geriatric sunglasses and put them on.

"That's her," she said.

She looked up at him a moment longer as he put the silver whistle to his lips and blew two short notes, like a songbird's call, and nodded to some action out in the pool. He looked like a Greek god on the mount, like Neptune.

"I thank you," Agnes said, and went back to her lounge chair.

Students from the college lay on their towels along the pool's edge. It was very hot, and every now and then one of the girls got up and stepped down the pool ladder into the water, holding her hair up on top of her head, until the water touched the back of her neck, then climbed out of the water, still holding her hair. Some girls liked to wet their heads, arching their necks back and lowering their long straight hair into the pool. The boys behind their dark glasses watched the girls lower themselves into the pool and emerge with water sparkling on their oiled bodies, then watched them walk to their towels again.

Agnes watched them all. They were all very nearly naked and all brown as the glazed donuts Pops used to bring home from Shipley's on Sunday mornings after his early drive to smoke his Sunday cigar. She thought about the students having sex, she knew they all did these days, and wondered if they had to get to know one another before they did it or if they just did it casual as dogs, without a thought. She remembered the taste of the hot soft donuts Pops would bring home and it made her so restless she sat up straight in the lounge chair.

Lura was still in the shade at the refreshment stand, fanning herself with a magazine. Agnes got up and eased herself over the pool's edge, let go, and sank to the bottom.

The water sent a great shock of cool through her body. She felt immersed in a great big glass of ice water. She looked around. Everything was green and bright. Way off down at the other end someone dove in and swam across, just thrashing arms and legs. She could see the legs of children dancing around at the shallow end. A cloud sailed over, made all jumpy by the waves. She could see people walk along the pool's edge, their bodies broken into pieces and quivering like Jell-O. The legs and bottom and shoulders and one arm of a girl came slowly down the ladder and slowly climbed back out, jerking like something big outside the water was taking her bite by bite. Agnes felt fine not breathing, as if there was a great supply of air in her lungs. She'd always had wonderful lung capacity. At some point, she thought, it seemed like a body would simply stop needing to take in so much air, stop needing to breathe all the time. Another girl came partially down the ladder, dipped her long hair back into the pool, and then walked back up into the air. Agnes felt as if they all belonged to another world, too thin and insubstantial to sustain her, and the one she was in, her world here deep in the clear green water, was much more pleasurable, much more peaceful. She remembered a dream, swimming in the ocean in a vast school of swift metallic fish, their eyes all around her, the feeling she got eye to eye with the fishes, and their effortless speed and flashing tails. She felt something stir in her, growing, until she felt filled with it. Her chest ached with it. Saturday nights, Pops would cook their meals. He loved to fry fish. Take Bob out to the lake and get on a bream bed. Pops would come home with a stringer, a mess, wet fish flopping and mouths groping for air. Made her chest ache, watching them. Pops would clean the bream out back, throw Bob a fish head. Bob tossing fish heads around the yard like balls. She was on the brink of a wonderful vision, as if in a moment she would know what Pops had seen as he passed through his own heart and a pile of washed foundry sand into the next world.

She thought she heard the distant trill of a bird and looked up as a crash of bubbles shot down from the surface. The bubbles cleared and she saw it was the lifeguard, his dark and curly hair about his face like a nest of water serpents. His eyes were a clear blue revelation, open wide and upon her. She held out her arms. He came forward and held her and pulled her gently upward. Her hands felt the muscles moving powerfully along his back. She thought that he must have wings, this angel, and he would take her on some beautiful journey.

AGNES LAY IN HER LAWN CHAIR, watching the last rays of the afternoon sift through tiny gaps between the leaves. The light shifted in an almost kaleidoscopic fashion as the leaves trembled in a breeze that seemed an augury of the evening. She did not fear them, the passing of the day nor the coming of the evening. She had never felt so relaxed or open to the world around her.

On the way home, Lura's words had been as distant and melodic as a birdsong. The drive had taken only seconds. Lura must have been driving all of thirty-five.

She heard Lura now, as she leaned over Agnes's lawn chair to look at her.

"I imagine you've had enough sun," Lura said. "You're addled. I'm lucky I'm not dead of a heart attack, you nearly scared me to death."

Bob ran full-speed in broad circles around the yard just inside the fence. He stopped and stood rigid beside the monkey grass patch beneath the pecan tree, then leapt stiff-legged into the middle of it. He thrashed around and came tearing out of it as if something were after him. A few feet away he stopped, turned around, and barked at it.

"Be quiet, Bob," Agnes said. Bob looked back at her, as if measuring her authority.

"You ought to let me take you to the doctor, anyway," Lura said. "You nearly drowned."

"I was all right."

"I don't know how you can say that. That boy had to pull you out of the water like an old log." She touched her hair. "I've left my hat."

"Lura, just sit down and be quiet or go home. I'm feeling so peaceful."

"You've had a near-death experience," Lura said.

"Oh, be quiet," Agnes said. Lura touched her hair again, started to say something, then sat down in a lawn chair, and Agnes again turned her attention to the sunset coloring the light behind the trees. The light deepened and the breeze ran through the leaves like the passing of a gentle hand. Agnes didn't know when she had felt so much at peace. It had not been her time to go. But she had been close enough to see into that moment, and she did not dislike what she had seen.

The bank of orange clouds behind and above the tree line began to fade into slate against the deepening blue of the sky. The loud and raucous birds of the day had retreated, and the quiet of evening began to settle in. The light faded measurably, moment by moment. It was so beautiful she did not think she was not seeing it with two eyes. She heard Bob and looked for him against the purpling green of the lawn and the shrubbery. He'd begun again his racing around and around. He'd worn a narrow path in the grass, a perfect oval like a racetrack. She found him, a speeding, blurred ball of black and white led by a wild and wide-open eye, and watched as he zipped past and approached the far fence. And then, in violation of what had seemed a perfect order, he suddenly leapt. He leapt amazingly high, and with great velocity. He leapt, as if launched by a giant invisible spring in the grass, or shot from a circus cannon, and sailed over the fence into the gathering darkness.

"My goodness," Lura said.

Agnes was stunned. In the empty space where a few seconds ago Bob had been pure energy in motion, had sped like a comet in his orbit, everything was still.

"Are you going to go get him?" Lura said.

After a moment Agnes said, "I imagine so," thinking, Now, why did he have to go and do that? but not really feeling all that disturbed, as if nothing could very much disturb her peace.

"You want me to drive you?"

"No," Agnes said. "He won't go far."

"It's getting dark."

"I can see in the dark as well as anyone."

"Well, I didn't mean anything. I just thought I'd offer to help."

"Go on home and get some rest, Lura. You've been through enough for one day."

She left Lura in the yard and went inside to pull on a pair of slacks and a blouse. She hesitated, then from the kitchen beside the refrigerator she got the nightstick Pops always used to carry in his car. She tapped it into her palm. "Damn old dog," she said.

She walked all the way down the street to the thoroughfare, calling, then crossed and turned into an older neighborhood with houses hidden in big heavy-limbed trees. The sidewalk was made of old buckled bricks. Dead downtown was a few blocks away, the air above it all blue and foggy with streetlamp glow. It looked underwater. She picked her way along the uneven brick path, the dry sound of roaches scurrying away from her flip-flops.

The old trees towering over her head were so thick with leaves they were spooky. Agnes harked back to fairy tales heard in her childhood and imagined that she was a child walking in a forest where someone had long ago cut the narrow rumbly streets along old trails.

Big roots hunched up through the crumbly pavement, and here and there a cozy house was nestled deep in among the trees like a forest cottage.

She and Pops were married forty-nine years. Sometimes it seemed like the whole thing actually took place, and then sometimes it didn't, as if there were a big blank between when she was a little girl and now. She was only twenty-one when they married. She remembered their honeymoon at the Grand Hotel in Point Clear. They'd walked those old paths draped with that moss like damp shadowy lace. In the room their love was quick and startling, their bodies drawn into it like a child's arm drawn briefly into a hard and painful little muscle.

Agnes slowed her steps as her heart sped up. She remembered kissing Pops in the late years and how it was just pinched-up lips and a dry peck, and remembered kissing him like that in his box, how his lips were like wood and how horrified she'd been. She'd had that craving for a child, briefly, a little bit late, and had not pressed it with Pops. He'd not had word one on the subject. He seemed at times such a passive man, and then at others all pent-up. If he'd had passions, she suspected he disapproved of their expression. Perhaps he told them to Bob in the intimacy between a man and his dog, who knows what a man told his dog? He'd always had Bob. There were two other dogs before him, but they were the same kind of dog, looked exactly the same. Every one named Bob. She wondered if he'd have done the same with her if she'd died, just gone out and got another Agnes. If there hadn't been Bob, maybe he'd have talked to her.

Seemed like they had the same dog for forty-nine years. One would die, Pops would get another one just like it the next day. Seemed to have the same obnoxious personality. She'd sometimes catch herself looking at that dog, or one of them, and thinking, This is the longest-living dog I ever saw. She laughed out loud.

She rounded a corner and looked down a narrow street lighted dimly by the old streetlamps. Far down, a little dog stood still in the middle of the road. From what Agnes could make out, it looked like Bob. He seemed to be looking back at her.

She leaned forward, squinting her good eye.

The dog stood very still, looking at her.

"Bob," Agnes said. Then she called out, "Bob! Come here, boy! Oh, Bob!"

She moved a little closer. Bob tensed up, stiffened his legs and his neck. Otherwise, he didn't budge.

Agnes clucked to herself and tapped the nightstick into her palm. "Damn old dog. I ought to let him run off somewhere.

"Go on!" she called to him then. "Go on, if you want to."

Bob took a little straightening step. He lifted his head and sniffed the breeze. He was poised there, under the streetlamp, looking proud and aloof, seeming in that foggy distance like the ghost of all the Bobs. She imagined that after fifty years he was asking himself if he wanted any more. Well, she thought, she wouldn't press it: she would let him go where he wanted to go.

She heard a car and looked around. There at the stop sign sat Lura's Impala, like some big pale fish paused on the ocean floor, the headlights its soft glowing eyes seeking. It nosed around the corner headed her way. At that Bob turned and trotted away. She watched him fade into the foggy gloom, just the hint of a sidling slip in his gait. Go on and look around then, she said to herself. Go see what you've been sniffing in the breeze. She couldn't see him then, his image snuffed in the fog.

She stood in the middle of the old quiet street and waited on Lura to pull up. On a lark she turned sideways and stuck out her thumb. The car eased up beside her. She opened the creaky old door and looked in. Lura appeared to be dressed for traveling.

"I got an idea," Agnes said.

At Lura's pace they reached the coast about dawn. They took the long winding road out to the fort, hung a left at the guard-house, and went down to the beach. Lura, woozy with fatigue, rolled on off the blacktop and into the sand for several yards before the Impala bogged down. She took the gearshift in one white-gloved hand and pushed it up into Park, pushed the head-lights knob to the dash, and shut off the engine. Gulls and wader birds called across the marsh. The sky was lightening into blue.

Frogs and more birds began to call, and redwings clung to stalks of swaying sea oats.

"Listen to the morning," Lura said.

And Agnes closed both eyes to sleep as the molten sun boiled up, cyclopic, from the water.

TERRIBLE ARGUMENT

ONCE THERE WERE A MAN, A WOMAN, AND THEIR DOG. NEI-
ther the woman nor the dog had ever conceived, so there were
no babies or pups. The man and woman drank heavily and often
had terrible arguments late in the evening, and raged back and
forth at one another for an hour or more, their fights often spilling out of the house and into the yard. If they had guests, which
was rare, they tried not to argue but usually failed, and then
they would argue in loud hissing stage whispers that inevitably
became loud hushed gargling voices like people being strangled.
They were sure that the guests heard almost every terrible word
they said to one another: the threats to leave, the vows of retribu-
tion and declarations of hatred, the sock-footed stompings in and
out of the room, and the openings and furiously careful closings
of the front door as one or the other went outside to smoke or
pace around in frustration and rage.

More than once, as he stomped out to his car intending to
leave her to her own insane devices, she leapt onto his back and
rode him around like a fierce, undisengagable monkey until he
fell down and promised that he wouldn't drive away. She demon-
strated a frightening strength when she was enraged, and all he
could do in the face of this was submit. Once, he managed to
throw her off in a jujitsu-type move onto her back, throwing his

own back out, and she was so astonished, outraged, and incredulous that she made him fetch the cordless phone from inside and called the police as she lay in the yard. When the police came, they argued so vehemently over who had attacked and hurt whom that the officers put them into the caged back seats of separate squad cars until they calmed down and then made them go back inside their home and behave.

Sometimes their lives entered less disturbing or fearful periods of relative calm. These times were most often disturbed in small ways, incrementally, subtly, and insidiously cracking the door to more serious arguments, awakening their hibernating ires. They might argue about the salt and pepper shakers, gone empty again, how the one never bothered to refill them and so the other always did. They argued about the recycling, how the one never bothered to take it to the recycling center. They argued about who failed to remove their hair from the shower drain sieve. About who snored or farted, frequently, in sleep. About who left the front door unlocked in the night. Who left the car windows down when it rained. They fought over the dog, over who loved the dog more or less, or walked it less, or yelled at it when angry, or did not love it, or traumatized it by yelling at the other, not at the dog. They fought over who had wanted the dog in the first place. About who picked up more of the dog's turds from the yard. Who had let the dog chew on the battery whose acid had eaten away part of its tongue. Who'd let it eat the mothballs that had nearly vaporized its anus.

For her part, the dog seemed traumatized by their constant fighting. She had a put-upon look on her face as if she wished they would just settle down. She had been a shelter rescue and although they knew nothing of her past they assumed it had not been good. She was an exceedingly good-natured, gentle dog, with big brown eyes she would level on them as if they were the saddest creatures in the world. But she was nervous, a little neurotic, and in truth such outright conflict increased her anxiety to the point where she had become a compulsive eater.

In addition to the battery and the mothballs, she had eaten a mole, a chipmunk, a piece of rope from a corner in the garage, the dried corpse of a mouse from the same place, a pine cone, several sticks of various sizes, a bunch of roses from the garage garbage pail, cat turds, dog turds, coyote turds, squirrel turds, a pair of severed crow's feet, a songbird's skull and beak, several small stones and one larger sedimentary rock, a rubber part from a motor mount, a valuable 1924 buffalo nickel, a utilities overdue notice, a box of wooden matches, a hot sausage right off the grill, many fleas, and of course hundreds of pounds of kibble. She shat approximately twice a day, in the best possible accessible places in the yard or the park or out on the prairie.

When she was on long trail walks she liked to shit on top of tiny shrubs, no one knew why. Sometimes when the dog held them in her long, inscrutable gaze, the man believed she was truly thinking about them, truly regretting being adopted by them, and he felt ashamed. Then he would think it was ridiculous to feel ashamed over what you thought a dog might be thinking of you, as if their thoughts could be anything but the simplest kind of reaction to your behavior or possibly your moods. A dog didn't know how to reprimand. He really should try not to have such absurd thoughts. It wasn't making things any better, that's for sure.

No matter how they tried, things seemed to get steadily worse. At least, he told himself at such times, we were never foolish enough to have children.

IT WAS NOT UNHEARD-OF FOR THEM to argue over the way in which one or the other took steps intended to ward off the possibility of an argument in the first place. One might do more than one's share of the cooking or cleaning, only to have the other accuse him or her of trying to gain the moral upper hand, of shoring up ammunition for or against some future assault.

Their therapist told them they were both emotional infants and this stung badly enough that for several days they were sullen and mute and limped about the house like injured pets who'd been kicked by their masters.

Sometimes, in their studied attempts to get along and avoid unnecessary argument, they argued over whether or not one or the other was, in fact, actually angry. The interpretation of a mood, a gesture or the lack of one, a meaningful look or a meaningful avoidance of eye contact or acknowledgment of a gesture or a mood. And then the one, indignant that the other was angry for no apparent reason, would begin to display obvious and intentional signs of frustration or anger, perplexing and then angering the other, all of which led to loud accusations of the one or the other and then of the one *and* the other having lost his and/or her mind.

Once they had a fantastic blowup over whether or not a certain actor in a particular movie was Albert Finney. She insisted the actor was Albert Finney, and he insisted that she was wrong, the man was not Albert Finney and possibly was not even English. They became impossibly enraged, out in the yard shouting at one another about Albert Finney, until one of their neighbors called the police.

He was essentially right in the end but it was spoiled because the other actor was in fact English, just like Albert Finney, and this tainted his victory with the faint odor of speculation, of luck. Afterward, they laughed over what the dog would think if she could understand that their argument was over the identity of an actor who resembled another actor, Albert Finney.

The dog lay on her pallet in the den, surrounded by her

comforts—her buddy toy, and her bunny which she'd had since she was in the shelter, and her ball and her bone—and gazed at them evenly, her snout resting on her paws, and said nothing.

They fought over sex, of course. Of course! Even so, it was horrible and humiliating all around. Each believed sex to be a great mediator, a mollifier, a rich black coal to stoke the fire of love. For they did love one another, in spite of their frequent and intense hatred. Their love and hatred were simply two sides of the same emotion, easily flipped. And so when they were enraged one with the other, and when the intense heat of the argument had cooled down, one or the other would sometimes attempt to blow gently into the embers, warm things up, maybe get it on. Timing was crucial, however, and almost never correct. You couldn't make your move a moment too soon, or the argument started right back up, and to wait a moment too late was futile, exhausting, as if years had passed, as if the one had spent much time in a coma, traveling eons in a cocoonlike, strange-dreamed world, awakening to this weirdly familiar stranger mooning and touching and whispering terrifying words into an ear.

Their secret, not necessarily kept from one another but an openly shared secret, was that each knew the other was the only kind of person either might be remotely capable of continuing to care about, much less stay with for any length of time. Each knew that the other was the kind of person who, little by little, inevitably, grew to hate whomever it was that they had once (perhaps) loved. That the other was just like them, the kind of person who hated him- or herself so deeply and thoroughly, and was so rottenly insecure of his/her intellect, moral fiber, looks, and so on, that it was impossible not to hate anyone who genuinely cared about them. And, if that person perhaps *did* come to genuinely despise them at some point, it only served to confirm their bitter certainty that such a betrayal was bound to happen. But—*but*—if you were with a person who was just like you, not only in those

ways but also in terms of being overly temperamental, extremely
hypercritical, constantly suspicious of one thing or another, and
who abused you verbally and sometimes, to some degree, physi-
cally, who in other words both treated you exactly as you deep-
down believed you deserved *and* gave you damn good reason
to think of him or her as the meanest, sneakiest (son of a) bitch,
well, it was a marriage made by the gods, that's all there was to
it. In her own humble and quiet way, the dog was in accord with
this assessment of the situation.

THEN THERE WAS THE BUSINESS of the gun. One could argue
that it would be insane for either of them to believe that one or
the other should bring a gun into their house, of all places. Even
so, when a colleague of his gave him the gun, he was delighted,
though later on he was mystified that he had been delighted over
the gift of a gun, that he had not thought it an unusual gift, a
dangerous gift, a gift almost never given, especially not to someone who is simply a colleague and not a frightened spouse who
must on a regular basis get to his or her car across a forlorn and
empty parking lot in a bad part of town, or deliver large bags of
cash from the till to the bank in the bleak evening, or rob a store
or a bank. It was not much of a gun, a little .25-caliber semiautomatic pistol, cheaply chromed, with a white plastic handle that
was a little loose in the screws.

The colleague had laughed and called it an Italian Assassin's
Gun, given to him by a friend after a poker game one night for
the same reason the colleague was giving it to him right now,
which was that his wife had demanded he get rid of the gun, she
would not have the thing in her house, and so would he like to
take it home and—HA HA HA, the colleague had laughed—try
it out on *his* wife?

And so quite possibly, of course, even he had to admit it, this was why he had accepted the gun and taken it home and pretended to be nonchalant about the fact that he was bringing a gun into their house. Their house, of all places. Because of the challenge, the bald-faced effrontery serving some vague, untethered resentment or another.

Of course they fought over it, the gun. Over the wisdom of having it and keeping it around. She was in the camp of those who believed having a gun would only, inevitably, put a gun in the hand of an intruder who otherwise might not have a gun. He was in the camp of those (or so he told himself conveniently at the moment) who believed that, whether or not one was especially handy with a gun, it was better to have a fighting chance with a formidable weapon in the admittedly unlikely but not beyond-the-pale chance that one would indeed be confronted by an intruder with a knife or a gun. I will not be a passive, helpless victim, he said. What difference would it make, she said, whether you had a gun in your hand when you got shot or did not have a gun in your hand? At least we'd have a chance! he said. What are the odds—the *chances*, if you prefer—of it ever coming *up*? she said. Then they fought over the quality of the gun, which was obviously not good, and over whether that mattered since it had been a casual gift from his colleague whose wife had told him it couldn't stay in *their* house any longer. I'm not talking about the manner in which we acquired the stupid thing! she said. And if *she* didn't want it around what makes you think *I* would, for God's sake? Well, it shoots just fine! he said. At aluminum *cans*, she said. CANS ARE NOT ARMED AND DANGEROUS!

Where are you going? he said.

To throw the goddamned thing away.

He ran ahead and blocked her from entering his study, where he had put the gun. She tried to get around him, and they began to wrestle. She dug her sharp fingernails into his arm, and instinctively he did something he'd never done before. He slapped her across the face. They both froze in disbelief of what had just happened, their faces two variations on some kind of horror. Then, giving him the coldest look she'd ever given him, she walked away.

It was late in the evening. She went into the bedroom and began taking clothes off the closet rack and from the dresser drawers and throwing them onto the rumpled bedcovers and took a duffel from the closet shelf and threw it onto the bed beside the clothes and began to stuff them into the bag. He followed her and stood in the doorway.

Where are you going?

I don't know, a motel, whatever. Maybe I'll just get into the car and drive, I don't know where.

You can't just do that.

Watch me.

She made for the front door with the unzipped bag in her hand, still in her pajamas and furry slippers.

Come on, she said to the dog, who had retreated from her pallet to a safer place beneath the coffee table. The dog looked from her to the man, and didn't move.

You're not taking the dog, he said.

She's my dog! she said. I'm the one who got her from the shelter. I'm the one who feeds her, gives her her medicine, brushes her coat. You don't give a damn about the dog.

I do, too! I do those things!

Where's the leash?

She found the leash and snapped it onto the dog's collar and started coaxing the dog from beneath the coffee table. The dog reluctantly began to creep from under the table to follow her, eyes frightened and moving rapidly from the woman to the man.

Stop that! he said. You're freaking her out.

Me! she said.

He went to stop her, trying only to restrain her from leaving the house, but they grappled in the foyer, her bag falling open into the living room and spilling her clothes, the dog trying to scramble out of the way but she was restrained by the leash held tight in the woman's hand. He knocked over a hat and coat stand with his elbow and sent it tumbling. She let go of the leash and the dog scrambled past them on clickity claws toward the rear of the house, trailing the leash.

Look at that! she shouted. You're traumatizing the goddamn dog again. Stop it. Just stop!

You can't just get into the car with a bag of clothes and head out into the night.

How do you know, how could you know? Let me go, you bastard. I'll kill you!

She twisted in his grasp and chopped at his throat with her fist. He deflected her blows, backing up.

Stop, he said. You'd better stop.

He backed away and she immediately stooped to gather her clothes back into the bag. He rushed into his study and snatched the little pistol off the shelf next to the dictionary and went back into the living room and stood over her. She looked up, saw the gun in his hand, and froze.

You don't have the guts to use that ridiculous thing, she said. Even you're not that insane.

He stepped back, shucked a round into the gun's chamber, and for a moment thought he would shoot a bullet into the floor near her, just to let her know he would do it. But at the last moment he pointed the muzzle toward his right foot and fired.

The pain was blinding. He fell to the floor.

Jesus! Jesus fucking Christ! she kept saying as he writhed on the floorboards, moaning, touching and then recoiling from his bleeding foot. Somewhere in another room the dog barked frantically, as if an intruder were breaking down the door.

———

ON THE WAY TO THE HOSPITAL, while he gritted his teeth and poured out a cold sweat, they did not fight verbally but carried on a battle of silence wherein each believed himself or herself superior to the other, she because he had been enough of a hysterical idiot to shoot himself in the foot in order to make a point, he because he was in agonizing pain and knew that anyone who could drive another person to shoot himself in the foot just to get her to shut up and stay put must be out of her mind.

The young, balding emergency room doctor ordered X-rays, anesthetized and cleaned the wound. The police came and required them to fill out a report. Luckily they were not police officers who had ever been to their house, called by one of them or by their neighbors. And then they went back home.

Miraculously, the bullet hadn't cracked through any bones.

It was five a.m. He hobbled off to bed, his foot bandaged and throbbing. He took one of the sample Percocets they'd given him and slept.

She stood over him for a long while, watching him sleep. It was difficult for her to gather her thoughts. She was rather stunned, a little in shock. She went into the kitchen to make a pot of coffee and forgot what she was doing and stood for a long while at the sink staring at her shaking hands and the stained porcelain in the basin of the sink.

In the afternoon he woke to find she was not there, had left a note that she was going away for a while, that she wasn't sure whether she wanted to come back or not, whether there was any point to coming back at all, and that the insanity with the gun was truly frightening to her and caused her to wonder whether things had finally gone too far, that if he could shoot himself in the foot in order to make a point, then who was she to say that one day, in order to make a point, he would not shoot her in the foot or the hand or point-blank right between the eyes?

He stood at the sink reading over the note, trembling at first with rage that she would leave while he lay wounded in the other room, then awash with a flood of shame and grief. He could hardly believe that she had gone and might not come back and that he hadn't been able to keep this from happening, yet another disaster, his third marriage down the drain.

He limped back to bed with the note crushed in his fist and lay down and stared at the ceiling. Theirs was an old house with real plaster on the ceilings and walls and he lay there for a long while looking at it, its hidden patterns slowly revealing themselves. How had the workmen made that simple but beautiful finish on the plaster? As if it had been pressed into place with crushed flowers. There were no craftsmen such as that at work anymore. He couldn't imagine how they might have done it, and he wondered for some minutes about the various ways in which they possibly had.

The dog, who'd been hiding somewhere in the house, crept into the bedroom, her head low, still trailing the leash clipped to her collar, her eyes wary and vulnerable. Then she crept backward from the room again and he heard her claws clicking across the kitchen linoleum and the sound of the leash dragging behind her on her way back to the den.

It was not all over, surely. She wouldn't stay away forever. He was fairly certain of that. She would've taken the dog, surely, if she meant to be gone for good. She was right that he should somehow get rid of the gun. The whole thing was at least as absurd as anything else they'd ever done, and the gun was the most absurd thing that he'd ever done, he'd have to grant that, and the painful embarrassment, the horror he was feeling, as he lay there, was nearly as excruciating as the throbbing pain returning to his foot. He fought against a great creeping weight of despair. What a fool he was. My God. He sighed heavily and reached for the foil packet of Percocets, popped one out, and swallowed it with water she'd left in a glass on the bedside table within reach. He took a pillow from her side and put it underneath his injured foot, to elevate it.

BACK IN THE DEN, the dog was not at all certain the woman would ever return. She had only watched the woman leave the house and drive sadly away in her vehicle, without saying a word to her, the dog. Now the dog didn't know what she would do. She thought all this was at least partly her fault.

With her previous owners, before she'd escaped and been taken to the shelter, she'd been beaten for simply crossing from one room to the next. For crapping in the very yard into which they had kicked her in order to crap. For barking when the very real threat of another dog entering their yard had been imminent. She had protected them! Defended their honor and territory! And they'd beaten her! It had scrambled her mind. She ran away. She was captured and put into yet another cage.

The man and woman came by one day and took her home, and were kind to her, but almost immediately the daily loud barking and snarling started up, and even if she could usually tell when it was about to start she was always frightened and wanted to run away. Now here she was beneath the coffee table, licking her paws, with their leash fastened to the collar about her neck, and nowhere to go. No walk. No drive up into the mountains to chase squirrels. No quick trip to the prairie to jump jackrabbits, harass the cowardly pronghorn herd. She could rip open the back screen, jump the fence, and walk until another man or woman or couple saw the leash and took it up. She could offer herself to someone else this way, take her chances.

But another couple, another family, would only present a new set of baffling circumstances. Of this she had no doubt.

In spite of their bad behavior, this couple had loved her and cared for her and served her well. She resolved to stay under the coffee table, the leash clipped to her collar in hope, and wait for the woman to return.

But she couldn't rid herself of the darkening fear that once again everything had gone to hell. She didn't know if she could take it all happening all over again. She had tried so hard to be smart, to stay out of trouble. But she had been distracted by her own anxiety, hadn't paid proper attention, and if the woman had been driven away, maybe she would have to go away now, too. She began to gnaw hopelessly at the end of her leash, but that didn't comfort her at all. For the first time in a long time, since she was very young and homeless and hungry, she raised her muzzle into the air and let out a long, mournful howl.

IN THE BEDROOM, THE MAN felt the howl penetrate to the very center of his wretched heart. He lay there looking at his discolored toes sticking out from the white gauze wrapping, blinking back tears, and tried to console himself. However horrible he had been, he had not actually harmed her and perhaps she'd consider this and come home. However colossally stupid he had been, concerning the gun, at least it had put an end to that terrible argument.

NOON

THE DOCTORS HAD DELIVERED BETH AND TEX'S ONLY CHILD stillborn, in breech, and the child had come apart. Their voices seemed to travel to her from a great distance and then open up quietly, beside her ear. She felt the strength leave Tex's grip on her hand as if his heart had stopped, the blood in his body going still. She looked up at him, but he turned away. Then the drugs had taken over, what they'd given her after so much reluctant labor, and she drifted off.

They allowed the funeral home to take their child, and to fix her, though they'd never had any intention of opening the casket or even having a public service. And neither did they view the man's work at all, despite his professional disappointment. He understood they wouldn't want others to view her, but seemed to think they'd want to see her themselves. He was a soft and pale supplicant, Mr. Pond, who kind of looked like a sad baby himself, with wet lips and lost eyes. They explained, as best they could, that they'd wanted only to have her as whole again as she could possibly be, never having been whole and out in the world. But Beth couldn't bear to see it, to see her looking like some kind of ghoulish doll.

They'd named her Sarah, after Beth's mother, who'd died the year before. Beth found a fading black-and-white photograph of her mother as an infant on a blanket beside a flowering gardenia bush. She placed it in her wallet's secret compartment. This was what her Sarah would have looked like.

They'd made him decide what to do, and he'd decided to save her more risk. She made him tell her about it, next day. He stood beside her hospital bed, hands jammed into the pockets of his jeans, hair lopsided from sleep.

"It was getting a little dangerous for you," he said. "It was either pull her out somehow or cut you, and they asked me what we wanted to do. You were kind of out of it.

"I understood what they meant," he said. "You were having some problems. It was dangerous. I said to go ahead and pull her out, to get it over with as quickly as they could.

"I was afraid for you," he said. "Something in the doctors' voices made me afraid. I told them to get it over with and to hurry. So they did."

What he was saying moved through her like settling, spreading fluid.

"I don't want to dwell on it," Tex said after a moment. He sounded angry, as if he were angry at her for wanting to know. "There wasn't anything they could do. She was already gone and it was an emergency. There was nothing anyone could do about that."

He stood there looking at the sheet beside her as if determined to see something in it, words printed there in invisible ink.

"She broke," she whispered. Her throat swollen and too tight to speak.

He looked at her, unfocused. She understood he could not comprehend what he'd seen.

"It doesn't mean anything," he said. "She was already gone."

"It means something," she said. "It means the world is a horrible place, where things like that can happen."

They went home. They arranged the funeral and attended it with his parents and her father, who came with her two sisters. No one had very much to say and everyone went home that afternoon.

In the house over the next few weeks they seemed to walk through one another like shadows. One night she woke up from a dream so far from her own life she couldn't shake it and didn't know herself or who slept beside her. A long moment of terror before she returned to herself with dizzying speed. She lay awake watching him as calm was restored to her bloodstream, quiet to her inner ear. Her heartbeat made an aspirant sound in her chest. She gently tugged the covers from beneath his arms. Their skins were a pale, granular gray in the bedroom's dim moonlight, which failed in silent moments as if an opaque eyelid were being lowered over its surface. She gathered his image to her mind swiftly, as if to save it from oblivion. But he seemed a collection of parts linked by shadows in the creases of his joints, pieces of a man put together in a dream, escaping her memory more swiftly than she could gather it in. In a moment he would be gone.

JULIE VERNER AND MAY MILLER had lost theirs, too, at about the same time. Miscarriages. They were all in their mid to late thirties, friends for close to ten years now, ever since they were young and happily childless.

It was May's first, but Julie and Beth had each lost two, so they were like a club, with a certain cursed and morbid exclusivity. Their friends with children drew away, or they drew away from the friends. They speculated about what it was they may have done that made them all prone to lose babies, and came up with nothing much. They hadn't smoked or drunk alcohol or even fought with their husbands much while pregnant. They'd had good obstetricians. They hadn't even drunk the local water, just in case. It seemed like plain bad luck, or bad genes.

On Friday nights the three of them went out to drink at the student bars near the college. They smoked, what the hell. Julie smoked now anyway but Beth and May smoked only on Fridays, in the bars. They smoked self-consciously, like people in the movies. Saturdays, they slept in and their husbands went golfing or fishing or hunting. Tex was purely the fisherman, and he would rise before dawn and go to the quiet, still lakes in the piney woods, where he tossed fluke-tailed artificial worms toward largemouth bass. When he returned in the afternoons he cleaned his catch on a little table beneath the pecan tree out back. He kept only those yearlings the perfect size for pan-frying in butter and garlic. On days he didn't fish he sometimes practiced his casting in the backyard, tossing lures with the barbs removed from their hooks toward an orthopedic donut pillow Beth had bought and used for postpartum hemorrhoids.

On the mornings he went fishing Beth rose late into a house as empty and quiet as a tomb. Despite the quiet, she sometimes put in earplugs and moved around the house listening to nothing but the inner sounds of her own breathing and pulse. It was like being a ghost. She liked the idea of the houses we live in becoming our tombs. She said to the others, out at the bar:

"When we died they could just seal it off."

Julie and May liked the idea.

"Like the pharaohs," May said.

"Except I wouldn't want to build a special house for it," Beth said. "Just seal off the old one, it'll be paid for."

"Not mine," May said. She tried to insert the end of a new cigarette into a cheap amber holder she'd bought at the convenience store, but dropped the cigarette onto the floor. She looked at the cigarette for a moment, then set the holder down on the table and pushed her hands into her hair and held her head there like that.

"And they shut up all your money in there, too," Beth said.

"Put it all in a sack or something, so you'll have plenty in the afterlife, and they'd have to put some sandwiches in there. Egg salad."

"And your car," Julie said, "and rubbers, big ones. Nothing but the big hogs for me in the afterlife."

"Is it heaven," May said, "if you still have to use rubbers?"

"Camel," Beth said.

"Lucky," May said. Julie doled them out. When they were in the bars, when they smoked, it was nonfiltered Camels and Luckies.

THEY WENT TO THE CHUKKER and listened to a samba band, the one with the high-voiced French singer. Beth danced with a student whose stiff hair stood like brown pampas grass above a headband, shaved below. Then a tall, lithe woman she knew only as Gazella cut in and held her about the waist as they danced, staring into her eyes.

"What's your name?"

"Beth."

Gazella said nothing else, but gazed frankly at her without flirtation or any other emotion Beth could identify, just gazing at her. Beth, unable to avert her own gaze, felt as exposed and transparent as a glass jar of emotional turmoil, as if the roil and color of it were being divined by this strange woman. Then the song stopped. Gazella kissed her on the cheek, and went back to the bar. Watching her, Beth knew only one thing: she wished she looked like Gazella, a nickname bestowed because the woman was so lithe, with a long neck and an animal's dispassionate intelligence in her eyes. Powerful slim hips that rolled when she moved across the room. And like an animal, she seemed entirely self-reliant. Didn't need anyone but herself.

She looked around. The pampas grass boy was dancing with someone else now, a girl wearing a crew cut and black-rimmed eyeglasses with lenses the size and shape of almonds. Beth went back to the table. Julie and May raised their eyebrows, moved them like a comedy team, in sync, toward Gazella. May had the cigarette holder, a Lucky burning at its end, clamped in her bared teeth. Then the two of them said the name, Gazella, in unison, and grabbed each other by the arm, laughing.

Beth said, "I was just wondering when was the last time y'all fucked your husbands?" May and Julie frowned in mock thought. May pulled out her checkbook and they consulted the little calendars on the back of the register. "There, then," Julie said, circling a date with her pen.

May spat a mouthful of beer onto the floor and shouted, "That's 1997! A fucking year!"

"I'M NOT GOING HOME NOW," Julie said. "Let's go where there's real dancing."

Because she'd been drinking the least, Beth drove them in the new Toyota wagon she and Tex had bought for parenthood. They went to Seventies, a retro-disco joint out by the interstate. There they viewed the spectrum of those with terminal disco fever, from middle-aged guys in tight white suits to young Baptists straight from the Northend Laundry's steam press, all cotton creases and hair-parts pale and luminous as moonbeams. Beth watched one couple, a young man with pointed waspish features and his date, a plumpish big-boned girl with shoulder-length hair curled out at her shoulders. They seemed somehow designed for raucous, comic reproduction. The man twirled the woman. She was graceful, like those big girls who were always so good at modern dance in high school, their big thick legs that rose like zeppelins when they leapt. Beth indulged herself with a Manhattan, eating the cherry and taking little sips from the drink.

May now drooped onto the table in the corner of their booth before the pitcher of beer she and Julie had bought. Julie whirled in off the dance floor as if the brutish, moussed investment banker type she'd been dancing with had set her spinning all the way back to the booth. She plopped in opposite Beth and said, breathless, "Okay, I think I'm satisfied."

"Not me," May intoned.

"Words from a corpse," Julie said. "Arouse thyself and let's go home."

"Oh," May said, and spread her arms as she sat up, then slumped back against the seat. She was crying. Too late, Beth thought, she's hit the wall.

"Better gather her in," she said to Julie.

"No, no," May said, shucking their hands off her arms. "I can get out by myself. Stop it."

"All right, but we'd better go home, honey."

"I just keep thinking something's wrong with me."

"Come on, none of that," Beth said.

"Oh, I'm sorry!" May said. "I know! It's not as bad as what happened to you. Shit. I'm sorry."

"Okay," Beth said.

" 'Cause, like, no one had it worse than Beth."

"May, shut up," Julie said.

"I have to shut up, I know that," May said, and let them guide her out to the car. They managed to tumble her into the back seat. Julie, drunker than Beth had realized, tossed a match from the flaming end of her Lucky Strike, spat tobacco flecks off the tip of her tongue, and said, "Let her sleep, let's go over to the

L&N and sip some Irish whiskey. Leave a note in her ear, she can
wake up and follow us inside if she wants to."

"She'll throw up in the car," Beth said.

They reached in and rolled May onto her belly.

"Okay, I'm all right," May mumbled.

"Good enough," Julie said. "She won't choke."

THEY DROVE TO THE L&N and plowed into the deep pea gravel
covering the parking lot. The streetlights cast a dim, foggy light
onto the building, an old train station that stood on the bluff
above the river like a ruined cathedral. May's voice came as if dis-
embodied from the back seat, "I'm sorry, Beth, goddamn I really
am sorry for that," and Beth was about to say, That's okay, but
May said, "I need to talk about all that. But y'all won't talk about
it. Y'all won't say shit about all that. Tough guys." She laughed.
"Tough gals."

Julie said, "May, I don't want to hear it."

"See, like that," May said, trying to sit up. "The strong, silent
type. John Wayne in a dress. No, who wears a dress anymore?
Why, only John Wayne. John Wayne with a big fat ass. John
Wayne with a vagina and tits. John Wayne says, 'Rock, I'm
havin' your baby—but there's complications.'" She got out of the
car and fell into the pea gravel, laughing. "It's so soft!" she said,
rolling onto her back. "Like a feather bed! Look, it just molds to
your body!"

Julie said something in a low voice to May but Beth had gotten out of the car, leaving the door open, and started down the
road. She called back, "I'm going to take a walk," and headed
down the hill toward the river, the sound of Julie now speaking
in an angry tone to May and May's high-pitched protests pinging
off the assault becoming distant, the beeping sound of Beth's keys
still in the ignition behind it all.

AT THE BOAT LANDING behind the Chevrolet dealer's lot the
river was broad and flat and black beneath a sky gauzy with the
moon's veiled light. Like old location westerns where they'd shot
night scenes during the day using something like smoked glass
over the lens. She stood there listening to the faint gurgling of
the current near the bank, seeing ripples from the stronger current out in the middle.

She waded in to her waist, feeling her way with her old sneakers, and stood feeling the current pull gently at her jeans and
the water soaking up into her faded purple T-shirt. The river
was warm like bathwater late in the bath. She leaned forward
and pushed out, swimming with her head above the water, and
turned back to look at the bank now twenty feet behind her. She
felt the need to be submerged for a moment, to shut out the upper
world. She dunked her head in and pushed the sneakers off with
her toes, then swam a few strokes underwater before coming up
again, where she heard a shout, "There she is!"

She threw a hand up. "Here I am!"

It was Julie shouting again. "Beth, that's too dangerous! Come
back to the goddamn bank, you idiot!"

"Beth!" May shouted. "I'm sorry! Come back!"

"Oh, for Christ's sake," Beth said to herself. Farther out the
water was still warm, though she passed here and there through
columns of cool. She called out to them, "I'm just going to float
along here for a while!"

More shouted protests, but she was farther out now, and moving downstream. She saw them start trotting along the bank,
then came a crashing of leaves and branches, a jumble of cussing
and some shouting, and then she couldn't see them anymore. She
was maybe thirty yards off the bank, mostly floating or treading
water, moving with the current. The moon was beautiful over-

head, its light on the water and the trees on either bank silver and weightless. The river was almost silent, giving up an occasional soft gurgling burp, and she could feel a breeze funneling through the riverbed, cooling her forehead when she turned her face back upstream. Nothing out there but her. There could be barges. This thought came to her. But she was lucky, none of that just then. Some large bird, a massive shadow, swooped down and whooshed just over her head, then flapped back up and away toward the opposite bank. "My God," she shouted. "An owl!"

"Beth!" she heard from the near bank again, and she saw them, jogging along in a clearing atop a little bluff no more than a few feet above the water level.

"Here I am!"

"Swim in!"

"Beth, please!" May struggled to keep up with Julie's long strides, and Beth heard them both, between shouting, panting, Shit Shit Shit. "Fucking cigarettes," she heard Julie say. They disappeared into a copse of thick pines. There must be a trail, Beth thought. From the pines she heard Julie's voice come up again. "Goddammit, Beth! Are you still floating?"

Their voices carried beautifully across the water, with the clarity of words transported whole and discrete across the surface, delivered to her in little pockets of sound.

"Still floating!" she called back. Then, "I'm not going to be able to hear you for a while, I'm going to float on my back. Ears in the water!" And then she turned over onto her back and floated, the water up over her ears to the corners of her eye sockets. Wispy clouds skimmed along beneath the moon, or was she moving that swiftly down the river? There was a soft roaring of white noise from the water beneath her. So much water! You couldn't even imagine it from the bank. You couldn't imagine it even here, in it, unless maybe you were a fish and it was your whole world. She heard a clanking, a moaning like whale sound-ings that could've been giant catfish she'd heard about, catfish big enough to come up and take her in one sucking gulp. Some huge, sleek, bewhiskered monster to swallow her whole, her body encased within its own, traveling the slow and murky river bottom for ages, her brain growing around the fish's brain, its stem lodged in her cerebellum.

Half ancient fish, half woman with strange, submerged mem-ories. She senses Tex on this river, in the early morning before first light, casting his line out into the waters. She follows some familiar current to where she hears the thin line hum past, trail-ing the little worm, fluke tail squibbling by. It's an easy thing to take it in, feel the hook set, sit there awhile feeling the deter-mined pull on the line, giving way just enough to keep him from snapping it. Rising beside the little boat and looking wall-eyed into his astonished face, wouldn't she see him then as she never had?

She remembered Tex fucking her the night she knew Sarah was conceived, their bodies bowed into one another, movements fluid as waves. Watching his face.

Tex saying two weeks after it happened, We could try again, Beth. But it was almost as if he hadn't meant to say it, as if the words had been spoken into his own brain some other time, recorded, and now tripped accidentally out. He sat on the sofa, long legs crossed, looking very tired, the skin beneath his eyes bruised, though she marveled at how otherwise youthful he was, his thick blond hair and unlined face, a tall and lanky boy with pale blue eyes. Though younger, she was surpassing his age.

"I had this dream," he said, "the other night."

In his dream he was talking to one of the doctors, though it wasn't one of the doctors who'd been there in real life. The doctor said that if they had operated and taken Sarah out care-fully, they could have saved her. *But she was dead*, Tex said in the dream. *Well, we have amazing technology these days,* the doctor said.

Tex's long, tapered fingers fluttered against his knee. He blinked, gazing out the living room window at the pecan tree in the backyard.

"I woke up sobbing like a child," he said. "I was afraid I'd wake you up, but you were as still as a stone."

"I'm sorry," Beth said.

Tex shrugged. "It was just a dream."

In a minute, she said, "I just don't think I could do it all again." Her voice quavered and she stopped, frustrated at how hard it was to speak of it at all.

"We're not too old," he said. "It's not too late."

But she hadn't said just that.

"I didn't mean that," she said.

SHE TURNED HERSELF OVER in the water and came up again into the air, and her knees dragged bottom, and she saw the current had taken her into the shallows along the bank. She floated there and then sat on the muddy bottom, the water lapping the point of her chin. She wished she could push from herself everything that she felt. To be light as a sack of dried sticks floating on the river. She heard the thudding weary footsteps of the others approaching through the clearing at this landing, breath ragged, and they came and stood on the bank near her, hands on knees, heads bent low, dragging in gulps of air. "Oh, fuck, I'm dying," Julie gasped. "Are you all right?" Beth raised a hand from the water in reply. May fell to her knees and began to throw up, one arm held flat-handed generally toward them. They were quiet except for the sound of May being sick, and when she was finished she rolled over onto her back in the grass and lay there.

Beth and Julie carried May, fortunately tiny, with one of her arms across each of their shoulders, back along the river to the downtown landing and then up the hill to Beth's car. They left her in the back seat and struggled to walk through the deep pea gravel of the lot into the bar and borrowed some bar towels for Beth and then sat at a table drinking Jameson's neat and not talking for a while. May dragged herself in and sat with them and the bartender brought her a cup of coffee. She laid her head beside the steaming cup and went to sleep again.

Julie reached out and took Beth's hand for a second and squeezed it.

Beth squeezed back, then they let go. Julie looked down at the floor and held out one of her feet, clad in a ragged dirty Keds.

"Pretty soon I'll need a new pair of honky-tonk shoes," she said sadly.

"I like them," Beth said. "My mother had a pair just like that. She wore them to work in the yard."

"I didn't cut these holes out, baby, I wore 'em out. I got a big old toe on me"—she slipped her toe through a frayed hole and wiggled it—"like the head of a ball-peen hammer."

"My God," Beth said. "Put it up."

"Billy says I could fuck a woman with that toe."

"Put it back in the shoe."

"I'm'on put it up his ass one day," Julie said.

Somehow they'd become the only patrons left in the place. The bartender leaned on an elbow and watched sports news on a nearly silent TV above the bar. Julie looked at the sleeping May and said to Beth, "Don't worry about all that, that shit May was saying. She's just drunk. She doesn't know what she's talking about."

"No," Beth said. "I know what she's talking about. She's right."

Julie stared at her blankly, then sat up and sighed.

"I can't even remember what all she was saying. Forget it. You should forget it."

"I don't want to forget it," Beth said, and set her shot glass down on the table harder than she'd meant to. "What do you mean?"

Julie didn't answer.

"It changes you," Beth said. "It's changed me. It's different," she said. "It is worse, Julie. It's not like the other time. It is worse. A real child."

So then she'd said it. Julie had started to say something, then turned her head away, toward the wall. Neither said any more after that. The bartender roused himself, flicked off the TV, and his heels clicked through the tall-ceilinged old station as he went from table to table, wiping them down.

They drank up, paid, and left, hefting May's arms again onto their shoulders, and put her into the car. Beth drove them to May's house, and they helped her to the front door, got her keys from her pocket, and let themselves in. Her husband, Calvin, was at the hunting camp building stands. They took her to the bed and undressed her, tucked her in, put a glass of water beside the bed and a couple of ibuprofen beside it, and drove to Julie's house. Julie started to get out.

"You okay to drive home?" She sat with one leg out the open door, in the car's bleak interior light.

"Sure, I'm fine," Beth said. She caught herself nodding like a trained horse and stopped. Julie looked at her a long moment and then said, "Okay." Beth watched her till she got inside and waved from the window beside the door. Then she drove home through the streets where wisps of fog rose from cracks in the asphalt as if from rumbling, muffled engines down in the bedrock, leaking steam.

SHE WAS PRONE THESE DAYS to wake in the middle of the night as if someone had called to her while she'd slept. A kind of fear held her heart with an intimate and gentle suppression, a strange hand inside her chest. She was terrified. Soft and narrow strips of light slipped through the blinds and lay on the floor. Their silence was chilling.

Just after four a.m. she woke and Tex was already gone. He hadn't moved when she'd come in, his face like a sleeping child's. She'd lowered her ear to his nostrils, felt his warm breath. He slept with arms crisscrossed on his chest, eyebrows lifted above closed lids, ears attuned to the voices speaking to him in his other world. She hadn't heard him rise and leave.

The covers on his side were laid back neatly as a folded flag. One crumpled dent marked the center of his pillow. He had risen, she knew, without the aid of an alarm, his internal clock rousing him at three so that he would be out on the lake at four, casting when he couldn't even see where his bait plooped into the water, playing it all by ear and touch. He knew what was out there in the water. If a voice truly whispered to him as he slept she hoped it spoke of bass alert and silent in their cold, quiet havens, awaiting him. She hoped it was his divining vision, in the way some people envisioned the idea of God.

For her the worst had been prior to the delivery, after she'd learned what she feared, that the child had died inside her and she would have to carry her until they could attempt a natural delivery, and that would be at least a month, maybe two. That had been worse than the delivery, because sometimes in her distraction she almost thought the delivery had not really happened, it had been only a nightmare that would momentarily well into her consciousness and then recede. This was not so with Tex, because he'd seen it all happen, it was imprinted in his memory as surely as Sarah had been implanted in her womb. It was what his mind worked to obscure, awake and asleep, in its different ways.

She lay in bed as dawn suffused the linen curtains with slow

and muted particles of gray light. The room softened with this
light, and she slept.

IT WAS NOON. The front that had kept them under clouds and
in light fog was moving, the same clouds she'd seen beneath the
river moon scudding rapidly, diagonally, to the northeast, and
occasional rafts of yellow light passed through the bright green
leaves and over the weed-grown lawn.

From the living room picture window she could see Tex in
the backyard cleaning his catch in the shade of the splayed pecan
tree. He worked on the plain wooden table he had built for that.
His rod and reel leaned against the table's end, his tackle box on
the ground beside it. A stringer of other fish lay on the ground
beside the box, and Beth could see, every few seconds or so,
a fish tail rise slowly from the mess—as if the tail had an eye
with which to look around, stunned—and then relax. Tex wore
a baseball cap and a gauzy-thin, ragged T-shirt. The muscles on
his neck and shoulders bunched as he worked away at one of the
fish, his back to the house. He left them gutted but whole, heads
on. He hadn't always. When he slit their undersides to gut them,
he did it carefully with just the tip of his sharp fillet knife. He
gently lifted out the bright entrails with a finger, the button-
sized heart sometimes still beating. Then he pulled them free of
the body with a casual tug, as if distracted, an after-action.

She watched now from the picture window as he almost rev-
erently palmed a cleaned fish into the pail of water. He rinsed his
hand before sliding another one off the stringer. The shadows of
patchy clouds moved across the yard and over him with the slow
gravity of large beasts floating by. She still felt the effects of sleep,
of the drinking and smoking, and a mild vertigo, as if she'd stood
up too quickly. That hungover sense of having waked into a life
and body that were not her own. She reached out to the window
and steadied herself.

As if he'd heard her, Tex turned to look, fish and knife poised in his hands, interrupted so deeply into his task he seemed lost, either not seeing or not recognizing her image behind the windowpane.

She had dreamed, reentering the waking dream she'd had of the catfish in the river. Her sight in the dream through the eyes of the fish. Tex had lifted her into the boat, taken her home, lain her on the old plyboard table, and carefully slit the fish skin covering the length of her belly, worked it away from her own true form. But he was unable to detach the fish's brain from her own. Her words, some gurgly attempt to say she loved him, bubbled out and then she died.

It was a whole world, the way dreams can be.

He buried her in the yard, with a stone on top to keep the cats from digging her up to sniff at the bones. But over time she drifted in the soil. The grass grew from her own cells into the light and air. She watched him when he passed over with the lawn mower. The times between mowings were ages.

VISITATION

LOOMIS HAD NEVER BELIEVED THAT LINE ABOUT THE QUAL-
ity of despair being that it was unaware of being despair. He'd
been painfully aware of his own despair for most of his life. Most
of his troubles had come from attempts to deny the essential
hopelessness in his nature. To believe in the viability of nothing,
finally, was socially unacceptable, and he had tried to adapt, to
pass as a believer, a hoper. He had taken prescription medicine,
engaged in periods of vigorous, cleansing exercise, declared his
satisfaction with any number of fatuous jobs and foolish relation-
ships. Then one day he'd decided that he should marry, have a
child, and he told himself that if one was open-minded these
things could lead to a kind of contentment, if not to exuberant
happiness. That's why Loomis was in the fix he was in now.

Ever since he and his wife had separated and she had moved
with their son to southern California, he'd flown out every
three weeks to visit the boy. He was living the very nightmare
he'd suppressed upon deciding to marry and have a child: that it
wouldn't work out, they would split up, and he would be forced
to spend long weekends in a motel, taking his son to faux-upscale
chain restaurants, cineplexes, and amusement parks.

He usually visited for three to five days and stayed at the same
motel, an old motor court that had been bought and remodeled

by one of the big franchises. At first the place wasn't so bad. The continental breakfast offered fresh fruit, and little boxes of name-brand cereals, and batter with which you could make your own waffles on a double waffle iron right there in the lobby. The syrup came in small plastic containers from which you pulled back a foil lid and voilà, it was a pretty good waffle. There was juice and decent coffee. Still, of course, it was depressing, a bleak place in which to do one's part in raising a child. With its courtyard surrounded by two stories of identical rooms, and excepting the lack of guard towers and the presence of a swimming pool, it followed the same architectural model as a prison.

But Loomis's son liked it so they continued to stay there even though Loomis would rather have moved on to a better place.

He arrived in San Diego for his April visit, picked up the rental car, and drove north up I-5. Traffic wasn't bad except where it always was, between Del Mar and Carlsbad. Of course, it was never "good." Their motel sat right next to the 5, and the roar and rush of it never stopped. You could step out onto the balcony at three in the morning and it'd be just as roaring and rushing with traffic as it had been six hours before.

This was to be one of his briefer visits. He'd been to a job interview the day before, Thursday, and had another on Tuesday. He wanted to make the most of the weekend, which meant doing very little besides just being with his son. Although he wasn't very good at that. Generally, he sought distractions from his ineptitude as a father. He stopped at a liquor store and bought a bottle of bourbon, and tucked it into his travel bag before driving up the hill to the house where his wife and son lived. The house was owned by a retired Marine friend of his wife's family. His wife and son lived rent-free in the basement apartment.

When Loomis arrived, the ex-Marine was on his hands and knees in the flower bed, pulling weeds. He glared sideways at Loomis for a moment and muttered something, his face a mask of disgust. He was a widower who clearly hated Loomis and refused to speak to him. Loomis was unsettled that someone he'd never even been introduced to could hate him so much.

His son came to the door of the apartment by himself, as usual. Loomis peered past the boy into the little apartment, which was bright and sunny for a basement (only in California, he thought). But, as usual, there was no sign of his estranged wife. She had conspired with some part of her nature to become invisible. Loomis hadn't laid eyes on her in nearly a year. She called out from somewhere in another room, " 'Bye! I love you! See you on Monday!" "Okay, love you, too," the boy said, and trudged after Loomis, dragging his backpack of homework and a change of clothes. " 'Bye, Uncle Bob," the boy said to the ex-Marine. Uncle Bob! The ex-Marine stood up, gave the boy a small salute, and he and the boy exchanged high-fives.

After Loomis checked in at the motel, they went straight to their room and watched television for a while. Lately his son had been watching cartoons made in the Japanese anime style. Loomis thought the animation was wooden and amateurish. He didn't get it at all. The characters were drawn as angularly as origami, which he supposed was appropriate and maybe even intentional, if the influence was Japanese. But it seemed irredeemably foreign. His son sat propped against several pillows, harboring such a shy but mischievous grin that Loomis had to indulge him.

He made a drink and stepped out onto the balcony to smoke a cigarette. Down by the pool, a woman with long, thick black hair—it was stiffly unkempt, like a madwoman's in a movie—sat in a deck chair with her back to Loomis, watching two children play in the water. The little girl was nine or ten and the boy was older, maybe fourteen. The boy teased the girl by splashing her face with water, and when she protested in a shrill voice he leapt over and dunked her head. She came up gasping and began to cry. Loomis was astonished that the woman, who he assumed to be the children's mother, displayed no reaction. Was she asleep?

The motel had declined steadily in the few months Loomis had been staying there, like a moderately stable person drifting and sinking into the lassitude of depression. Loomis wanted to help, find some way to speak to the managers and the other employees, to say, Buck up, don't just let things go all to hell, but he felt powerless against his own inclinations.

He lit a second cigarette to go with the rest of his drink. A few other people walked up and positioned themselves around the pool's apron, but none got into the water with the two quarreling children. There was something feral about them, anyone could see. The woman with the wild black hair continued to sit in her pool chair as if asleep or drugged. The boy's teasing of the girl had become steadily rougher, and the girl was sobbing now. Still, the presumptive mother did nothing. Someone went in to complain. One of the managers came out and spoke to the woman, who immediately but without getting up from her deck chair shouted to the boy, "All right, God damn it!" The boy, smirking, climbed from the pool, leaving the girl standing in waist-deep water, sobbing and rubbing her eyes with her fists. The woman stood up then and walked toward the boy. There was something off about her clothes, burnt-orange Bermuda shorts and a men's lavender oxford shirt. And they didn't seem to fit right. The boy, like a wary stray dog, watched her approach. She snatched a lock of his wet black hair, pulled his face to hers, and said something, gave his head a shake, and let him go. The boy went over to the pool and spoke to the girl. "Come on," he said. "No," the girl said, still crying. "You let him help you!" the woman shouted then, startling the girl into letting the boy take her hand. Loomis was fascinated, a little bit horrified.

Turning back toward her chair, the woman looked up to

where he stood on the balcony. She had an astonishing face, broad and long, divided by a great, curved nose, dominated by a pair of large, dark, sunken eyes that seemed blackened by blows or some terrible history. Such a face, along with her immense, thick mane of black hair, made her look like a troll. Except that she was not ugly. She looked more like a witch, the cruel mockery of beauty and seduction. The oxford shirt was mostly unbuttoned, nearly spilling out a pair of full, loose, mottled-brown breasts.

"What are you looking at!" she shouted, very loudly from deep in her chest. Loomis stepped back from the balcony railing. The woman's angry glare changed to something like shrewd assessment and then dismissal. She shooed her two children into one of the downstairs rooms.

After taking another minute to finish his drink and smoke a third cigarette, to calm down, Loomis went back inside and closed the sliding glass door behind him.

His son was on the bed, grinning, watching something on television called *Code Lyoko*. It looked very Japanese, even though the boy had informed him it was made in France. Loomis tried to watch it with him for a while, but got restless. He wanted a second, and maybe stronger, drink.

"Hey," he said. "How about I just get some burgers and bring them back to the room?"

The boy glanced at him and said, "That'd be okay."

Loomis got a sack of hamburgers from McDonald's, some fries, a Coke. He made a second drink, then a third, while his son ate and watched television. They went to bed early.

THE NEXT AFTERNOON, SATURDAY, they drove to the long, wide beach at Carlsbad. Carlsbad was far too cool, but what could you do? Also, the hip little surf shop where the boy's mother worked during the week was in Carlsbad. He'd forgotten that for a moment. He was having a hard time keeping her in his mind. Her invisibility strategy was beginning to work on him. He wasn't sure at all anymore just who she was or ever had been. When they'd met she wore business attire, like everyone else he knew. What did she wear now, just a swimsuit? Did she get up and go around in a bikini all day? She didn't really have the body for that at age thirty-nine, did she?

"What does your mom wear to work?" he asked.

The boy gave him a look that would have been ironic if he'd been a less compassionate child.

"Clothes?" the boy said.

"Okay," Loomis said. "Like a swimsuit? Does she go to work in a swimsuit?"

The boy stared at him for a moment.

"Are you okay?" the boy said.

Loomis was taken aback by the question.

"Me?" he said.

They walked along the beach, neither going into the water. Loomis enjoyed collecting rocks. The stones on the beach here were astounding. He marveled at one that resembled an ancient war club. The handle fit perfectly into his palm. From somewhere over the water, a few miles south, they could hear the stuttering thud of a large helicopter's blades. Most likely a military craft from the Marine base farther north.

Maybe he wasn't okay. Loomis had been to five therapists since separating from his wife: one psychiatrist, one psychologist, three counselors. The psychiatrist had tried him on Paxil, Zoloft, and Wellbutrin for depression, and then lorazepam for anxiety. Only the lorazepam had helped, but with that he'd overslept too often and lost his job. The psychologist, once she learned that Loomis was drinking almost half a bottle of booze every night, became fixated on getting him to join AA and seemed to forget altogether that he was there to figure out whether he indeed no longer loved his wife. And why he had cheated on her. Why he had left her for another woman when the truth was he had no faith that the new relationship would work out any better than the old one. The first counselor seemed sensible, but Loomis made the mistake of visiting her together with his wife, and when she suggested maybe their marriage was indeed kaput his wife had walked out. The second counselor was actually his wife's counselor, and Loomis thought she was an idiot. Loomis suspected that his wife liked the second counselor because she did nothing but nod and sympathize and give them brochures. He suspected that his wife simply didn't want to move out of their house, which she liked far more than Loomis did, and which possibly she liked more than she liked Loomis. When she realized divorce was inevitable, she shifted gears, remembered she wanted to surf, and sold the house before Loomis was even aware it was on the market, so he had to sign. Then it was Loomis who mourned the loss of the house, which he realized had been pretty comfortable after all. He visited the third counselor with his girlfriend, who seemed constantly angry that his divorce hadn't yet come through. He and the girlfriend both gave up on that counselor because he seemed terrified of them for some reason they couldn't fathom. Loomis was coming to the conclusion that he couldn't fathom anything; the word seemed appropriate to him, because most of the time he felt like he was drowning and couldn't find the bottom or the surface of this body of murky water he had fallen, or dived, into.

He wondered if this was why he didn't want to dive into the crashing waves of the Pacific, as he certainly would have when he was younger. His son didn't want to because, he said, he'd rather surf.

"But you don't know how to surf," Loomis said.

"Mom's going to teach me as soon as she's good enough at it," the boy said.

"But don't you need to be a better swimmer before you try

to surf ?" Loomis had a vague memory of the boy's swimming
lessons, which maybe hadn't gone so well.

"No," the boy said.

"I really think," Loomis said, and then he stopped speaking, because the helicopter he'd been hearing, one of those large,
twin-engined birds that carried troops in and out of combat—a
Chinook—had come abreast of them a quarter mile or so off the
beach. Just as Loomis looked up to see it, something coughed or
exploded in one or both of its engines. The helicopter slowed,
then swerved, with the slow grace of an airborne leviathan,
toward the beach where they stood. In a moment it was directly
over them. One of the men in it leaned out of a small opening on
its side, frantically waving, but the people on the beach, including Loomis and his son, beaten by the blast from the blades and
stung by sand driven up by it, were too shocked and confused to
run. The helicopter lurched back out over the water with a tremendous roar and a deafening, rattling whine from the engines.
There was another loud pop, and black smoke streamed from the
forward engine as the Chinook made its way north again, seeming hobbled. Then it was gone, lost in the glare over the water.
A bittersweet burnt-fuel smell hung in the air. Loomis and his
son stood there among the others on the beach, speechless. One
of two very brown young surfers in board shorts and crew cuts
grinned and nodded at the clublike rock in Loomis's hand.

"Dude, we're safe," he said. "You can put down the weapon."
He and the other surfer laughed.

Loomis's son, looking embarrassed, moved off as if he were
with someone else in the crowd, not Loomis.

THEY STAYED IN CARLSBAD for an early dinner at Pizza Port.
The place was crowded with people who'd been at the beach all
day, although Loomis recognized no one they'd seen when the

helicopter had nearly crashed and killed them all. He'd expected everyone in there to know about it, to be buzzing about it over beer and pizza, amazed, exhilarated. But it was as if it hadn't happened.

The long rows of picnic tables and booths were filled with young parents and their hyperkinetic children, who kept jumping up to get extra napkins or forks or to climb into the seats of the motorcycle video games. Their parents flung arms after them like inadequate lassos or pursued them and herded them back. The stools along the bar were occupied by young men and women who apparently had no children and who were attentive only to each other and to choosing which of the restaurant's many microbrews to order. In the corner by the restrooms, the old surfers, regulars here, gathered to talk shop and knock back the stronger beers, the double-hopped and the barley wines. Their graying hair frizzled and tied in ponytails or dreads or chopped in stiff clumps dried by salt and sun. Their faces leather-brown. Gnarled toes jutting from their flip-flops and worn sandals like assortments of dry-roasted cashews, Brazil nuts, ginger roots.

Loomis felt no affinity for any of them. There wasn't a single person in the entire place with whom he felt a thing in common—other than being, somehow, human. Toward the parents he felt a bitter disdain. On the large TV screens fastened to the restaurant's brick walls, surfers skimmed down giant waves off Hawaii, Tahiti, Australia.

He gazed at the boy, his son. The boy looked just like his mother. Thick bright orange hair, untamable. Tall, stemlike people with long limbs and that thick hairblossom on top. Loomis had called them his rosebuds. "Roses are red," his son would respond, delightedly indignant, when he was smaller. "There are orange roses," Loomis would reply. "Where?" "Well, in Indonesia, I think. Or possibly Brazil." "No!" his son would shout, breaking down into giggles on the floor. He bought them orange roses on the boy's birthday that year.

The boy wasn't so easily amused anymore. He waited glumly for their pizza order to be called out. They'd secured a booth vacated by a smallish family.

"You want a Coke?" Loomis said. The boy nodded absently. "I'll get you a Coke," Loomis said.

He got the boy a Coke from the fountain, and ordered a pint of strong pale ale from the bar for himself.

By the time their pizza came, Loomis was on his second ale. He felt much better about all the domestic chaos around them in the restaurant. It was getting on the boy's nerves, though. As soon as they finished their pizza, he asked Loomis if he could go stand outside and wait for him there.

"I'm almost done," Loomis said.

"I'd really rather wait outside," the boy said. He shoved his hands in his pockets and looked away.

"Okay," Loomis said. "Don't wander off. Stay where I can see you."

"I will."

Loomis sipped his beer and watched as the boy weaved his way through the crowd and out of the restaurant, then began to pace back and forth on the sidewalk. Having to be a parent in this fashion was terrible. He felt indicted by all the other people in this teeming place: by the parents and their smug happiness, by the old surfer dudes, who had the courage of their lack of conviction, and by the young lovers, who were convinced that they would never be part of either of these groups, not the obnoxious parents, not the grizzled losers clinging to youth like tough, crusty barnacles. Certainly they would not be Loomis.

And what did it mean, in any case, that he couldn't even carry on a conversation with his son? How hard could that be? But Loomis couldn't seem to do it. To hear him try, you'd think they didn't know each other at all, that he was a friend of the boy's father, watching him for the afternoon or something. He started to get up and leave, but first he hesitated, then gulped down the rest of his second beer.

His son stood with hunched shoulders waiting.

"Ready to go back to the motel?" Loomis said.

The boy nodded. They walked back to the car in silence.

"Did you like your pizza?" Loomis said when they were in the car.

"Sure. It was okay."

Loomis looked at him for a moment. The boy glanced back with the facial equivalent of a shrug, an impressively diplomatic expression that managed to say both I'm sorry and What do you want? Loomis sighed. He could think of nothing else to say that wasn't even more inane.

"All right," he finally said, and drove them back to the motel.

WHEN THEY ARRIVED, Loomis heard a commotion in the courtyard and they paused near the gate.

The woman who'd been watching the two awful children was there at the pool again, and the two children themselves had returned to the water. But now the group seemed to be accompanied by an older heavyset man, bald on top, graying hair slicked against the sides of his head. He was arguing with a manager while the other guests around the pool pretended to ignore the altercation. The boy and girl paddled about in the water until the man threw up his hands and told them to get out and go to their room. The girl glanced at the boy, but the boy continued to ignore the man until he strode to the edge of the pool and shouted, "Get out! Let them have their filthy pool. Did you piss in it? I hope you pissed in it. Now get out! Go to the room!" The boy removed himself from the pool with a kind of languorous choreography, and walked toward the sliding glass door of one of the downstairs rooms, the little girl following. Just before reaching the door the boy paused, turned his head in the direction of the pool and the other guests there, and hawked and spat onto the concrete pool apron. Loomis said to his son, "Let's get on up to the room."

Another guest, a lanky young woman whom Loomis had seen beside the pool earlier, walked past them on her way to the parking lot. "Watch out for them Gypsies," she muttered.

"Gypsies?" the boy said.

The woman laughed as she rounded the corner. "Don't let 'em get you," she said.

"I don't know," Loomis said when she'd gone. "I guess they do seem a little like Gypsies."

"What the hell is a Gypsy, anyway?"

Loomis stopped and stared at his son. "Does 'Uncle Bob' teach you to talk that way?"

The boy shrugged and looked away, annoyed.

In the room, his son pressed him again, and he told him that Gypsies were originally from some part of India, he wasn't sure which, and that they were ostracized, nobody wanted them. They became wanderers, wandering around Europe. They were poor. People accused them of stealing. "They had a reputation for stealing people's children, I think."

He meant this to be a kind of joke, or at least lighthearted, but when he saw the expression on the boy's face he regretted it and quickly added, "They didn't, really."

It didn't work. For the next hour, the boy asked him questions about Gypsies and kidnapping. Every few minutes or so he hopped from the bed to the sliding glass door and pulled the curtain aside to peek down across the courtyard at the Gypsies' room. Loomis had decided to concede they were Gypsies, whether they really were or not. He made himself a stiff nightcap and stepped out onto the balcony to smoke, although he peeked through the curtains before going out, to make sure the coast was clear.

THE NEXT MORNING, SUNDAY, Loomis rose before his son and went down to the lobby for coffee. He stepped out into the empty courtyard to drink it in the morning air, and when he looked into the pool he saw a large dead rat on its side at the bottom. The rat looked peacefully dead, with its eyes closed and its front paws curled at its chest as if it were begging. Loomis took another sip of his coffee and went back into the lobby. The night clerk was still on duty, studying something on the computer monitor behind the desk. She only cut her eyes at Loomis, and when she saw he was going to approach her she met his gaze steadily in that same way, without turning her head.

"I believe you have an unregistered guest at the bottom of your pool," Loomis said.

He got a second cup of coffee, a plastic cup of juice, and a couple of refrigerator-cold bagels (the waffle iron and fresh fruit had disappeared a couple of visits earlier) and took them back to the room. He and his son ate there, then Loomis decided to get them away from the motel for the day. The boy could always be counted on to want a day trip to San Diego. He loved to ride the red trolleys there, and tolerated Loomis's interest in the museums, sometimes.

They took the commuter train down, rode the trolley to the Mexican border, turned around, and came back. They ate lunch at a famous old diner near downtown, then took a bus to Balboa Park and spent the afternoon in the Air & Space Museum, the Natural History Museum, and at a small, disappointing model railroad exhibit. Then they took the train back up the coast.

As they got out of the car at the motel, an old brown van,

plain and blocky as a loaf of bread, careened around the far corner of the lot, pulled up next to Loomis, roared up to them, and
stopped. The driver was the older man who'd been at the pool.
He leaned toward Loomis and said through the open passenger
window, "Can you give me twenty dollars? They're going to
kick us out of this stinking motel."

Loomis felt a surge of hostile indignation. What, did he have
a big sign on his chest telling everyone what a loser he was?

"I don't have it," he said.

"Come on!" the man shouted. "Just twenty bucks!"

Loomis saw his son standing beside the passenger door of the
rental car, frightened.

"No," he said. He was ready to punch the old man now.

"Son of a bitch!" the man shouted, and gunned the van away,
swerving onto the street toward downtown and the beach.

The boy gestured for Loomis to hurry over and unlock the
car door, and as soon as he did the boy got back into the passenger seat. When Loomis sat down behind the wheel, the boy hit
the lock button. He cut his eyes toward where the van had disappeared up the hill on the avenue.

"Was he trying to rob us?" he said.

"No. He wanted me to give him twenty dollars."

The boy was breathing hard and looking straight out the
windshield, close to tears.

"It's okay," Loomis said. "He's gone."

"Pop, no offense"—and the boy actually reached over and
patted Loomis on the forearm, as if to comfort him—"but I
think I want to sleep at home tonight."

Loomis was so astonished by the way his son had touched him
on the arm that he was close to tears himself.

"It'll be okay," he said. "Really. We're safe here, and I'll
protect you."

"I know, Pop, but I really think I want to go home."

Loomis tried to keep the obvious pleading note from his voice. If this happened, if he couldn't even keep his son around and reasonably satisfied to be with him for a weekend, what was he at all anymore? And (he couldn't help but think) what would the boy's mother make of it, how much worse would he then look in her eyes?

"Please," he said to the boy. "Just come on up to the room for a while, and we'll talk about it again, and if you still want to go home later on I'll take you, I promise."

The boy thought about it and agreed, and began to calm down a little. They went up to the room, past the courtyard, which was blessedly clear of ridiculous Gypsies and other guests. Loomis got a bucket of ice for his bourbon, ordered Chinese, and they lay together on Loomis's bed, eating and watching television, and didn't talk about the Gypsies, and after a while, exhausted, they both fell asleep.

WHEN THE ALCOHOL WOKE HIM at three a.m., he was awash in a sense of gloom and dread. He found the remote, turned down the sound on the TV. His son was sleeping, mouth open, a lock of his bright orange hair across his face.

Loomis eased himself off the bed, sat on the other one, and watched him breathe. He recalled the days when his life with the boy's mother had seemed happy, and the boy had been small, and they would put him to bed in his room, where they had built shelves for his toy trains and stuffed animals and the books from which Loomis would read to him at bedtime. He remembered the constant battle in his heart, those days. How he was drawn into this construction of conventional happiness, how he felt that he loved this child more than he had ever loved anyone in his entire life, how all of this was possible, this life, how he might actually be able to do it. And yet whenever he had felt this he was always aware of the other, more deeply seated part of his nature that wanted to run away in fear. That believed it was not possible after all, that it could only end in catastrophe, that anything this sweet and heartbreaking must indeed one day collapse into shattered pieces. He had struggled to free himself, one way or another, from what seemed a horrible limbo of anticipation. He had run away, in his fashion. And yet nothing had ever caused him to feel anything more like despair than what he felt just now, in this moment, looking at his beautiful child asleep on the motel bed in the light of the cheap lamp, with the incessant dull roar of cars on I-5 just the other side of the hedge, a slashing river of what seemed nothing but desperate travel from point A to point B, from which one mad dasher or another would simply disappear, blink out in a flicker of light, at ragged but regular intervals, with no more ceremony or consideration than that.

He checked that his son was still sleeping deeply, then poured himself a plastic cup of neat bourbon and went down to the pool to smoke and sit alone for a while in the dark. He walked toward a group of lawn chairs in the shadows beside a stunted palm, but stopped when he realized that he wasn't alone, that someone was sitting in one of the chairs. The Gypsy woman sat very still, watching him.

"Come, sit," she said. "Don't be afraid."

He was afraid. But the woman was so still, and the look on her face he could now make out in the shadows was one of calm appraisal. Something about this kept him from retreating. She slowly raised a hand and patted the pool chair next to her, and Loomis sat.

For a moment the woman just looked at him, and, unable not to, he looked at her. She was unexpectedly, oddly attractive. Her eyes were indeed very dark, set far apart on her broad face. In this light, her fierce nose was strange and alarming, almost erotic.

"Are you Gypsy?" Loomis blurted, without thinking.

She stared at him a second before smiling and chuckling deep in her throat.

"No, I'm not Gypsy," she said, her eyes moving quickly from side to side in little shiftings, looking into his. "We are American. My people come from France."

Loomis said nothing.

"But I can tell you your future," she said, leaning her head back slightly to look at him down her harrowing nose. "Let me see your hand." She took Loomis's wrist and pulled his palm toward her. He didn't resist. "Have you ever had someone read your palm?"

Loomis shook his head. "I don't really want to know my future," he said. "I'm not a very optimistic person."

"I understand," the woman said. "You're unsettled."

"It's too dark here to even see my palm," Loomis said.

"No, there's enough light," the woman said. And finally she took her eyes from Loomis's and looked down at his palm. He felt relieved enough to be released from that gaze to let her continue. And something in him was relieved, too, to have someone else consider his future, someone aside from himself. It couldn't be worse, after all, than his own predictions.

She hung her head over his palm and traced the lines with a long fingernail, pressed into the fleshy parts. Her thick hair tickled the edges of his hand and wrist. After a moment, much sooner than Loomis would have expected, she spoke.

"It's not the future you see in a palm," she said, still studying his. "It's a person's nature. From this, of course, one can tell much about a person's tendencies." She looked up, still gripping his wrist. "This tells us much about where a life may have been, and where it may go."

She bent over his palm again, traced one of the lines with the fingernail. "There are many breaks in the heart line here. You are a creature of disappointment. I suspect others in your life disappoint you." She traced a different line. "You're a dreamer. You're an idealist, possibly. Always disappointed by ordinary life, which of course is boring and ugly." She laughed that soft, deep chuckle again and looked up, startling Loomis anew with the directness of her gaze. "People are so fucking disappointing, eh?" She uttered a seductive grunt that loosened something in his groin.

It was true. No one had ever been good enough for him. Even the members of his immediate family. And especially himself.

"Anger, disappointment," the woman said. "So common. But it may be they've worn you down. The drinking, smoking. No real energy, no passion." Loomis pulled against her grip just slightly but she held on with strong fingers around his wrist. Then she lowered Loomis's palm to her broad lap and leaned in closer, speaking more quietly.

"I see you with the little boy—he's your child?"

Loomis nodded. He felt suddenly alarmed, fearful. He glanced up, and his heart raced when he thought he saw the boy standing on the balcony looking out. It was only the potted plant there. He wanted to dash back to the room but he was rooted to the chair, to the Gypsy with her thin, hard fingers about his wrist.

"This is no vacation, I suspect. It's terrible, to see your child in this way, in a motel."

Loomis nodded.

"You're angry with this child's mother for forcing you to be here."

Loomis nodded and tried to swallow. His throat was dry.

"Yet I would venture it was you who left her. For another woman, a beautiful woman, eh, *mon frère*?" She ran the tip of a nail down one of the lines in his palm. There was a cruel smile on her impossible face. "A woman who once again you believed to be something she was not." Loomis felt himself drop his chin in some kind of involuntary acquiescence. "She was a dream," the woman said. "And she has disappeared, poof, like any dream." He felt suddenly, embarrassingly, close to tears. A tight lump swelled in his throat. "And now you have left her, too, or she has left you, because"—and here the woman paused, shook Loomis's wrist gently, as if to revive his attention, and indeed he had been drifting in his grief—"because you are a ghost. Walking between two worlds, you know?" She shook his wrist again, harder, and Loomis looked up at her, his vision of her there in the shadows blurred by his tears.

She released his wrist and sat back in her chair, exhaled as if she had been holding her breath, and closed her eyes. As if this excoriation of Loomis's character had been an obligation, had exhausted her.

They sat there for a minute or two while Loomis waited for the emotion that had surged up in him to recede.

"Twenty dollars," the woman said then, her eyes still closed. When Loomis said nothing, she opened her eyes. Now her gaze was flat, no longer intense, but she held it on him.

"Twenty dollars," she said. "For the reading. This is my fee."

Loomis, feeling as if he'd just been through something physical instead of emotional, his muscles tingling, reached for his wallet, found a twenty-dollar bill, and handed it to her. She took it and rested her hands in her lap.

"Now you should go back up to your room," she said.

He got up to make his way from the courtyard, and was startled by someone standing in the shadow of the Gypsies' doorway. Her evil man-child, the boy from the pool, watching him like a forest animal pausing in its night prowling to let him pass. Loomis hurried on up to the room, tried to let himself in with a key card that wouldn't cooperate. The lock kept flashing red instead of green. Finally the card worked, the green light flickered. He entered and shut the door behind him.

But he'd gone into the wrong room, maybe even some other motel. The beds were made, the television off. His son wasn't there. The sliding glass door to the balcony stood open. Loomis felt his heart seize up and he rushed to the railing. The courtyard was dark and empty. Over in the lobby, the lights were dimmed, no one on duty. It was all shut down. There was no breeze. No roar of rushing vehicles from the 5, the roar in Loomis's mind canceling it out. By the time he heard the sound behind him and turned to see his son come out of the bathroom yawning, it was too late. It might as well have been someone else's child, Loomis the stranger come to steal him away. He stood on the balcony and watched his son crawl back onto the bed, pull himself into a fetal position, close his eyes for a moment, then open them. Meeting his gaze, Loomis felt something break inside him. The boy had the same dazed, disoriented expression he'd had on his face just after his long, difficult birth, when the nurses had put him into an incubator to rush him to intensive care. Loomis had knelt, then, his face up close to the incubator's glass wall, and he'd known that the baby could see him, and that was enough. The obstetrician said, "This baby is very sick," and nurses wheeled the incubator out. He'd gone over to his wife and held her hand. The resident, tears in her eyes, patted his shoulder and said, for some reason, "You're good people," and left them alone. Now he and their child were in this motel, the life that had been their family somehow dissipated into air. Loomis couldn't gather into his mind how they'd got here. He couldn't imagine what would come next.

ALIENS IN THE PRIME
OF THEIR LIVES

THE DAY WE RAN OFF WAS HOT, EARLY AUGUST, NO AIR CON-
ditioner in my 1962 VW bus. It topped out at forty miles per
hour, so the forty-mile journey took us more than an hour,
during which we drove along, kind of stunned by what we were
doing, sweating, saying little, staring ahead at the highway, other
cars and trucks blasting past us in the left lane. Just over the state
line we stopped at a Stuckey's and bought a pair of gold-painted
wedding bands for a dollar apiece.

Olivia wore her favorite pair of red and white polka-dotted
bellbottoms. None of her other pants fit, by then. The bellbottoms were low-waisted, and Olivia was carrying high, so she
wore them often. She never did gain weight. She seemed to lose
it. She threw up every day, throughout the day, from the beginning. How she'd been hiding that from her mother, I had no
idea. She'd begun to look like one of those starving children in
the CARE commercials, all big eyes, gaunt face, stick limbs, and
a little round belly up high underneath her ribs.

We parked on the downtown square and started up the old
brick walk to the courthouse door. But halfway to the building,
Olivia headed back toward the bus.

I caught up with her, took her by the hand.

"Look," I said, "what else are we going to do?"

She took a deep breath and then looked directly at me for the first time that day. The skin beneath her eyes seemed bruised from lack of sleep.

"I don't know what else to do," she said. "I want to do the right thing."

"I know," I said. "I do, too."

We stood there listening to songbirds in the oak trees in the square, watching cars make their slow, heatstroked weave through downtown. A couple of old men wearing fedoras, sitting on a park bench in the shade, stared speechlessly at us, their old mouths open to suck a last strain of oxygen from the incinerated air.

She came along reluctantly. Once, she tried to go back to the bus again, but I held on to her hand. When we got inside the courthouse, she stopped trying to run away and sat like a chastened child in one of the hard wooden chairs in the anteroom outside Judge Leacock's chamber as we waited our turn. Judge Leacock was known to marry just about anyone who asked. Two other couples sat there like us, silent, jittery. A third couple—a soft, pale, fat girl with pretty blond hair and a thin, pimply boy with a farmer's haircut—waited in their seats with strangely beatific, vacant smiles on their faces, their hands on their knees. They seemed like Holy Rollers or something, but I didn't imagine Holy Rollers would get married in a courthouse by a judge.

The ceremony took about five minutes. Judge Leacock was an older man with a slackened face and tired-looking folds beneath and at the corners of his eyes. But the eyes themselves were alert, even crafty, as he leaned back in the chair behind his desk and looked at us for a long moment.

"How old are you?" he said to Olivia.

"Eighteen," she lied.

"You?" he said to me.

I lied and said I was eighteen, too. We were both heading into our senior year.

He asked us if we were sure we wanted to get married. I said yes. He asked us to sign the certificate, then asked us to stand up before his desk. He remained seated.

"Do you take this little gal to be your lawfully wedded wife?"

"Yes," I said.

"Do you take this young fellow to be your lawfully wedded husband?"

Olivia stood there looking stunned, her lips parted, and stared at him.

"You need to be able to say it, darlin'," Judge Leacock said.

"Yes," Olivia whispered.

"I now pronounce you man and wife," the judge said. "That'll be five dollars, please."

"Can I kiss the bride?" I said.

"Go right ahead."

I kissed Olivia, pulled out my wallet, handed the judge a five-dollar bill. He gave us our copy of the certificate. We drove back home at forty miles per hour, windows down, sweating, not saying a word.

A FEW WEEKS EARLIER, we'd secretly rented an attic apartment over a small frame house on the south side of town, a block from the state mental institution. They had drug cases over there, dementia, catatonics. Maybe a schizophrenic or two. Retarded people. People with injured or disoriented brains who thought themselves to be other people, elsewhere. No hard-core psychotic criminals like they had in Whitfield over near Jackson.

During the weeks we'd spent cleaning and painting the

apartment, I took breaks and walked over to the hospital property for a smoke and a stroll. The grounds were beautiful,
populated with big, dark, seductive oaks and magnolia trees,
and you could imagine being very happily insane if you were
allowed to walk their grassy, shaded slopes every day. Once I
saw an old man, apparently a patient there, who crept along as if
he were hunting something. He wore a pale blue robe over pink
pajamas, torn paper slippers, and a broad-brimmed tan cowboy
hat. He held an imaginary rifle in his hands and a look of mischievous anticipation in his watery eyes. It never occurred to
me to wonder how he'd gotten out onto the grounds. Stealthy,
I guess.

"What are you hunting?" I said.

He froze as if he hadn't seen me standing there. He turned his
little bald head very slowly and put a finger to his lips. He moved
his fuzzy eyebrows toward the little glen that lay just beyond us,
its grass deliciously lush and green in the afternoon light. Then
he scrunched his eyes tight shut and whispered, "*Lions.*"

THE ONLY PLACES YOU COULD stand upright without knocking
your head on the apartment's attic ceiling were in the middle
of the living room, the hallway, and the middle of the bedroom. You had to crouch to get to the sofa or the bed. The
bathroom and kitchen were small but okay for standing upright
because they were built into dormers. The bathroom had an old
wood-frame window fan the size of a ship's propeller. When
you switched it on the blades began to turn slowly at first, and
as they picked up speed they huffed and pushed out the wooden
slats that stayed folded shut on the outside when the fan was off.
Now that we were in mid-August, the temperature inside the
place rose above a hundred during the day. Turning on the fan
at night flushed that still, stifling air and pulled a slightly cooler
breeze of about eighty-five degrees (on a good night) through

the apartment's open windows, small rooms, narrow hallway, and out the bathroom window. If you closed the bathroom door, the fan created a near-vacuum in there, so your ears sucked in and went deaf, and the whole house shook with the fan's effort to pull wind through the little crack at the bottom of the bathroom door.

While we were fixing up the apartment, we'd be up there every late afternoon and early evening during the week, after our summer jobs, and all day on Saturdays and Sundays, sweat soaking our shorts and shirts, stinging our eyes and dripping from our chins. We scrubbed every surface clean. We painted the walls, the old brown wooden floor, and hung curtains. We made trips to K-Mart, half for the relief of the store's air-conditioning, half to get cheap aluminum cookware and plates and cutlery, sheets and bedspread, towels, though some of this we filched from our parents' houses.

And sometimes in the late afternoon, in spite of the heat, we'd go at each other in the little bedroom in the back of the apartment, right under the rear gable. The bed frame was imitation brass, so I could hang on to the headboard rungs with my slippery, sweaty hands. Olivia was getting so round in the belly, and we had to take care in how we did it, and I needed some independent purchase. We sweated deep into the bedding, the creaky set of old steel springs screeching and squawking at even our most discreet, restrained, ecstatic movements. The scrawny, bitter landlady downstairs shouted up through the floor, "HEY! HEY!" Banging on her ceiling with a shoe or something.

We'd lie there catching our breath, cooling off as much as we could, with the old fan huffing to pull a hot breeze across our reddened, sticky-slick skin, and then we'd dress, turn off the fan, lock up, get into the car. I'd drop her off at her parents' house, and drive to my parents' house. I would go inside, speak to my parents and my brothers, if they were home. Then we would all sit down to supper. Or if I was late, I would sit down by myself at the kitchen table and eat some of what was left, and maybe my mom would sit there and talk to me while I ate, if she had a minute. Then I would go to the bedroom I shared with my little brother, maybe listen to the radio for a while, and then I would go to bed.

I WAS UNDER A SPELL, those days. I had been ever since I'd first seen her.

I was with my friend Wendell Sparrow, that day, skulking about the pool at the local run-down country club my parents managed to belong to. Sparrow and I sat in the oak shade between the pool and the tennis courts, smoking cigarettes and waiting for girls to enter the dressing rooms to change for a swim.

We did this because we knew there had been, at some unrecorded time in this old pool's history, peepholes drilled in the wall between the men's dressing room and the women's. The holes were artfully hidden beneath metal soap dishes attached to the shower's water pipes that ran from the ceiling down this wall, ending in the hot and cold handles. Just below the handles were the little soap trays. And just beneath the soap trays, so that you wouldn't notice as you stood there taking your shower, someone had drilled single peepholes about a half-inch in diameter that went through to the other side of the wall, which was the wall inside the women's dressing room. If you held on to the water pipes and leaned down, peered just below the soap dishes, you could look through the peepholes into the dressing stalls there. It was ingenious and simple. Most people who weren't in the know never noticed the peepholes, since you'd have to bend down in the shower to see them, and as these were mostly rinsing showers, few ever did. Those who did guarded the secret as if they were the only ones who knew it, for fear of such fantastic information getting out to the authorities, who—being at an age and level of respectability that it would never do for anyone to catch them peeping into the women's dressing room—would probably plug the holes with concrete from sheer jealous outrage against youth and the effrontery of its prancing, tawdry, exuberant libido.

So, as Sparrow and I were sitting in the lawn chairs beneath the oak outside the dressing rooms, around three o'clock, the pool all but deserted, no one on the tennis courts, who should walk past us in her street clothes, holding a little bundle of swimwear, smiling a little half-shy smile, but Olivia Coltrane, on her way to the women's side. We smiled and nodded to her. As soon as she'd cleared the door into the dressing room we shot out of our chairs and ran into the men's dressing room and took up stations, Sparrow at the left showerhead peephole, me on the right.

She was in my stall already.

"You see anything?" Sparrow said.

"No, not yet."

"Me, neither."

Olivia had such a playful, placidly languorous look on her face through the peephole, I couldn't imagine she didn't know we were there.

She bent over, out of view. Then she straightened up. She raised her arms and slipped off her blouse. I could see everything from her beautiful rib cage up: her brassiere, her long, pale neck, her coy expression. I was trembling just a little bit.

"See anything?" Sparrow stage-whispered. He sounded desperate.

"Nothing yet."

"Shit. Where the hell is she?"

She took off her brassiere. My God. Her little breasts were beautiful: small, a little heavy on the bottom, sloping down and then up to what looked to be a pair of hard, erect, hazelnut nipples. I was shivering, my body was all but bucking against my grip on the pipes against the wall above my head.

"See anyth— You son of a bitch!" Sparrow said, and he was on me. "Let me see, goddammit!"

But I was stronger and in fact I could not let go of the pipes. Sparrow pummeled me and made far too much noise. Through the peephole, Olivia's face seemed to register just the slightest increase in some kind of strange satisfaction as she slipped the bikini top over her beautiful little breasts, roughed up her hair, turned, and walked out of the dressing stall, its door slapping shut against my eyes. I let go and sat down heavily on the shower floor. Sparrow grabbed the pipes and jammed his forehead against the soap dish.

"Shit! Son of a bitch. Goddamn you son of a bitch!" and so on for a good five or ten minutes, as he slammed things around the dressing room, lit a Marlboro, and smoked it in that way he had, sucking the life from it, his long scrawny neck flaring tendons, the bony Adam's apple bobbing. He was bleeding from a cut on his forehead where he'd jammed it against the soap tray. He stopped pacing and glared at me. One eye twitched at the little drop of blood leaking into it from his brow. He took off one of his tennis shoes and hurled it through the high window of the dressing room. It crashed through, sending glass shards out into the grass beside the pool apron. He stood there, his breath heaving in and out. He stomped over to one of the toilets and threw his cigarette into it and banged out through the dressing room door.

I sat there on the shower floor, entirely unfazed by Sparrow's tantrum. You could not have shaken me from what I was feeling, not with the strength of a hundred men. That was when, pretty much, I knew that I had to have Olivia Coltrane. I was just about dying for her, right then.

SHE WAS SLIM, TALLISH, with a thick clump of short black hair that framed her small, delicate face, black bangs against her milky forehead. She was pale and pretty, if not conventionally so. Her teeth were a little too big for her mouth, so she may not have been smiling so often as she appeared to've been. She was a little nearsighted, but vain about wearing her glasses, so the crinkling around her eyes may have been more of a squint than the mirth you might have taken it for. You wouldn't have put her in a magazine to model clothes or makeup. But you might have put her in an ad for some other product, say a snappy new red convertible, because she had a wholesome natural beauty in her, hard to say just what it was except maybe happiness. I think it was that sense of her natural happiness, really, that attracted me to her. I was never a very happy or contented person, and people like Olivia tended to ignite in me a secret, almost feverish desire to absorb whatever it was that made them so different from me. So at ease with the world and themselves in it.

She had a way of looking at me, straight-on, and seemed incapable of the usual emotional evasion, as if she had nothing to fear. It didn't bother me in the least that she wasn't the smartest girl around. She struggled in English, was competent in math. If you drew her as partner in biology lab, you would surely do most if not all of the work. She was a little bit lazy. She tended to spend her spare time reading ridiculous magazine articles like big spreads on the lavish lifestyle and strange marital relations of Jackie and Aristotle Onassis. But I really didn't care. Most people thought me a little dim, too. I was ridiculously earnest and deliberate. I wasn't the handsomest boy she could have dated, either, but I had a kind of appealing, homely kindness in my features, or so people would note from time to time, in one awkward way or another.

Soon after we'd started going out, I took every cent I had in my savings account at Citzens Bank and bought the ten-year-old VW bus, took the back seat out, padded the floor with old blankets and a flannel-lined sleeping bag, and began my serious courting of Olivia. I took her out as many nights as her parents would allow, and on Saturdays and Sundays, too. I started picking her up after church, in the bus, and either taking her on a picnic or over to Sunday dinner at my parents' house. We did this every other week, alternating with her family's Sunday dinners at her maiden aunt's house, which I didn't attend. I wasn't exactly ever invited. Olivia enjoyed the picnics, and she loved the dinners at our house. My mom was an old country girl and a fantastic cook, whereas the Coltranes' fare reflected Mr. Coltrane's salt-free diet and the family's general lack of interest in food.

She liked my folks, too, and kidded my little brother about his long, pretty hair and his dreamy, calflike brown eyes. She called him "Beautiful." "Hey, Beautiful," she'd say, and he'd frown and leave the room, but soon he'd be back in, grinning, and we knew he loved it. Once he slipped up to her and said, "Hey, Beautiful, to you," and blushed so deeply I thought he might burst into tears of embarrassment. We all burst out laughing instead, and it saved him. Olivia spent the whole Sunday dinner in the chair next to him, her slim left arm over his shoulder while they ate. It almost seemed she loved him so much because he was still such a boy, and part of her still wanted to just be a girl, with crushes on beautiful boys. She would pet him, then look up at me with an expression of earnest if simulated heartbreak, as if she wanted to possess him somehow, possess his innocence and strange beauty.

When I picked her up at the church on Sundays, morning service over and all the Baptist folk standing out on the lawn feeling good about the world and their lives, it was dismaying to see the vague pall of anxiety that seemed to settle over them when they saw me pull up in the old VW bus, and on some of the faces you could see it was a type of anger or disgust. And Olivia, in her yellow or powder-blue Sunday dress and white shoes, throwing her hand up in a wave, saying goodbye to her family over a shoulder, running on her toes out to meet me and climb up into the bus, me and my jeans and T-shirt and long hair—you'd think they were standing in the yards of their beloved homes watching some heartless foreclosure agent auction them away. It was always a rotten feeling, just barely made bearable by the vision of Olivia, how pretty and fresh she always looked, and I was always glad to round the corner, away from all those disapproving Christian eyes. The only thing I'd ever liked about church was the stained-glass windows in the sanctuary, with the human-looking animals and the people in colorful robes, and their pale, luminescent faces, yearning.

She was a good Baptist girl, but she wasn't a prude, and she liked to drink a beer here and there, and go to parties, and she generally liked my rowdy crowd. She was a virgin, though, and determined to stay one until she married. After a few months, I'd just about given up on that, and then one night on the way home she told me to pull over somewhere, anywhere, and I did, and everything changed. I'm not sure what had changed for her. She was a nice girl, but nice girls liked fooling around, too, once they were able to arrange the justification for it in their minds.

AND THEN IT WAS LIKE we'd turned on the power and couldn't find the switch to turn it back off. We started doing it everywhere. Out in the VW bus in the parking lot during study hall. On the visitors' side of the stadium, beneath the bleachers, during lunch period. Sometimes, at night, we'd just pull the bus over to the side of the road, traffic swerving past, people hooting and

honking. We did have a favorite private spot, for a while, a little cubbyhole of a niche in the brush along a sparsely populated
street on the north end of town. You could pull in there and it
was like the brush closed up behind you, it was that inconspicu-
ous. We'd pull in there and take our time, like real lovers, then
collapse to either side of one another, giving our bodies time to
stop humming.

We didn't realize that people living in a new subdivision one
block over had noticed our lights pulling in there night after
night, shutting off, clicking on again, pulling out. Maybe they
thought we were burglars working a plan. Maybe they just didn't
like the idea of young, careless couples fornicating, rocking the
vehicle, practically in their new backyards. At any rate, one night
as I leaned on an elbow admiring her pale, slim, spraddled legs,
a flashlight shone its beam directly into my naked lap. A man's
voice said, "Looks like we missed the action," and another one
said, "Get dressed and step out of the love machine, son." I could
make out the uniform and the badge, the heavy gun belt, the
gun, even in the darkness.

Olivia scrambled for her panties and bra. I groped for my own
underwear and pants, pulled them on, opened the side door of
the bus, and stepped barefoot onto the cool ground. I closed the
door behind me, for Olivia's sake.

The two cops shone their flashlights on me, keeping
their distance.

"What are you doing here?" one said.

"Well," I said, gestured, shrugged. I hiccuped out a nervous laugh.

"He thinks it's funny," the one cop said.

"I do, too," the other cop said. He was older than the first cop,
and a little shorter and stouter. That's about all I could tell, in the
dark with only their flashlights in our faces for light.

"The people who live in those houses right over there don't

think it's funny," the younger cop said. "They thought maybe you were parking here to case their houses."

"Rob them," the older cop said. "Break in, steal things, or worse."

"Much worse."

"I didn't know they could see us," I said.

They said nothing. The first cop leaned his head toward the bus window to look in at Olivia, trying to cover herself, cowering on the floor in there.

"All right, miss, get out and get your clothes on."

They stepped back to let her out and kept their flashlights on her as she got dressed. They were quiet, as if they were studying her. This made me angry and I almost said something. She was crying. I moved closer and stood beside her. Something about looking at her in the small harsh glare of the cops' flashlights made her seem all the more vulnerably beautiful to me. When she was dressed the cops switched off their flashlights. Every now and then they'd switch them back on and shine them into our eyes as we spoke. They asked us who our parents were. Where we lived. How old we were. But they didn't really seem to care about any of that, hardly waiting for our answers, seeming bored. In the end they let us go with a warning not to park there again and a few halfhearted words about hauling us in if they ever caught us doing this again, and told us to go home.

"You know what's going to happen, you keep doing this," the younger cop said. "You know how it is that people make babies? With the old in and out?"

"*A-makin' whoopee*," the older cop said, and laughed.

"Seriously," the younger cop said. "We're gonna keep an eye on you."

" 'Bye, now," said the older cop, giving us an odd little wave. Then they got into their squad car, backed out onto the road, and drove away. Strange cops.

———

WHEN WE GOT BACK TO TOWN after eloping, the apartment all ready for us to live there officially, we went to tell our parents what we'd done.

We went to Olivia's house first.

"Oh," her mother said, deflating into the sofa cushions, a hand over her mouth. "Oh, oh, oh."

"WHAT?" her father said. He was a tall, good-natured man with a heart condition, who spoke very loudly and was a little bit deaf. He'd been an artilleryman, when he was young, in the war.

"THEY'RE MARRIED, IKE," Olivia's mother said loudly back to him.

It took a moment to register. He stood there vacantly, looking at her, then cast an embarrassed glance at us before jamming his hands into his trouser pockets.

"Well," he said softly, "no use crying over spilt milk."

THEN WE WENT TO MY PARENTS' HOUSE. My mother was at the kitchen table, in a very good mood, nibbling peanut brittle. My father was in the back bedroom, reading a magazine. The kitchen opened up to the den, and Olivia sat in there on the couch, her knees pressed together in terror.

I sat down opposite my mother at the table, under the bright bulb of the hanging lamp. I didn't want to go through with it. But it was too late for that.

"I have to tell you something," I said.

Her nibbling slowed. She could tell something was wrong.

"Olivia and I got married," I said. I said it quietly. So quietly that Olivia and my younger brother, Mike, sitting on the sofa on the other side of the den, couldn't hear it. Of course, Olivia knew what I was saying. She sat there and stared into something only she could see. I said to my mother, "We went over to Livingston and did it this afternoon."

She said nothing for a moment, unable to swallow the brittle in her mouth. When she finally could, she whispered, "Is she pregnant?"

It was awful to look at her eyes just then. A sudden grief had filled them, laced with a terrible dread, a horror, really, as if I'd just told her that one of us, one of her children, had died.

I nodded.

She got up from the table and walked to the back of the house. I looked over at Olivia. She had closed her eyes and grabbed on to my little brother's hand. He looked confused but not displeased to have Olivia holding his hand.

In a minute, as I was pacing in the living room, my father came in and asked me if what my mother had just told him was true. I nodded.

He didn't say anything, looking as if he couldn't comprehend it.

"What are you going to do?" he said.

"We have a place, an apartment over by East Mississippi," I said. It's what everyone called the asylum. "We're going on over there, I guess."

"How far along is she?"

"About five months, we think."

"Damn," he said. He shook his head, jingled the coins in his pocket. "Well, go on over there, then," he said. "We'll talk about it tomorrow. I have to go see about your mother. I think this is about to kill her."

Olivia and I drove to our little apartment, mounted the rickety steps to the deck, and went inside. I turned on the big, chuffing fan, to pull out the stifling air. We sat down on the sofa, nothing but the engulfing huff of the fan for sound, the hot breeze searing our skin, beneath the bare bulb of the overhead light.

THE BARE BULB LIGHT WAS SO HARSH, I lit candles instead and set them on the coffee table. Olivia had brought over her old cat, Max, and he rubbed against my leg, hungry. I fed him, and checked the seedcake in the cage of her parakeet, Donald, who whistled and made as if to bite my finger. She'd left her pet rabbit, an old Easter gift, with her parents, because she'd never liked it, with its weird red eyes and bland personality. I think she felt guilty about it, though. I'd told her to leave them all, afraid the heat in the place would kill them during the day, but she couldn't.

She'd been sitting on the sofa, that slightly stunned and day-dreamy look on her face I loved so much, and I'd taken heart. But then she seemed to come to, got up from the sofa, and began pacing up and down the little hallway from the living room to the bedroom and back. She took off her Keds and walked bare-foot on her longish narrow feet, with the pretty toes I liked to roll between my fingers and call them her peanuts. She was cry-ing quietly. At first I couldn't tell. The place was so hot, before the fan had a chance to help out a bit, that we'd started sweat-ing the moment we walked in, my T-shirt and Olivia's peasant smock blotched with dampness, and our faces shone with perspi-ration. When I saw she was crying, I held her for a minute, but it was still too hot for that. I got her to sit at the kitchen table in front of the dormer window there for the breeze. I brought one of the candles in from the living room and set it beside the fridge, on the counter away from the window so it wouldn't blow out.

There wasn't much to eat, but there was a fat ripe tomato on the counter, and a new unopened jar of mayonnaise, and a loaf of white bread. I tore off a square of paper towel for a plate and made each of us a tomato sandwich, and got two beers from the fridge, all the while keeping an eye on Olivia to see if she was cheering up at all. We ate the sandwiches and sipped the beers, not talking. Olivia was still sniffling a little bit but she was coming around. When we'd eaten, I took her by the hand

and led her to the living room, and put a record on our little record player, some easy stuff. Maybe it wasn't the best choice. It was by that singer, Melanie, and when she sang "Look What They've Done to My Song, Ma," Olivia started sniffling again. I was holding on to her and shuffling us around in the old Teen Center slow dance, and she dug her chin into my collarbone and started to bawl.

"This isn't what I wanted," she said between sobs. "I wanted to go to college. I wanted to date lots of boys. I wanted to graduate and marry somebody successful and live in a big two-story house and have lots of children but not like this, and not in a shitty old attic that's hot as an oven, and not even graduate from high school. And poor." She punctuated her sentences with little bops of her fist against my other shoulder.

"I know," I said. "I'm sorry."

"Are you?" she said, as if accusing.

"I do love you, though," I said.

She drew in a big slow breath and let it out, still leaning against me.

"Oh, God," she said. Then, "God, please forgive me."

I said, "God doesn't mind people having babies."

"This isn't funny," she said, crying again.

"I mean it," I said.

"Just stop."

I shuffled us around for a minute, while she settled down.

"Well, wait and see," I said. "I'm going to work hard, and build us a beautiful house—it'll be like a mansion, to us anyway—and we'll have beautiful children, starting with this one, and they'll be so beautiful that people will hardly even recognize them as ordinary human beings, like a whole new amazingly beautiful and intelligent subspecies or something. Coltranians. Like you. And we'll have dogs, and horses. A couple of fat, arrogant cats.

And I'll drive a cool Ford pickup, a good, solid, settled-down man, and you'll have something like a Mercedes station wagon to haul around all the kids in style. And we'll have a boat, if you want, and take it to the reservoir, and ski, and maybe even build a cabin beside my grandmother's little lake up in the country, looking out over the water."

Olivia gave a quietly derisive snort when I was done, but I could tell she was lightening up.

I said, "We've got all the time in the world. Look how young we are. Look how much time we have to try to get all the things we want." I stepped back so I could look at her.

"It's going to be all right," I said.

She nodded, looked at me for a moment, then looked down again.

"Okay," she said. The tears were there again, but quiet ones. They were tears of sadness, I thought, instead of fear. That was better, I hoped.

ABOUT AN HOUR LATER my older brother showed up, with his fiancée.

They came into the little living room, and I turned on the bare, bright bulb again, and after some sympathetic and concerned small talk from them, questions about how this came about and what our plans might be, they got down to business.

Olivia and I knew that his fiancée, Ruth, had been whisked to New York the previous year by her parents for an abortion. We knew what was coming. As soon as they even hinted at the idea that we should consider doing the same, Olivia leapt up and stomped to the bathroom and slammed the door. Immediately, the house began to shudder from the force of the chugging fan in there trying to pull wind through the little space under the door, which made a weird kind of howling sound.

Curtis and Ruth seemed astonished, looking from the hall-way where Olivia'd disappeared, back to me, back to the hallway. Almost instantly after Olivia shut the bathroom door, cutting off the fan breeze, our sweating increased, beads popping out on our foreheads and running down our faces. It tickled me trickling from my armpits down over my ribs.

I went into the tiny hallway and knocked on the bathroom door, having to shout to be heard over the noise of the fan and the wind howling through the little space below the door.

"Olivia, would you just come out, please?"

"Tell them to go away!"

"Don't worry, we're not going to do that."

"I'm not listening!"

I made my apologies to Curtis and Ruth and, after a moment, realizing that Olivia was not coming out of the bathroom until they left, and maybe worrying that the fan's desperate huff-ing might destabilize the old frame house itself, they got up to go. When Ruth had stepped out onto the deck, Curtis came back to me.

"Just think about it, okay?" he said.

"Curtis, for Christ's sake," I said. "Were you here just now? Did I imagine that you and Ruth were just in there talking to me while Olivia shut herself in the bathroom and lost her mind?"

He frowned, gave me a hug, and they left.

"Are they gone?" Olivia shouted from the bathroom.

"Yes!" I shouted back.

She opened the door and stalked back to the bedroom and fell onto her side into the bed. The house stopped shaking and the hot air in the apartment began to move again. When I followed her into the bedroom she looked up at me, her face puffy and streaked with tears.

"I'm not going to do that, I'm not," she said.

"It's okay," I said, "I know. We're not."

"I couldn't do that," she declared.

"Me, neither," I said. "And it's way too late for that, anyway. They didn't realize. Don't worry."

There was a knock on the door.

"*Tell them to go away*," Olivia said, and burrowed herself beneath the bedsheet, clamping a pillow over her head.

It was the landlady from downstairs, standing in the weak yellow glow of the deck light, her scrawny arms crossed, a scowl on her face.

"If every night is going to be some kind of commotion like this," she said, "I am not going to stand for it. You can take your kind of behavior to some other place."

"I'm sorry," I said. "I promise we're not usually like that."

"Or loud *other* kind of behavior, either," she said, narrowing her eyes and arching her thinning brows.

I nodded, mumbled, "Okay, right." Then she stomped down the deck stairs.

"Was it them?" Olivia said, her voice muffled beneath the pillow.

"Just Curtis," I said. "Forgot his keys."

Olivia stayed beneath the pillow. I watched her side move up and down with breathing for a moment, until it began shaking with sobs, and I went into the darkened kitchen and sat there alone for a while, sweating in the warm breeze the fan pulled through the kitchen window. I smoked a cigarette. I'd been there a good hour, knowing Olivia had cried herself to sleep, when an old Chevy Bel Air station wagon idled up to the stop sign on the quiet street below. I couldn't see who was in it but I recognized it from the student parking lot at school. I knew the boy who drove it. I heard loud stage-whispers, and made out some girl's voice saying, *Is that it? Is that where they're living?* And other loud whispers, unintelligible. And then the wagon rattled off down the street.

This is about as strange as it gets, I said to myself.

But for the sound of the fan huffing away, then, the apartment was quiet. It was quiet on the little streets in our new neighborhood, down below. The streetlamps stood silently above their diaphanous pools of yellow-gray light. The neighbors' houses were quiet, sleeping. The inmates at the asylum down the street were quiet, sleeping or lying awake, wondering how this had happened to them, or who they were, or where. Our parents were home, in their beds or sitting at kitchen tables, drinking coffee, sleepless.

I opened the refrigerator and took out a bottle of beer. The fridge was a small old Frigidaire, with the locking handle. It cast its chilly bright block of light onto me and into the tiny kitchen, which still smelled strongly of fresh paint and Formula 409 and Comet from all our cleaning. The cold air rolled into the hot room in a little cloud of condensation and rolled away toward the huffing fan. I closed the fridge, sat at the table in the dark, and drank the beer. It was so cold, and bitter, and delicious. I was bathed in sweat. I drank the beer down in big long gulps, then sat there blinking my eyes from the cold, the carbonation, the alcoholic buzz.

I set the empty bottle on the kitchen counter and took off my clothes and laid them on the chair, then went into the bedroom. Olivia breathed long and slow in her sleep. I carefully pulled the covers away from her, so as not to wake her. It was still so hot in the place. She made a little sound and smacked her lips, rolled herself slowly over to face the other direction. She was so pretty. I lay down beside her and snuggled up, rested my hand on her hip, and we slept, the fan rocking the attic apartment like we were inside some gentle engine, cradled and safe.

———

SOMETHING WOKE ME UP a few hours later. I saw I'd left a light on in the living room, so I shuffled in there to turn it off. That's when I saw the man and woman sitting on our sofa. They wore identical pairs of white cotton pajamas and looked sleep-rumpled, and older, in their forties or fifties. They looked familiar, though I couldn't say I'd ever seen them before. I didn't know them, that's for sure. A rush of fear went through me. My scalp prickled, I felt myself shrink up in my boxers. I kind of hunched over, ready to run or fight. But then the woman raised her eyebrows like she'd forgotten something, and waved a hand at me, as if passing something before my vision, and I felt myself relax somehow.

"Who are you?" I said.

The man and woman just sat there smiling at me.

"I don't want any trouble," I said. "My wife's pregnant. She's asleep."

I felt foolish and confused. I realized it was the first time I'd called Olivia "my wife."

"Oh, we know all that," the woman said. She had a kind of grumbly voice that, even so, wasn't unpleasant. And it sounded kind of familiar, I didn't know from where.

"That's right," the man said.

"I really think you need to leave," I said, wishing Olivia and I had a phone, but we didn't. We couldn't afford it.

"I'm very thirsty," the woman said.

"Who are you?" I said.

"We're what you might call aliens," the woman said.

"Really," I said. "You're from the hospital, aren't you?"

"No," the man said. "We're from a planet in another solar system only about five million light-years from here." He held his hand up, palm toward me, and then slowly pointed a finger upward as if toward the very solar system he was talking about.

"Really," I said, feeling so strangely calm all of a sudden that I didn't quite know what to do with myself.

"If we fizzle and fizz out on you, don't be disturbed," the woman said.

"If we get a CME, we might revert," the man said. "Kind of like a solar flare, but worse."

"Much worse," she said, as if bitterly amused.

"Why don't you get yourself a cold beer," the man said, "sit down and join us for a while?"

"Would you like one?" I said.

The man seemed as surprised as I was that I'd said this, then said, "I sure *would* love a beer, come to think of it."

"Yes, I'm just dying of thirst and I would love a cold beer," the woman said.

I went into our little kitchen and got three bottles of Budweiser from the refrigerator. On the way back to the living room I looked in on Olivia. She was still sleeping soundly, on her back, her mouth slightly open. At least she looked peaceful, though. The furrow was gone from her brow. I took the beers into the living room, opened them, and gave one each to the man and the woman. We raised them slightly to one another, in a little toast.

"How did you get here from that far away?" I said. I didn't know much about physics and astronomy, nothing, really, but I was smart enough to know how long it would take even a ray of light to get here from five million light-years away.

"Can't really explain it," the man said. "We don't normally have bodies like this, not limited to this."

"Are you normally made of light?" I said.

"No," he said, shaking his head and laughing, not unkindly.

"It has more to do with the fabric of the universe," the woman said. "Sort of."

"Negative energy," the man said.

"Cosmic inflation," the woman said. "Kaluza-Klein."

"These are just terms some people are using these days," the man said. "Their ideas are a little wacked, but they're going in the right direction."

"Okay," I said. "But if that's the case, where did you get those bodies you're in?"

The woman grinned.

"Well, we did get these from the hospital, so in that sense we came from there."

"It's just easier, logistically," the man said. "If there's trouble with the police, or if the hosts have a little problem with the occupancy. And it's just down the street."

"I thought you both looked a little familiar."

"I used to be an usher at the Royal Theater," the woman said. "This body did, I mean."

"I was a policeman," the man said. "A homicide detective, actually. Busted down to traffic cop. I may have given you a ticket."

"How did you end up in the hospital?" I said. I'd almost said "asylum," and just caught myself.

"Drugs," said the woman.

"Depression," said the man. "Really bad depression."

I said, "Do you know the old man who hunts imaginary lions on the grounds?"

"Oh, sure," said the man.

"Imaginary?" said the woman, and she laughed.

"Mr. Hunter, believe it or not," said the man. "He never got to hunt, before he went crazy."

"He's bagged two since then," the woman said. She laughed again.

"Really."

"You wouldn't be able to convince him otherwise," she said.

"You'll have to forgive us," the man said. "Sometimes we take on certain characteristics of the hosts."

"Like crazy," the woman said, bumping her eyebrows up and down. "You're awfully young," she said then, grinning. "I'll bet you two ran off."

"Yes," I said. "We did."

"Where are your parents?" she said. "Are they in another *state?*"

"No."

The man and the woman looked at each other for a moment, then nodded. Whatever they were thinking seemed to make them very happy.

"May we have it, when it's born?" the woman said.

"What?" I said. "No. Of course not."

"Oh," she said, disappointed.

"Well, let's think this over," the man said. "We don't have to actually have it."

"No, I suppose not," the woman said, cheering up just a bit.

"But you could let us have it now," she said, leaning forward. "We could take it, and it would be like it was never there."

"Not like an abortion," the man said.

"No, not like an abortion," the woman said. "Just zip, gone," and she snapped her fingers. "Gone! Into me, I mean. This lady's not as old as she looks."

"No side effects," the man said.

"No," I said. "I don't know what you're talking about. We want to keep it."

"All right," the man said.

"But if you change your mind," the woman said, "just let us know."

"Okay, but we won't."

"All right," the man said. "But maybe you could let us be close to the child, somehow."

"Like godparents," the woman said.

"Yes," the man said. "We'll be available for advice. And if anything happens to you, we can take care of it."

"Or help take care of it."

"We're from a very advanced civilization, for lack of a better term."

"All right, sure," I said.

"Don't worry," the man said, "we won't interfere."

"We have so much to offer," the woman said. "And this place is our interest. It's our subject, if you will. Like God."

"You believe in God?" I said.

"Of course," the man said.

"Well, not in the same way people here do, of course," the woman said.

"Did you come from God?" I said. It seemed a logical question at the moment.

"Oh, let's just not get into that," the woman said.

"Right, yes," the man said, laughing, closing his eyes and shaking his head, "let's not."

None of us said anything for a moment, me standing there in my boxer shorts holding the sweating beer bottle, them sitting on the sofa in their aged bodies and white pajamas, seeming to glow with heat and a strange satisfaction.

"It's a glorious time for us, you see," the woman said. "I suppose you could say we're in the prime of our lives."

I didn't know what to say. I turned up the bottle and finished my beer. When I looked down at them again, they were still there, looking at me. Then she sighed and looked at the man.

"We should go now," she said.

"Thanks for the beer," he said.

"It was delicious," she said. "Nice and cold."

They said goodbye again and stepped out onto the deck. I hadn't noticed earlier that they were barefoot. They made their way carefully, even tiptoeing on the balls of their pale, blue-veined feet, down the rickety staircase. They crossed the yard and walked down the street in the hazy light of the streetlamps, now blueish with the mist of early morning dew. I watched them from inside the screen door. At one point she turned and gave me a little wave, and I waved back.

AFTER SHE WAVED, AND I had waved back, something changed. It didn't look as if anything had changed, but it felt as if something had changed. I looked back down at the street. The strange crazy man and woman were gone. Everything else looked the same.

I went out onto the deck. If there had been a breeze, the old structure would have been swaying in it. But everything was very still. Almost as if before something terrible, like an explosion or the ground collapsing in on itself, sucking everything in. The trees stood massive, dark, and still, not daring to tremble their thin hard leaves. A vast cloud limned about its edges with moonlight seemed not to move even glacially across the sky.

I remembered my best friend Scotty and I once saw the strangest thing on a night that wasn't so very different from this. It was clear, we could see lots of stars, and we lay on our backs on my parents' patio, in sleeping bags, looking up. We were camping out in the backyard. And then, as we lay there, an odd thing zipped across the little opening of sky above us between the clusters of tall neighborhood trees. It was, or seemed to be, the lighted outline of a rocket, a classically shaped rocket I should say, heading from south to north, there and gone in less than a heartbeat.

We leapt from our sleeping bags and stared, and then began shouting, and kept shouting until my parents shouted at us from their bedroom window to pipe down.

It never made any sense. An illuminated outline of a cartoon-style rocket, zipping by faster than the speed of sound, without a sound, not even in its wake? A lighted outline of a rocket? Not even anything in the middle? It made no sense whatsoever. But even to this day we both still agree that we saw it, saw the same thing.

I went back inside. I was feeling hungry now. I opened the refrigerator, even though I knew there was nothing in there but beer, an aging tomato, and some milk, maybe a couple of eggs. We'd forgotten to go shopping on our wedding day. But I was wrong. There was a wide bowl of cold fried chicken down on the bottom shelf, and a Tupperware container of potato salad next to that. I rejoiced. Olivia must have gone to Kentucky Fried Chicken that morning, thinking ahead. I didn't know just when she could have gone, but that was the only possible explanation.

Or maybe Curtis and his fiancée had brought it, and in all the anxiety of their visit I just hadn't noticed.

I sat at the little kitchen table in the dark, and ate three pieces of chicken and two servings of potato salad, and drank another cold beer. It was delicious. I sat there for a while, digesting, feeling good, and finishing the beer. I checked the clock on the wall. Three o'clock in the morning. But I didn't feel sleepy. I crept into the bedroom and looked in on Olivia. In sleep, her face seemed younger than ever, like a child's. Just down the hill from the mental hospital, a few more blocks away, was the city park where each of us had spent time when we really were children, with our parents, swimming in the public pool and riding the famous old carousel. It seemed a long time ago, though of course it wasn't. Now we'd be taking our own child there, soon enough. I crept back to the kitchen, got another beer from the fridge and took it into the living room, sat on the sofa and drank it. The apartment was much cooler now. In fact, it didn't seem hot at all. All the heat from the day, the blasted fucking insane heat in that attic apartment, was whooshed out and replaced by what seemed a perfect temperature, somewhere in the seventies, a nice cool breeze now gliding through the place. That was a fine development.

I started thinking about Olivia lying in there, so pretty, asleep. I wished she would wake up, come into the living room, and start to love on me a little bit, even though she'd recently called a halt to fooling around. I waited for a few minutes, actually thinking against reason that this might happen, and then I gave up and crept in to have another look at her lying on the bed, asleep.

But she had wakened, atop the rumpled covers, and had removed her sleep-creased clothing, and lay on the bed in a pale beauty, in the scant light through the open window.

"Come on over here," she said, barely louder than a whisper.

THE NEXT MORNING, I WOKE before Olivia and lay there in bed beside her for a while.

It was still August, school hadn't started yet, and I was working full-time at the construction job Curtis had gotten me in June. But I didn't feel like going in, so I just lay in bed with Olivia. When she woke up and snuggled against me, I said I thought we both should skip out today, and she didn't give me any argument or worry about it. She just said, "Okay." She sat up against the pillows and roughed her tangled black hair with both hands, bunched it up on top of her head, and held it there a moment. It brought her nice face out, like an old painting.

"What are you thinking about?" I said.

She seemed a little surprised by the question. Then she smiled in a kind of goofy way and said, "I don't know. Blueberries, I think." We had to laugh at that.

I said, "Why don't we just go on a picnic up at the old pond on my grandparents' property? It's nice up there in summer. Maybe I'll catch a fish."

202 | THERE IS HAPPINESS

"That sounds good."

"We'll take that chicken and potato salad along, and a few beers."

"Okay."

"It'll be our honeymoon," I said, and laughed.

She was still half asleep, lying back against the pillows. I pulled myself up onto an elbow and faced her.

"Did you know we had fried chicken and potato salad in the fridge?" I said.

Olivia opened her eyes and seemed to think about it for a moment.

"I think so," she said. Then she shrugged and closed her eyes again.

I went into the kitchen. The chicken and potato salad were still in there, minus what I'd eaten the night before. There were several eggs, too, and an unopened package of bacon.

"Wow," I said. I called out to Olivia that I was going to make us a nice breakfast.

"Okay," she said. "I could eat. I'm starving."

I put the bacon into a pan and began to heat it, and waited for the smell of it to make Olivia sick. I listened for the sound of her getting up and running into the bathroom, but it didn't happen. When I called out that the bacon, eggs, toast, and coffee were done, she came shuffling into the little kitchen in her robe, still sleepy, sat down at the tiny table across from me, and began to eat as if she were indeed the hungriest I'd seen her in a long time.

When we finished, she smiled at me across the table, and I smiled at her, and we went back into the bedroom for another little romp before making the preparations for our picnic.

She was beautiful, hungry, glowing, ecstatic. I've never felt more in love in my life. I wanted to swallow her whole, like a loving, cannibalistic god.

WE DROVE UP INTO THE COUNTRY in the VW bus, trundled it down the two-track path to the little lake, hardly bigger than a pond. I parked in a clearing beside the bank, and spread out a blanket on the grass.

We went for a walk in the woods and along the edge of the pasture on the nearby hill. Cattle grazed on the green slope there. A small herd of deer trotted through the trees in the ravine below us. A flicker chattered high up in an old pine, and flew away down the wooded decline, flashing the spot on its tail.

We went back to the lake and Olivia sat on the blanket and read a thick, steamy romance novel while I walked the bank and fished for bass. I was fishing with an artificial worm, one of the long thick purple ones with the big hook. Nothing was happening in the middle, so I walked on down to the narrow end, and cast across to the opposite shallows.

It was a beautiful day, cloudless, cool in the shadows along the bank. The trees filtered light where they stood on the gentle hill across the water, releasing it in stripes and patterned patches onto the leaf- and pine-straw-carpeted ground. Back where I'd walked from, at the other end of the lake, Olivia lay on her side, up on an elbow, and read her novel. She'd worn a light blue sundress, and it lay easily across the barely perceptible mound of her belly. I hadn't noticed it this morning, for some reason, the dress. I hadn't known she'd even owned it. Looking at her in it, reading there on the blanket in the shade, made me feel happy.

In a perfect cast I bumped the worm off a stump near the opposite bank and dropped it into the shallows there with a tiny sploosh. A fish hit it, I popped the rod, and it went wild, bent deep. The bass ran, stripping line from the whining reel, toward the bank where Olivia lay. When it paused, I reeled and it jumped, clearing the pond's surface. It seemed to pause at the top of its leap, and even from that distance I could see its huge eye on one side, looking at me, as if it sensed its trouble came from the other world, the one that was not water, and wanted to see. When it slapped down into the water again Olivia looked up and watched me fight it for a minute, then went back to reading.

I brought it in, grabbed it by its broad, hard bottom lip, and walked it around the bank to where she was. It was at least a six-pounder. Now its big round eyes seemed to take in the whole world, and we were insignificant in it.

"Ooo!" she said, looking up. "What a fish!"

"I know what we're having for supper tonight," I said.

I tethered the fish on a stringer tied to a log at the water's edge, and we had our picnic on the blanket, cool fried chicken and potato salad and a couple of cold beers. We climbed into the back of the VW and partially closed the doors and had us a little midafternoon play, sun-dappled leaves winking outside the old windows. We lay there awhile and had a deep nap. It was late afternoon when we woke, feeling sleepy but rested.

I laid the fish in the cooler we'd brought, on top of the melting ice, and drove us slowly home, down the dirt and gravel roads as far as they would take us, then on the old two-lane blacktop, and we pulled into the driveway of the house with the attic apartment and went upstairs and went immediately to bed and to sleep again.

I WAS SETTLING INTO THINGS, it seems to me now. Shaping up our little world a bit at a time. A modest measure of the American dream. I spent the next day just goofing off, resting, and in the afternoon I filleted the fish, marinated it in lemon juice, sliced some potatoes for frying, and made a salad.

"Oh, fan*tas*tic," Olivia said. "I'm starving again." She stood in the door to the tiny kitchen, cupping her little belly in both hands and grinning.

We went out onto the deck. Low thin clouds to the west hugged the horizon, glowing a strange and bloody blend of deep pink and fiery orange, as if distant lands were engulfed in a vast chemical inferno.

I fried the potatoes while the coals were burning down, then cooked the fish steaks on a little grill on the deck, and we ate out there in folding lawn chairs, the plates in our laps, and washed it down with some cheap wine from the liquor store that I'd put in the freezer for a while to make it cold and drinkable. The icy alcoholic coldness made frozen lumps in our brains, so we walked it off over to the mental hospital.

It was twilight, the strange glow gone from the horizon. No one was about on the hospital grounds. We strolled onto the broad front lawn, with its old magnolias limbed and leafed so low they covered the ground beneath them like huge mutant shrubs, and ancient live oaks, their massive limbs like the knotted arms of giants bent and lowered to lift some smaller creature into the sky.

We had our arms around each other's waist, and I kissed her on the cheek, and she stopped and we kissed there in the failing light beside one of the magnolias. She had a strange but pleasant musky taste I'd never noticed before. We knelt and crawled beneath the magnolia's sheltering low limbs, pushed aside the soft, fallen cones, and got lost in one another, everything around us disappearing, ceasing to exist, and we were a long few minutes catching our breaths in the dank, earthy air beneath the limbs and thick waxy leaves and letting the warm rushing feeling slowly leave our blood. It was as if time had changed, somehow, and we were alone in the world. I heard something outside the leafy cave we were in, and in the next moment something startled us pushing its way through the lowest limbs, too dark to see just what it was, but God what a stench. Olivia sucked her breath in surprise, and we lay very still because the broad, stinking muzzle of the lion was snuffling us, pushing its warm dry nostrils against our hair and our cheeks, running them down our bodies and back up to our mouths, a low quiet growl like a basso purr in its throat, and I dared to look into its burning yellow-green eyes, and when I did that the lion jerked its head up and backed rapidly out of the sheltering leaves and was gone.

I couldn't speak. It took me a moment to get my breath back. Olivia said, "My God, oh, my God. That was fantastic."

I realized I was excited, on fire. She had me in her cool slim hand. We went at it again, immediately, just as lost in it as we were before. I don't know how long it was before we made our way back to the apartment. I can't even remember that we did.

I WENT BACK TO MY JOB the next day. I hadn't really thought about it for a while.

Curtis was there, on the site, standing in a foundation ditch with a shovel. This was a job I was supposed to be handling, shaping up the ditch started by the backhoe, which he'd operated.

"I'm sorry, Curtis," I said. "I hope Arlo's not mad." Arlo was the young contractor we worked for.

"He's not," Curtis said, and I realized that Curtis didn't seem angry, either. Normally, after such a stunt, he would be. Then again, normally he'd have come to the apartment the day I didn't show to see what was keeping me. But he hadn't even called.

I decided not to say anything more about it, in case I'd break the spell of good luck. I found a shovel and hopped into the ditch and we worked at trimming and shaping the ditch all morning, and in the afternoon we laid and tied off the rebar, and when we were done the foundations were ready to pour the next morning.

"Are you coming in?" Curtis said, meaning the next morning. He was asking, as if there were an option.

"Sure," I said after a moment.

"Okay, buddy," he said, climbing into his green Bronco. "See you at seven." He headed off to his fiancée's place.

I hadn't seen or heard from my parents since we'd broken the news, either, which suddenly seemed very odd, and so I thought I'd drop by the house on my way home, check in.

They were both at home, although my little brother was out with some friends. Mom was watching the news from the big lounge chair while she let a casserole cook in the oven. Dad was out on the back patio, sipping a bourbon and water. He held up the glass in salute when he saw me through the plate-glass window to the patio. I leaned over and kissed my mother on the cheek and she kissed me back on my cheek and said, "Hey, hon."

I sat on the sofa and watched the news with her for a bit.

"Listen," I finally said, "are you doing okay?"

She turned her attention from the news to give me a nice warm smile.

"Of course," she said. "How are you? How's Olivia feeling?"

"Oh, she's fine, I guess," I said. "I mean, she's been fine. We went on a picnic."

"That sounds like fun." And she turned her attention to the news again.

I went out back onto the patio.

"Hello, son," my dad said. He wore an old pair of dress pants with a sheen worn into the thighs, his favorite high-top sneakers, and a guayabara shirt. "Drink?"

He'd never offered me bourbon before. He'd let me have a beer before, the previous year, and that had been a big deal. I guess the idea was I was grown up now, for all practical purposes.

"Sure."

He went in and came back out with a second drink, handed it to me.

"Cheers."

"Cheers."

We drank the bourbon and talked about golf. He'd been watching a tournament that day, at one of the local country clubs, following the leaders in a cart and drinking beer. I remembered how I used to go to the tournaments as a kid and put together long, elaborate strands of beer can pop tops and wear them around like primitive necklaces.

"So," I finally said. "Are y'all okay?"

He looked at me with the sort of indulgent smile a father can give.

"Sure, we're okay," he said. "How about you? How's Olivia?" he said suddenly, as if he'd just that second remembered our whole predicament.

"She's good," I said. "We went on a picnic, at Mom Bertha's lake. I caught a pretty good bass."

"Yeah? How big?"

"Maybe six pounds, I think."

"Damn. You going to mount it?"

"We ate it."

"Good for you."

After the drink, I said my goodbyes and went on home to Olivia. She was in the little kitchen, making biscuits. I didn't know she could bake anything. In fact, I'd never seen her cook anything. It was a pleasant surprise. I gave her a kiss on the cheek. The room was filled with a late, glowing, warm yellow light.

"What's going with the biscuits?" I said.

She shrugged.

"Want breakfast for supper?"

"Always," I said. I sat down at the table. "It's so cool in here. Crazy. Just a couple of days ago, it was unbearable."

"I know. Must be a cool front."

"Well, it feels pretty much the same outside. As it was a couple of days ago, I mean."

"It's bearable out there," she said.

"Yeah," I said. "That's not what I mean."

She didn't really seem to be listening. She was brushing the tops of the unbaked biscuits with melted butter before putting them into the oven, just like my mom would do.

"I guess the rent's due," I said.

"Mmm."

"I've got the cash," I said. "I'll go down and pay it."

I didn't relish any contact with our landlady, but seeing her in order to pay the rent was preferable to having her pound on the door, pissed off, to demand it. I checked my wallet, pulled out three twenties and a five, folded them, walked down the deck stairs and around to the front door of the house, and knocked. No one answered. I knocked again, and heard no steps of anyone approaching the door.

I cupped my hands against the door's glass window and looked inside. No one home. I'd never known the landlady not to be home. Aside from our measly rent, I didn't know how she survived.

I looked through the windowpane again. In some strange way, the place looked as if no one had been home in a long time.

WE ATE SUPPER AT OLIVIA'S PARENTS' HOUSE the next night. As with my parents, it was like nothing had happened. Or it was like everything had happened, but no one was upset or even concerned. It was as if Olivia and I not only had been married a number of years, but had gotten married in an entirely conventional way.

Olivia's mother's cooking, normally unsalted green beans and white rice and bland baked chicken because of Mr. Coltrane's blood pressure problem, was much better, too. It was a rich lasagna, with a green salad drenched in tangy oil and vinegar dressing, and French bread slathered with butter and garlic. We all ate like gluttons.

Mr. Coltrane ate like a man just released from a concentration camp, all but shedding tears of pure joy and gratification.

AT SOME POINT IN THERE, because I knew Olivia and her parents would like it, I joined their church, the Baptist church, and signed up to sing in the choir, and taught a Sunday school class to seventh-graders, and went out on witness nights with other men of the church, to convert and save souls. I didn't particularly believe any of the things I was supposed to believe in as a Baptist, but I didn't feel especially bothered by pretending to believe them, either.

Unbeknownst to myself before, I had a very nice singing voice.

We went to the Sunday morning service, the evening Sunday service, and the spaghetti suppers on Wednesday nights.

WE ENTERED A VERITABLE DREAM of days. At work, Curtis convinced the carpentry crew to take me on as apprentice, so I spent my days cutting studs to length, and joists, and hauling them up to the carpenters. I nailed the least attractive jobs, such as overhanging eaves, squeezing my legs around the two-by-six boards and leaning out over a drop of forty feet so we wouldn't have to erect scaffolding. But I loved it. I'd always been afraid of heights but that seemed to have vanished. The crew voted to hire me on as a real carpenter after only six months. I decided I wanted to be the best carpenter in town, I would devote my working life to it. I took the GED and sailed through it, nights.

Our little boy was born in December. He came out with a full head of thick tawny hair like a lion's mane, so we decided to call him Leo: William Leonardo Caruthers.

The next year, with a loan from our parents, Olivia and I bought a piece of land with a small stand of woods next to a pasture, and I began to build our house there in the late afternoons and evenings. Curtis helped me when he could. It was a simple but free-ranging design of our own. I wanted it to be at least part treehouse, remembering the ones I'd helped build as a child, so after the basic structure was done I began to expand it up and into a huge live oak we built next to for that purpose. Within two years we had our wish-home, all wood, with a broad front porch looking out over the pasture, a screen porch off our treehouse bedroom looking down into the woods out back. I was a good carpenter, as it turned out, and good at scavenging surplus and scrap materials from work sites, so when we were done the debt was minimal, and Olivia worked only part-time at home transcribing medical records, and sold rugs and coverlets and other nice things she wove herself on a big loom she kept in her workroom. She took long walks in the woods, early mornings, Leo toddling along or strapped in a carrier on her back, though he'd really gotten too big for that, to gather roots, nuts, flowers, and berries for natural coloring of the wool. Her body, which had been the lithe but soft body of a high school girl before, was now supple and muscular, beautifully toned. She was amazing in the sack.

I went on the walks with them, when I could. And lifted weights in the shed out back. I'd never felt stronger. I had my Ford pickup. She didn't have the Mercedes, but she did have a pretty cool little VW station wagon, baby blue.

It was a good life. I was astonished and deeply grateful that we'd made it happen. Leo was growing into a strong and happy child, soon he'd be going off to kindergarten and school. I could see our whole lives ahead of us, peaceful and full of light. We were lucky.

———

I WAS STANDING ON OUR FRONT PORCH looking out over the pasture at the end of a day, sun going down behind the pines and oaks and pale green sweetgum trees to the west.

Leo was inside reading *Where the Wild Things Are* to himself. He had learned to read just after turning four. Olivia and I had vowed to avoid treating him like a genius. No skipping grades, things like that. We would supplement his school at home, however we could. Give him novels, books about history and current events. Math problems from our old high school texts.

Olivia had a venison stew in a pot on the stove. I'd shot the doe not half a mile from our house, in the woods. Olivia had helped me butcher it. She was in her workroom weaving something new on her loom while the stew simmered.

The chickens pecked about the yard, an eye always on their rooster. He strutted the yard's edge, very intelligent for a rooster. He'd killed two hawks in just the past month. Killed them before they could kill the chickens they'd swooped down upon to lift away. He and the hens fell upon the hawks and tore them to pieces.

Our dog, an Aussie mix, looked on from the other end of the porch. She kept away the foxes and coyotes. She understood the most subtle of questions and commands. I'd never owned a better dog in my life.

She was my first dog, in fact. I kept forgetting that.

I saw someone walking across the pasture toward the house. When the person got closer, he looked familiar, although I still couldn't tell or remember just who he might be. He smiled and waved when he was just a stone's throw away, maybe, and I waved back, and he walked up to the house and stood in the yard a few feet away from the edge of the porch and looked up at me. He was a tall man, dark hair cropped short and receding in a widow's peak, heavy beard shadow, horn-rimmed glasses, a kind expression. He wore a conservative, narrow-lapeled suit and a modest narrow necktie.

"You look familiar," I said.

He said, "I'm Lowell Bishop, your sixth-grade teacher."

"Oh," I said. "My God. Mr. Bishop. I always wondered what happened to you."

Mr. Bishop had been a substitute, that year, for another teacher who'd gone on unexpected maternity leave. He hadn't been a very good teacher, kind of lazy, actually, but I'd liked him and always hoped he'd had a good life after leaving our school and going on to whatever his next, probably temporary, job may have been. He'd been the only teacher who hadn't treated me as if I were invisible.

"I did all right," Mr. Bishop said. "I went back to school. Psychology. I was still fairly young."

"I'm glad to hear that," I said. "I'd kind of worried about you."

He laughed. "I don't doubt you did."

Mr. Bishop had rented a garage apartment a block or so from my home while he'd lived in town. And on the day after school ended, I'd gone over there to say goodbye. When I knocked, he came to the door wearing his school trousers and an undershirt, the kind without sleeves, and he needed a shave, and behind him in the little kitchen area were two other men in similar shape, sitting at the dining table with hands of cards before them, a whiskey bottle and glasses on the table, and cigarette smoke filled the dingy light in there.

"Hey there!" Mr. Bishop had boomed at me. "Come on in!"

I declined and told him I just wanted to say goodbye.

"Suit yourself," Mr. Bishop said. "But you be good, be a good student, now. If I come back through here in a couple of years and you're not being a good student, I'm going to beat the crap out of you!" And he laughed. I all but ran away from his place.

So I had worried that Mr. Bishop was just an affable, unfortunate drunk.

I said to him now, standing there somehow in my front yard at our house in the country, some nine years later, "What are you doing here, Mr. Bishop?"

He smiled up at me in a curious and almost sad kind of way for a long moment before replying.

"I've come to tell you that now you have to go back to where you came from," he said.

"What do you mean?"

"You'll know when you get there," he said. "We just want you to know that we appreciate your cooperation."

After a moment, I said, "With what?"

Olivia stepped out onto the porch beside me then. She smiled and nodded to Mr. Bishop. She was holding Leo against her hip, and he was clinging to her as if something had upset him, inside.

"Is everything okay?" she said to me.

I was gazing at them, my beautiful little family, and so in love I thought I might be drawn into their eyes and entirely absorbed, and disappear from the world, and be nothing but some barely traceable element in their very cells.

And then the light began to fade from the sky as if the arrival of evening had accelerated, the turning of the earth somehow sped up, and the image of Mr. Bishop before us darkened along with the rest of the world and was gone.

OLIVIA WAS STILL PREGNANT, of course. We'd been out for only a couple of days. Our parents stood next to our hospital beds. Our mothers were tearful, holding our hands. Our fathers seemed stunned, hands in their pockets, standing behind our mothers, rocked back on the heels of their shoes. The nurse disappeared and a few moments later came back in with a doctor.

"Well, well, what have we here?" the doctor said. He checked Olivia's pulse, looked at her pupils, then did the same with me. He turned to our stunned parents and said, in a bright manner, "May we have a few minutes alone with these two?"

Our parents, like confused tourists in a foreign country, stared at him for a moment and then nodded and shuffled out of the room, bumping into each other trying to let one another out of the door before them.

The nurse stepped forward to stand beside the doctor. They stood there looking at us, smiling in an odd kind of way, I thought.

"Hello," the doctor said then. Olivia and I looked at each other from across the little space between our beds.

"How've you been?" the nurse said then.

They looked nothing like the couple from the asylum, except there was something in their manner that was exactly that way.

Olivia watched them, a kind of vacant look on her face.

"I've been fine," I said then, carefully.

"How did you like your experience?" the nurse said.

The doctor raised his eyebrows, waiting for one of us to reply. He tapped at his clipboard but didn't necessarily seem impatient.

"What do you mean?" Olivia said.

The doctor laughed softly to himself, and scratched at an ear.

"Very different," the nurse said, looking from the one of us to the other. "You'll have to discuss *that*, soon enough."

"What are you talking about?" Olivia said. "What are they talking about?" she said to me.

"You should have told her about us, I suppose," the doctor said to me.

"Told me what?" Olivia said.

The strangest thing was, I was pretty sure I'd seen this doctor, off duty of course, around the old country club. He had a rather stolid expression, but also a head of neatly clipped, boyish blond hair. I'd never seen the nurse before. She was older than the doctor, with an old-fashioned perm, reading glasses perched on the end of her nose, but with red lipstick and bright red nails, and a querulous expression.

"We just woke up," I said.

"It's not important," the nurse said to the doctor.

"I will attempt to be more patient with the patient," the doctor said. "How'd you like the lion?" he said to me then.

After a moment, I said, "It was amazing," and then I felt something like a deep sadness well up in me.

"Very creative," the doctor said. "Impressive."

"And the fish," the nurse said.

"And the frequent, vigorous intercourse," the doctor said, raising his eyebrows again and smiling.

That made me a little bit angry, that.

"Don't be embarrassed," he said. "We're scientists. I was only joking."

"I'm not embarrassed," I said.

He seemed amused.

"The house in the country, though, and the various elements of sentimental perfection," he said. "Something of a disappointment, there."

"They're very young," the nurse said to him. "It's a long shot, to expect much better."

"Interesting, isn't it," he said to me, "how curiously time moves when it's decoupled from physicality."

"Yeah," I said vaguely.

"What in the world are y'all talking about?" Olivia said. She looked frightened.

"The sixth-grade teacher, though," he said. "That was a nice touch."

"Touch*ing*, actually," she said.

The doctor laughed his quiet laugh again.

"*You* did that," I said.

"Not exactly," he said.

"It was all certainly more substantial than hers," she said.

"How *did* you like your experience, sweetheart?"

Olivia's expression went flat again, but with something like irritation behind it.

"What experience?" she said.

The nurse had taken on an inscrutable smile.

"The mansion, the yacht, the handsome wealthy Greek husband." She accompanied her words with a little swaying motion, a casual parody of romantic reverie.

"How do you know about my dream?" Olivia said in a small, quiet voice.

My heart got even heavier inside of me.

"Much more than a dream, dear," the nurse said with a wry twist of her lips.

"No children, we noticed," the doctor said in a pensive voice. He was looking down at the chart in his hand as if studying something there instead of talking to us.

"A little overload on the substitutions, maybe," the nurse said. "Those strange house servants."

"What do you mean?" Olivia said.

"That was actually pretty good," the doctor said.

"Just a theory I have," the nurse said.

"I was really upset," Olivia said. She looked like she was about to cry.

"It's all right," I said to her.

"Nothing to be overly concerned about," the doctor said.

"You simply have to approach these things with a measure of intelligence," the nurse said. "Remove the emotional veil, so to speak."

"That's good," the doctor said to her.

"I'll make a note," she replied. "Now we really must go."

"The doctor and the nurse have many rounds to make," he said.

"Would you like any drugs?" she said. "The doctor can prescribe."

"Maybe some Valium," I said. "For both of us."

"Done," the doctor said, writing something on the clipboard.

"Take care," the nurse said.

Giving us those little sideways waves, they backed in shuffling backwards steps out the door.

IN THE MOMENT AFTER THE COUPLE from the asylum had left us that previous night, when I had begun to construct our little paradise in my mind, Olivia had awakened, dressed quietly, crept from the house, down the steps from the rickety deck, and walked away.

As she walked, and as dawn seeped into the cooled August air, the landscape began to change until she knew she was no longer in our little hometown. It was as if she didn't know where she was, or where she wanted to be, and the landscape continually reshaped itself with the beautiful, disorienting whorl of a kaleidoscope turned by an invisible hand.

She put her own hand to her belly as she walked. It was flat and soft. Well, that was gone. That had ceased to exist. That was not a problem anymore.

She walked on. There was a vista now, improbably so. The trees had thinned out. There was a horizon, seemingly with nothing beyond the rise.

She heard a distant, quiet, susurrant sound, which grew louder the closer she got to the rise. And before she reached the rise she saw water, and when she stepped to the edge of the bluff she now stood on she could see it was the ocean, vast and blue-gray, with gulls sailing in the sky above it, and white breakers on the narrow beach below, and just beyond them in the water there was a very large yacht. There seemed to be no one on the yacht, which was at anchor in the swells. It was new, its hull made of polished, coffee-colored wood. And then there was someone on the yacht. She could see that a man dressed in a white jacket stood on the broad rear deck, facing her, a neat, sky-blue towel draped over his arm, which he held crooked in front of him in the manner of an old-fashioned waiter. Which he apparently was.

There was a stepped path down the face of the bluff and she took it, counting her steps as if she were a child with no more on her mind than the descent itself. One hundred and twenty-seven. She walked across the beach, the warm sand pushing up between her bare toes. She no longer had any need of shoes. She waded into the surf and swam through the breakers to the yacht, pulled herself onto the ladder hanging down from its gunnel, and climbed up onto the deck.

The waiter nodded to her. He was an older man, a soft and large and comforting man, dark-complexioned, and his expression was as somber as the expression on a tilefish. She wondered for a moment how she knew that, and then she remembered being amused by the photo of a somber tilefish in the margin of a page in her dictionary, when she was a little girl. And she had said to her father at dinner that night, when he seemed troubled by something and would not speak, You look just like an old tilefish! And after everyone had gotten over their astonishment at where this expression may have come from, they all laughed.

The waiter nodded toward a deck chair and said something to her in a language she didn't understand. She sat in the chair and fell asleep and when she woke up her summer dress was dry and the waiter had placed a cold drink on the little table beside her. It was delicious and tasted like crushed watermelon on ice. The waiter was nowhere to be seen but there was another man across the deck from her, in another chair, watching her.

He was the most beautiful man she'd ever seen. More beautiful than any man she'd ever seen in a movie. Or in a magazine photograph. Or on a billboard or the cover of a record album. He was impossibly beautiful and impossible to describe. She blushed and could not say any more to me about how beautiful this man was, and I didn't ask her to try.

She said, We went away on the yacht to another country.

The country was something like she imagined Greece to be, or possibly southern Italy. It was very sunny, the warm air brimming with golden light, and there were mountains in the distance you could see from the villa on a hill above the shore. Below the villa there were steep rocky cliffs and a wide blue sea. The villa had a broad terrace that overlooked a white swimming pool. There were large, slow ceiling fans turning in all the rooms. There was a constant cool breeze that blew in from the sea. There were servants as beautiful and slender and brown and silent as some kind of near-human, intelligent animal. Their eyes clear and limpid with an animal-like devotion in their gaze. They transformed into other, similar creatures when they moved from one room to another.

There were dogs the size of small slender horses that roamed the grounds and guarded them against intruders, and killed rabbits and could be seen loping across clearings with these rabbits in their jaws.

There were great outsized housecats that lay draped over balustrades and the arms of stuffed sofas and chairs and they didn't seem to acknowledge the existence of other creatures, not even the dogs.

The birds in the trees in their gardens watched her as she walked beneath them and they spoke to her in a silent language about things she could not translate to normal speech or even thought, and so these things remained entirely between her and the birds.

She and her Greek or Italian lover never spoke to one another, and yet they grew older, without appearing to. They only became more beautiful.

I became more beautiful, she said, until I wasn't at all the person I had been before. I was entirely changed.

And that was good? I said.

She nodded, her attention distracted in the memory of her dream.

Yes, it was.

OUR PARENTS, HAVING BEEN TERRIFIED back to their senses, wasted no time seeking an annulment of our marriage. We'd lied about our ages, had no parental consent. Seeing us unconscious and possibly dying (as far as they knew or feared), they were sure we were being punished by God for being so young and so foolish, for thinking we could bring a child into the world when we were nothing but children ourselves. We were going to serve as a ghoulish example to other young people, the young couple who eloped and went to sleep and never woke up. Their child delivered by the doctors although the couple themselves would never know. Would never see that child, who would never see his or her parents, either—not awake and in the world, in any case.

Within days of our awakening, we were no longer married, no longer legal tenants of our apartment. Olivia was taken away to live with relatives in another state, I was never certain if it was Louisiana or Texas. I suppose it could have been a state even farther away, with a relative she'd never happened to mention in our brief time together. I don't really think she put up much if any resistance.

I heard from someone a year or so later that she—we, I guess, but it no longer felt like that—had delivered a little boy, after all.

Then someone else told me they'd heard it was a girl.

In any case, I presume it went straight to adoption.

On the other hand, I once heard she never even had the child. She either miscarried or had what people called a phantom or false pregnancy.

I never spoke with Olivia again, so I never knew for sure.

Once, a few months after she'd been taken away, I saw her downtown, on the sidewalk, walking along as if nothing like what happened to us had ever happened to her, as if she were just another one of the people walking along, window-shopping, another person with no history at all.

It was winter, January. She wore a long, heavy coat and some kind of colorful hat, from which her dark hair just peeked at the bottom, even shorter than before. She wasn't pushing a stroller or anything like that. Just by herself.

I looked different. I'd gained a lot of weight and some of my hair had fallen out, ridiculously, just from stress. I was depressed, I guess, what a joke of a word. And I was just driving by in a car, not our old VW bus. She wouldn't have recognized me, anyway.

I tried not to worry or feel guilty about the child. He would always have someone looking after or over him. He would most likely have some very interesting fairy godparents, for lack of a better term.

LOOKING BACK NOW, OF COURSE, it's obvious we got off pretty easy. There was always some young mindless dying in that town, those days. Cars flinging themselves into groves and against large stalwart roadside trees, the residents in their myopic ranch-style houses hardly bothering to venture out to the carnage.

During the year all this took place, one boy I knew was flung from a friend's truck and crushed between the truck and a tree. A girl I knew and liked a lot died when an addled motorist drove the wrong way on the interstate. Another night, a guy who'd been on my Little League baseball team heckled a drunk stumbling into a pizza parlor and the drunk walked over and shot him in the heart. He'd been bored, the boy had, hanging out with a bunch of other bored boys in the parking lot, and too easily amused by potentially violent drunks hungry for pizza. Not long after all this, my own brother Curtis died in a head-on collision with a car driven by another young man his age. They'd gone to high school together, had known each other most of their lives.

I knew a boy who shot himself in the head, in front of his mother, in their front yard, because he was so sick and goddamn tired of her drunken bitching cruel ways.

The funerals of these young people were awful affairs, with parents wailing, suffering, siblings slouching about in angry grief, not a little frightened over their own suddenly looming mortality, friends fairly creeping around as if to avoid the contamination of bad luck.

Then of course there were the teen couples who ran off to get married, so alluring the delusion of greater freedom. They were so phenomenally bored with being *nothing*, and high school seemed little better than a minimal-security prison. They were almost literally mad to chain themselves to lives of eight-to-five jobs, punch-clock paychecks, puttering home to the little postwar starter bungalow, and having a couple of beers, cooking burgers on the grill, being grown-ups.

I was kind of mad to find something of significance, anywhere, though I was into the delinquency, too. It was the most obviously interesting thing going. There was plenty of good, cheap marijuana, the kind that made you laugh a lot. Quaaludes. Mescaline. Plenty of acid. A few people blossomed into full-blown junkies. It even went that way for my little brother, Mike. But, instead of smashing up my car and friends, or overdosing on one concoction or another, I fell in love with Olivia Coltrane.

IT'S NOT LIKE THAT ANYMORE in that town. There's more to do, inside the house, inside the magnificent motherboards of the new machines. Young people don't just drive around, bored, drinking beer and crashing into trees and other vehicles, slashing and flailing away at one another in parking lots and vacant lots out of rage or boredom. If they get pregnant, they get a quick and easy abortion at the local clinic, the boy waiting outside for the girl who doesn't want him to come in, and then she staggers slightly back to the car, a stunned look on her face, something in herself suddenly evaporated, beyond her ken. No one seems to get all excited over the drugs, even though there are more of them to choose from. They're just not the big deal they were. I suppose there's the usual brittle coterie of meth-heads, if you look.

You can get just about anything you want, these days.

But nobody runs off and gets married anymore. Nowadays, if you did that, you'd be greeted upon your return as if you were declaring, after an unexplained absence, that you'd been abducted by aliens, taken aboard their spaceship, and probed in various humiliating ways.

THE YEAR OR TWO AFTER we woke up was a kind of limbo. I would live out some alternative life, and then come to on a park bench, or in the hospital again, or in my car somewhere, ignition on, engine dead, gas tank empty. I'll admit that at one point my family had me admitted to East Mississippi. That was ironic, I thought. The old man who hunted lions, Mr. Hunter, was no longer around. None of the inmates remembered him, and no one on the staff would discuss him with me. I'm not sure how long I was in. I may have been used, myself, for a visitation or two. Fuzzy memories, as if from deep dreams. I was disciplined, once, for going AWOL and walking around. I was in a locked, padded room for two days. It was like being inside a white dream, or in a pure fog or cloud.

When I got out of the hospital, I would see other people with these lost, somewhat sad looks on their faces, and I would think that similar things were happening to them. But you didn't ask. You didn't want to get them started. There was the fear of the destabilizing admission. We left one another alone.

I went through a brief period when I wanted desperately to see Olivia again, and not just to see her but talk to her, too. But her parents would hang up on me when I called. A couple of times she answered the phone, but she wouldn't speak after I said hello. And then her mother or father would take the receiver from her, tell me not to call again, and hang up.

I sneaked up to the house one night. I didn't really know what I was going to do. Maybe I fantasized that she'd step outside for something, to take out the garbage or just sit out in the night air looking up at the stars. She didn't, of course. I crept into the shrubbery near their living room window and peeked in. Mrs. Coltrane was on the sofa, knitting something, and Mr. Coltrane was watching TV. I crept out and around to what used to be Olivia's bedroom and peeked in there.

She was sitting on the bed, reading something, dressed in a pink nightgown, her legs beneath the covers. My heart fluttered. I stared for a long time, trying to see what she was reading, before I realized it was that green, faux-leather edition of *The Living Bible*. Her brow was lined with concentration. She seemed to be moving her lips a little bit as she read. I backed quietly from the window and crept to my car and drove home, to my own parents' house, and went to bed.

I could see her whole life ahead of her, then, and it seemed kind of simple. She'd been saved, from me and from everything else. She'd been pretty shocked by the whole affair, and wanted to do everything the proper way now. She'd marry, eventually, someone safe and predictable, and kind. Fold herself into her parents' church. Develop a particularly amnesiac cartography of her past. Our past.

Obviously, I haven't done that so well. I haven't wanted to. Even now, when I think of Olivia, I'm looking at her sitting naked and unselfconscious on our creaky old bed in the attic apartment, lost in some thought that is destined to escape her. Maybe it'll wander in the breeze and lodge itself in some poor thought-crazed head in the asylum down the street, maybe worm its way into the bitter landlady downstairs, maybe squeeze into the head of a scatterbrained cardinal in the pecan tree just outside the gable window. She wrinkles her pretty brow in thought, literally puts a finger to her bottom lip, but it's hopeless, the thought is gone, never to be aired before me or anyone else in her line of mortal acquaintance. Her pale skin is beautiful, smooth and lightly blue-veined, a barely visible pale blue line at one temple, another across her growing tummy, and one on the back of the hand that holds the finger to her moistened lower lip, which cannot voice her fleeting thought, lost now to her before she even knows it.

I wondered what our lives would really have been like, had we gone on together, stayed married, kept the child, tried to deal with the kinds of things that always work like an underground

river to undercut people's happiness. I wonder if she ever won-
ders the same.

I DID, ONCE, LIVE OUT that life. It was while I was in the hospital, early on in my stay.

We stayed married, for a while anyway. Instead of becoming
a professional carpenter, I worked a wood-shop job and attended
the local branch of the university in my spare time, because
Olivia and her parents and my parents convinced me to do so.
Olivia stayed home and took care of our child, who was a boy
but whose name was Jackson, we called him Jack.

I was good at academics, as it turned out. This surprised me,
but pleased me, too. I'd never thought I was very smart. You
might think I'd have studied the hard sciences, maybe astronomy,
but I chose anthropology, a so-called social science. I wanted to
know about people.

The more I studied, of course, the more my sense of who
I was began to change. It changed who I *thought* I was or was
becoming, anyway. Olivia clung all the more stubbornly to who
she thought I was, or had been. Naturally my skepticism toward
organized religion only continued to deepen and grow. I began
to lose interest in Olivia, who it seemed to me had no interest
in growing, learning, changing with the times. We grew apart.
And one day, though she did so kindly and without anger, she
took Jack and moved back home to her parents' house. We were
still only twenty-two years old.

She remarried a few years later, to a prosperous local businessman, had two more children, belonged to the newer, richer
country club, the larger and more exclusive Episcopalian church
in town, and drove a Mercedes station wagon. I was amused to
see that.

I eventually finished the PhD and did fieldwork for a number
of years in Wyoming on prehistoric settlement sites, then took a

228 | THERE IS HAPPINESS

job at a university not too close, but not too far from our home-town, so I could visit Jack more easily when he was visiting his mother during holidays from school. He was a sensitive young man, with a forgiving nature, and we were close. I remarried, twice, but neither one worked out. I fathered no more children, though I kept in touch with the daughter of my third wife, a girl she'd had during her first marriage, under circumstances not so different from mine and Olivia's.

I grew old not so gracefully. I was a little bitter, though I had a dark sense of humor my students seemed to like. I drank far too much, pretty much every night. Stopped and started smoking in what seemed like regular seven-year intervals. I had an old dog, a pound mutt of inconceivable lineage. I died while out on a walk with the dog one afternoon in winter, of exposure, because of a mild heart attack that nonetheless left me unable to get back to my vehicle, parked half a mile away.

When I woke from this one, who should be sitting on the hospital cot across from me but Wendell Sparrow, looking strange as ever, but worse. He seemed to have aged to some-thing like forty or fifty, though he was surely only twenty, just a couple of years older than me. Judging by the white orderly uniform he wore, and his crew-cut, balding head, he was now an employee of East Mississippi. He was smoking a cigarette, in the same famished way, and looked to weigh about a hundred and ten pounds. I couldn't imagine him overpowering even the tiniest crazy person.

No, he said when I asked, he was a respiratory therapist. They need that in here, too, he said.

"Ever use the machine on yourself?" I said.

"I figure it'll come in handy, one day," he said.

"It's good to see you," I said then. "Even if it is in here."

He didn't answer for a moment, just watched me with a kind

of detached or absent look on his ravaged face. I figured he was doing a lot of speed, maybe junk. Or maybe something he could only get in here.

"So," he said. "How was that?"

"How was what?" I said. And then a little chill ran through me. He was looking at me in that way.

"That was real," Sparrow said then. "That's the way it would've really been."

I didn't say anything for a minute.

"What about the rest of it?" I said. "All the stuff after the divorce."

Sparrow put out his cigarette on the floor, dug into his therapist coat pocket for the pack, niggled another one out of it, and lit up, put the pack back into the pocket.

"Yeah," he said. "Could be pretty much that way. Probably a few minor differences. Might look a lot different at times, along the way. But in the end, not a whole lot."

I didn't say anything to that.

"Gotta go," Sparrow said, getting up. "So many lungs, so little time."

He walked out. I never saw him again, after that.

IT HAD BEEN SPARROW, in a perverse concession, who'd driven us on our first date. He drove us around in his mother's humongous emerald-green Electra 225. I say date, although really it was a contrived, rolling parking session, Sparrow sitting alone up front behind the wheel while Olivia and I made out in the back seat.

I'd begged him. My father was on the road again and my brother had our mother's car. Sparrow agreed only because he needed to be angry, he hadn't gotten it all out. I could see his beady, furious eyes watching us in the rearview mirror. He chain-smoked, hardly ever taking the cigarette from his mouth, just sucking hard and burning it a half inch at a time. But after a while the strange rhythms of his driving began to rock us into a kind of submissive stupor. He drove with his left foot on the brake, right foot on the accelerator, so that we moved through the evening like a big green fish swimming in fluid lunges against the current. The effect was lulling, hypnotic. After a while we forgot he was up there, forgot we were in his car. We fell almost into sleep into one another's kisses.

Later, when we dropped Olivia off at her home, I stayed in the back and Sparrow drove me home in silence, fuming tobacco smoke and rage. I felt pretty good, like a rich man's son, Sparrow my father's powerless chauffeur, forced to drive me on a date with his own beautiful daughter.

That had basically been the end of my friendship with Sparrow. I haven't seen him in decades, now. But the funny thing is that he'd looked kind of like an alien, I mean like the ones in abduction stories. He had the teardrop-shaped head already balding at eighteen, the long skinny neck, the long thin hands and fingers, and his eyes just enormous. Except that Sparrow's eyes were normally very expressive, very human. Normally, he was just an alien of the everyday variety.

A YEAR OR TWO AFTER all of this, after I'd gotten a little better, I was tending my dad's bar, the one he opened up after Curtis died in the accident and he lost his job from drinking too much. He bought the bar, and ran a little liquor store in a corner of the building, and I ran the bar, evenings. I took classes at the junior college during the day.

One night when almost no one was in the bar, a weeknight, a man came in by himself and sat on a stool and asked for a beer. I'd never seen him before. He was maybe forty, forty-five. Hard to tell, as I was still only nineteen, myself, legal age in Mississippi in those days, but far from having any view over the nearer horizon.

He was a pleasant man, with a small, pleasant, unremarkable face. He was dressed in what looked like business attire minus the jacket and tie he'd left either in the car or at the house. His collar was pressed but knocked awry. His medium-length, but definitely barbered hair was just the slightest bit mussed up. Mine wasn't the first bar he'd been to that evening.

When he'd ordered his second beer, he said this was his one night in the year to go out and get drunk.

"I don't drink, otherwise," he said. "Just one night a year, though, I go out and I get plastered. It's a safety valve."

"Well, that sounds okay," I said. "Can't fault you for that."

"No, you cannot, that's true," the man said.

He reached across the bar to shake my hand.

"Monroe Clooney," he said. "My friends call me Mo."

"Call me Will, Mo," I said.

"I will, Will," he said, and laughed. "Sorry."

"No, no, Mo," I said, and we both laughed.

Then Mo Clooney told me his story. He was a civil engineer, made a good living, but he and his wife couldn't have children, they'd tried, and so about ten years earlier they'd started taking in foster children from the local orphanage. There were mostly boys in the orphanage, and so they decided to take only boys, just to keep things simple as possible. But here they were ten years down the road, and now they had ten boys running about their house, which was fairly large, but still.

"They're great boys, mostly," Mo said. "But even so, you got to blow off a little steam every now and then. Hence," he said, raising his beer, and then draining it. I got him another, on the house.

"Thank you," he said, as if I'd paid him a compliment. He spilled a little of his beer on the counter and mopped it with his shirtsleeve.

"My boys need a project," he said then. "Always have to keep them busy. So I've decided to buy some kind of old car that they can take apart. Doesn't really matter if they can put it back together again."

"They get the 'exploded view,'" I said. I loved that term. So did Mo Clooney, because he was an engineer, I guess. Most people don't know it. It's the simulated photo of something, like an engine, as if it's just been blown into pieces that happen to be all its component parts, and they're suspended just inches away from one another, as if in the act of flying apart, so that you can see all the parts separately and where they fit into the whole. Mo Clooney could hardly stop laughing. He probably didn't get to hear much engineer humor. I knew the term only because I tended to thumb through dictionaries when I was bored sometimes, a habit I'd picked up lately. When Mo Clooney finally could stop laughing, he asked me about the old VW bus I'd parked in the corner of the bar's dirt and gravel parking lot.

"Doesn't run anymore," I said.

"Doesn't matter," he said. "What'll you take for it?"

I shrugged. "Fifty bucks."

"Deal," Mo Clooney said.

He pulled out his wallet, peeled off fifty dollars and handed the money to me, and shook my hand.

"No need for a bill of sale," he said. "I trust you." He laughed. "I trust everybody. It was nice to meet you. I'll have someone tow the vehicle to my house by tomorrow afternoon."

And then he left, giving me a little wave over his shoulder, and walking only a little bit unsteadily.

Next afternoon when I got to the bar, the bus was gone.

I'd had a thought, when he was walking out the night before, that he was a pretty odd guy, and so I'd gone outside to the parking lot, to see if he was really there.

Or to see if I was, I suppose.

Mo Clooney was there, fumbling with the keys to his car, and then getting into it, cranking it up, and driving it slowly away down the darkened, lamp-lined street.

I'd thought for a moment that he was one of them. But his sense of humor had been too normal, his laughter too real. And the look in his eyes had been so vulnerably human. It seemed filled with a kind of muted loss.

No, I said to myself then, he's one of us.

BILL

WILHELMINA, EIGHTY-SEVEN, LIVED ALONE IN THE SAME TOWN as her two children, but she rarely saw them. Her main companion was a trembling poodle she'd had for about fifteen years, named Bill. You never hear of dogs named Bill. Her husband in his decline had bought him, named him after a boy he'd known in the Great War, and then wouldn't have anything to do with him. He'd always been Wilhelmina's dog. She could talk to Bill in a way that she couldn't talk to anyone else, not even her own children. Not even her husband, now nearly a vegetable out at King's Daughters' Rest Home on the old highway. She rose in the blue candlelight morning to go see him about the dog, who was doing poorly. She was afraid of being completely alone. There were her children and their children, and even some great-grandchildren, but that was neither here nor there for Wilhelmina. They were all in different worlds.

She drove her immaculate ocean-blue Delta 88 out to the home and turned up the long, barren drive. The tall naked trunks of a few old pines lined the way, their sparse tops distant as clouds. Wilhelmina pulled into the parking lot and took two spaces so she'd have plenty of room to back out when she left. She paused for a moment to check herself in the rearview mirror, and adjusted the broad-brimmed hat she wore to hide the thinning spot on top of her head.

Her husband, Howard, lay propped up and twisted in his old velour robe, his mouth open, watching TV. His thick white hair stood in a matted knot on his head like a child's.

"What?" he said when she walked in. "What did you say?"

"I said, 'Hello!' " Wilhelmina replied, though she'd said nothing. She sat down.

"I came to tell you about Bill, Howard. He's almost completely blind now and he can't go to the bathroom properly. The veterinarian says he's in pain and he's not going to get better and I should put him to sleep."

Her husband had tears in his eyes.

"Poor old Bill," he said.

"I know," Wilhelmina said, welling up herself now. "I'll miss him so."

"I loved him at Belleau Wood! He was all bloody and walking around," Howard said. "They shot off his nose in the Meuse-Argonne." He picked up the remote box and held the button down, the channels thumping past like the muted thud of an ancient machine gun.

Wilhelmina dried her tears with a Kleenex from her handbag and looked up at him.

"Oh, fiddle," she said.

"Breakfast time," said an attendant, a slim copper-colored man whose blue smock was tailored at the waist and flared over his hips like a suit jacket. He set down the tray and held his long delicate hands before him as if for inspection.

He turned to Wilhelmina.

"Would you like to feed your husband, ma'am?"

"Heavens, no," Wilhelmina said. She shrank back as if he intended to touch her with those hands.

When the attendant held a spoonful of oatmeal up to her husband's mouth he lunged for it, his old gray tongue out, and slurped it down.

"Oh, he's ravenous today," said the attendant. Wilhelmina, horrified, felt for a moment as if she were losing her mind and had wandered into this stranger's room by mistake. She clutched her purse and slipped out into the hall.

"I'm going," she called faintly, and hurried out to her car, which sat on the cracked surface of the parking lot like an old beached yacht. The engine groaned, turned over, and she steered down the long drive and onto the highway without even a glance at the traffic. A car passed her on the right, up in the grass, horn blaring, and an enormous dump truck cleaved the air to her left like a thunderclap. She would pay them no mind.

When she got home the red light on her answering machine, a gift from her son, was blinking. It was him on the tape.

"I got your message about Bill, Mama. I'll take him to the vet in the morning, if you want. Just give me a call. Bye-bye, now."

"No, I can't think about it," Wilhelmina said.

Bill was on his cedar-filled pillow in the den. He looked around for her, his nose up in the air.

"Over here, Bill," Wilhelmina said loudly for the dog's deaf ears. She carried him a Milk-Bone biscuit, for his teeth were surprisingly good. He sniffed the biscuit, then took it carefully between his teeth, bit off a piece, and chewed.

"Good boy, good Bill."

Bill didn't finish the biscuit. He laid his head down on the cedar pillow and breathed heavily. In a minute he got up and made his halting, wobbling way toward his water bowl in the kitchen, but hit his head on the doorjamb and fell over.

"Oh, Bill, I can't stand it," Wilhelmina said, rushing to him. She stroked his head until he calmed down, and then she dragged him gently to his bowl, where he lapped and lapped until she had to refill it, he drank so much. He kept drinking.

"Kidneys," Wilhelmina said, picking up the bowl. "That's enough, boy."

Bill nosed around for the water bowl, confused. He tried to squat, legs trembling, and began to whine. Wilhelmina carried him out to the backyard, set him down, and massaged his kidneys the way the vet had shown her, and finally a little trickle ran down Bill's left hind leg. He tried to lift it.

"Good old Bill," she said. "You try, don't you?"

She carried him back in and dried his leg with some paper towels.

"I guess I'd do anything for you, Bill," she said. But she had made up her mind. She picked up the phone and called her son. It rang four times and then his wife's voice answered.

"You've reached two-eight-one," she began.

"I know that," Wilhelmina muttered.

". . . We can't come to the phone right now . . ."

Wilhelmina thought that sort of message was rude. If they were there, they could come to the phone.

". . . leave your message after the beep."

"I guess you better come and get Bill in the morning," Wilhelmina said, and hung up.

Wilhelmina's husband had been a butcher, and Katrina, the young widow who'd succeeded him at the market, still brought meat by the house every Saturday afternoon—steaks, roasts, young chickens, stew beef, soup bones, whole hams, bacon, pork chops, ground chuck. Once she even brought a leg of lamb. Wilhelmina couldn't possibly eat it all, so she stored most of it in her deep freeze.

She went out to the porch and gathered as much from the deep freeze as she could carry, dumped it into the kitchen sink like a load of kindling, then pulled her cookbooks from the cupboard and sat down at the kitchen table. She began looking up recipes that had always seemed too complex for her, dishes that sounded vaguely exotic, chose six of the most interesting she could find, and copied them onto a legal pad. Then she made a quick trip to the grocery store to find the items she didn't have on hand, buying odd spices like saffron and coriander, and not just produce but shallots and bright red bell peppers, and a bulb of garlic cloves as big as her fist. Bill had always liked garlic.

Back home, she spread all the meat out on the counter, the chops and steaks and ham, the roast and the bacon, some Italian sausage she'd found, some boudin that had been there for ages, and even a big piece of fish fillet. She chopped the sweet peppers, the shallots, ground the spices. The more she worked, the less she thought of the recipes, until she'd become a marvel of culinary innovativeness, combining oils and spices and herbs and meats into the most savory dishes you could imagine: Master William's Sirloin Surprise, Ham au Bill, Bill's Leg of Lamb with Bacon Chestnuts, Bill's Broiled Red Snapper with Butter and Crab, Bloody Boudin à la Bill, and one she decided to call simply Sausage Chops. She fired up her oven, lit every eye on her stove, and cooked it all just as if she were serving the king of France instead of her old French poodle. Then she arranged the dishes on her best china, cut the meat into bite-sized pieces, and served them to her closest friend, her dog.

She began serving early in the evening, letting Bill eat just as much or as little as he wanted from each dish. "This ought to wake up your senses, Bill." Indeed, Bill's interest was piqued. He ate, rested, ate a little more, of this dish and that. He went back to the leg of lamb, nibbling the bacon chestnuts off its sides. Wilhelmina kept gently urging him to eat. And as the evening wore on, Bill's old cataracted eyes gradually seemed to reflect something, it seemed, like quiet suffering—not his usual burden, but the luxurious suffering of the glutton. He had found a strength beyond himself, and so he kept bravely on, forcing himself to eat, until he could not swallow another bite and lay carefully beside the remains of his feast, and slept.

Wilhelmina sat quietly in a kitchen chair and watched from her window as the sun edged up behind the trees, red and molten like the swollen, dying star of an ancient world. She was so tired that her body felt weightless, as if she'd already left it hollow of her spirit. It seemed that she had lived such a long time. Howard had courted her in a horse-drawn wagon. An entire world of souls had disappeared in their time, and other nameless souls had filled their spaces. Some one of them had taken Howard's soul.

Bill had rolled onto his side in sleep, his tongue slack on the floor, his poor stomach as round and taut as a honeydew melon. After such a gorging, there normally would be hell to pay. But Wilhelmina would not allow that to happen.

"I'll take you to the doctor myself, old Bill," she said.

As if in response, a faint and easy dream-howl escaped Bill's throat, someone calling another in the big woods, across empty fields and deep silent stands of trees. *Ooooooo*, it went, high and soft. *Ooooooo*.

Wilhelmina's heart thickened with emotion. Her voice was deep and rich with it.

Hooooo, she called softly to Bill's sleeping ears.

Ooooooo, Bill called again, a little stronger, and she responded, *Hooooo*, their pure wordless language like echoes in the morning air.

UNCLE WILLEM

I REMEMBER UNCLE WILLEM FROM WHEN I WAS VERY YOUNG, how he would bring bushels of vegetables from his big garden he kept on their family's land in the country. I thought Willem was just a nice man with a funny, kind of nasal voice, a strangely rapid way of speaking, tall and slim with stooped posture, a large round Elmer Fudd bald head on top of a skinny neck. But then he disappeared at some point and when I asked about him, my mother said simply that he'd had to go into the hospital. Then when he came out, he had been prescribed some kind of heavy medication that had left him in an alternate reality all his own. I assume it was nice in there, quiet and peaceful, like sitting in a little boat by yourself in the middle of a small lake in the woods, with only birdsong and the occasional plop of a fish sucking a bug off the surface of the water breaking the breezy softness of that world. After all that, Uncle Willem mostly just sat around the house or in a chair on the porch, staring at nothing, like a terminal heavy-duty daydreamer. He didn't smile or frown. He dozed off a lot. The one time I went over to see him and Aunt Sadie with my mom, he didn't seem to recognize us. Aunt Sadie tried to make the best of it but just our being there, seeing him like that, made her tear up. So I never went over again, and my mom rarely went herself. Aunt Sadie blamed my father for Uncle

Willem's condition, and never forgave him, so she never visited our house. Uncle Willem died of a stroke a few years later. My mom said the doctors thought he had suffered from a kind of mild schizophrenia, and that only the heavy drugs he was taking kept him from being afraid all the time.

Afraid of what? I asked her.

Everything, I guess, she said.

It's too bad because although Uncle Willem had been a kind of a classic simpleton, he was also smart in lots of ways. No one could grow a vegetable and make a garden thrive like Uncle Willem. And his job as an accountant at the creosote plant was apparently as steady as it could be, since once Uncle Willem got himself lost in a mess of figures, you couldn't distract him. It was said that he never made a mistake, ever, in all the years he worked there. I imagine the owners of the creosote plant were almost as sorry to see Willem come to his sad end as we were.

Apparently all his funny gestures and way of speaking, his tendency to come into the house grunting under the weight of all the garden bounty he was bringing, to talk really fast to everyone for a brief while and then leave suddenly as if he were running away, or running to something, some very important errand like the rabbit in *Alice in Wonderland*—apparently, these were signs of his vulnerability. Then he went into his own rabbit hole and couldn't get out. In those days, most people did not understand the idea of someone having a vulnerable mind, one that could become terribly confused and lost if the wrong thing happened.

My father blamed himself for Uncle Willem losing his mind. He was fond of Uncle Willem, and loved talking to him, and thought his peculiarity, his tics, his apparently complete lack of self-consciousness, kind of childishly charming. He loved taking advantage of Uncle Willem's naivete in various ways. For instance, when Willem would come to the door unannounced to bring us some vegetables, my father would shush us and sneak us out the back door, sneak us around front to gather quietly around Willem's pickup truck while Willem stood at the door knocking and ringing the doorbell in a querulous way. Then, when Willem came slouching back to his truck, eyes down, shaking his round head back and forth in perplexity over both our vehicles being in the carport but no one home, he'd look up and see us and nearly fall over backwards in some kind of attack of astonishment, and start cussing, and then get embarrassed about that and apologize over and over for the rest of the time he was there, even through a piece of pie and cup of coffee, shaking his head and laughing at himself for being fooled yet again by the same old trick. My father loved it.

The coup de grâce came when my father and Willem were scheduled to go fishing one Sunday morning. Dad was to pick up Willem at four in the morning, and they would make it out to the pond by five, just before dawn, and catch a mess of bream that we would use for a great big fish and hush puppy fry that evening. The bream were on their beds so it was a sure thing. They were both excited. But my father was excited not just about the bream. He was also excited because of the ingenious trick he'd worked out to play on Willem. Part of its genius was that Willem was probably the only person it would work on.

Whenever they went fishing early in the morning like that (I'd gone along once or twice, just to enjoy sitting in the middle of the johnboat between them, wearing an orange life jacket that felt like a neck brace or something it was so poofed up, of course, watching them cast and listening to them crack jokes and tell stories), the routine was that my father would cut the lights before pulling into their driveway and walk quietly up to Uncle Willem and Aunt Sadie's bedroom window, and tap on the screen. This was to keep from disturbing Aunt Sadie, who loved her sleep, and it worked because Willem was such a light sleeper (I imagined him never really being asleep, but only in some kind of state just shy of his daytime or waking state of extremely attentive anxiety) that just a little tap or scratch on the window screen would wake him, which my father knew. A few minutes later Willem would come sneaking out to the car and wouldn't say a word until we were at least a block away from their house, because (I think) he believed if he spoke in his regular voice or even a whisper, even inside the car, somehow Sadie would hear it and wake up and be afraid before she remembered why he was gone and where he was going. Or she would be mad.

So, as my father told it, everything went as usual, the quiet pick-up, the silent drive out into the country to the little pond on Mom and Uncle Willem's family's old land, down the little dirt road, all in the dark, the two men sipping coffee my father had brought along in a thermos, with a paper sack of fried egg sandwiches wrapped in wax paper for later on, when they got hungry. They parked in their usual spot next to the bank near the dam, got their rods and reels from the back seat, found the john-boat and pulled it into the water, pushed off, and paddled out to the middle of the pond, where they usually fished in the deeper water until sunrise, when they would switch to fishing the shallows. There was a good moon up, so they could see pretty well.

They fished in the yellow glow of the moonlight for an hour or so. Then another hour or so. Uncle Willem began to get nervous. Ought to be getting light by now, he said at some point. My father didn't say anything, casting and cranking the jig back to the boat. Then he said, You're right, that's odd. He made a show of looking at his wristwatch in the moonlight. Damn, he said. It's seven o'clock in the morning. This is strange.

Uncle Willem, who never wore his watch when they went fishing (my father knew this), said, Damn! Seven o'clock in the goddamn morning? And the sun's not up? What the hell is going on, what's happening?

By the time another half hour had gone by, and it was still

full-on dark with a full moon still in the sky, Uncle Willem had become truly frightened. Was it the end of the world? Had the sun died, frozen over, and by midday everyone would be frozen to solid ice in a frozen world, like some outer planet? Or had we moved away and become an outer planet? Holy Christ, Mack! he said. It's the fucking end of the world!

Only then did my father let up, laughing, and tell him he'd tricked him by picking him up at midnight instead of four o'clock in the morning, and that it was really only three in the morning right then. But Willem couldn't calm down. He was shivering, and shouting out things that made no sense. He grabbed the oars, rowed them in, ran to the car, got in the back seat and curled up on himself, shivering and shaking and moaning and crying. My father drove them into town and made Uncle Willem look at the clock on the bank, which by then showed it was four in the morning, and even went by the bootlegger joint that stayed open all night and got a six-pack of beer and made Uncle Willem drink one to help calm him down. Normally Uncle Willem didn't drink, but he drank the beer and began to calm down a little bit, my dad trying to talk him down.

They drove out on a lonely country road with my dad talking to Willem the whole time, "saying things like you'd say to a frightened child," he told me later. The light finally started to come into the sky, and then the sun shone behind the trees to the east. Uncle Willem turned in his seat and stared at it, gripping the door at the open window with one hand and the dashboard with the other. And when the ball of the sun finally did rise up over the trees and cast its long yellow light fully over the land, Uncle Willem began to weep, sobbing like a wretched child into his hands. By the time my father took him home to Aunt Sadie, Willem was a man you'd think had just been through a horrific battle in war or an encounter with a monster of some kind, he was so shaken and pale. What in the world! Aunt Sadie said, and put him to bed. When my father confessed to her about his practical joke, she became furious and told him to get the hell out, he was a fool, and didn't he realize Willem wasn't the kind of man you could do that kind of thing to? She slammed the door in his face and never spoke to him again. Things would never be the same again between Aunt Sadie and my mother.

The only time I thought I might be experiencing the end of the world involved a slight overdose of psychedelic mushroom tea, but unlike with Uncle Willem, the tea high wore off and I felt all right again. I recognized the world again. But some people never do.

LAST DAYS OF THE DOG-MEN

WHEN I WAS A BOY MY FAMILY ALWAYS HAD HUNTING DOGS, always bird dogs, once a couple of blueticks, and for six years anywhere from six to fifteen beagles. But we never really got to where we liked to eat rabbit, and we tired of the club politics of hunting deer, so we penned up the beagles, added two black Labs, and figured we'd do a little duck.

Those were raucous days around the house, the big pen in the back with the beagles squawling, up on their hind legs against the fence, making noises like someone was cutting their tails off. It was their way. At night when I crept out into the yard they fell silent, their white necks exposed to the moon, their soft round eyes upon me. They made small, disturbed, guttural sounds like chickens.

Neighbors finally sent the old man to municipal court charged with something like disturbing the peace, and since my mother swore that anyway she'd never fry another rabbit, they looked like little bloody babies once skinned, she said, he farmed out the beagles and spent his Saturdays visiting this dog or that, out to Uncle Spurgeon's to see Jimbo, the best runner of the pack. Or out to Bud's rambling shack, where Bud lived with old Patsy and Balls, the breeder. They hollered like nuclear warning sirens when the old man drove up in his Ford.

After that he went into decline. He liked the Labs but never took much interest, they being already a hollow race of dog, the official dog of the middle class. He let them lounge around the porch under the ceiling fan and lope around the yard and the neighborhood, aimless loafers, and took to watching war movies on TV in his room, wandering through the house speaking to us like we were neighbors to hail, engage in small talk, and bid farewell. He was a man who had literally abandoned the hunt. He was of the generation that had moved to the city. He was no longer a man who lived among dogs.

It wasn't long after that I moved out anyway and got married to live with Lois in a dogless suburban house, a quiet world that seemed unanchored somehow, half inhabited, pale and blank, as if it would one day dissolve to fog, lines blurring, and seep away into air, as indeed it would. We bought a telescope and spent some nights in the yard tracking the cold lights of the stars and planets, looking for patterns, never suspecting that here were the awful bloody secrets of the ancient human heart and that every generation must flesh them out anew. Humans are aware of very little, it seems to me, the artificial brainy side of life, the worries and bills and the mechanisms of jobs, the dolt-ish psychologies we've placed over our lives like a stencil. A dog keeps his life simple and unadorned. He is who he is, and his only task is to assert this. If he desires the company of another dog, or if he wishes to mate, things can get a little complex. But the ways of settling such things are established and do not change. And when they are settled and he is home from his wandering he may have a flickering moment, a sort of Pick-ett's Charge across the synaptic field toward reflection. But the moment passes. And when it passes it leaves him with a vague disquietude, a clear nose that on a good night could smell the lingering presence of men on the moon, and the rest of the day ahead of him like a canyon.

———

WHICH IS HOW I'VE TRIED to view the days I've spent here in this old farmhouse where I'm staying with my friend Harold in the country. I'm on extended leave of absence from the *Journal*. But it's no good. It's impossible to bring that sort of order and clarity to a normal human life.

The farmhouse is a wreck floating on the edge of a big untended pasture where the only activities are the occasional squadron of flaring birds dropping from sight into the tall grass, and the creation of random geometric paths the nose-down dogs make tracking the birds. The back porch has a grand view of the field, and when weather permits we sit on the porch and smoke cigarettes and sip coffee in the mornings, beer in the afternoons, often good scotch at night. At midday, there's horseshoes.

There's also Phelan Holt, a mastiff of a man, whom Harold met at the Blind Horse Bar and Grill and allowed to rent a room in the house's far corner. We don't see a great deal of Phelan, who came down here from Ohio to teach poetry at the women's college. He once played linebacker for a small college in the Midwest, and then took his violent imagination to the page and published a book of poems about the big subjects: God, creation, the confusion of the animals, and the bloody concoction of love. He pads along a shiny path he's made through the dust to the kitchen for food and drink, and then pads back, and occasionally comes out to the porch to drink bourbon and to give us brief, elliptical lectures on the likes of Isaac Babel, Rilke, and Cervantes, gently smoking a joint which he does not share. In spite of his erudition, thick, balding Phelan is very much a moody old dog. He lives alone with others, leaves to conduct his business, speaks very little, eats moderately, and is generally inscrutable.

One day Harold proposed to spend the afternoon fishing for bream. We got into the truck and drove through a couple of pastures and down an old logging road through a patch of woods to a narrow cove that spread out into the broad sunlit surface of a lake. The sun played on thin rippling lines that spread from the small heads of snapping turtles and water moccasins moving now and then like sticks in a current.

Harold pulled a johnboat from the willows and rowed us out. We fished the middle, dropping our baits over what Harold said was the old streambed where a current of cooler water ran through down deep. The water was a dark coppery stain, like thin coffee. We began to pull up a few bluegill and crappie, and Phelan watched them burst from the water, broad flat gold and silver, and curl at the end of the line, their eyes huge. They flopped crazily in the bottom of the boat, drowning in the thin air. Phelan set down his pole and nipped at a half pint of bourbon he'd pulled from his pocket.

"Kill it," he said, looking away from my bluegill.

"I can't stand to watch it struggling for air." His eyes followed the tiny heads of moccasins moving silently across the surface, turtles lumbering onto half-submerged logs. "Those things will eat your fish right off the stringer," he said. He drank from the little bottle again and then in his best old-fashioned pedagogical manner said, "Do we merely project the presence of evil upon God's creatures, in which case we are inherently evil and the story of the garden a ruse, or is evil absolute?"

From his knapsack he produced a pistol, a Browning .22 semiautomatic that looked like a German Luger, and set it on his lap. He pulled out a sandwich and ate it slowly. Then he shucked a round into the gun's chamber and sighted down on one of the turtles and fired, the sharp report flashing off the water into the trees. What looked like a puff of smoke spiffed from the turtle's back and it tumbled from the log. "It's off a little to the right," he said. He aimed at a moccasin head crossing at the opposite bank and fired. The water jumped in front of the snake, which stopped, and Phelan quickly tore up the water where the head was with three quick shots. The snake disappeared. Silence, in the wake of the loud hard crack of the pistol, came back to our ears in shock waves over the water. "Hard to tell if you've hit them when they're swimming," he said, looking down the length of the barrel as if for flaws, lifting his hooded eyes to survey the water's surface for more prey.

HAROLD HIMSELF IS SORT OF LIKE a garment drawn from the irregular bin: off-center, unique, a little tilted on his axis. If he were a dog, I'd call him an unbrushed collie who carries himself like a chocolate Lab. He has two actual dogs, a big blond hound named Otis and a bird dog named Ike. Like Phelan, Otis is a socialized dog and gets to come into the house to sleep, whereas Ike must stay outside on the porch. At first I could not understand why Otis received this privilege and Ike did not, but in time I began to see.

Every evening after supper when he is home, Harold gets up from the table and lets in Otis, who sits beside the table and looks at Harold, watching Harold's hands. Harold's hands pinching off a last bite of cornbread and nibbling on it, Harold's hands pulling a Camel cigarette out of the pack, Harold's hands twiddling with the matches. And soon, as if he isn't really thinking of it, in the middle of talking about something else and not even seeming to plan to do it, Harold will pick up a piece of meat scrap and let it hover over the plate for a minute, talking, and you'll see Otis get alert and begin to quiver almost unnoticeably. And then Harold will look at Otis and maybe say, "Otis, stay." And Otis's eyes will cut just for a second to Harold's and then snatch back to the meat scrap, maybe having to chomp his jaws together to suck saliva, his eyes glued to the meat scrap. And then Harold will gently lower the meat scrap onto the top of Otis's nose and then slowly take away his hand, saying, "Stay. Stay. Stay. Otis. Stay." Crooning it real softly. And Otis with his eyes cross-eyed looking at the meat scrap on his nose, quivering almost unnoticeably and not daring to move, and then Harold leans back and takes another Camel out of the pack, and if Otis slowly moves just an eighth of an inch, saying, "Otis. Stay." And then lighting the cigarette and then looking at Otis for a second and then saying, "All right, Otis." And quicker than you can see it Otis has not so much tossed the scrap up in the air as he has removed his nose from its position, the meat scrap suspended, and before it can begin to respond to gravity Otis has snatched it into his mouth and swallowed it and is looking at Harold's hands again with the same look as if nothing has happened between them at all and he is hoping for his first scrap.

This is the test, Harold says. If you balance the meat scrap, and in a moment of grace manage to eat the meat scrap, you are in. If you drop the meat scrap and eat it off of the floor, well, you're no better than a dog. Out you go.

But the thing I was going to tell at first is about Ike, about how when Otis gets let in and Ike doesn't, Ike starts barking outside the door, big woofing barks, loud complaints, thinking (Harold says), Why is he letting in Otis and not me? Let me IN. IN. And he continues his barking for some couple of minutes or so, and then, without your really being able to put your finger on just how it happens, the bark begins to change, not so much a complaint as a demand, I am IKE, let me IN, because what is lost you see is the memory of Otis having been let in first and that being the reason for complaint. And from there he goes to his more common generic statement, voiced simply because Ike is Ike and needs no reason for saying it, I am IKE, and then it changes in a more noticeable way, just IKE, as he loses contact with his ego, soon just Ike!, tapering off, and in a minute it's just a bark every now and then, just a normal call into the void the way dogs do, yelling HEY every now and then and seeing if anyone responds across the pasture, HEY, and then you hear Ike circle and drop himself onto the porch floorboards just outside the kitchen door. And this, Harold says, is a product of Ike's consciousness, that before he can even finish barking Ike has forgotten what he's barking about, so he just lies down and goes to sleep. And this, Harold says, as if the meat scrap test needs corroboration, is why Ike can't sleep indoors and Otis can.

THE OTHER DAY, HAROLD SAT IN A CHAIR in front of his bedroom window, leaned back, and put his feet on the sill, and the whole window, frame and all, fell out into the weeds with a crash. I helped him seal the hole with polyethylene sheeting and duct tape and now there's a filtered effect to the light in the room that's quite nice on cool late afternoons.

There are clothes in the closets here, we don't know who they belong to. The front room and the dark attic are crammed with junk. Old space heaters in a pile in one corner, a big wooden canoe (cracked) with paddles, a set of barbells made from truck axles and wheel rims, a seamstress dummy with nipples painted on the breasts, some great old cane fly rods not too limber anymore, a big wooden Motorola radio, a rope ladder, a box of *Life* magazines, and a big stack of yellow newspapers from Mobile. And lots of other junk too numerous to name.

All four corners of the house slant toward the center, the back of the foyer being the floor's lowest point. You put a golf ball on the floor at any point in the house and it'll roll its way eventually, bumping lazily into baseboards and doors and discarded shoes and maybe a baseball mitt or a rolled-up rug slumped against the wall, to that low spot in the tall empty foyer where there's a power-line spool heaped with wadded old clothes like someone getting ready for a yard sale cleaned out some dresser drawers and disappeared. The doors all misfit their frames, and on gusty mornings I have awakened to the dry tick and skid of dead leaves rolling under the gap at the bottom of the front door and into the foyer, rolling through the rooms like little tumbleweeds, to collect in the kitchen, where then in ones and twos and little groups they skitter out the open door to the backyard and on out across the field. It's a pleasant way to wake up, really. Sometimes I hang my head over the side of the big bed I use, the one with four rough-barked cedar logs for posts and which Harold said the mice used before I moved in, and I'll see this big old skink with pink spots on his slick black hide hunting along the crevice between the baseboard and the floor. His head disappears into the crevice, and he draws it out again chewing something, his long lipless jaws chomping down.

The house doors haven't seen a working lock in thirty or forty years. Harold never really thinks about security, though the bums walking on the road to Florida pass by here all the time and probably used this as a motel before Harold found it out here abandoned on his family's land and became an expatriate from town because, he says, he never again wants to live anywhere he can't step out onto the back porch and take a piss day or night.

The night I showed up looking for shelter I just opened up the front door because no one answered and I didn't know if Harold was way in the back of the big old house (he was) or what. I entered the foyer, and first I heard a clicking sound and Otis came around the corner on his toes, claws tapping, his tail high, with a low growl. And then Harold walked in behind him, his rusty old .38 in his hand. He sleeps with it on a bookshelf not far from his bed, the one cheap bullet he owns next to the gun if it hasn't rolled off onto the floor.

The night that Phelan arrived to stay, fell through the door onto his back, and lay there looking up into the shadows of the high old foyer, Otis came clicking in and approached him slowly, hackles raised, lips curling fluidly against his old teeth, until his nose was just over Phelan's. And then he jumped back barking savagely when Phelan burst out like some slurring old thespian, "There plucking at his throat a great black beast shaped like a hound, 'The Hound!' cried Holmes, 'Great Heavens!' half animal half demon, its eyes aglow its muzzles and hackles and dewlap outlined in flickering flame."

"Phelan," Harold said, "meet Otis."

"Cerberus, you mean," Phelan said, "my twelfth labor." He raised his arms and spread his fingers before his eyes. "I have only my hands."

HOW HAROLD CAME TO BE ALONE is this: Sophia, a surveyor for the highway department, fixed her sights on Harold and took advantage of his ways by drinking with him till two a.m. and then offering to drive him home, where she would put him to bed and ride him like a cowgirl. She told me this herself one night, and asked me to feel her thighs, which were hard and bulging as an ice skater's under her jeans. "I'm strong," she whispered in my ear, cocking an eyebrow.

One evening, after she'd left, Harold stumbled out onto the porch where I sat smoking, bummed a cigarette, braced an arm against a porch post, and stood there taking a long piss out into the yard. He didn't say anything. He was naked. His hair was like a sheaf of windblown wheat against the moonlight coming down on the field and cutting a clean line of light along the edge of the porch. His pale body blue in that light. He kept standing there, his stream arcing out into the yard, sprayed to the east in the wind, breathing through his nose and smoking the cigarette with the smoke whipping away. There was a storm trying to blow in. I didn't have to say anything. You always know when you're close to out of control.

Sophia left paraphernalia around for Harold's fiancée Westley to find. Pairs of panties under the bed, a silky camisole slumped like a prostitute between two starched dress shirts in Harold's closet, a vial of fingernail polish in the silverware tray. It wasn't long before Westley walked out of the bathroom one day with a black brassiere, saying, "What's this thing doing hanging on the commode handle?" And it was pretty much over between Westley and Harold after that.

I must say that Sophia, who resembled a greyhound with her long nose and close-set eyes and her tremendous thighs, is the bridge between Harold's story and mine.

Because at first I wasn't cheating on Lois. Things had become distant in the way they do after a marriage struggles through passionate possessive love and into the heartbreak of languishing love, before the vague incestuous love of the long-together. I got home one night when Lois and I were still together, heard something scramble on the living-room floor, and looked over to see this trembling thing shaped like a drawn bow, long needle-nose face looking at me as if over reading glasses, nose down, eyes up, cowed. He was aging. I eased over to him and pulled back ever so softly when as I reached my hand over he showed just a speck of white tooth along his black lip.

"I read that story in the *Journal* about them, and what happens to them when they can't race anymore," she said. She'd simply called up the dog track, gone out to a kennel, and taken her pick.

She said since he was getting old, maybe he wouldn't be hard to control, and besides, she thought maybe I missed having a dog. It was an attempt, I guess, to make a connection. Or it was the administration of an opiate. I don't really know.

To exercise Spike, the retired greyhound, and to encourage a friendship between him and me, Lois had the two of us, man and dog, take up jogging. We'd go to the high school track, and Spike loved it. He'd trot about on the football field, snuffling here and there. Once he surprised and caught a real rabbit, and tore it to pieces. It must have brought back memories of his training days. You wouldn't think a racing dog could be like a pet dog, foolish and simple and friendly. But Spike was okay. We were pals. And then, after all the weeks it took Spike and me to get back into shape, and after the incidental way in which my affair with Imelda down the street began out of our meeting and jogging together around the otherwise empty track, after weeks of capping our jog with a romp on the foam-rubber pole vault mattress just beyond the goalposts, Lois bicycled down to get me one night and rode silently up as Imelda and I lay naked except for our jogging shoes on the pole vault mattress, cooling down, Spike curled up at our feet. As she glided to a stop on the bicycle, Spike raised his head and wagged his tail. Seeing his true innocence, I felt a heavy knot form in my chest. When Lois just as silently turned the bicycle and pedaled away, Spike rose, stretched, and followed her home. Imelda and I hadn't moved. "Oh, shit," Imelda said. "Well, I guess it's all over." Imelda merely meant our affair, since her husband was a Navy dentist on a cruise in the Mediterranean, which had put Imelda temporarily in her parents' hometown, temporarily writing features for the *Journal*, and temporarily having an affair with me. It was Imelda's story on greyhounds that Lois had seen. It was Imelda who said she wanted to meet Spike, and it was I who knew exactly how this would go and gave in to the inexorable flow of it, combining our passive wills toward this very moment. And it was I who had to go home to Lois now that my marriage was ruined.

IMELDA LEFT, AND I LAY THERE awhile looking up at the stars. It was early October, and straight up I could see the bright clusters of Perseus, Cassiopeia, Cepheus, Cygnus, and off to the right broad Hercules, in his flexing stance. I remembered how Lois and I used to make up constellations: There's my boss, she'd say, scratching his balls. There's Reagan's brain, she'd say. Where? The dim one. Where? That was the joke. Looking up at night usually made me feel as big as the sky, but now I felt like I was floating among them and lost. I got up and started the walk home. There was a little chill in the air, and the drying sweat tightened my skin. I smelled Imelda on my hands and wafting up from my shorts.

The door was unlocked. The lamp was on in the corner of the living room. The night-light was on in the hallway. I took off my running shoes and walked quietly down the hallway to the bedroom. I could see in the dim light that Lois was in bed, either asleep or pretending to be, facing the wall, her back to the doorway, the covers pulled up to her ears. She was still.

From my side of the bed, Spike watched me sleepily, stretched out, his head resting on his paws. I don't imagine I'd have had the courage to climb into bed and beg forgiveness, anyway. But seeing Spike already there made things clearer, and I crept back out to the den and onto the couch. I curled up beneath a small lap blanket and only then exhaled, breathing very carefully.

When I awoke stiff and guilty the next morning, Lois and Spike were gone. Some time around midafternoon, she came home alone. She was wearing a pair of my old torn jeans and a baggy flannel shirt and a Braves cap pulled down over her eyes. We didn't speak. I went out into the garage and cleaned out junk that had been there for a couple of years, hauled it off to the dump in the truck, then came in and showered. I smelled something delicious cooking in the kitchen. When I'd dressed and come out of the bedroom, the house was lighted only by a soft flickering from the dining room. Lois sat at her end of the table alone, eating. She paid me no attention as I stood in the doorway.

"Lois," I said. "Where's Spike?"

She cut a piece of pork roast and chewed for a moment. Her hair was wet and combed straight back off her forehead. She wore eye makeup, bringing out the depth and what I have only a few times truly recognized as the astonishing beauty of her deep green eyes. Her polished nails glistened in the candlelight.

The table was set with our good china and silver and a very nice meal. She seemed like someone I'd only now just met, whom I'd walked in on by her own design. She looked at me, and my heart sank, and the knot that had formed in my chest the night before began to dissolve into sorrow.

"He was getting pretty old," she said. She took a sip of wine, which was an expensive bottle we'd saved for a special occasion. "I had him put to sleep."

I'M SURPRISED AT HOW OFTEN dogs make the news. There was the one about the dog elected mayor of a town in California. And another about a dog that could play the piano, I believe he was a schnauzer. More often, though, they're involved in criminal cases—dog bitings, dog pack attacks on children. I've seen several stories about dogs who shoot their masters. There was one of these in the stack of old *Mobile Registers* in the front room. "Dog Shoots, Kills Master," the headline read. Way back in '59. How could you not read a story like that? The man carried his shotguns in his car. He stopped to talk to his relative on the road and let the dogs run. When his relative walked on, the man called his dogs. One of them jumped into the back seat and hit the trigger on a gun, which discharged and struck him "below the stomach," the article said. The man hollered to his relative, "I'm shot!" and fell over in the ditch.

There was another article called "Death Row Dog," about a dog that had killed so many cats in his neighborhood that a judge sentenced him to death. And another one sentenced to be moved to the country or die, just because he barked so much. There was another one like that just this year, about a condemned biter that won a last-minute reprieve. I'm told in medieval times animals were regularly put on trial, with witnesses and testimony and so forth. But it is relatively rare today.

One story, my favorite, was headlined "Dog Lady Claims Close Encounter." It was about an old woman who lived alone with about forty-two dogs. Strays were drawn to her house, whereupon they disappeared from the streets forever. At night, when sirens passed on the streets of the town, a great howling rose from inside her walls. Then one day, the dogs' barking kept on and on, raising a racket like they'd never done before. It went on all day, all that night, and was still going the next day. People passing the house on the sidewalk heard things slamming against the doors, saw dog claws scratching at the windowpanes, teeth gnawing at the sashes. Finally, the police broke in. Dogs burst through the open door never to be seen again. Trembling skeletons, who wouldn't eat their own kind, crouched in the corners, behind chairs. Dog shit everywhere, the stench was awful. They found dead dogs in the basement freezer, little shit dogs whole and bigger ones cut up into parts. Police started looking around for the woman's gnawed-up corpse, but she was nowhere to be found.

At first they thought the starving dogs had eaten her up: clothes, skin, hair, muscle, and bone. But then, four days later, some hunters found her wandering naked out by a reservoir, all scratched up, disoriented.

She'd been abducted, she said, and described tall creatures with the heads of dogs, who licked her hands and sniffed her privates.

"They took me away in their ship," she said. "On the dog star, it's them that owns us. These here," she said, sweeping her arm about to indicate Earth, "they ain't nothing compared to them dogs."

ON A WARM AFTERNOON IN NOVEMBER, a beautiful breezy Indian summer day, the wind steered Lois somehow in her Volkswagen up to the house. She'd been driving around. I got a couple of beers from the fridge and we sat out back sipping them, not talking. Then we sat there looking at each other for a little while. We drank a couple more beers. A rosy sun ticked down behind the old grove on the far side of the field and light softened, began to blue. The dogs' tails moved like periscopes through the tall grass.

"Want to walk?" I said.

"Okay."

The dogs trotted up as we climbed through the barbed-wire fence, then bounded ahead, leaping like deer over stands of grass. Lois stopped out in the middle of the field and slipped her hands in the pockets of my jeans.

"I missed you," she said. She shook her head. "I sure as hell didn't want to."

"Well," I said. "I know." Anger over Spike rose in me then, but I held my tongue. "I missed you, too," I said. She looked at me with anger and desire.

We knelt down. I rolled in the grass, flattening a little bed. We attacked each other. Kissing her, I felt like I wanted to eat her alive. I took big soft bites of her breasts, which were heavy and smooth. She gripped my waist with her nails, pulled hard at me, kicked my ass with her heels, bit my shoulders, and pulled my hair so hard I cried out. After we'd caught our breath, she pushed me off of her like a sack of feed corn.

We lay on our backs. The sky was empty. It was all we could see, with the grass so high around us. We didn't talk for a while, and then Lois began to tell me what had happened at the vet's. She told me how she'd held Spike while the vet gave him the injection.

"I guess he just thought he was getting more shots," she said. "Like when I first took him in."

She said Spike was so good, he didn't fight it. He looked at her when she placed her hands on him to hold him down. He was frightened and didn't wag his tail. And she was already starting to cry, she said. The vet asked her if she was sure this was what she wanted to do. She nodded her head. He gave Spike the shot.

She was crying as she told me this.

"He laid down his head and closed his eyes," she said. "And then, with my hands on him like that, I tried to pull him back to me. Back to us." She said, No, Spike, don't go. She pleaded with him not to die. The vet was upset and said some words to her and left the room in anger, left her alone in her grief. And when it was over, she had a sense of not knowing where she was for a moment. Sitting on the floor in there alone with the strong smell of flea killer and antiseptic, and the white of the floor and walls and the stainless steel of the examination table where Spike had died and where he lay now, and in that moment he was every-thing she had ever loved.

She drained the beer can, wiping her eyes. She took a deep breath and let it out slowly. "I just wanted to hurt you. I didn't realize how much it would hurt me."

She shook her head.

"And now I can't forgive you," she said. "Or me."

IN THE OLD DAYS WHEN HAROLD was still with Westley and I was still with Lois, Harold had thrown big cookout parties. He had a pit we'd dug for slow-cooking whole pigs, a brick grill for chickens, and a smoker made from an old oil drum. So one crisp evening late in bird season, to reestablish some of the old joy of life, Harold set up another one and a lot of our old friends and acquaintances came. Then Phelan showed up, drunk, with the head of a pig he'd bought at the slaughterhouse. He'd heard you could buy the head of a pig and after an afternoon at the Blind Horse he thought it would be interesting bring one to the barbecue. He insisted on putting it into the smoker, so it would have made a scene to stop him. Every half hour or so, he opened the lid with a flourish and checked the head. The pig's eyelids shrank and opened halfway; the eyes turned translucent. Its hide leaked beaded moisture and turned a doughy pale. People lost their appetites. Many became quiet and left. "I'm sorry," Phelan stood on the porch and announced as they left, stood there like Marc Antony in Shakespeare. "No need to go. I've come to bury this pig, not to eat him."

Finally Harold took the pig's head from the smoker and threw it out onto the far edge of the yard, and Phelan stood over it a minute, reciting some lines from Tennyson. Ike and Otis went sniffing up, sniffing, their eyes like brown marbles. They backed off and sat just outside of the porch light and watched the pig's head steaming in the grass as if it had dropped screaming through the atmosphere and plopped into the yard, an alien thing, now cooling, a new part of the landscape, a new mystery evolving, a new thing in the world, there whenever they rounded the corner, still there, stinking and mute, until Harold buried it out in the field. After that we pretty much kept to ourselves.

We passed our winter boarded up in the house, the cracks beneath doors and around windows and in the walls stuffed with old horse blankets and newspaper and wads of clothing falling apart at the seams, the space heaters hissing in the tall-ceilinged rooms. We went out for whiskey and dry goods and meat, occasionally stopped by the Blind Horse of an early afternoon, but spent our evenings at home. We wrote letters to those we loved and missed and planned spring reunions when possible. Harold's once-illicit lover, Sophia the surveyor, came by a few times. I wrote Lois, but received no reply. I wrote to my editor at the *Journal* and asked to return in the late spring, but it may be that I should move on.

It is March just now, when the ancients sacrificed young dogs and men to the crop and mixed the blood with the corn. Harold is thinking of planting some beans. We've scattered the astonished heads of bream in the soil, mourning doves in their beautiful lidded repose. The blood of the birds and the fishes, and the seeds of the harvest. I found the skin of our resident chicken snake, shed and left on the hearth. He's getting ready to move outside. The days are warming, and though it's still cool in the evenings we stay out late in the backyard, sipping Harold's Famous Grouse to stay warm, trying in our hearts to restore a little order to the world. I'm hoping to be out here at least until midnight, when Canis Major finally descends in the west, having traveled of an evening across the southern horizon. It rises up before sunset and glows bright above the pastures at dusk, big bright Sirius the first star in the sky, to wish upon for a fruitful planting. It stirs me to look up at them, all of them, not just this one, stirs me beyond my own enormous sense of personal disappointment. And Harold, in his cups, calls Otis over and strikes a pose: "Orion, the hunter," he says, "and his Big Dog." Otis, looking up at him, strikes the pose, too: Is there something out there? Will we hunt? Harold holds the pose, and Otis trots out into the field, restless, snuffling. I can feel the earth turning beneath us, rolling beneath the stars. Looking up, I lose my balance and fall back flat in the grass.

If the Grouse lasts we'll stay out till dawn, when the stellar dog and hunter are off tracing the histories of other worlds, the cold distant figures of the hero Perseus and his love Andromeda fading in the morning glow into nothing.

And then we will stumble into the falling-down house and to our beds. And all our dreams will roll toward the low point in the center of the house and pool there together, mingling in the drafts under the doors with last year's crumbling leaves and the creeping skinks and the dreams of the dogs, who must dream of the chase, the hunt, of bitches in heat, the mingling of old spoors with their own musty odors. And deep in sleep they dream of space travel, of dancing on their hind legs, of being men with the heads and muzzles of dogs, of sleeping in beds with sheets, of driving cars, of taking their fur coats off each night and making love face-to-face. Of cooking their food. And Harold and I dream of days of following the backs of men's knees, and faint trails in the soil, the overpowering odors of all our kin, our pasts, every mistake as strong as sulfur, our victories lingering traces here and there. The house is disintegrating into dust. The end of all of this is near.

Just yesterday Harold went into the kitchen for coffee and found the chicken snake curled around the warm pot. Otis went wild. Harold whooped. The screams of Sophia the surveyor rang high and clear and regular, and in my half-sleep I could only imagine the source of this dissonance filling the air. Oh, slay me and scatter my parts in the field. The house was hell. And Ike, too, baying—out on the porch—full-lunged, without memory or sense, with only the barking of Otis to clue his continuing: already lost within his own actions, forgetting his last conscious needs.

APOLOGY

I'VE BEEN HERE IN THE DESERT, IN THIS LITTLE TOWN, FOR
two months now. I don't know if you would like it out here on the
high southwestern plains but I suspect not. Such windblown open
spaces. The trees in town give way to endless arid prairie. The
constant passage of long, loud trains, busy, muscular, saddening.

I know our little boy would like that, at least. The trains.

Yesterday, along the tracks west of town, the Union Pacific
boomed down with five engines and three hundred double-
stacked cars. Six hundred cars, if a piggyback is two. You can
believe that or not.

The mares and foals were gone from their pasture. Eight large
crows flew from the cistern there, silent, blown by the southwest
gray-blue wind.

A pronghorn stood alone on the hill, just inside the barbed
wire fence, alert and anxious, making that strange call they make.
Like a wind-up party favor, or the stripped gears of a lawnmower
crank yanked hard and whirring sharp and short. A cough from
rusting metal lungs.

Farther down, on the tracks' north side, another pronghorn
sprawled out dead in a dusty two-track road, eyes and tongue
hollowed, devoured by flies, still swarming. Something had
yanked his colon out and left it two feet from the carcass, the

round cavity beneath his tail empty and wet with bright fresh blood. A strange mutilation. No obvious sign he was hit by the train, or shot, or chased and torn apart by lion or coyote or some extraordinarily numerous murder of crows. Only the bloody colon, and the coat along each side of his spine roughly shorn, as if grazed by the sharp front teeth of his own kind.

Pronghorn, jackrabbit, horses, crows. Trains, clouds, the occasional car. You rarely see people if you don't go downtown. Which is good.

I SPEND ALL MY TIME at this house I occupy up on the hill, or walking the trail out into the desert along the railroad tracks, or at the liquor store or grocery store, or drunk and wandering one of the desolate dirt tracks spurring from town into the prairie. All else is gone, like the pronghorn, like the little bird I will tell you about, like my former ambition, which now seems to have been tied far too closely to a lack of imagination, so, gone.

I did make a friend, Marie, who works in the coffee shop in town. This is not her great ambition. Like a lot of people here, she's lying low for a while. She does occasional favors for the movie people who are in town making, of course, a movie. The regular movie people live in the motel. The big shots and stars rent estates and have their personal assistants plus special assistants who live in this town. Marie is sometimes one of those.

In fact, we met when I went into the coffee shop where Marie works, and she mistook me for a movie person because I was a new face in town. We laughed about that and I got a free coffee. Should I have been flattered to be mistaken for a movie person, or is it just that movie people, everyone except the most famous or the prettiest actors, look like ordinary people out of their element?

Marie even has a sense of humor, in her own way, about her cancer. She still calls it her cancer even though it's officially gone. She says it's like a bad boyfriend—you never know when he might show up again, asleep or passed out there, in the back-yard, but alive. I went over to her house for dinner, and she didn't mind talking about her cancer, or her boyfriend who had a harder time with her cancer than she did, or how long she will stay here before going back to civilization, which for her is California, and how nice it was to spend time with a man (me) without all that shit going on. Infatuation, sex, anticipation. We sat in her backyard, in dim starlight. She gave me a little whiskey to sip on, although she doesn't drink, herself. Not good for the immune system.

I said, I hope you don't mind if I go on being an alcoholic for the time being.

She said that she could understand that, wouldn't judge me for it.

So she poured me another drink. She's a good and beautiful person. I'm glad I'm not in love with her. Although her name means "bitter," she is anything but that.

I remember when I said to you, a bit shocked, You want me to stop at just two drinks before dinner? And you said, One would be best. Inconceivable at the time. Your pragmatic sister, staying with us then, suggested we could save money if I stopped drink-ing, and I replied quite righteously that for God's sake I drank the cheapest stuff I could stand. Your father, on the telephone before he passed, said gently, Take it easy on the booze, buddy, okay? That kind of broke my heart but not enough. Because I was thinking, That fucking sharp-tailed Gordon's martini is my only friend in the hard-slanting light of the afternoon through the casement windows of our beautiful old home after another day of nodding my head and writing down everything this or that windbag said to me so that I could translate it into a paean to his supposed innovative intelligence and distribute said propaganda to the world. Public relations, so to speak. Not a good career for

a misanthrope. Writing that nasty, acidic book about public relations was my only means of escape. I've made one hundred and
twenty-two thousand dollars and seventy-seven cents on advance
and royalties but there's not much left, so I found this old, abandoned house on the south end of town and quietly moved in.
Unless or until someone objects, I claim squatter's rights. Most
of the windows are sheets of plastic stapled onto casings, though
a few are intact and give a view of downtown and the prairie.
No power, so I use kerosene lamps. A paid-for Port-a-John out
back. An oil drum that catches rare rainwater that I pipe in to the
shower and toilet using PVC and simple lawn faucets. A plastic
farm water tank in case the oil drum goes dry. A doorless wood
stove that was already here. An old fridge converted to an ice
box. A mangy sofa and a little table and a chair and Nikon binoculars that belonged to my dead father who, as I recall, never
used them. Neither do I.

Did I ever tell you about the day I took a break from the office
and went for a tall cup of ice water at the café across the street
and sat on the patio there drinking it through a straw, thinking
bitterly that things would never change, I'd never get out of that
job, and walking across the street I refused to yield to a car that
would not yield to my crossing and so, seeing the driver's window down and without losing stride, I casually tossed the remains
of my water through the window and *kersplash* caught the son of
a bitch right in the face? That felt good. The kersplashed fellow
wheeled around and pulled up beside me, red-faced, shaking,
and said, If you ever do that again (I was thinking, What are the
odds?), I'll take my 9mm and blow you fucking away. I leaned on
his driver's door and said, very calmly, Well that would be two
strikes against you, given that I had the right-of-way. Then the
young man (he was very young) banged his fists on the steering
wheel, nearly losing control of his car, nearly crashing, before
roaring away. Did I tell you about that? I must have, unless by

that time I was only really speaking to my friend Gordon's London Dry Gin.

I recall that in the afternoons, roughly an hour or half an hour before it was time to go home from that job, in the passageway between the receptionist station and my little office, I would experience these strange and amusing olfactory hallucinations, as if the air in that passage were infused with the sharp scent of juniper berries. When I told this story to my new friend Marie, she laughed, then apologized. What is her actual ambition, you say? I think it is 1) to keep on living, and 2) to enjoy it.

Unlike us in that dream I had last night, when we were in some great hall in the New York Public Library where I'd given a speech and you were half-drunk on white wine, raging through the place, having finally had enough, the halls ringing with the sound of your anger, telling everyone that it was you I was talking about in that speech, you were the source of all this fucking pseudo-fame, and then I could not find my voice at all, no matter how fine the quality of the earphones they found and placed upon my head—I could not even keep them in place, they kept dislodging and becoming ineffective as I watched you raging up this staircase or that, hair and skirt flying as if in the wind, and all the library ladies and gentlemen horrified and helpless over who to go to for help, much less who to blame for the whole terrifying business.

THIS MORNING, A SMALL BIRD flew into one of the remaining windowpanes and fell stunned into the Stipa grass, one wing awry, so small and light that the tuft it lay on did not bend to the ground. A look of astonished befuddlement in its eyes. There you go, I said to it, halfway hammered, myself, at 11 a.m., that's it all right.

I picked it up, no alarm or struggle. I stroked the purple feathers on its tiny skull, about the size of a chickpea. I gently pressed the skewed right wing into a proper fold against its side. Bird in open hand, I walked into the weedy backyard, to the bench beside the crumbling barbeque pit. I held it up to the fruitcake feeder, at which it cocked its head and flinched. We walked to the old iron birdbath and took that in. We walked to the seedcake feeder and checked that out. We sat at the leaning picnic table beneath the leaning trellis covered with some kind of climbing vine, and soon the bird began to look around. When a big dove flew up, fanned, and flew away from our surprise presence, the little bird startled and crouched against my palm and curled its left talon into the crevice between two of my fingers and began to watch the bolder, closer flights of red finches and sparrows flicking in to the fruitcake feeder. Flycatchers alighting on the tops of the pecan tree rising golden green in the yellow light of late morning. A crow cranking by at an angle overhead like a shadow or memory.

This bird was mystified. I believe it suffered amnesia. I think it had forgotten not only that it was a bird, but also that there are birds in the world. I believe it thought, like Adam, that it had awakened from a scattering of inanimate particles into a collection, which, possibly, was similar to these wild things flicking and fluttering and chittering and cooing with such supreme confidence. I suppose if this bird had religion, it might've assumed that I was God. Its bird descendants, distorting the story over years, would eventually see it that way. And then one day, when I was very old, they would have to kill me.

Was Adam's first thought, looking around and blinking, surrounded by birdsong, that these creatures were the embodied voices of God?

As I was distracted, dreaming, the bird flew from my hand and into a bush behind the seedcake feeder. He perched there on a slim branch swayed by the breeze for another few minutes. A bold dove grabbed onto the fruitcake feeder, a look of defiance in his eye, and when I looked back the little bird was gone.

I know that my love for birds is one of the few things you truly loved about me. As opposed to my birdlike indifference to your unhappiness. Although you will recall the time, when we lived in our old house near downtown, the little brown female cardinal went mad, and her mate followed her from perch to perch, circling the house, bush to bush to little tree, chirping in what seemed such obvious distress. It may have been some cat had robbed their nest, devoured their hatchlings. But we preferred to think she had gone mad, the way people sometimes do, for no reason.

I DROVE WEST OUT OF TOWN on the highway, through a commotion of trucks and cars and lights and cameras and cables and movie people on the side of the road, fucking around the way they seem to always be doing, past the large commercial greenhouse, to the airport, and put down my money for a glider ride. When I told the pilot that I had my private pilot's license, though lapsed, he kicked his head back like a startled horse and said, Well hell, then, you can take front seat.

He attached the cable from the Cessna that would pull us into the sky, we climbed in, latched the hatch shut. He said, I'll take it till he cuts us loose, and then we were rolling down the runway behind the Cessna, its prop kicking up dust. The glider pilot lifted us a few feet off the ground and we were flying behind the Cessna even as it still rolled out, our nose a little heavy so that it seemed always as if we were about to plow into the runway. Then the Cessna lifted off and pulled us high into the air over the desert. At around three thousand feet we saw the tow pilot's hand lift in a little wave. I released the cable and we watched it whip away in the air behind the plane as he banked down back toward the airport.

Take the stick, said the pilot, and I did.

When you feel a bump and lift from a thermal, turn hard into it, he said, and I did. We lifted up on the thermal a good thousand feet.

Okay, let's fly a little here, he said, so I steered a south heading and we sailed toward Mexico.

You still got the stick-and-rudder skills, he said.

Thanks. I wanted to be a fighter pilot.

What happened?

They wouldn't let me.

We caught another thermal, and another, for an hour. The desert and its low hills and black volcanic outcroppings below us, stretching forever into what seemed a beautifully desolate Earth.

I'll take it for the landing, the pilot said.

And then we were on the ground again, the sky beyond us. So heavy, as if our bodies were just sacks in the shapes of limbs, etc., filled with hot yellow sand.

I'M SORRY FOR SHOUTING and throwing things, drunk. For wanting to fuck you more often when you were skinny than when you were not. For fucking you the same old way for about fifteen years. I was a monster in my pretty skin, two or three thousand years of age, stumbling and grumbling through my twenties and thirties.

I'm sorry for bringing you coffee in bed, so I could see that lazy beauty about you, your hair all down and thick and mussed and tangled, the way you would never let yourself go out, brushing it to implacable perfection.

I'm sorry I wasn't enough to make you want to wear it like that, all disheveled, all the time. For getting sweetly drunk every afternoon and cooking you dinner. That was for me, more than for you. I did it all for myself, so I could feel a little bit better or a whole lot worse. I know and don't know. I can and I cannot. Could and could not. I did it all in a blind lack of faith. I'm not saying I have any now.

The *Alpine Avalanche*
Thursday, May 11, 2006
Sheriff's Blotter
Loose Buffalo (Marathon)
Owner Notified—Cattle put up;
Possible Domestic (Alpine)
Parties Separated;
Loose Cattle (Marathon)
Owner Notified;
Ambulance Request (Alpine)
No Transport;
Possession of Marijuana (Alpine)
Two Arrests;
Injured Cat
DOA;
Disturbance (Alpine)
Unable To Locate;
Possible Fight (Alpine)
Unable to Locate;
Suspicious Person (Alpine)
Under Investigation;
Possible Overdose (Marathon)
Refusal for Transport

THE LITTLE BIRD WAS A TREE SWALLOW, according to Sibley, migrating from Mexico to Canadian summer grounds. They usually travel in large flocks, but I've seen none.

You would love all the birds and church bells. You would hate the wind as much as I love it. You would love the arid air as I do. And the trains going through, which I have described in my letters to our son. I wonder if you've read them. I wouldn't mind.

I am cobbling myself back together from the pieces lying about the room. Every evening they fall apart again. I can't help but wish such a thing were possible, a second life emerging from the ruin of our first. A new sense of our selves seeping into our present stunned states of mind. I can't help but believe we have within us some genetic compass marked north, south, east, west.

Love, loss, anger, grieving.

Loving-anger, grieving-loss.

Bird brains harbor tiny grains of magnetite, imagine that. Only constant calibration avoids endless misdirection and the end of the world.

These are very responsible creatures. I believe we owe these birds our very lives.

PRONGHORNS EITHER WILL NOT or cannot leap the fences. They get down onto their bellies and crawl under the lowest wire, repeatedly scraping the coats along their spines with the twisted barbs. The death of the pronghorn beside the tracks remains a mystery, thus, but now the marks on his back are less mysterious, a less interesting story, I'm sorry to say.

I read a book on them. The reason they can run twice as fast as any of their predators is that there used to exist, here, an American cheetah, larger than the present African species, but just as fast. Does give birth to twins that, together, can weigh as much as the calf of an elk cow, which can be five times as large as the pronghorn. The mother and father hide their fawns in the grass, and the fawns learn to stay very still. The mother will take her fawns' feces into her mouth and deposit it elsewhere, to keep predators from locating them by the scent of their poop.

I told Marie all this and more. That's fascinating, she said, staring in wonder. What a mother! Then she said, I think I would like to eat one.

I'm sorry for my great fucking ambition. For always wanting to be something or someone else. Something more, and something less of whatever it was I could not stand.

This morning I would like to be elsewhere, cannot stand the cacophony of birdsong: the chatter-squawking of sparrows, the hyper-chittering of a swallow and its rattling footnote, the coo-coo-c'coo of white-winged doves, the incessant aggressive appropriation of mockingbirds, and the monotonous, mindless repetition of a wooing Inca dove's *POO! poo!*, which Sibley transliterates as "No hope!" Forgive me, but I'd like the two cats who prowl the yards around here—the fluffy, cool Siamese and the scrappy, lean, and feral black—to make a few sensational kills and silence all these mad, insufferable creatures for a while. I'd mate with the fucking dove myself if I thought it would mollify.

On the other hand, I watched for weeks as two barn swallows built what seemed to be their first nest. I say so because they seemed so inept, so tentative at first in their mud-daubing around the metal cage protecting my defunct porch light.

Sibley says their nest-building takes ten to fourteen days, but these swallows took that long just to get a good foundation up, and two more weeks to shape it into the classic cup you see in photos.

Every day I watched them work, watched them pad the bottom of the nest with cottony wads from some plant out here, maybe cottonwood fluffs blown from the river to the north. As they worked they chattered back and forth, one impatient for the other to daub the load and get out of the way, cocking a head, looking up as if to say, what's taking so long? I'm waiting here with my little ball of mud drying up while you get all artistic.

And in the evenings now they sit, heads together, the long pinfeathers in their tails extended right and left like the whiskers on the cats they've built their nest so carefully to confound. And more, of late, the female sits alone there during the day, warming a hatch that should arrive pretty soon.

Sometimes a lone male barn swallow will destroy the eggs of a mated couple, which often drives the mated male to something like despair, a thing I can thus ascribe to barn swallows if not to mindless, whooping doves, and so he leaves. Perhaps he thinks the mission is aborted and his work done. But the interloper's work has just begun, and he often mates with the mother bird, whose second clutch she lays in the nest she built with the other male, who may himself, for all I know, have become an interloper, too, across the meadow, on the other side of the Inca's tireless, futile siren song.

I suppose you'd find this bit of lore, this speculation on my part, a bitter metaphor, a bitter observation about birds.

ALTITUDES OF VARIOUS FAMILIAR THINGS:

517 miles	Spy satellite (debris, dead souls)
62 miles	Outer space
60,000 ft	Tops of cumulonimbus clouds
29,000 ft	Bar-headed geese, Himalayas
21,000 ft	Mallard duck, Nevada
11,000 ft	Monarch butterfly, glider pilot
6,500 ft	Low cloud bases, God
379.7 ft	Tallest living tree
200 ft	Crows
151 ft	Statue of Liberty
0 ft	Fog

DO YOU CARE THAT I'VE QUIT SMOKING? Of course not, no real reason you should. The elevation here is five thousand feet, fifteen hundred feet below God. You get away with very little, here. It's difficult enough just to breathe.

I got drunk in town and slept on the church lawn beneath the sermon sign and no one noticed. Sign said: WELCOME, PILGRIMS. I got up in the morning and walked back up the hill and to bed. Later I woke to the smell of fresh coffee in a paper cup someone had placed on the floor beside the sofa. I opened an eye to see Marie sitting at the little table beside the wood-stove, reading a book, the wind blowing dust against the popping Visqueen windows. I took a sip of the coffee, still warm, and she looked up, and though I knew she was Marie, there was a moment when I was confused, unsure, maybe she was someone else I'd known somewhere else, and a fear ran through me. But then she said, You don't have to get up, and went back to her book, and I turned over facing the back of the couch, as it was all I could do not to start bawling like a child.

Do you dream of me as a different person, with different habits, who wouldn't recognize you in your dream if your life depended on it?

I get these hate letters, digitalized, radio waves, invisible radioactive clouds of vapor. I know they don't actually come from you. They have no words. Pure invective—purified! Made of blinding, blinding light. And darkness. Blindness. An endless falling into the black depths. It was a void I hoped we'd long caved in, filled with rubble, forgotten, before I reopened it walking away.

What do you do with your days now that you are alone with our son near the edge of the continent with no real vista, land or sea? No sense of the future beyond some kind of black hole, no desire to escape or embrace, no forgiveness, not just of me but also yourself and the rest of the world. I picture you in a room I've never seen, in a car I've never sat in or driven, in a store buying groceries and I cannot walk up and say hello in the white light-washed aisle, on the beach searching for the shell fragments the Gulf begrudges its spoiled shores except after the storm that time when, wading in the rough surf, I stepped on something hard and came up with that beautiful, perfect conch. You must remember that day. The light was dazzling, as if life were dazzling. All I can say is in memory it seems as dazzling as older memories of smoking some kind of fantastically magical weed.

Do you remember those first days, when we would pack a simple meal and a bottle of wine and drive down the peninsula to the beach house still under construction, and set up our portable grill in the dunes, and set fat steaks on the coals and drink the wine and nestle into a sleeping bag on the beach-house deck and watch the sky wheel by all evening, and rise at dawn before the workers arrived and drive our sleepy way back to town?

And the trysts when one would say to the other, quietly come noon, Would you like to go and get some lunch?

How you loved, when we had the apartment on the beach, to go early before work and search for rare shells, and I would watch from the balcony as you walked, hair down and wind-blown, head down, bending at the waist, finding the occasional whelk, auger, cone, or olive, and bringing them back in your pocket or in a fold of your skirt like some country maiden gathering berries and plums.

The old house outside Montgomery where, enraged for no reason, I slung and smashed a glass of scotch against the wall and you calmed and shamed me with your silence, pulling the covers up to your chin against the madman.

In the big house upstate on the wide double lot, sun slanting in on the lawn, casement windows open for the attic fan to pull great huffing breezes through the house and through the attic and out the vents, entirely changed, and how our son would release a balloon to watch it bump against the fan guard, and spin like a mad child beneath it howling, arms up, diaper sagging, feet dancing on the shiny hardwood floor.

And Christmas, the large tree, your heirloom decorations from the Old World and the new, brought out as the sweets rolled into little morsels baked in the kitchen, bright with warbled light through the molded panes.

Though I left all that, I cannot for the life of me leave it in my heart and mind. Our two cats stalking in formation, heads high through the grass, summoned by the tangled shrubbery on the other side. Big, splayed pecan tree, dogwood tree, garden plot, patio. Playhouse made from discarded pallets. Sunset refracted through shrubbery leaves and the cone of a classic martini glass. The incredible quiet of an afternoon, both of you napping, my mind fraught with a strange, muted panic. Those who say they have erased their pasts, how can they truly believe it? Who would want to die such a death? Who knew we could fall so long and so far from those days, refusing to speak, touch, send tenderness through the actual wires, remember sweet times untainted with rage, invective, madness, murderous, amnesiac, wretched desperate hoarding of once-full hearts now heavy only with emptiness, trying like craven saints to feel nothing?

THERE IS HAPPINESS

THE OFFICIAL REPORT: A MAN, A WOMAN, AND A SIXTEEN-
year-old girl were in an automobile accident suspected to have
been caused by the woman, who apparently was the man's wife
and the girl's mother and is believed to have been driving the
vehicle when it crashed into a tree on State Boulevard Extension.
No other vehicles were involved.

Eyewitness accounts suggested, and hospital and morgue
reports confirmed, that the man died in the accident and the
girl was maimed for life. Those same eyewitnesses reported to
police that the woman fled the scene carrying a shoulder bag of
some sort in one hand, by its strap. Police confirmed that someone, presumably the same woman, entered the family's home,
apparently to gather some items into a suitcase. Minutes later,
she entered a nearby branch of Citizens Bank, indeed carrying a
small suitcase, cashed out her and her deceased husband's check-
ing and savings accounts, and left the bank on foot.

The cause of the accident is unknown, according to authorities who declined to be identified. Other sources close to the case
suggested the crash was intentional, although those same sources
provided no suggested motive for such behavior and declined to
speculate. According to those same authorities, the incident is
now classified as a cold case.

They also said that, after the man's death and the woman's disappearance, the girl was given over to authorities to become a ward of the state.

Administrators at the hospital have declined to reveal when the girl was released and officials at the State Ward for Children have declined to comment on whether she is in their custody.

In an odd development some months after the incident, a spokesperson for the state police suggested there may be a connection between the accident and a series of murders, according to reports from survivors of the attacks as well as witnesses, by a young woman dressed as a man and strongly resembling the girl in the accident (a beautiful and happy girl, by all accounts, who wore her hair cut very short in the style recently favored by the comedian Ellen DeGeneres). Bizarre rumors surfaced, suggesting the child may have escaped the care of the state at some point and committed the series of murders carried out in a strange and gruesome fashion. State police dismissed the idea as highly unlikely, and one spokesman, off the record, called it "preposterous."

The spokesman declined to comment upon the girl's whereabouts, calling it "a family matter." He did confirm that the whereabouts of the woman were still unknown.

The motive for the murders has never been determined. One investigator who declined to be identified told reporters that, if the murders were indeed the act of a single individual and are indeed classifiable as "serial killings," then the motive for the killings may never be satisfactorily revealed or understood.

That's the nature of the beast, the investigator said. This isn't the movies or TV.

Our theory:

The woman believed to be the mother of the girl who was taken away and the wife of the man who died in the accident, and who is suspected of having caused the accident in some way, through neglect or despair, actually steered the vehicle into the thick trunk of the oak tree, head-on, on purpose, intending to kill not just her husband but herself and her daughter, as well. She failed, and instead of remaining at the scene of the accident or crime, and instead of going to check on her daughter, still in the hospital with serious injuries, and failing to show up at her husband's funeral, and having never returned to live in the home where all three were thought to have lived together as a normal, nominally happy family, she disappeared.

When she fled the accident, she entered the family's home, threw some items into a suitcase, left on foot, and made her trip to the bank. She then took a bus to Jackson, where she knew no one, and checked into a Motel 6. There she lived under an assumed name and existed for a while on nothing but take-out pizza and Chinese, which she always had delivered and for which she always paid in cash, tipping just enough to be proper but not so much as to make the delivery people more suspicious of her than they might be simply because she was living in a Motel 6. There are enough pizza and Chinese delivery joints in Jackson to make it possible to stay for at least three weeks without ever ordering from the same place twice, so her strategy with the tipping was unnecessary. She had begun to undergo a curious change during this time, a transformation so profound it was affecting even her physical features. She began to look, in the cloudy mirror of the motel room, younger, until she resembled herself before her marriage to the man more than herself after having been married to the man for seventeen years, bearing and raising their child. The transformation was the result of a deep and exhilarating sense of freedom, as marriage and family had seemed to her an oppressive, state-sanctioned bondage. She felt an almost uncontrollable joy of which she was so ashamed that in addition to feeling free and light she was invaded by a creeping insanity. One evening she took the straight razor from her deceased husband's toiletry kit, which she had put into her suitcase along with a set of his clothes and a set of her clothes including a black dress, a pair of tennis shoes, and a hat with veil that her mother had worn to her father's funeral, and hacked off her hair until it was shorter than her husband's had been when he died in the crash. As short as her daughter's. The straight razor wasn't something the husband had shaved with. It was an heirloom, the razor his grandfather had used which had been passed along first to his father and then to him. But it was still sharp. The act of cutting off her hair with it was one of the ways in which her insanity manifested itself. However by this time, in her mind, it was not insanity, it was purely reason, which is the way that insanity works on the person in possession of its peculiar qualities.

The insanity was necessary to deal with the great burden of shame that threatened to ruin her newfound happiness and sense of freedom. And so the insanity slowly enveloped her shame and began to mold it into something altogether different, a form of clairvoyance, clairaudience, including the ability to read auras, so that she could see people on the sidewalk or in stores or in cars or on bicycles, in a new and profound way. She could tell which of these people were either evil or possessed the capacity for evil. She could sense and hear their thoughts, which were like words but not exactly, a glottal mutter disturbing an aura like a veil of swarming, translucent flies. These evil people she began to follow. She would follow them to their cars, to see where they parked every day for work, or if they were just out for walks she would follow them to their favorite cafés or shops and then follow them to their homes. If they were children or teenagers she followed them to their schools and then to their homes, as well. If they were older people who simply sat on their porches or stoops or in lawn chairs on their lawns, she would stay at a distance and observe them, when they came out and went in, how long they stayed on their porches or stoops or lawns and when they retired to their backyards to do yard work or seek privacy from their neighbors. After she had observed someone she believed to be evil long enough to be sure of it, she would return to the motel room, put on the set of her husband's clothes (which were not overly large on her, as he had been a fairly small man), and her tennis shoes, and with a deftness surprising in someone who had never practiced it before, she would surprise them in their back-yards or, during a shortcut on their routes, she would dash up— or hiding in the back seat of their cars, she would rise up—and slit their throats with the razor.

She moved from town to town or city, never murdering more than two people in a place, never more than one in a smaller city. When she traveled she wore a wig she'd bought, and made up her face to look older, and wore the black dress, the hat and veil, and a pair of cheap number-one-strength reading glasses which did not significantly affect her vision.

The police and the authorities for the various agencies, for reasons of their own, were lying about witnesses and survivors of the attacks. None of those who were attacked survived, and there was only one witness, a woman who heard someone following her down a suburban alleyway and turned to see a person stand-ing there, about ten feet distant, in strange-fitting men's clothing and short hair but, the witness said, definitely a woman, possibly a young woman and, yes, she looked a little like the photo they showed her of the girl in the accident but also a little like the woman in the accident but with shorter hair and not as old. This person stared at her, hands thrust into the pockets of her baggy pants, but did not move toward her or act aggressively except to stare at her in a steady way that was unsettling. The woman was spooked enough to file a police report, but of course by that time the murderer had moved on to another place.

As for the murders being described as "strange and grue-some," never explained or defined by investigators on the case, there is this: She used the old razor to remove from each victim, after they had expired, a certain part of their cephalic anatomy: an ear from two different victims, a nose, a mouth, the skin of a chin, one cheek each from two others, eyebrows and forehead skin from another, the entire scalp from one. She took a blue eye from one and a brown eye from another. All these she kept in two Mason jars filled with saline solution, in order to preserve them as best she could. The scalp took up its own jar, but the other items nestled together into one jar.

And then one day, after many months of being consumed by her obsessive mission, the clairvoyance, clairaudience, and auras disappeared. She could no longer look at someone and detect goodness or evil, and realizing this she also realized that she could not remember why she had taken on her mission, nor anything of her past before the accident beyond the occasional fleeting mnemonic ghost. She no longer possessed the shame that had led to the defensive development of her insanity. She was possessed, however, of an almost feverish desire to be in a desert environment, somewhere vast and dry, so she threw away her husband's things, put on her wig, bought a fresh set of women's clothing at a secondhand shop, and rode the train to New Orleans. From there she took another train to a small city in southern New Mexico, and from there took a bus to a small town in the high desert, where she worked as a waitress in a diner that catered almost exclusively to Mexican Americans, about whom she knew nothing and had never encountered before in any intimate way, and whom she believed would be less likely or willing to identify her from a poster somewhere such as a post office or other federal building, and in fact they did not. And that is where she stayed. The original, local investigators in the case had no idea where she was and considered the case to be open but not active. Federal and state authorities, with no real leads, either, considered it active and urgent. She wasn't worried, and in fact was more at peace than she had ever been. Whatever happened, whether she would be captured and punished or not, was immaterial. Her hair had grown out. She had burned the wig. She felt flushed and brimming with humanity, and just about anyone who set eyes upon her, took a cup of coffee or a beer or a plate of food from her, received even an accidental brush of her hand against hand, wrist, or shoulder, felt happier for it, quietly elated. Some of the older, more religious and sentimental people in the community believed that this strangely beautiful, even beatific, seemingly ageless Anglo woman was possibly an angel in the form of a regular human being, and secretly they worshipped her, and gave thanks in their prayers to the Virgin for sending them this creature who must surely have formerly sat at Her very feet, and was sent down to be among them in order to give them happiness.

And there was happiness. Every evening, alone in her adobe bungalow on the outskirts of town, she opened the hinged lid of a small wooden crate that sat upright on a bookshelf next to a comfortable chair, where she rested and had a beer, a glass of white wine, or a cup of tea. Inside the small wooden crate was a Styrofoam wig stand, the stand that came with the wig that she bought and then burned, to which she had affixed with pins and glue the various parts she'd removed from her victims. She had no vivid memory of any individual victim but this figure served as an emblem of their collective memory for her, reconfigured or even reborn into a figure devoid of evil and filled with an all-but-incomprehensible empathy and compassion for humankind in general and the woman in particular, who engaged in conversation with this figure, which was her only friend. She called the figure Elizabeth Bob, and she loved Elizabeth Bob in the way that other people, people not like her, might love their child, or their spouse. It seemed perfectly normal, reasonable to her. She knew that no one else could understand, so Elizabeth

Bob was her secret companion, and together they lived for a long while a contented and peaceful life, a life that seemed graced with unconditional love.

Many years later, having worked in the diner through her last day, she died in her sleep in her home. The people who worshipped her prepared her body for burial and left her in the earth beneath the desert. They had become concerned about her for she had seemed over the years to grow saddened, remote in a different way, but not aloof or unkind. They did not condemn or claim and sell her little adobe house but left it to its own devices and to fate, with the doors knocked from their hinges and the windows crowbarred into the dusty yard, open to whatever creatures that might wander in and occupy it in any way they wished.

In fact, over the years, her great unburdened happiness had been gradually eroded, and her conversations with Elizabeth Bob had taken a melancholy turn. "I don't think I can go on much longer," she said one late afternoon as she carried Elizabeth Bob with her on a long walk beside the railroad tracks leading into the desert south of town. "I do not truly understand, but something has wormed its way into my heart and I am burdened with a burgeoning sadness." Elizabeth Bob, whose skin had shrunken and hardened, and whose eyes had at first gone milky like a blind seer's but were now black as if burned in a fire of deep understanding, spoke to her then, and told her that many years ago she had left everything behind, erased her past, so that she could feel alive again, but that death is inescapable, and death had made its way back into her heart because she had underestimated its tenacity, its insidious presence in the air and in the features of every creature one might encounter in the world. It had crept into her walks into the desert along the long freight tracks, among garrulous ravens, the beautiful delicate barking pronghorns, the curious bluebirds, ubiquitous cottontails, horses with their knob-kneed foals, dry and empty brick cisterns, tumbleweeds, the sotol shrubs with their great stalks that stand both dead and alive, the dead stalks leaning to make way for the new—these things were no longer enough to sustain her. The wind billowing white curtains into the house full of hard bright light as if wind and light were one. And the unrecognizable ghosts of her husband and child drifted into every shadow, every rise and fall in the breeze, every rustle of a leaf, every dove, swallow, flicker, sparrow, every distant or curious raven or crow, every glance from a stranger, every voice, every scarce drop of hot black rain. "You may leave me here, beside this beautiful flowering yucca," Elizabeth Bob said to her, and so she did.

Elizabeth Bob remained there beside the yucca for a while, then tumbled in the wind across the desert landscape, lodging here and there against vegetation or rock or crevice, silent but sensing the tentative approach of wildlife, undisturbed except for the occasional small bird that would perch on the starchy hair of the scalp for a moment, cock an eye, and fly away. Elizabeth Bob traveled far, until out of reach of the woman's thoughts, although the woman was never far from Elizabeth Bob's, until the woman expired and her spirit drifted into the atmosphere to dissipate in diaphanous vapor into time.

As for the woman's daughter, her child, who can say what will happen to a child? Children are all the children of fate.